Twinter
the first portal

Library and Archives Canada Cataloging in Publication
Knox, Veronica, 1949- TWINTER : the first portal / V Knox

ISBN: 978-0-9937380-4-3

Editor: Silent K Publishing
Cover design: Veronica Knox and SpicaBookDesign
Cover illustration: Veronica Knox
Typeset at SpicaBookDesign in Times
Second Edition
Printed with www.createspace.com

Silent K Publishing:
Victoria, British Columbia, Canada
www.veronicaknox.com

V KNOX

Twinter
the first portal

for sarah and david

Table of Contents

WINTER WONDERLAND

HOLLYWOODLAND

THE PROMISED LAND

LAND'S END

THE SHADOWLAND

LAND AHEAD

PART ONE

DREAMLAND

"The holidays have begun.
The dream is over.
This is the morning."

- CS LEWIS
'THE CHRONICLES OF NARNIA'

There are three generations
of Stratford-Smyths
'living' in Bede Hall.
The fourth is the ghost
of a nine-year-old girl,
which makes them
four generations
spanning four dimensions.

CHAPTER ONE

The Mummy's Curse

The most extraordinary thing about the twins, Kit and Bash, was the ghost of a little girl in their grandmother's deserted stately home, Bede Hall. That, plus their ability to know what each other was thinking... and sometimes sharing the same dreams.

Kit stood in the center of an Egyptian tomb and directed his sister's attention away from the sad sight of three skeletons jumbled together in a discarded heap of bones. "It's all right," he comforted, "we're only dreaming, and they're safe now." But his voice couldn't reach Bash because she was waking up. He pinched her dream arm seconds before she faded. "Bash? Can you hear me? Whatever happened here took place a long time ago. Their suffering is over."

It was too late. Kit was alone.

Livingston, Surrey, England
JUNE 29 – 2013

Bash should have known something terrible was about to happen because she woke from a disturbing dream where skeletons chased her. She dressed for school with a wobbly feeling in her legs as if she was a skeleton herself.

Her brother Kit felt uneasy too, but then, sharing feelings was fairly normal for twins.

"It was awful," she told Kit, "I was trapped in a dark room. The air was all musty and I think there were bats because I could hear them squealing, and something was crawling in my hair." She rubbed a small bruise on her arm. "It felt like the fingers of the skeletons. I couldn't breathe."

"It's only nerves," Kit reassured her. "You're just worried about the science exam," but he felt anxious too. He hadn't wanted to alarm his sister that they'd been dream-sharing because after Bash left, a sad voice declared *"our suffering is NOT over, and yours is about to begin."*

The twelve-year-old twins each had a soft-boiled egg for breakfast with bread and butter cut into 'soldiers.' Bash barely tasted hers, eating with her science textbook open, desperately scanning the pages.

Kit was looking forward to acing another test on his favorite subject, and savoured the salty taste of the bread strips dipped into the runny yolk. He even polished off two slices of toast spread with marmalade, and, as always, he cut his toast into several isosceles triangles, leaving one of them plain for their lanky deerhound, Jack.

The open window brought the sounds of early morning traffic drifting into the cozy kitchen the same way it always did. It was unusually bleak for the last week of June, with the sort of grey sky that promised drizzly rain all day. Already the first drops were spattering the pavement below.

Pigeon, their father's ancient parrot, resumed sharpening his yellow beak on a new cuttlebone after loudly reproaching the family's ginger cat, Feathers, for nibbling a plant.

It was always unnerving when Pigeon mimicked someone's voice, but with the nightmare fading, nothing unusual warned the twins that a message would bring their safe world tumbling down like a pyramid made of sand.

Feathers continued to paw the pot of mint growing on the windowsill hoping it would turn into its catnip cousin while Jack kept his unblinking eye on Kit's toast with the anticipation only a dog can know of a treat from a human's plate.

4

Mrs. S sipped her tea and smiled happily as she opened the letter with the foreign stamp that arrived in the morning post.

"It looks like your father will be home soon," she read. "His dig is over for the summer. He writes that the June heat is quite unbearable, so the authorities are shutting things down early this year. He sends his love and some photos of the pyramids."

"At least *someone* is having sunny weather," Kit said. "Although to be scientific, weather isn't the same anymore. I think the planet's in for it. The climate's gone all topsy-turvy. Only yesterday the news reported a snowstorm up in Northumberland that lasted for a few hours. Maybe it's lucky we aren't going up there this summer."

"Bede Hall is magic in any weather," Bash said. "I wish we could live there all the time."

The kettle shrilled and sent Pigeon into a flap. *"Kettle's boiling ... Polly take the kettle off... please!"*

Mrs. S put down her letter and filled the teapot. She stopped to soothe the bird. "It's all right Pidgy Pollykins. The kettle's all gone."

"Polygon," Pigeon said. *"Poo... perfect... peace."*

"I'm afraid we've had our last summer in Bede," Mrs. S said, picking up her letter. "There's another promising buyer sniffing around. A group of developers or some such, and as much as I love the place, it has to go."

Bash stared hard at Kit. "The seasons are *erratic*," she said. "Besides, rain is good for the gardens. In fact, I find it..." She tilted her head, searching for the perfect word that momentarily escaped her. *"Invigorating."*

No-one was prepared for the bomb of devastating news that dropped into the unsuspecting kitchen when the telephone jangled.

Mrs. S's cup of tea crashed to the floor in mid-conversation, startling poor Feathers into the next room in a blur of orange fur and sent Jack slinking under the table. Pigeon squawked a louder version of *"stop eating that plant, you!"* and flapped his bright, red and green wings.

"Mum what is it?" Bash said, "You've gone white as a ghost."

Kit, who had been about to give Jack his treat, nearly knocked over his chair getting up too fast. "What's happened?" he cried.

Mrs. S slumped back into her chair. "Your father... is... missing," she said in a barely audible whisper quite drained of emotion. "He never showed up in Cairo," she continued weakly. "The museum thinks he may have been... kidnapped."

The twins stared at each other in disbelief.

"I have to call Rupert," Mrs. S said, getting up suddenly. "He will have to come home. Oh dear, I've broken one of my best cups. Be careful. Mind your feet, and watch out for Jack."

"Don't worry," Kit said, "I'm sure they'll find Dad. He'll be all right. Egypt's a funny old place. There's been a mistake."

Bash's knees were more wobbly than ever as she settled her mother in a chair and poured her a fresh cup of tea.

But Mrs. S abandoned her tea, jumped up again, and busied herself, cleaning up the broken china, all in a rush as if someone's life depended on it.

"Leave that Mum," Kit said. "Sit down and drink your tea. I'll call Rupert."

Mrs. S obeyed, still in shock, and stared dry-eyed at a photograph of her husband waving in front of the sphinx.

Kit looked over at Bash and their eyes met, widened with fear.

Neither of them had any idea that their lives were about to become more extraordinary than they could ever have imagined.

CHAPTER TWO

News Travels Slow

The twins used to look forward to their summer holiday, but sadly they were no longer spending their school breaks at Bede Hall. For the moment, Bede Hall belonged to no-one. The three-hundred-acre estate had been on the market for three years with only one interested party, but last month the deal had unexpectedly fallen through for unknown reasons, and with the market for large stately homes slow at the best of times, it looked as though it wasn't going to sell anytime soon.

For three years, Lady Nan had been half-asleep, fading away in 'The Beehive Nursing Home,' no longer in residence at her grand manor.

Lady Nan's dreams were deeper than the usual twilight wanderings of her elderly companions. Most of them slept adrift in a pleasant happy-go-lucky sea randomly replaying their good old days, but Lady Nan had always been different. Sometimes being of sound mind was too upsetting to bear.

She made every effort to control her sadness by concentrating on one of her favorite daydreams. She conjured up amazing images of the golden sands of Egypt and the glory days of its ancient past. She dreamed creatively in order to live there and leave England behind.

Lady Nan begged her dreams to erase her sad memories. She dreamed purposely to forget, yet she dreamed selectively to remember something wonderful. It was easier to slip away to Egypt than face the heart-breaking truths that haunted her, but as hard as she tried, old-family loyalty was in her blood, and messages of responsibility crept in to disturb her night travels. The winter scene inside the snow globe on her bedside table wavered between an English Christmas and a desert sandstorm that threatened to cover the Great Sphinx. And often, the flakes of fake snow swirled into warm rain.

Her beloved old manor house was ever more insistent she return home. It began to send her pleasant invitations and then ever more urgent messages and stronger pleas until at last it had no choice but to order her return.

But it was the fretful voice of a lonely little girl she once knew, calling out for help who disturbed Lady Nan's sanctuary the most.

CHAPTER THREE

Looks Like Snow

Bede Hall, Northumberland, England
AUGUST 1, 2013

The over-excited little ghost rubbed a small hole in the window frost and peered down into a summer that shouldn't be there. A thin slick of ice defied the blistering heat of August and crept over the sundial's weathered face. The rest of Bede Hall's garden grew perfectly wild the way an abandoned landscape should.

She saw the same things she always did: a marble sundial leaning slightly towards the stables, a maze that looked like a giant green puzzle, and a bright carpet of flowers that shimmered like jewels. Beyond them, a topiary sphinx basked under a blazing sun.

For as long as she could remember, she expected someone to arrive in the in-between time to fulfill a promise made yesterday. August was her special window of time and she tried to keep her hopes up.

As the morning passed she allowed herself to anticipate the thrill of meeting her friend again, but the garden remained deserted. For the third year in a row the girl had not come. Sadly, the ghost melted back into her wintry room. Haunting, as she knew only too well, was mostly a tedious business.

Fourth Time's the Charm

Livingston, Surrey, England
AUGUST 1, 2013

The winter dream had come again – the fourth time in four years. Kit woke, shivering, overheated from clutching his hot water bottle like a teddy bear that had somehow migrated from his feet to become a security blanket. Happily, it anchored him to the safety of home, and according to its heat, only a short passage of time had elapsed since he closed his eyes.

Traffic sounds dispelled the nightmare of feeling completely alone and in despair. The clock showed he'd drifted off for only a minute. Time was strange stuff. Surely his dream had lasted ten days. Maybe more.

The word drift recalled nightmare drifts of blue snow as far as his eye could see. He remembered feeling abandoned on an arctic expedition. But no. Had he abandoned someone else? He'd been an explorer trekking through a frozen landscape, slowly running out of energy. Sleep, a winter hiker's worst companion, had shadowed him for the last mile, urging him to sleep and overtaken him with his last heavy steps. He'd finally collapsed to his knees, chilled to the bone, set his pack in the snow, and leaned against it fighting to stay awake. Happy thoughts of his childhood tucked up in a cozy bed with a hot water bottle filled his mind. And then he WAS home with a dream too real to set aside.

The shapes of familiar objects illuminated by the moonlight reassured him he was back in Livingston, a million miles from the North Pole. He counted them to ground himself: microscope, telescope, bookcase, globe, desk lamp, and his robe hanging on the closet door. But wait. The door was all wrong. Painted wood had

10

been replaced with metallic sliding doors. Two buttons with arrows supplanted the light switch and a gentle rumbling sound issued from the wall. The down arrow stopped blinking red as the doors slid open with a pleasant *whoosh*.

For a second time, Kit descended the elevator of sleep and felt a blast of icy wind. But instead of waking him it alerted him to action. The rules of survival were clear. He must pitch his tent and build a fire. He pictured himself going through the motions until an imaginary fire crackled before him and lit up the horizon. Like all weary travelers, he gazed into the hypnotic flames.

A vision of a shining pyramid in the heart of the fire burned so bright it woke him with a jolt. He'd fallen asleep again. Perhaps counting things had not been the best thing for staying awake. This time, by the clock, two hours had passed. But surely he'd only closed his eyes by the fire for a second. Then he reasoned it out. He had dreamed the fire inside the dream of winter and the horror struck him that imagined campfires never saved anyone from freezing.

Perhaps even now he was only dreaming he was awake in his bed-room. As a boy mad for science he intended to work out which sleep was real. Some dreams happened after too much sugar and late-night snacks, but his grandmother used to say that some dreams happened for a reason. She called them portents, a word that delighted his sister, but he didn't believe in things he couldn't prove. That's why he loved science. That's why he was going to be a scientist.

Kit closed his eyes to think and found himself back near the Great Pyramid of Giza. The winter landscape had gone. But this time he was ready. He knew he was dreaming. This time he scanned the horizon for clues and promised himself to remember everything. The sand was pale pink under the setting sun, and as he walked towards the sphinx it turned bluish-white and his feet left deep footprints as if it were snow. He appeared to be alone, so when a childlike voice called behind him, he startled.

He turned, determined to follow. "Hello," he called out. "Show yourself. Who are you? What do you want?"

The voice sounded close to tears. It came from inside the Great Sphinx, an unlikely sound for a lion with a pharaoh's head to make, so he paid closer attention.

For a twelve-year-old English boy Kit knew a lot about Egypt. His father studied the place and all three of his children had grown up with stories of animal-headed gods as commonplace as other children read fairy tales about ghosts and goblins. *"Please come home,"* the sphinx said. *"Daddy."* He knew that voice. Almost.

Kit waded through the snow until he stood between the sphinx's paws and looked up at the giant face. "Do I know you?" he shouted, but a strong wind howled the sand into a tornado and he had to step back. Sand swirled in the air and fell to earth as snowflakes. He caught the brief flash of a levitating doll with tall ears, instantly obscured in a blizzard whiteout. Unlike the winter dream, this storm was hot and dry.

Back in his room, Kit made notes. AUGUST 1, 2013 - DREAM ANOMALIES: *a blizzard of snow in the Sahara Desert? A lion statue with the voice of a child? Hot snow and freezing sand? Someone calling for their father. A clue to Dad's whereabouts? Dad's been missing four weeks. A stuffed rabbit doll?* He knew that toy. Almost. It belonged to... Who? And when?

Time was a funny thing. Funny ODD.

The words *please come home* and *Daddy* haunted him all day, even during science class.

Withering, Surrey, England
AUGUST 1, 2013

Two miles from the twins' house in Livingston, the 'Beehive Nursing Home' on Young Street was a hive of inactivity, tucked into a forgotten corner of Withering, Surrey. Lady Nan lingered in her own impatient dreamtime. Bede Hall fussed three hundred miles to the north, and it was in trouble. *"Please come home,"* it called, and when she drifted off into a lapse of deeper memory its pleas grew more demanding, sounding more like a father ordering his daughter. *"Come home this instant, young lady!"*

When she woke, another delivery of white carnations had arrived. As always the card read, *Eternally Yours – P.B.* But this time there was more. The sender had written *please come home* and underlined the word please three times.

It was curious how the word 'present' had a double meaning, referring to a gift as well as the time called now. It was significant that the word 'myth' was 'present' in her family name, Stratford-Smyth. Truly amazing. The words 'a maze' flashed once and disappeared. Words delivered magic if you knew how to listen.

Words were funny things. Funny STRANGE.

Bede Hall, Northumberland, England
AUGUST 1, 2013

The little ghost bundled into her red coat and trudged a fresh path through the snow that stretched to the horizon. Bede Hall's tower was gone today, so she climbed the woodpile as high as she dared. Her view was always the same on wintry days. The sun painted a crystallized world into a vast field of diamonds that hurt the eye and made her miss her father more than ever.

The wind whipped through her thin coat. She felt as if she lived in the center of a blank sheet of white paper. But some days the garden was there. Some days the tower stood tall and she didn't need her coat. Some days she ran over the grass and climbed to the top to look for her father. And best of all, she visited the green sphinx made of leaves and picnicked between its paws.

Back inside, drowsy from the cold, the ghost cuddled under a blanket and drew herself into a ball to keep warm. A clock missing its hands tick-tocked her into drowsiness. She closed her eyes – only for a minute.

It took no time at all to scramble up the sphinx's body using the secret steps carved into the stone, craftily concealed behind its tail. The desert night was cool. A wind off the Sahara blew her white hair into a halo lit by the fading moon. Soon she tiptoed along its back and used deep footholds in the headdress until she stood on its head, arms outstretched, embracing the plateau. From here, the pyramids were her playground.

An age went by before she bowed solemnly to the rising sun and lay face down where she fell into a trance, all the better to ask a big question. "Dear lion," she whispered, "can you please find my father?"

The sphinx's purr sounded like a growl. *"Child, have you brought me water?"*

The ghost emptied a small bundle carried on her back. "I've brought you snow, she said," and waited patiently while the heat melted the snow into a pool that trickled down the sphinx's shoulders.

"That feels refreshing. "I will answer your request. Let me look."

All was quiet while the great sphinx searched the horizon. *"I see a man. He's not far from here as Horus flies. Do you see him?"*

The girl squinted into the pool. "That looks like him but my father is much younger."

The sphinx laughed so hard she had to grab onto the stone to stop from falling. *"Men say time passes. I say, man passes."*

"Can I stay here with you? I remember once you said..."

"You're already home, child. Can you not smell the flowers in your garden?"

For a moment, the ghost-child leaned out her window to inhale the delightful fragrance of carnations that wafted up to the attic from below. Any day now her father would be home. Her eyes searched in vain for his familiar figure until snowflakes obscured her view. She sent her best wish into the blue sky. Please come home. She knew he would return. The sphinx always told the truth even if she didn't always understand its riddles, besides, time in Bede didn't always behave as it should.

A movement of green caught her eye as the sphinx made of leaves sprang to its feet, shook off a blanket of snow and ran behind the house.

Bede Hall was a funny old place. Funny WEIRD.

In the meantime, the mystical 'rule of three' charmed itself around Bede Hall in a tangled knot. The old lady, her grandson Kit, and the great estate slumbered restlessly in similar states of fretful dreaming while its ghost pined, anticipating another lonely summer.

CHAPTER FIVE

Kindred Spirits

Bede Hall
AUGUST 1 - 1949

The ice on the sundial had sealed time in a narrow wedge of mauve shadow.

It had been a scorching August day, sixty-four years ago, in the afternoon to be exact, when Bede Hall first heard two little girls crying. One was distraught with an alarming headache; the other from the worst sort of fear – that of being lost and alone.

The 'little girl lost' had looked down on the maze from her window, and beckoned the other with a frantic wave but had hidden when the door opened, only venturing a timid look at the unwell girl when she was sleeping.

For a while they remained alone yet together, dreaming now-and-again in the same wintry room, both in search of comfort. One girl sought refuge to *avoid* her father; the second searched in vain, hoping to *find* her father.

They were connected by a secret neither of them knew and a window of friendship they pledged would survive forever even though they were separated by a hundred boring tomorrows that reached into an uncertain future.

In spirit years, yesterday often seemed like a lost trail of pale dreams and the present was most often a confusion of restless memories, but this time the house had promised to intervene.

The old sundial continued to wait patiently in a sea of emerald grass like a lonely gravestone, sun-drenched yet frozen, and for many years time jumped ahead in erratic leaps like a frightened rabbit. And then the unthinkable happened – a third girl lost her father.

CHAPTER SIX

Old Beginnings – New Endings

It was the year 1949, when Lady Nan was nine-years-old, that her embarrassment thrummed itself into a drumming headache. She had felt ill from anger long before she left the house and the scene of an argument with her father. There was nowhere to hide from the pounding humiliation she felt, but there was a place she could go.

An invisible cat trailed after her like a pale cloud scudding over the grass as Beryl Stratford-Smyth haphazardly plucked a handful of sweet peas on her way to her green sanctuary.

The embracing arms of the maze welcomed her as she made a beeline (as much as one can inside a puzzle of tricky corridors) to the small shrine at the center. A plaster statue of a unicorn set on a low plinth marked the grave of her beloved cat.

Unicorn had been laid to rest there with the help of her good friend, Stanley, groundskeeper Park's fourteen-year-old son.

Before collapsing in a heap of tears, Beryl pulled the pink and purple heads from the flower stems and scattered them in a circle of bright petals the way she always did.

After sobbing for a while she curled into a defiant ball of rage. 'Grownups. They never listen!'

Her head ached in dull dry throbs as she lay spread-eagled under the noonday sun. One of her hands rested in the petals; the other, reached for a cat that wasn't there.

But it *was* there. Unicorn the cat rubbed his ghost-nose into Beryl's fingers and purred into the girl's body until more tears trickled slowly from the girl's eyes and into her ears. Unicorn licked at them and his raspy ghost-tongue made Beryl sit up and wipe her face with her pinafore.

Groundskeeper Parks took immense pride in the geometric precision of his corners, and was about to clip a few stray twigs from the far side of the hedge when he heard Beryl crying. It was his regular Monday task of taming the box hedges from outgrowing the square shapes he had pruned so carefully.

"There there, lass," he called through the foliage. "I heard about all the fuss indoors. It'll be all right, now. Let's get you back to the house. They're looking for ye. Wait there lass."

Parks found Beryl easily.

"I... *um*... have sunstroke," Beryl said, sniffing. "It doesn't usually make me cry. I'm not a baby. I'm nine you know. And, by the way, sometimes a person doesn't *want* to be found."

"Well, I expect it's this place that made you cry," Stanley's father said kindly, pulling a weed from Unicorn's grave. "Old Corny were your best friend, weren't he?"

"He was my *only* friend," Beryl replied. "Apart from Ben."

"Well now, you have Stanley and me don't you?" he said.

His kindness made Beryl's chin begin to tremble again.

"Look here, you've just had a mite too much sun. You need to rest somewhere cool. You're all flushed and bright-eyed."

"There's no shade at this time of day," Beryl said.

"Doesn't have to be shade. You look up yonder, there." He pointed to the house. "See that pointy window under the eaves?"

"The one with the girl in the window?" Beryl replied.

Parks reacted with surprise. "You can see her can ye? I thought you might. At your age... well, things happen."

"What things?"

"Nothing to worry your head about, young miss. Let's just say there's a time for most things and now it's time for this one."

"Time?"

Stanley's father winked. "Time to give you a special present," he said, smiling.

Beryl's eyes were dry, and seeing her strong again, Unicorn chased after a passing butterfly.

"But no-one lives up there," Beryl said.

"True enough; they don't," he said. "That young lady is a visitor and she needs a friend as much as you. It's high time you two met. You know the blue door down from the nursery? The door that's always locked?"

"The Winter Door?"

"The very one. This is the key," he said, holding up a long silver key by its blue tassel. "It belongs to you now." He smiled. "I've been keeping it for you. Now, run along Miss Beryl and say hello. It's the best place for curing sunstroke – a cooling-off room for hot tempers, I calls it."

The key tingled in Beryl's hand. "But I'm not allowed, am I? Is it a secret?"

Parks removed his battered gardening hat and stared up at the window with tears in his voice. "It's someone else's secret," he said.

The key had a will of its own and Beryl's mood lifted slightly but Parks was right, she'd had too much sun and she didn't want to run into Nanny. Her bedroom was no place to hide. "Thank you Mr. Parks," she said. "I believe I will hide up there for a while until I feel better." Suddenly, inside was the place she wanted to be.

The house loomed golden and sleepy in the sunshine. For a place bustling with servants it looked deserted. It reminded Beryl of the palace in Sleeping Beauty that slept under a spell. Strange that a house could be as sleepy as she felt. It was a comforting old house, but lonely with Ben away at school.

Parks leaned on his spade and watched her go. "And take Unicorn with you," he called after her.

Beryl replied without turning around. "Corny is always with me," she said feeling dazed and feverish.

The steep climb to the fourth floor made Beryl's head all thumpy again, and not at all inclined for visiting, but she opened the blue door and peered inside.

The Winter Room was empty of strangers; it was filled with piles of books and boxes and broken chairs, and Beryl was pleased to see

19

an inviting uncluttered cot with a plump pillow in the far corner that invited her to lie down.

The moment her head touched the pillow, Beryl's headache ceased and she felt a soothing dream lift her high away from her problems – to fly over Bede like a seagull. She would have her own adventures and never tell Ben. Who needed school anyway!

Unicorn kneaded the blankets and curled into the curve of Beryl's arm as the girl ghost peered down at him. "Hello," she said, petting Unicorn behind the ears, "I wondered where you'd gone."

It took a second visit for the ghost to show herself to Beryl and a third visit for them to become best friends, and soon afterwards, to Beryl's delight, she was able to see Unicorn even though it was only inside the magic of the Winter Room. Still, she was always able to feel the weight of her old cat whenever he snuggled into her at night.

Beryl confided to her new friend how life was unfair for girls. "I'm much more curious than my brother and yet he gets to go to school and learn about the world. But I'll show them. I'm going to break the rules. You see if I don't."

The ghost hugged her knees and listened. "You're so brave and I'm not," she said, "But..."

Beryl opened the book on her lap. "Now, I'm going to read you an adventure about a girl named Lucy who visited a wintry world inside a wardrobe..." she paused. "But what?"

The ghost hesitated and her form flickered out from anxiety. "It's just that I know a secret." Her voice grew faint. "Be careful of what you wish for," she said from far away, and then there was silence.

"Oh, please come back," Beryl shouted. "I didn't mean to upset you."

The ghost remained invisible but her voice rang clear and strong from behind the wall. "Death is the biggest adventure of all."

CHAPTER SEVEN

The Rule of Nine

MARCH - 2014

Other than two last names, which made them sound rather glamorous and a distant claim to a spectacular address, most things about Kit and Bash Stratford-Smyth (that rhymes with myth) were ordinary.

It was rather tricky for new acquaintances to describe them. They were of average height, neither fat nor thin, and had brown hair and brown eyes. They were never 'alike as two peas in a pod,' but they did share the same cheery enthusiasm and infectious good nature. Kit, short for Christopher, was exceptionally curious about everything, and his sister Bash, short for Bathsheba, was single-mindedly devoted to interesting words and anything to do with gardens. The best thing one could say about them was that they were the sort of people you'd want for a friend, however; other than tongue-in-cheek, this could never be said about their older brother, Rupert.

By contrast, the twins' brother Rupert, older by ten years, and happily installed at Oxford University, always stood out in a crowd. Partly because he delighted in drawing attention to himself but mostly because, regardless of the weather or the time of day, he always wore a pair of flashy sunglasses. He was tall with deep-blue eyes and had long blond hair worn in a trendy ponytail. He was arrestingly handsome. The trouble was, he knew it.

Rayne Stratford-Smyth, the twin's mother, was a tall brunette and quite pretty, but she lacked her eccentric mother's drive as well as her confidence and flamboyant style. To this end Mrs. S always wore nondescript pastel outfits and the palest of pale-pink lipsticks, so that when she smiled it often disappeared from her face. She purposely blended into the background of any room filled with people, and even when times were exceedingly pleasant, she always looked slightly careworn and worried about something.

Lady Nan, the twin's grandmother, the former 'Miss Beryl Stratford-Smyth,' was quite the opposite of her retiring daughter. She was a 'queen' – rooms had to become larger when she entered them. She was once, as the men in her youth described her, a 'cracker' who wore the most daring shades of bright lipstick, always immaculately turned-out in crisp tailored suits and sophisticated dresses with matching shoes, scarves, and hats.

The hats of the vivacious young Beryl Stratford-Smyth were confections of wonder. 'Positively stunning,' folk had said repeatedly, vying for the first look at the latest creation.

Even now, fashionably silver-haired in her advanced years, Lady Nan had a soft elegant glow of timeless beauty about her that still commanded respect, deference, and awe, although not necessarily in that order. That is, until she decided it was high time she pretended to lose her mind.

Extraordinary events like to take their time. It had been nine months since the devastating news of Professor Cornelius Stratford-Smyth's disappearance had brought so much sadness and disruption to the house on Stanley Street, but the family had adapted slowly through the stages of grief to acceptance, where more practical choices had to be made for a future without him.

Official search parties had been called off, although there was always the faint chance that he could still be alive. But if so, he was surely lost in a country of scorching deserts and underground tombs where tunnels dug in the sand were forever in danger of collapsing. Egyptology was a demanding business.

Charles Digby, the professor's right-hand man, had been found wandering in the desert with a large gash on his forehead, and was declared to be in a permanent state of amnesia.

Digger, as Mr. S had called him, was slowly piecing his own life together and was unable to supply any information on his partner's whereabouts or the location of the tomb they'd staked out only the year before.

Pharaoh Smenkhkare's tomb had had to remain secret from the public until formal permission to excavate the following season could be arranged, and the Egyptian authorities still moved at the speed of the eighteenth century when investigating the eighteenth dynasty.

The twins couldn't help but overhear the many heated discussions between their mother and Rupert over the long months of waiting. It had been a grim time, and all the talk of clues, and false sightings, and motives, had finally shifted to how they were going to pay the bills.

Then Lady Nan decided to wake up.

CHAPTER EIGHT

Waking-up is Hard to Do

Livingston
MARCH - 2014

The kitchen table was strewn with terrifying papers. Mrs. S looked more defeated than ever as Rupert tried to backpedal his way out of the threat of employment and back into the spotlight of Oxford University. He was so disconcerted he had removed his sunglasses and stared myopically into the hopeless future – the reality of making ends meet.

Oxford wavered like a cooling mirage behind heavy theatre curtains descending at the end of a play.

Every solution ended in a wall of thorns like a false passage inside the maze of Bede Hall. Somewhere in the center was a Minotaur who looked an awful lot like a realtor, or an accountant, or a lawyer, or a bank manager.

"Your father would want us to... oh dear, I don't know what he would want," Mrs. S cried. "I have to find a job. *You*'ll have to find a job. Your grandmother will have to move into our... the *big* bedroom. I can share with Bash. You and Kit can..."

"Father would want me to finish my degree," Rupert cut in frantically, retying his ponytail using his reflection in the kettle.

"Yes, yes. Quite right. He would," Mrs. S agreed. "And you will, but for now, don't you think we should cut every expense we can? Your grandmother keeps insisting we should go to the Hall and live *there*. Your fath..."

"Mother, they could still *find* him," Rupert interrupted again. "We have to wait. I should stay in Oxford. For sure, Grandmamma's not 'coming back,' from Doolally-land. Surely you're not going to *listen* to her? I mean, why don't we just ask the ruddy parrot?

"I can help you move in and be down in half-a-shake if there's a problem," Rupert whined. "I will visit whenever I can. Maybe bring a friend as well. I can fix up a room somewhere upstairs out of the way. It's the best of both worlds. And... the Pater would approve. I'm sure of it."

"I've decided to plant more carnations," mocked Pigeon in Lady Nan's voice.

Mrs. S gave Pigeon an icy stare. "Lady Nan says the Hall wants us to move back," she said looking appropriately flustered.

"Of course it does! Does it want modern wiring, fresh gravel, and new wallpaper as well?" Rupert offered sarcastically. "It's already in debt."

Mrs. S dithered, not listening.

"Your father always knew how to handle her. But she's different, Rupert. At times she's her old self again, and she seems up to it. Goodness knows how; she was always a mystery."

"At *times* Mother," Rupert sighed. "This is *not* one of those times."

"Ruddy parrot," Pigeon chortled under his wing.

"I don't know. She was very insistent. Quite like the mother I remember," Mrs. S fluttered. "This place is far too small."

"Mater, the Hall is our *identity*. Our *heritage*. Sell most of the land. We don't need *that*. But keep the house. I can get old Tweedy on the phone, and..."

"No. Absolutely not. Your grandmother was quite insistent that there would be no more realtor nonsense, and especially with *that* man. She says we should move first and something will turn up."

"Great! I mean, really! What sort of job could I possibly get if I forfeited my degree? Bagging groceries? Holding a stop sign? What? Surely you don't expect me to work in a factory! We'll just leave it up to a miracle then, shall we, and maybe Pigeon will know..."

Rupert's rant stopped mid-sentence as an obvious opportunity presented itself.

"Wing and a prayer," spluttered Pigeon with his mouth full of birdseed.

"Perhaps Grandmamma *has* got a point after all," Rupert said, "but I still say we can do both. I can stay at college, and Bede Hall can remain ours if we play our cards right because the work thing does seem a bit hasty. No need to go overboard, Mater.

"Rents in Livingston are far too high even if each of us took a manual job. The Hall is even wheelchair friendly for Lady Nan.

"So, stop renting this place, and eventually, when the Bede land sells, there'll be enough money left after over after the debts are paid to get the old place in shape. Then we can make a new start for... for the *next* generation. Maybe we can raise funds by opening the house to the public again. That almost worked once before.

"Later, after Lady Nan has... *moved on*, and the deeds are in your name again, there's bound to be at least one developer who'll want the land without the house. I can help with that. No need to worry.

"I can finish college and visit all of you on weekends... well, *some* weekends. We can all shift *together* and pull through. I should really be carrying on Father's legacy. I can be there all of August break and I'll take an extended leave to get everyone settled in."

When Rupert finished there was a silent pause before the cackle of maniacal laughter issued from Pigeon's beak. *"Together ... birds of a feather, wake up,"* he muttered. *"Just peachy... perfectly peachy... ruddy parrot!"*

"Things can happen that one doesn't expect," Rupert resumed gingerly, draping a tablecloth over the parrot cage, snarling at Pigeon under his breath: "Button your beak you pathetic creature."

"Like your father disappearing?" Mrs. S said, a tad crossly.

"Like him coming home," Rupert said rather too brightly, looking unconvinced.

"Lady Nan won't sign anything that divides the estate," Mrs. S repeated. "She says, it would be tantamount... to murder. We'll have to wait and see."

"Pathetic...dirty rascal... murderer!... poo... king of the castle... all together now ...p ...p ... pathetic...old b...b..buttons!" shrieked Pigeon from underneath the tablecloth.

Behind Rupert Stratford-Smyth's heavily tinted shades, his eyes were a remarkably vibrant shade of turquoise blue. He was the spitting image of his father as a young man. Cornelius had aged only slightly – his hair going grey, and worn somewhat shorter.

Rupert had followed Cornelius' footsteps into Oxford University, where he planned to become an archaeologist and join his father in the field, but there the two men's similarities ended.

Professor Cornelius Stratford-Smyth built his scholarly reputation from the ground up, and was, by nature, a kind generous soul. Rupert felt entitled, and hoped to bypass the dreariness of time-consuming experience by standing on his father's shoulders, zooming unchecked through as many open doors as possible.

In fact, Rupert thought himself quite perfect, but in Lady Nan's opinion there was still hope for him; she often said that no matter how bad things seemed, there was always hope.

The summer of 2013 had dragged on with hopes for the archaeologist's safe return rising and falling, and then permanently fading. Christmas passed with no tree or presents, until finally in late March, the Stratford-Smyths had no choice but to vacate their three-bedroom townhouse and join forces together under Lady Nan's bold new plan. Most of Rupert's scheme had been outright rejected by the awakened matriarch, but, much to his relief, Oxford remained his personal stomping ground until further notice.

In any case, they still needed the extra space. Their townhouse had been much too small to hold the increasing number of family members. Lady Nan no longer desired to live in her nursing home, so there were four of them. Five when Rupert came home.

It was decided that they would take up temporary residence in a few rooms at Bede Hall until the great mansion could be sold.

Mrs. S, having once been a teacher, would reopen the Red Library as a schoolroom and take on some private students (including the twins) and Rupert would help as often as his studies permitted. Bash would help take care of her grandmother, and a home-visiting nurse would drop by once a week. It was a shaky start.

Apart from the second-floor schoolroom, Mrs. S decided the ground floor kitchens would be the most central and practical place to set up residence.

A long corridor leading to the old domains of the 'help' ran parallel behind the grand dining room to a complex of workrooms on the main floor. These connected to the basement in what was collectively referred to as 'below stairs.'

Two people objected to sleeping there.

Lady Nan insisted on being installed in her old third-floor bedroom, and after scouting the entire building, Rupert chose the grandest space for himself – the ballroom on the east wing's second floor. It was the size of a large loft apartment, and Rupert, who dreamed big (as in posh) envisaged swanky partitions that divided it up into a bedroom, a computer room, a living room with an enormous wall-mounted TV, and an eating area overlooking the front of the grounds.

"I know it will be colder up there," he said, "but I can use a couple of extra hot-water-bottles and an electric fire when I visit, and there's bound to be warmer weather soon."

Mrs. S indulged him; it had always been difficult not to, and now that he had promised to disrupt his studies by sacrificing his weekends in order to help, she felt her eldest child deserved some extra privacy.

"As long as you take your meals downstairs with us while you're there," she insisted, "and you agree to only go up there at night. I don't want to traipse upstairs whenever I want you... and none of that ringing the bell for one of the twins to jump at your beck and call. They aren't your servants."

In the meantime, the vegetable gardens of Bede Hall and a few hens could provide some of their food, while the rent-free accommodation would keep their expenses low and give them time to consider their future in relative peace.

The old almost-retired gardener Stanley Parks, who had been a lad of five when Lady Nan was born, and being unusually sprightly for a man of seven-nine, had been persuaded to return for a few days with his son – the heir to his vast knowledge of horticulture in general and Bede Hall in particular, in order to give Rupert a few gardening tips 'just in case' he grew interested... or so he said. He really wanted to continue teaching Miss Bash, who he had declared his youngest protégé and a natural botanist when she was only seven.

For Mrs. S it was the least expensive solution. For the twins (other than being home-schooled by their mother) it was an adventure. For Rupert it was the fragile edge of his worst nightmare. For the Red Library it was a new beginning. But for Lady Nan it was, quite literally, a dream come true.

In the end, the only sensible thing was to move on to Bede Hall, so Kit and Bash learned to hope for the best, all the while realizing they may never see their father again.

Mrs. S handed Rupert a picnic lunch for the road. Your grandmother is having a wee nap," she said. "I'll tell her you said goodbye. You will come back to help with the packing won't you dear?"

Rupert adjusted his sunglasses in the hall mirror and checked his school scarf was arranged around his neck in a suitably rakish fashion. "Of course Mamma, you can always count on me. I'll be down the available next weekend. Start without me."

Rupert pecked his mother's cheek and headed for the door. "I'm off siblings," he said over his shoulder.

Kit giggled. "*Very* off if you ask me."

Kit and Bash waved to Rupert without looking up from their books. Once the noise of his car merged into the general blur of Livingston traffic, Kit nudged Bash. "Careful what you wish for, eh?"

Bash's eyes flashed angrily. "Whatever do you mean? I didn't wish for dad to go missing."

"Not that, silly goose. You wished we could live at Bede Hall forever."

CHAPTER NINE

Ben Again

Livingston
MARCH - 2014

Lady Nan smiled as she dozed in her four-poster bed, breathing in an Egyptian landscape. The vista of the great pyramids and their crouching guardian always soothed her.

The brass metal of Lady Nan's hourglass was too hot to touch even under the shade of her fan made of ostrich feathers. A hundred slaves hovered in the distance as far as they dared so as to still hear her if she called, but far enough away as she had ordered. She wanted to be alone with the great oracle that had a lion's body and a pharaoh's head.

She had come with a question and traditional offerings of bread and beer.

She sat on the sand close to the Sphinx's chin because the desert had covered its long paws in a deep sand dune. The pale gold hills in the distance strangely reminded her of another landscape. A far-off home that called like a green oasis.

Lady Nan stared into the crumbling eyes of the monument for a sign, and when she grew tired of waiting she wriggled two wide cuffs of gold from her wrists and laid them with the food and drink.

The Sphinx remained aloof and unimpressed, but the sand stirred beneath her as if the beast had stretched its body.

"Mighty One, I have nothing else to give you. How else may I serve?" she asked.

"*I thirst,*" said the Sphinx, "*bring me water.*"

Lady Nan took advantage of the desperation in the Sphinx's voice.

"If you save my brother, I will cause my magicians to make it rain every day," she bargained, and as she promised it began to rain.

The first drops of rain sizzled as they made contact with the metal casing of Lady Nan's hourglass and hissed away like tiny snakes, but soon its glass bowl was chill to the touch, and filled with powdery snow the color of lavender.

The echo of a refusal filled the air as gentle rain turned to a lazy flurry of snow. Shimmering drifts softly melted on the scorching stone of the Sphinx's back and ran down its sides forming a small lake. To Lady Nan, the great beast looked like an island castle surrounded by a moat.

She caught a snowflake on her tongue and made a wish.

Bede Hall
MARCH - 1959

The nineteen-year-old Lady Beryl woke in the Winter Room, terrified and alone. Beside her cot, the white pool of melted wax from a candle looked like a miniature frozen pond with a small lump shaped like the sphinx in the center.

"Ben! Perry!" Wait ... come back!" she shouted helplessly, but the only sound she heard was the cold north-wind eerily tinkling the winter trees like a forest of giant wind chimes.

She ran downstairs to the crisp morning. Frost had painted the landscape into a frozen blue nightmare.

"Have you seen Ben?" she shrieked at Cook.

"We're far too busy, Miss," came Mrs. Lamb's sharp reply.

"The mistress was calling him, Miss," a kitchen maid said. "Master Ben and his friend ran off soon as they heard her. Left their breakfast as well, they did."

Beryl raced to the boot entry. The curvy wrought-iron hooks that usually held the boys' ice skates were empty. It was too late.

Another dream within a dream had claimed Lady Nan and pushed her further away from a perfect second childhood.

CHAPTER TEN

Promises to Keep

Bede Hall

The blue door had a charmed key. But there was no need; the child ghost was alone and the door was unlocked.

Inside, a low nursery table was laid for two. Two bowls painted with yellow bees sat beside two plastic serving spoons, Egyptian mummy salt and pepper shakers, and a cracked doll's teapot shaped like a beehive used for pretend cream. The little girl's imaginary breath formed tiny clouds as she fussed, pulling and pushing her father's great stuffed armchair into place. Everything was ready. She glanced at the clock. He would be home soon.

Unicorn, an albino cat, the child's sole companion, lay, curled into himself like a fluffy hedgehog in the center of a worn red velvet cushion tossed on the bed. The two had discovered each other one thin August morning, wandering the deserted halls of the rooms below. Since then, they'd become inseparable. He was made as she was: solid most of the time but transparent as gauze when startled.

Every day had been the same for a very long time. She opened her morning eyes giddy with the expectation that her father would be there making her favorite breakfast of boiled eggs and bread and butter cut into soldiers. But this dream was soon dashed by the familiar scene of her lonely room, the white hills, the biting cold, the empty horizon, and a world where a bruised blue sun still delighted in playing tricks on the eyes.

Until she could sit and read one of her favorite books, she focused on her dreary list of daily chores. The ones her father had said were her responsibility while he was away. He had made her promise. He wouldn't be gone but a few days, he'd said, but the marks she scratched on the wall each night were finally too numerous to count and she didn't want to measure her loneliness anymore.

Her first task of the day was to poke the sleeping fire awake before grabbing a large battered saucepan and the reins to a miniature sled. Then she headed outdoors.

She heaved her shoulder against the weight of the snowdrift blown into the door during the night, and it squeaked outwards like the arm of a giant's compass etching an arc on the threshold – one quarter of a snow angel's wing. The old snowman she and her father had built a lifetime ago still stood sentinel at the edge of a picket fence that looked like a comb with missing teeth. How the wind loved to whistle through it, but today it was silent.

Every morning was the same. She tramped a fresh carpet of dry powder over yesterday's beaten path, dragging the sled behind her. A corridor of frozen steps led straight to the woodpile where she collected new-fallen snow for melting and a few sticks of broken furniture to feed the fire.

The ghost-child felt the icy pain from staring into the distance too long for a first glimpse of a navy-blue coat approaching across the frozen lake.

The flowing hills looked like the dunes of a white desert, shape-shifting into swirls and strange mounds like melted whipped-cream animals.

She held her breath as a dark dot moved slowly behind a curtain of fresh snowflakes and refused to look away until her eyes watered from the strain... but it was a only a crow, and it swooped away laughing as it flapped across the murky sky. It landed to mock her atop a stone circle that barely showed above the deep snow banks.

Her fingers peeped raw from her red mittens, almost as blue as the phantom coat she hoped to see. She shaded her eyes and squinted through the bitter sting of wintry air.

She huffed on her numb fingers to thaw them. Then, shading her eyes, she squinted through the bitter sting of icy wind, and pulled her wool scarf closer over her mouth, breathing through it like a mask. There was nothing to see but the cheerless panorama of a forever Christmas without the fun.

She sighed, and clear sad pearls formed at the corner of each eye before she allowed the cruel wind to push her back inside.

She threw her coat onto a hook to dry and pulled on two sweaters. The last of these was one of her father's pullovers and reached to her knees. She loved that she could draw her legs up inside it and release her arms from its sleeves and sit, cocooned inside one of her father's bear hugs.

Her fur-trimmed boots shuffled to the window where the warm smoke from the fire's breath had puffed its way over to the sheet of ice causing it to glisten, slick as a puddle. She liked to pretend a two-dimensional world existed in the landscapes of crystals joining hands on the windowpane. It was a world of her own making and she gave it a wipe with the woolly elbow of her sleeve, fracturing the thin continent that lived there.

As she boiled a kettle for her father's tea, a hot blast from the stirred flames shot from the fire and hit the glass forming new hoar frost. To make a window within a window, she used a kitchen spatula to scrape the baby ice. It was soft. Crystallized paper.

The food was running out. The ghost wanted to sleep all the time, now. Only the scent of summer and a new friend broke her slumbers, but she often heard the flutter of voices from the walls telling her to be brave and promising that help was on its way.

But every night was the same. The possibility of a navy-blue coat trudging over the wasteland towards the light from her window faded as the night dropped down and the wind moaned around the moon wrapping it in gray bandages. Her last task was banking the fire into a red glow before snuggling her way under the covers with Unicorn nestled under her chin like a scarf. She slept with her nose in his fur, and girl and cat dreams mingled together so that she stretched whenever Unicorn did, and she felt her tail twitch when the storm scraped its icy fingers on the windowsill and the bed springs groaned like weary bones.

But her last thought before she drifted into sleep, was the heavenly comfort of a blue coat that smelled of stars, and the possibility of *'daddy what did you bring me? And a happy, 'but where have you been?'* and the best tears of all, from the waiting being over.

PART TWO

NORTHUMBERLAND

*"Sometimes
I've believed as many as
six impossible things
before breakfast."*

- LEWIS CARROLL

CHAPTER ELEVEN

Alarming Clocks

Bede Hall
APRIL 1, 2014

On the first day of April, the bewildered Stratford-Smyths found themselves shivering in the chilly courtyard in front of Bede Hall beside a large moving van, shoulder-deep in a confusion of wind-whipped cardboard boxes, cages, and mounds of furniture.

Three over-excited pets stirred-up by the crisp cold air made a barnyard din of squawks and meows and barks in addition to the bustle of unpackings and goings-on necessary to tame an ornery deserted mansion into a new home.

"They're far too invigorated," Bash declared, carrying Feathers in her cat carrier, and Jack, not being an adventurous breed of dog, followed close behind her, tail between his legs, without the need of a leash.

It took Kit and Rupert all their strength to lug the enormous parrot cage muffled in blankets into the Hall, but in a matter of hours the family was alone with all their belongings inside filling several passageways, while a huge saucepan of milk simmered gently on the stove for cocoa.

Mrs. S rinsed out the last cocoa mug and set it on the draining board.

"I'm too tired to wash these tonight," she yawned, folding a tea-towel over them.

"Sweet dreams Mum," Bash said, giving Mrs. S a hug.

"I don't dream anymore," Mrs. S sighed, "I suppose it's a blessing really. At least the nightmares have stopped."

"Dreaming is good for you," said Kit. "It's a scientific fact that dream-deprivation makes you ill."

"You and your science," Rupert said, "it's *sleep*-deprivation. The fewer dreams the better as far as I'm concerned."

Lady Nan was adamant. "Well I for one, plan to have a jolly good dream after today. We're in, so the house should be satisfied. Just listen to that storm. Isn't it wonderful? It's the best sort of lullaby; I won't have any trouble sleeping."

"Perhaps everyone should turn-in early." Mrs. S sighed. "Kit, don't forget to give Jack a short run outside. There's no need to take Lady Nan upstairs. I'm afraid you'll have to sleep in my room tonight, Mamma. Bash and I can share. Storms might be thrilling, but the power has been dodgy all day. Parks says he'll have it under control soon, but we don't want to take any chances getting stuck in the lift."

"Will do," Kit answered, already offering his arm to help Lady Nan into her wheelchair.

"And please bank the fire before you go up will you Rupert?" Mrs. S said over her shoulder.

"I'll do the stove now," Rupert crowed. "I'm hitting the headphones for a couple of hours. Hands up who wants a hot-water-bottle," he said with both hands in the air.

"Feathers is probably already on my bed, sound as a pound – she always gets there ahead of me," said Lady Nan. "She'll keep me warm enough. Can you fetch her for me Sheba?"

Bash nodded that she would, and patted her mother's arm.

"Maybe the house will send you a nice dream tonight, Mum," she said kindly, "it feels like home here."

"Homing pigeon," shrieked Pigeon, *"home sweet home...more cocoa... more pooh... time flies...cats meow... the bees knees... pop goes the weas...!"*

The sizzling sound of several overhead light-bulbs on the back stairs and hallway interrupted Pigeon, by popping in a dramatic explosion when Bash flicked them on.

"Wooooooooo!" taunted Rupert. "Your childhood ghost is still awake then, Lady Nan?"

Lady Nan gave him a sympathetic stare.

"Don't be an ass," Kit said. "There's no such thing as ghosts. Scien..."

"There's more science in heaven and... um... something I forget," misquoted Rupert, snickering. "Goosebumps that pass in the night and all that. The unexplained defies science... oooooooh... waaaaaah...ooooooo – the beyond! Can't you feel it calling?"

"You know, you're quite mad, don't you," Kit said.

"Just kidding. April Fools," Rupert said lamely, polishing his sunglasses.

"Ghosts don't like to be mocked," Lady Nan said, giving Kit a wink.

Rupert gave a hollow laugh, but looked a little unsettled.

The family did their best to ignore him. Candles were distributed in silence against future *pop-outs*, and Kit and Lady Nan disappeared down the hall in a murky sphere of candlelight.

"Pooooooo...waaaaaah...pooooooo," Pigeon screeched in Rupert's voice.

Bash threw a cloth over Pigeon's cage, and left with a sputtering candle to find Feathers, and Mrs. S filled five hot-water-bottles in case Feathers abandoned Lady Nan by taking a nocturnal prowl around her new home. Jack was content to remain sprawled asleep by the stove.

Rupert headed up the shadowy stairs, his long legs taking two at a time, armed with a sixth hot-water-bottle and a temperamental flashlight whose feeble energy sent out a fragmented S.O.S. beam only slightly ahead of him. Halfway up the dark passage, the batteries hesitated, coughed a few times, and died.

He gave it a good smack with his hand, but all that happened was a cold draft shuddered past him, and he bolted back to the kitchen where Jack blended into the hearth rug.

Rupert felt bruised and shaken from colliding with the corner of a heavy hallstand, and quickly grabbed his own low-tech candle which offered a more reliable light source.

"C'mon Jacko," Rupert cajoled, heaving the reluctant Jack to his feet. "You can come upstairs with me tonight, mate."

But Jack remained cemented to the floor, and Rupert bunked in the living room. A strange name to call a room where the image of a ghost's face peered in the windows every night at 9 o'clock.

"There's no fool like an April fool... Nighty-night Horatio," Pigeon cackled softly to himself within his tablecloth cocoon.

In spite of the bad weather and the electrical circuits mysteriously fluttering on and off every few minutes, the ordeal of moving had been relatively smooth.

The glow of a new hearth-fire and candlelight felt peaceful, and the fatigue from hard work mixed with cocoa sent everyone off to bed at eight o'clock. The next day would be the start of a new life, rain or shine, even if the electrics were determined to have a mind of their own.

It had been a chore to pack Mr. S's study and undo all the things which had made their home the special place where they'd so recently been together.

Each artifact of his personal collection had been handled with care and cataloged against the day they would be donated to a museum. His awards and honors were carefully packed in tissue paper, and his favorite books were crated and labeled 'Kit's room' where they would continue to be read and treasured. But it was decided that his priceless scarab-beetle collection would be kept on permanent display in a place of honor.

Although drastic changes had occurred, there had been nothing out of the ordinary to announce the supernatural events which were to come. In fact, astounding events were already silently brewing high above Bede Hall like the proverbial storm in a teacup. Timing, apparently preferred to take 'its own sweet time.'

The twins hadn't a clue that their personal teacup was about to expand to the size of a bathtub or that even a bathtub would be unable to contain the bizarre experiences that were about to unfold. But then, that's what supernatural means: not natural... not usual... and as far beyond normal as they could possibly have supposed in their wildest imagination.

Besides, they had no idea that Bede Hall had absolutely no intention of being sold.

CHAPTER TWELVE

Cozy is as Cozy does

Bede Hall groaned wearily in its old foundations and sighed with relief, satisfied it could rest for a while. Humans, it thought, were slow creatures, but it was delighted to feel the warmth rising from the ground floor, spreading down to the cellars like the roots of a tree. Its service elevator had anticipated the return presence of Lady Nan's wheelchair and behaved itself in deference to its queen. The rows of dusty books in the Red Library shuffled together and the clock began to tick softly again as time returned to the manor.

The building snapped and creaked from age and memories, occasionally stirring from prolonged semi-hibernation, feeling friendly. In one of its crofter's cottages, barely half-a-mile away, its old gardener, Stanley Parks, along with his son Stanley Parks, his grandson Stanley Parks, and his great-grandson Stanley Parks, had settled in, eager to dig and till, trim and clip, and prune and plant. The gardens stirred in anticipation. Fresh cool winds dropped from the brewing tempest above and breathed new hope into the flowerbeds choked with weeds. The long grass rippling like a restless sea under the full moon, dreamed of its former smoothly-mown lawns, while the giant sculptured topiaries rustled their shaggy overgrown leaves with excitement.

The conjured gale lashed fiercely enough to cleanse the countryside below from years of neglect, and howled its pleasure through the towering columns of poplar trees that encircled Bede Hall like a giant green Stonehenge.

Icy fingers of wind slipped through the Hall's keyholes and worried its locks, and whistled under its doorways rattling the latches, and pummeled the windows, and creaked the stairs, until all the anger inside had been blown away like cobwebs.

After two years of neglect there was so much work to do, that the wind wouldn't fully moan itself out until after May Day.

The Red Library received Mr. S's scarab collection with pleasure. It eagerly unlocked the glass doors of its rare books cabinet with open arms, and spent happy hours counting and admiring the rows of shiny beetles nestled on a large wooden tray. It loved each of them – the common clay beetles, the carved bone and quartz beetles, and the precious-stone beetles of blue lapis lazuli and turquoise, and the most valuable of all, the solid gold beetle in the center. It gloated over the smallest, the size of a fingernail, to the life-sized ones that filled the palm of a child's hand, and reveled in their iridescent colors as much as the plain gray ones.

Mr. S had put on his professor hat many times and made history sound like the best stories.

Carved beetle-shaped ornaments had been sent far and wide throughout upper and lower Egypt because they were more durable than papyrus scrolls. 'The ancient Egyptian's telegrams,' he had called them, with their carved hieroglyphic messages on the undersides, were 'e-mails' of great deeds that were commemorated as engravings in tribute to the real-life beetles which represented sun worship.

'The scarab beetle rolled a ball of its eggs in front of it as it traveled,' he had told them... 'and always towards the sun,' and so it was pictured with its front legs outstretched holding a sun disk.

Mrs. S hastened towards the library rattling the key to the glass cabinet in order to choose two scarabs from her husband's collection. It was the twins' birthday soon, and although the professor's collection would always be theirs as a family heirloom, she wanted them to have one scarab each for their own. In the evening light the rows of beetles glimmered like the lines of chess piece armies waiting to play.

"Bother!" she said, discovering she'd brought the wrong set of keys.

For a moment she considered using the elevator but thought better of it and took the servants' stairs.

The return journey to the kitchen was swift. On her way, Feathers crossed Mrs. S's path who nearly tripped over her from being distracted with birthday cake recipes.

Feathers shadowed Mrs. S back up the stairs hoping for a chance to show the woman how hungry she looked. In the library, Mrs. S gave a little cry. The door to the cabinet was gaping open.

"I'm sure I didn't open that," she said to Feathers.

"You shouldn't have done that," Feathers said to Bede Hall.

"She wanted it open. I was only trying to help," came the reply.

Mrs. S glanced at the wrong set of keys in her hand. She confessed to Feathers, patting her head. "I must have had the right keys in the first place. Goodness, I'm getting as forgetful as Lady Nan."

The thought caused her some dismay and she dithered all the way to the teapot and sipped a tipple of sherry to calm her nerves while the kettle boiled.

Rupert continued to tease the twins that a poltergeist was playing tricks with the power but they scoffed, and in the end he only unnerved himself.

The erratic crash of thunder from the unseasonably harsh spring storms didn't help relieve his anxiety, and during his first stay he bedded down in the living room, citing he should be downstairs in case of an emergency.

Rain and sleet interfered with the gardening, but it was cozy inside the ground floor kitchen with one of its three massive wood stoves blasting enough heat to fill the cavernous room which was almost as big as the Stratford-Smyth's old house.

Luckily, the main fireplaces hadn't been boarded up, and wood fires blazed wherever they could in makeshift bedrooms, thawing the damp brick walls into a snug nest.

The complex warren below-stairs was soon converted into a delightful rambling apartment with odd pockets of space for closets, as the former servants' dining hall was reborn as a makeshift living room, and a cluster of abandoned workrooms were given beds and wardrobes and dressing tables, and sets of drawers and shelves, and whatever else pleased the new inhabitants that was portable enough to shift from the rooms above, which had become a veritable department store of unique treasures.

Chaos may have ruled outside, whipping the trees into a frenzy, but little-by-little, the interior of the new family headquarters, for that's what a corner of the cold mansion was, buzzed with energy and the old Hall which had been slowly dying came back to life.

From a distance, golden light could be seen through the wind and rain spilling from the lower windows of Bede Hall, an electric lamp flashed erratically in the Red Library like an S.O.S message, and one pale blue light flickered softly in a small arched window high under the eaves.

It had been so long since anyone had sighted the ghost of Bede Hall that she had become a fanciful illusion. Certainly the twins had never tried to make contact with her. Not from fear, because it's said she's a friendly child, but because they didn't really believe she existed. Although to be fair, Bash remained open to anything Lady Nan believed. Besides, it was April, and the apparition was known to only appear in the month of August.

In any case, the Stratford-Smyths were far too busy to think about an unlikely invisible inhabitant, and time continued to cast a sleeping spell over the room under the roof and its childhood memories frozen for sixty-five years. But Lady Nan had never forgotten. Sometimes she remembered like it was yesterday.

For eleven months of each year, the ghost continued to call for her lost father. She sent messages to her friends and took comfort from weaving her own dreams about a happy family who shared the warmth of a safe winter hearth.

She remained aware of the Hall and knew it was mindful of her because her room flared with blue power from time to time, and a light bulb that hadn't worked for years fluttered from the ceiling like a trapped white bird.

Still, she was contained by a magic calendar, and there was nothing to do but wander invisible throughout the house and wait for a better summer.

CHAPTER THIRTEEN

The Name Game

The sound-word myth inside the name Smyth, bothered Rupert no end since he wanted to pronounce the name Smyth the more snooty way: Smythe that rhymed with scythe.

Words and names held power, Lady Nan liked to say.

Vocabulary, she insisted, was critical if one wanted to be a writer, and she was intent on training her granddaughter to assist her in writing the history of Bede Hall. Bede Hall had deemed it so. To practice, Lady Nan dictated her own stories and Bash wrote them down in a large black hardcover notebook.

It was the Stratford-Smyth family's view that although an extra 'last' name had a distinct social ring to it, a first name was much more powerful when condensed as short as possible, like using a single initial as was the custom in old genteel households. It was this logic which had earlier reduced Christopher to C if he was in a particularly scientific mood, and finally settled on, Kit.

The name Bathsheba had easily been shortened to Sheba and then B, but Bash seemed just right, and as no other nickname presented itself, Bash it was and Bash it stayed.

However, grandmothers have very different ideas about their grandchildren's names; Lady Nan was no exception. To her, Kit would always be Christopher, and although she often addressed Bash as Sheba, if she really wanted to make a point, Bash was once again Bathsheba – but with an added exclamation point.

Rupert lorded it over everyone, and Kit and Bash dubbed him Boss, which Rupert rather liked in spite of it being awarded in the spirit of blazing sarcasm.

The name caught on, even by Mrs. S who wanted to believe someone else was in charge at least some of the time.

In deference to her ancestral status, the twins' quirky Grandmother had always been Lady Nan, but on the days she reverted to her second childhood she would only answer to Beryl.

The twins had called their grandfather Hilton, Captain Hilltop or Captain Hilly, and in private, tongue-in-cheek, just plain, Top. Partly to spite his austere naval career and commanding nature, and partly because of Hilly being a nickname for Hilton, but also because their earliest memory of him was the time they went climbing the nearby Box Hill on a wintry day when he bossed them about calling them his little soldiers, marching them through the snow banks and giving them instructions on how to survive if they were ever caught off-guard in a blizzard. Kit had remarked he would never feel his toes again.

Grandfather Hilton had taken the title Captain as a compliment but it was delivered in a mocking tone by Lady Nan, his long-suffering wife, who had never called her husband anything else.

All three Stratford-Smyth children had the middle name Carter because Carter was Mr. S's real last name. Stratford-Smyth was only his latest name, due to marriage in the Stratford-Smyth tradition.

Old Aloysius, Lady Nan's great-grandfather who'd had no sons, decreed that if there were no male heirs to carry on the family name then the daughters must. So when necessary, the ruling hand of male power passed like the ancient Egyptian kings, through their womenfolk.

It seemed that Egyptian dynasties and the old families of England had one thing in common: a goal to preserve the family name at all costs.

Lady Nan was caught between her only child, a daughter named Rayne, and the death of her brother, Bentley. She rarely discussed Ben. Some things were better left as haunting memories.

In order to marry Rayne, Cornelius Carter willingly signed the papers that changed his name and was formally recorded on the Stratford-Smyth genealogy chart.

It was a great testament to Mr. S's affection for his wife, as he had been particularly attached to the name Carter. It had inspired him to become an archaeologist because it had been Howard Carter, his distant third-cousin several times-removed, who had discovered King Tutankhamun's tomb in 1922.

Cornelius Stratford-Smyth resigned himself to marrying his delicate fiancé, Rayne, and in due course, had been proud to bequeath his former surname to his children. And up to his disappearance, his new name hadn't appeared to hamper his efforts to successfully excavate his own findings in the Valley of the Kings.

So, truth be told, the latest generation of Stratford-Smyths had three last names.

Rupert found it especially gratifying to flaunt his last name at every opportunity.

He had certainly dropped his personal ties to the country estate of Bede Hall into as many of his college chums ears as often as he could, and he found it particularly satisfying, now that he'd actually become an official resident of Bede Hall, that he was in an even better position to lord it over any acquaintances worthy of impressing.

Postcards of Bede Hall still paved Rupert's way like prestigious calling cards, but he steamed and complained bitterly about his boring train journeys to Bede, and watched the clock, counting down the seconds till it was time to leave.

But the most peculiar names of all belonged to the family's elderly parrot named Pigeon, who not only answered to any word beginning with P, but especially liked to squawk the word 'poo' when he was particularly upset, although he also enjoyed inserting it into his regular rantings at random intervals any old time of the day, if you please.

Inherited, was not quite the word for Pigeon's ownership so much as a gift. He had once belonged to the twin's Great Uncle Bentley, and was much pampered and encouraged to speak his rather spontaneous mind.

It had not been easy for Lady Nan to part with the eccentric bird, but she gave him to her son-in-law Cornelius, as a wedding gift. 'From one Egyptologist to another,' she had said, although her teenage brother had never been to Egypt and had only had a few years in his short life to express his most earnest and budding desire to be an archaeologist.

Bentley Stratford-Smyth, the perpetual boy, had taken to Egyptian history with such enthusiasm, that after he died, Parks created the sphinx topiary in his honor. He positioned it to guard the maze, that had taken him twenty years to finish.

Pigeon was a chatty addition to the family, and at the ripe old age of one-hundred-and three, he had witnessed the events of Bede Hall like a colorful tape recorder from the unique advantage of his inconspicuous perch.

He was like one of the old faithful servants waiting in the wings, the kind who were trained to blend into the woodwork so well that their ears and eyes were forgotten – dismissed like wallpaper, yet all the time they were privy to private conversations that were expected to travel in one ear and out the other without leaving a trace.

Pigeon had heard every kafuffle and hushed secret, and savored each juicy tidbit of gossip, and more importantly, he had sensed every appearance of the Winter Child as she accompanied Lady Nan as a girl, down the stairs to the gardens below, leaving a faint frosty chill in the air behind her.

Lady Nan's old friend, Dr. Brooks, joked that the bird had 'Parrot Turrettes' and that the little bird-brain needed to wear a muzzle.

But Pigeon Carter Stratford-Smyth took his duties seriously; he listened in the shadows, out of sight and slightly out of his mind.

Stanley Parks, the elder, had been rewarded for his long service as head gardener and overseer with the deeds to his 'grace and favor' cottage the day he retired, and the men in his family had continued to inhabit it from time-to-time whenever they visited the village of Bede.

Citrine, Parks' daughter-in-law, always stayed back in Scotland and was heard to say that it was the 'boys' special time to be alone, and didn't she love to have her highlands to herself for a bit, anyway.

Since all four generations of Parks were named Stanley, the Stratford-Smyths added a number to their name in order to distinguish one from the other: the most senior Parks had earned the title of number one so he was plain 'Parks'. Next in line was his son, Parks 2, his grandson, Parks 3, and his teenage great-grandson was, in the natural order of things, Parks 4. He was the latest Stanley being trained in the tradition of Bede Hall conservation, and it was clear by the cheerful dedication of all four, that they not only respected the estate immensely, but cherished it as their second home as well. Parks 6, Parks' nephew, was scheduled to be his apprentice next year. Parks 5 had decided to stay in school to study animal husbandry at college.

Bede Hall recalled the date July 30th, 1958 very well. It was the day Master James Bentley Stratford-Smyth turned eighteen, and it was fair to say that most of his gifts had something to do with Egypt.

He had sat browsing through the book given to him by his best friend, Perry, with his back leaning against the sundial, and a few feet away, Parks had been trimming the topiary shaped like a chesspiece knight.

"Parks, I've got to get to Egypt any way I can," Ben said. "I'm simply dying to go."

"Well, young sir, that's easy enough," Parks replied, "but I don't advise it."

Ben held up the cover of his new book so Parks would see. It showed the Great Sphinx of Giza under a bright blue sky. "You mean I have to just wait and see if something happens? I don't think much of that," he argued. "I mean, it's hardly a plan of attack is it?"

Parks removed his cap and twisted in his gnarled work hands staring off into the future before answering. "I mean, you don't want to tempt providence," he said with a firm eyeball-to-eyeball stare for emphasis.

"Providence?"

"Yes m'lad," Parks said. "Providence. It's a newfangled word of Miss Beryl's that means fate."

CHAPTER FOURTEEN

Homecoming Queen

Bede Hall
APRIL 3, 2014

A moving van in Bede had been big news, and news traveled fast in the sleepy village where time seemed to have stopped, when Sylvia Fox, who owned Twigglys Tea Shop, and Enid Tweedy, the wife of the local realtor, shared their regular cup of tea at the meeting of the 'Who's Who and Who's Better Club.' The pair represented the beginning, the middle, and the end of the village's grapevine, but they were terrible at math. More often than not, their two-plus-two conclusions ended up in a very large wobbly number beginning with five and had several zeros at the end.

One-by-one the villagers gravitated to Mrs. S and said their hellos. Sprightly Mr. Vincento Leoni, the venerable chemist, who was surely as old as Lady Nan herself, restated his sincere condolences and had snapped a photograph of Jack's ear.

One or two of the townsfolk looked uncomfortable and talked about the weather, saying how atrocious it had been for it to snow in April, and Mrs. Tweedy almost tripped over, Ritzy her poodle, to get to Mrs. S's side before her chum, Sylvia, beat her to it.

Mrs. Spoondance, the rotund postmistress, waved a letter from behind her counter.

"Hellooooo. Something here for you already, Rayne," she called out over the heads of the queue lined up for stamps and parcels.

"Hello Cora," Mrs. S acknowledged, waving back the shopping list in her hand like a small flag.

The cramped corner store looked as if it might burst with customers. Patrons jostled old-fashioned wicker baskets and shopping bags with wheels, maneuvering them down the narrow aisles trying to avoid the people clutching the official wire baskets provided at the door.

Judging by the variety of merchandise on its crowded shelves, the shop seemed as if it couldn't quite decide if it was a grocery store, a chemist, a newsagent, or a post office.

Mrs. Spoondance moved to the checkout counter, leaving young Freddie Allen, a bewildered new employee, to face the post office queue, alone.

"Well, we're finally here," Mrs. S announced breathlessly to the postmistress, setting down her purse and shopping basket. "As you can imagine, we need supplies, but I'm only doing a small shop today," she said consulting her list. "Let's see... just tea and milk... Oh, and some lamp oil, and Mama's chocolate biscuits. The special ones that come in a tin that she likes so much."

"Naturally. Can't do without *those*," Cora quipped.

By the look of Cora Spoondance's plump shape, she knew all about the perils of chocolate biscuits and perhaps several assorted candy bars and cakes as well.

"And a half-dozen boxes of matches," Mrs. S finished. "And I'm also going to need one of those change-of-address forms."

"How are your old wood stoves holding up?" Cora asked placing the items on the counter.

"*They're* not the problem, the electricity is playing up. Playing *with* us more like, as old houses are wont to do. Parks thinks it's either the storms blowing the power-lines about, or a pesky fuse.

"Rupert isn't going to be home that often, and he doesn't even know where the fuse box *is*, and if he did, he wouldn't dare tinker with it; he'd just call Parks anyway.

"The extra matches are for oil lamps and candles and to light the fires. We're back in the bad old days I'm afraid, but it's really a very welcoming house when all is said and done. Candlelight is actually rather comforting, and we need that. It's been a terribly difficult time."

"We were all shocked when we heard about dear Cornelius," Cora said, totting up the bill. "He had many admirers here. You just take things one day at a time and feel better, and don't forget... you have lots of friends in Bede."

"That's very kind," Mrs. S replied. "I wish it were under better circumstances, but even the most well-meaning visitors would be too much at the moment. I think it's best we keep a low profile for at least a few weeks.

"Oh, I nearly forgot. I have a little ad to put up on the notice board. I'm looking for a few private students for the summer," she said, looking uncomfortable. "Just until things sort themselves out you understand ... one or two children the twin's age who need coaching before next term.

"Rupert can't possibly take on a part time job with his full-time studies, but I didn't think I would ever need to go back to work," she finished lamely, nearly in tears.

"The twins have grown."

Mrs. S welcomed the diversion. "Yes. They'll be thirteen in a few days. Growing like a couple of weeds, although Bash would find fault with that word. Parks has told her there's no difference between hothouse flowers and weeds growing wild under the sun. Our dinner-table discussions are quite diverse. We get botany lectures from Bash when Kit isn't explaining geology and the weather." Her voice faltered. "And my husb... their father used to tell us about Egypt."

"I see Queenie is well," Mrs. Spoondance said quickly, inclining her head towards Lady Nan examining the biscuit selection.

Mrs. S brightened. "I haven't heard anyone call Mama that for years."

Cora patted Mrs. S's arm.

"Rayne, I assure you it's said with great affection. My mother always called her Queenie. Beryl was the 'Queen of Bede,' not just the Hall, and no mistake. It's grand that she can use a walker again."

A shout from Sylvia Fox, the vet's wife, interrupted their conversation. "Drop by the teashop," she sputtered, arriving breathlessly, patting Mrs. S's arm as if they were old friends. "Bring her Cora. You must. So much to catch up on my dear."

How is your husband?" Mrs. S asked, just to be polite. She'd always liked Mr. Fox, the vet.

"My husband is a saint," Mrs. Fox gushed, "an absolute saint." And with that, she rushed off to another face in the crowd the way a bee buzzes from flower-to-flower. She returned almost immediately, to eavesdrop. Juicier gossip required a dedicated ear.

"That woman will wear herself out one of these days," Cora laughed. "Well, we can always hope. She's very curious about you lot. Her *and* Enid Tweedy. Those two are always plotting together about something. Now, what was it we were saying before the old bat pushed in?"

"I was about to say that Mamma is her old self once-in-a-while, and that she's had more good days ever since we decided to move back here, but she's still very muddled most of the time. She told me the Hall ordered her to come home. But, you know? It *does* feel like home, and if any place could literally call us, Bede Hall could. I'd quite forgotten how the place used to energize us. Even with all the moving pains, and... well, *everything*, it almost feels as if we never left. Some things and people stay the same don't they? Which reminds me. I just ran into Vincento and his irrepressible camera. He'll never change either."

"That digital camera thingy certainly changed the art of photography," Cora chuckled. "He hardly ever puts the flaming thing down. The chap takes pictures of the most unlikely things at the drop of a hat. He's a bit of an eccentric old bird, but I've never met anyone so affable in my life."

Mrs. S nodded agreeably.

"I speak for the whole village when I say we've missed the Hall being open," Cora said, gazing out the door with a look of wonder. "Will you look at that sky! I do believe there's snow up there. So much for April showers. By the way, how is Parks? It's amazing he's still alive. I haven't seen him for years, not since I went up to the Hall when your mother was taken to the hospital that last time. Not long afterwards we all heard he'd gone up to Scotland to live with his son, Stanley Jr. He never would venture into town. He's an odd duck."

"Parks went all the way to Withering to visit Mamma, once. Her doctors told me. I tried to call and thank him, but he wasn't in the phone book."

"He's devoted to Bede Hall," Mrs. S said. "It's rather sweet really. He told me he's never happy anywhere else. He and Bash get along like a house on fire. What ever happened to Mrs. Parks?"

Cora smiled and totalled the bill. "It's said she died not long after they were married. Sad business. Parks won't talk about it. Will you be wanting the newspapers sent up?" she asked, pen poised in the air.

Mrs. S hesitated, checking her list. "*Um*... no thanks. I think we can do without them. We've seen enough bad news lately." She shuddered and pulled her coat closer. "It's awfully chilly in here," she said. "I just felt a shiver."

"That means someone's just walked over your grave," Cora said and immediately wished she hadn't.

Mrs. S looked uncomfortable and gathered her belongings clumsily. "Parks is still a godsend," she said quickly, "and he's brought his family business down with him to get us started. He seems quite indestructible. Pity I can't claim the same for our electrics."

Bash held a large curious-looking parcel when she met up with her mother and brother under the town clock.

Mrs. S consulted her shopping list.

"Next stop: the pet shop for bird seed and cuttlebones and those instant I.D. tags. Jack and Feathers need new ones," she said.

"We should get one for Pigeon," Bash piped up, he almost got out yesterday."

"That poor bird needs space to exercise his wings properly," Mrs. S said. "The library is big enough. I just have to remember to double-lock the windows. Pigeon's crafty, and he's been at Bede Hall longer than any of us – certainly long enough to discover the best ways to get out."

"I doubt they make a tag big enough for all *his* names," Kit chuckled. "Mum? Can I go to the sweet shop for a bit? I could meet you after. Where will you be in half an hour?"

"That's an awful lot of sweets," Mrs. S said, imagining her son wolfing down sugar the entire time.

"I'm not going for the sweets," Kit said. "I saw Dr. Brooks go in there. I doubt he'll even remember me. So can I?"

"Half-an-hour only, mind. I know what you get up to when you start on about science," Mrs. S said. "Talk the leg of a chair, you can."

"You scientists," Bash declared, and quickly added. "Can I look in on Charlotte, then?"

"You should call her *Miss Findhorn*," Mrs. S said. "She may be your friend, but she's also an adult. It's disrespectful to address her by her first name."

"Oh Mum," Bash said.

"You *botanists*." Kit said.

Bash fingered the necklace she always wore, a copper disk threaded onto a gold chain. "Charlotte's a *florist*, and she's my best friend as much as my teacher. And she said this button is my lucky talisman."

"That *button* is a Roman coin," Kit said. "And there's no such thing as luck."

"That's what you think. Charlotte said it was a Roman *button* and I believe her. She said it was..." she stopped. Kit would laugh at her. "Never mind. I found it in the maze when I was with Charlotte and it's special." Kit would tease her mercilessly if she told him that Charlotte called it a fairy penny. That had been nearly four years ago on her ninth birthday.

"You kids," Mrs. S said. "I'll be at Twigglys. I have to pick up Lady Nan there. She's having tea with her old friend, Miss Goodman."

"I still think Twigglys is a stupid name for a tea shop," Bash commented. "It's so weird naming it after a cat."

"Maybe it's because Mrs. Fox looks like a twig," Kit joked.

"Sarah Goodman wouldn't think it was stupid," Mrs. S rebuked, giving Kit another warning look. "Mrs. Fox is naturally tall and on the thin side."

"I just got a strong feeling she wants to see me," Bash said.

"Miss Goodman?"

"No. Char... I mean *Miss Findhorn*," Bash said.

"That's funny, I just had the same feeling about Peregrine," Kit added.

"Kit!" Mrs. S said, with a stern expression.

"Okay okay. *Dr. Brooks*. I just like to say Peregrine."

But Dr. Peregrine Brooks had already left the sweet shop, and it would be weeks before Kit had the opportunity to meet up with him.

Just some white carnations please, Charlotte," Dr. Brooks said cheerily. "I think an old-fashioned nosegay would be an excellent choice."

"For Miss Beryl?"

He smiled. "They're her favorites. Maybe I will actually get to give them to her this time."

"Perry, she's just across the street. She's in Twigglys," Charlotte said pointing. "Look. You can see her through the window from here; she's with Sarah."

"The twins are coming," the doctor said, suddenly brightening as a black and white tomcat sauntered tail up through the open door.

The cat stared up at Dr. Brooks and yowled a startlingly intense meow.

"Hey there Lucky old chap. Found a home yet?" the doctor said, changing the subject abruptly.

"Where?" Charlotte said, still looking into the street for Kit and Bash. "I don't see them."

"Sorry, I saw them in my mind," Dr. Brooks replied, grinning. "It's so good to have the family around again. Kit is hardly recognizable. We haven't had the chance to reacquaint ourselves yet. I doubt he'll even remember me."

"He'll remember," Charlotte said, bending down to pet the cat. "Come on Lucky me old beauty, if that's what your name is. I saw a mouse in here this morning and I'm pleased to say it's all yours."

The cat leaped gracefully onto the windowsill happy to be out of the cold and in a place where the conversation was decidedly interesting. *No thanks, I can get a mouse any old time of the day,* he thought. *Humans are such simpletons.*

Peregrine Brooks scratched behind the cat's ear. "If this fellow does have a home, you'll have to get a mouser from Sarah," he commented. "I'm sure she has one to spare. I think she has ten cats now."

"She'd never give up one of her 'babies,'" Charlotte smiled. "She does love those cats of hers. They seem to find her."

"Cats are extremely psychic," Perry said. "If they're drawn to someone in particular, it's a sure bet that person is of a high order."

"You and your high orders," Charlotte said chuckling. "*Your* order comes to 50p so I guess it's *your* lucky day."

"Any day Miss Beryl comes home is a lucky day," Dr. Brooks replied wistfully. "Could you send them to the Hall for me, please?"

The doctor scribbled a message on a small white card and tucked it into the bouquet. "Put this on my tab please and thanks. My regards to Beegle. Is it too cold for him to be out today?"

Charlotte plucked a miniature rose from an enormous healthy-looking plant and threaded it into Dr. Brook's buttonhole.

"Monkeys need to keep warm. The 'Beeg' is happy to stay at home these days with all the cold weather, and it gives me a bit of a break. School kids are always dropping by to see him when he's here, and he loves to eat their sweets. So it saves me a trip to the vet," Charlotte said.

The tab was a running joke between them. For years Dr. Brooks had given Charlotte a complimentary fifteen-minute hypnosis session once a week, in exchange for what he referred to as the 'B flowers.' B for Bede Hall and B for Beryl, and for the last three years, 'B for the Beehive Nursing Home,' where Beryl Stratford-Smyth had received them in silence, not remembering his name on the card at all.

The cat, hearing everything he needed to know, slunk down from the window and bolted across to the churchyard, where he lived snug as you please, down an abandoned burrow amongst the gravestones.

Lately, the weather was too miserable for long-distance travel, but it couldn't stop him feeling a new sense of excitement. Doctor Peregrine had said the 'people' were back at the Hall which made him more eager to return.

Lucky told himself he would take a stroll up there as soon as it stopped raining and see if Feathers was back too. But his empty tummy told him something else. Soon it would be the time Miss Sarah put food out for the colony of feral cats living behind the church, and if he was quick, he sometimes got in a few savory mouthfuls before they ran him off. They were a tough lot.

But it didn't stop raining for two days, and Feathers looked out her own window in vain, peering through the downpour for a familiar sleek black shape waiting as it had always done, between the paws of the giant green sphinx.

CHAPTER FIFTEEN

Childish Things

Bede Hall had never been a child, although it knew what children liked. It had seen many generations of Stratford-Smyths born and raised to defend its borders.

So far, the Hall had been safe. It had been respected and admired, but for the last three years it had wasted away. It had tried to be patient, but it was constantly humiliated by feeble inspectors and greedy developers and hungry realtors.

The Hall, fussed after every obnoxious visitor. Corridor wind-tunnels of frantic air howled down the passages, and opened the windows and slammed doors in a dramatic temper, and disturbed the rows of long white curtains into a frenzy that flapped and waved like ghosts.

It grew increasingly alarmed as it overheard the various plans to divide its acres of unspoiled landscape into a cold map of cement squares crammed with rows of houses, with its stately rooms converted into flats, or a hotel, or a country club, or even a fancy restaurant.

It heard how its stables were to be torn down and its vegetable gardens ploughed over to become parking lots, and its proud formal gardens violated from the addition of a miniature golf course, and a playground with a waterslide that would end by spilling loads of stranger's children into its glorious fountain after the stone dolphins and mermaids were removed.

The topiaries were considered too high-maintenance and would be razed to the ground, these invaders had said.

Naturally it was confused, but most of all it was angry. The nursery on the third floor was full of ancient toys still treasured as keepsakes, archived for future generations, so why wasn't the same consideration being given to its bricks and mortar, and the precious land?

Bede Hall knew exactly how it felt to be deserted. Most of the time it felt like a dead museum about to be plundered by marauders.

It had served the Stratford-Smyths for centuries, and now it had been betrayed.

When it heard the suggestion that it would make a good retirement home or mental institute, Bede Hall knew it was time to put a stop to such nonsense and fight back with all its might. It summoned up its remaining energy and blasted out a distress signal to any family member sensitive enough to still hear its voice.

It had called out to its reigning queen, Beryl Stratford-Smyth, slumbering in a fairy-tale movie, and recalled its most faithful servant, Parks. It sent out a clear S.O.S to another of its former residents – a villager, sometimes called Tom, who had already lived four lives, and it called upon the frozen little ghost as well.

The Winter Child had never left. She had once been told to be seen and not heard, so the top floor where her presence was most felt was always silent.

The Hall had tried to console her, but now it was time to free her at last, and it was time to wake up the ones who were still obligated by Bede Law to preserve its nobility.

And due to its extreme efforts, Bede Hall overloaded its electrical circuits and lay exhausted in a fever-dream on its low hill, curled like a sleeping cat.

In its comatose state, it had called upon the dormant spirits of the surrounding winds to rouse themselves into a wild tempest that would confound the intruders who wanted to wipe out its history. And so it slumbered, fitfully dreaming of storms for ten long months.

Bede Hall didn't actually mind if it crumbled in time; that was a building's natural fate, but it wasn't going to be dissected or painted pink or endure any other such ludicrous 'improvements.'

Children didn't require a waterslide or games; they wanted trees and gardens to play in; they wanted a maze and a giant green sphinx made of leaves; they wanted to see fairies waving from amongst the flowers and to glimpse the Green Man inspecting his trees; they wanted the rabbits and the deer to leap across the lawns and to watch the swans glide silently on the lake.

Most of all, children wanted to dream their dreams where they lived in grand mansions like Bede Hall, and rode horses from stables like the ones at Bede Hall, and to play hide-and-seek through rooms full of treasures like those of Bede Hall, and to never be afraid of natural things like ghosts or the spirits of the wildwood.

Children were able to see fanciful creatures with gleeful appreciation, but the adults refused to listen about such things. Adults were determined to erase anything imaginative and force progress on their children. It was a sign of the times, they said; fantasy was best left to the movies.

Bede Hall agreed it was a sign to take back its power. Time to reclaim its glory days, even if it had to invoke heroic measures. It was time for war.

All families have at least one secret. The Stratford-Smyth's just happened to be an invisible child stored in a locked room behind a door painted ice-blue. A door sealed long ago when its current matriarch, Lady Nan, was a girl.

Lady Nan called it the Winter Door because its hallway was always chilly, even when the heat of summer turned the attic into a hothouse.

Today, the ghost of Bede Hall seemed more like a childhood fantasy of Lady Nan's, who was never sure what year it was although her fanciful daydreaming made her stories far more interesting... and Lady Nan loved to tell amazing stories.

The insatiably inquisitive Kit, was always interrupting them to ask lots of questions like a reporter, which gave Bash the time she needed to write them all down.

One of Lady Nan's stories was gaining steam.

"Wait just a minute!" Kit said, his eyes agog. "You saw the sphinx, the *topiary* sphinx, the one in *our* garden, the one made of, you know, *leaves*, run off into the woods?"

Lady Nan looked affronted. "I believe I said so quite clearly," she said peevishly.

Kit remained unruffled, allowing his grandmother's sarcastic tone to wash harmlessly over his questions.

"And you were awake?" he persisted.

"Of course I was."

"How do you know?"

"Because," Lady Nan sighed. "I wasn't the only one who saw it."

Kit was more determined than ever to discover the truth.

"But this was in your childhood, right?" he asked.

Bash scribbled non-stop, biting her lip trying to keep up.

"Goodness child! You really should pay attention. I said it was last *week*!"

"Okay, sorry... I missed that. One more question please," Kit insisted. "*Who* was it that saw it with you?"

Lady Nan looked a tad exasperated, but she spoke deliberately, pausing between each word as if Kit were a simpleton.

"It...was...Pigeon," she finished.

Bash guffawed and gave Kit a 'you asked for it' kind of grin.

Kit had already decided he wanted to study quantum physics in order to discover time-travel and said it was important to practice how to investigate everything scientifically in order to get one's facts straight, and since Lady Nan's bizarre tales often sounded highly unlikely, they prompted buckets of questions.

Bash raved about being a botanist, and still thought of the planet as her personal magic garden. She especially liked to collect big words for everyday things, and dropped her favorites into conversations as often as she could.

Her latest word was panache.

Lady Nan had spelled it out and made Bash look it up in the Hall's massive leather dictionary in the library.

Kit made a race out of the assignment and found it first, online, but both definitions the twins found described panache as another word for elegance and something posh that was fairly bursting with style.

Kit said science had panache, and both twins agreed it described Bede Hall perfectly. Bash added that Lady Nan had the most panache of anyone she had ever met.

CHAPTER SIXTEEN

Lucky Thirteen-ish

Bede Hall
APRIL 6, 2014

The twins turned thirteen during their first week in Bede Hall, and Kit had asked for a proper file cabinet with a lock; Bash said she wanted a wheelbarrow more suited to her size.

Bash gave Kit an extra-large, blue, wall clock whose hands had fallen off sometime in the distant past. She found it in Mr. Clutterbuck's 'Junk Emporium' her first afternoon in Bede, browsing for treasure while Mrs. S shopped for supplies. Perfect symbol for time-travel, she'd thought, and purchased it instantly.

Mr. Clutterbuck had rooted around in several cupboards claiming he knew where the hands of the clock were, until Bash explained that she would have taken them off anyway as the clock was meant to signify timelessness. "Rather like the 'The Stopped Clock' pub in Bede," she said.

"Of course," he replied, not understanding at all.

Joseph Clutterbuck was a slightly balding man who always wore exceptionally bright-colored waistcoats, and liked to refer to his business as an 'antique shop.'

Lady Nan affectionately called his business 'an establishment of disembodied collectibles,' and Kit called it heaven, as he loved to spend time there rummaging for odd bits of paraphernalia for his ongoing science projects.

Kit gave Bash a pair of green gardening gloves and matching socks so she would have green toes as well as green thumbs, and Lady Nan gave each of them the most amazing gift of all: two small parcels of land – one each, for their very own.

Bash's was a walled herb garden with a fishpond and a rope

swing, near the glass greenhouse shaped like a pyramid. Kit's was a stone tower behind the stables. The space at the top of the tower was the perfect spot to conduct his more secretive experiments and to gaze down at the stables where he hoped his own horse would be someday, and most important of all, it was a special place away from everyone when he wanted to be alone. He explored it immediately, racing to the top, leaving Jack behind.

Curiously, someone had painted a bold red number on each of the four corner crenelations forming a grid. The numbers 2 and zero made two diagonals. Could it be a signal for planes?

$$2 \qquad\qquad 0$$

$$0 \qquad\qquad 2$$

Mrs. S had been teary-eyed, and in addition to a file cabinet and wheelbarrow, had given each of the twins an Egyptian scarab, thousands of years old, from their father's collection along with framed photographs of the professor smiling with his arms around each of them.

Rupert's gift had been having a couple of second-hand bicycles repaired that he'd found in the classifieds of the 'Daily Bead,' the local newspaper. They'd been spray-painted; one fiery red for Kit; the other lime-green. "Now that you're older," he had declared haughtily over chocolate birthday cake, "you can go to the village for Mother and help Parks more with the grunt work."

Kit's turquoise scarab was given a place of honor on top of his favorite book, 'Ripley's Annual Believe it or Not.' Bash put hers, carved from rose quartz, on her dressing table beside her old rabbit doll, named Pookie – a stuffed toy that had seen better days, and an Egyptian mummy-shaped music box that her father had brought home as a souvenir.

Lady Nan still had her own children's books and toys. Her favorite was a snow globe that contained a tiny cabin and an evergreen tree. She would gaze into it for hours, and Bash kidded her that it was a crystal ball. Sometimes Lady Nan even sought 'readings' in the sand of a brass hourglass, and often turned the instrument on its side, which was, she said, more like a real landscape that way, rather than just an escape of time because both horizons stayed level and looked like parallel deserts separated by a glass tunnel.

Lady Nan had agreed that once in a while the future could be seen in her snow globe, and that holding the world in one's hands was a very big responsibility.

Many times, when Bash tiptoed in to say goodnight, the snow globe was still in Lady Nan's hands.

This particular morning it was the globe that had captured Lady Nan's attention.

Lady Nan was entranced, tilting her snow globe the better to interpret its message.

"What do you see in there this morning?" Bash asked cheerfully.

"There's been a sandstorm; I can just make out the pyramids," Lady Nan said continuing to peer closely. "The whirling sand is so white it looks like... oh dear, it looks like snow. There's a couple of horses galloping in the distance... oh, blast! They're gone. Fetch me my stronger glasses will you dear. I want to see who's riding them. Bother! Now it's snowing again."

This meant the prophecy was over for the moment. A snow globe that snowed was nothing unusual.

Most mornings began with Lady Nan studying her 'crystal ball'. She would sip her first cup of tea with a happy smile on her face, declaring she was searching the miniature landscape for signs of life.

Bash rarely asked what her grandmother saw. It was usually the past – a shaken mini-world of sandstorms and blizzards, but always, afterwards, the little house stood safe inside and the spruce tree remained 'ever green.'

Bede Hall listened attentively to every conversation floating through its furnace brain, emitting sparks and clanks as every old pipe and wire zapped new information from the library, and Lady Nan's crystal 'snowball' generously provided glimpses of a future it could live for.

It was possible, it thought with a chuckle, to tolerate almost anything for the sake of one's long term dignity... and panache.

Fortunately for Mrs. S and her brood, all four Parks had agreed to join forces and spend the entire spring season helping the new residents of the Hall, which they said, would blend in nicely with their annual summer visit.

Most days, Parks showed up to teach Bash the secrets of listening to the garden, but sometimes he was too tired, and she caught up on her schoolwork and writing Lady Nan's story, which she had insisted be called her memoirs.

But sometimes Bash used her spare time to visit Charlotte Findhorn, her quirky florist mentor in the village of Bede, who shared her progress using the tried and trusted New-Age techniques of growing things that Parks jokingly referred to as his *old-age* techniques.

All four Stanleys kept to their self-appointed tasks: Parks 4 handled all the mowing and weeding (engaging Rupert when he was home) Parks 2 and 3 managed the clipping of the hedges and the maintenance of the building, and Parks delighted in his labor of love: teaching his favorite Stratford-Smyth the forgotten art of gardening, with what Miss Charlotte and he discussed as supernatural which meant above and beyond natural.

Lady Nan had begun to use a walker for exercise, but her wheelchair was used for longer distances in the house or the village. She circumvented Bede Hall's sweeping staircases by using a rickety elevator that looked more like Pigeon's cage than a box.

For the most part, Lady Nan was still bedridden by choice, but she continued to take 'walking inspections' of the house and grounds in her imagination, and Bash wrote her accountings and stories down each morning after breakfast, in the large black book.

Quite often there was a list of duties for Parks that had to be couriered to the garden. "Any Parks will do in a storm," Lady Nan would always say.

70

CHAPTER SEVENTEEN
Cabbages & Queens

"Let's conduct an experiment," Parks said, staring knowingly at the cabbage seedlings and then at Charlotte. "You work on all these rows," he said to Bash, "and Charlotte will concentrate on one plant in the center. We'll give it more room than the others, and mark it with a red ribbon."

"That's what Kit would suggest," Bash said. "Well, perhaps not the ribbon."

Bash had long-term plans to plant masses of sweet peas against her garden's brick wall and restore the overgrown roses which had been left to struggle by themselves.

"They look dead," Bash said to Parks, as they inspected the garden under umbrellas. "Can we bring them back to life?"

"Of course," Parks replied. "They only *look* dead. Plants are much smarter than people. Never let the look of something fool you. Underneath that gnarled old bark there, it's green as Spring. Up there," he pointed to the sky, "it looks like the sun might break through."

"But they're choked with weeds," Bash argued.

"Weeds! Parks exclaimed, grinning. "What's a weed?"

"Now you're teasing me," Bash said.

"D'you think a weed knows itself as being any different than any other plant? A weed is an ambitious flower, that's all. A weed isn't even a plant at all," Parks insisted.

"It isn't?"

"No miss. It's something all plants *do*. Any plant can *weed* if it finds itself in the wrong place. Oh dearie-me no," he chuckled. "It be humans who decided way back, which plants were 'good' and which ones were 'bad.' They mostly got em wrong too. Only an herbalist or a true apothecary truly knows what's what. Mr. Leoni, in the village... he knows."

"But he's just a chemist," Bash said.

"Just!... he's much more'n that! *Just* indeed," Parks mocked. "Vincento Leoni has spent his life studying nature, and, well everything, really. He takes his studies most seriously, he does. And so should you. Plants are the best medicine," he went on. "And do you remember what Miss Charlotte taught you about the world of plants?"

Bash searched her memory when the florist had first talked to her about magic gardens.

"That plants are a kingdom?" she said.

"Righty-o. Learned that from me, she did. She's a pearl that girl. But you get the prize." Parks cackled, presenting Bash with a broken stem sprouting a lone rosebud that looked like a brown nut clinging to a stick. "Your scepter milady," Parks chortled, and patted Bash on the head affectionately. "You'll learn youngen. It takes years. Don't I look hundreds of years old?"

Bash accepted the rose and held it aloft like a queen.

"I reckon we should be planting reincarn... I mean *carnations*," Parks said. "They're Miss Beryl's favorites. "Did I ever tell you bout' the Green Man? Older than me, he is. Well, he can make anything grow. He's the king of the forests. Hair of leaves he has, and skin greener than your thumb. That's why we celebrate him on May Day."

"I'll have you know I have 'ten green fingers and ten green toes, thank you very much," Bash said with a smile.

"All right then," Parks said, "let's see how you do with these gladiola bulbs. Make sure the holes are nice and deep, mind."

The three gardeners said farewell to the cabbages as the first drops of rain fell. The tender leaves turned a brighter green under the damp breeze, and the earth released a spicy scent as the drops turned into a fine sprinkle.

"I can feel how happy they are," Bash said to Parks as they admired the healthy rows of plants.

Charlotte looked pleased. "Yes, the promise of a shower excites them," she agreed. "I'm glad you're beginning to feel that. You're starting to open."

"Open?"

Parks tapped a rose in bud. "Just like a flower," Parks said. "You're growing and listening to the elements."

"You mean the weather?" Bash asked.

"The energies surrounding us," Charlotte said, beaming at Parks.

"I wonder, do either of you have time for a cup of tea?" Bash asked. "Mum's made some scones, and we've still got fresh cream and a pot of your homemade fig jam, Charlotte."

Parks doffed his cap. "Not I Missy. Much as I love a cream tea, I promised my grandson we'd go into Bede."Well, I'd love one," Charlotte said. Bash smiled with relief. "I've been wanting to show you something inside. Something very special."Bash and Charlotte linked arms and waved to Parks who was across the lawn brushing some leaves from the sundial.

"Speaking of energy," Bash said, "Parks sure walks fast for someone of his age. He's already by the sundial."

"As long as I get the grand tour as well," Charlotte said, changing the subject.

Bash showed Charlotte her prize find on the third floor while the kettle boiled.

"This is what I wanted to show you, Bash said. "It's too bad it's so big and heavy. I can't ask Parks to shift it, but I'd like it down-stairs for my room."

"The fairy bed," Charlotte gasped. "It's legendary you know. I've heard of it. Miss Goodman told me about it once. Parks' father had a hand in the making of it."

"Lady Nan told me it's Art Nouveau," Bash said. "That's a style of design based on plants. All curvy and entwined. The shapes are supposed to move like water."

Charlotte ran her hands lovingly over the carving of the goddess's face, her long flowing hair woven with leaves and flowers, and her wings. The figure was surrounded by vines and birds. "Her name is Chloris," Charlotte marveled. "This bed is fit for a queen. Truly magnificent."

"It was Lady Nan's," Bash said. "Her father had it made for her. Apparently as an apology after they had a quarrel or something."

"Well, it's magic," Charlotte said. And just as she spoke, they were summoned by the far-off whistle of the kettle from two floors below.

When Kit wasn't dreaming about unlocking the secrets of space-time, he visited the long rows of stables imagining the horse he would own one day. It would be midnight black and parts of its coat would gleam like navy-blue silk.

The twins had their best dreams at Bede, and their grandmother made sure they heard how wonderful the estate was in the grand old days.

It had once bustled with servants and horses and carriages, and the hedges had been trimmed square as boxes, and the fanciful topiaries were so meticulously manicured by Parks that it had looked as if some escaped pieces from a chess board and a zoo of giant green animals had been enchanted into frozen shapes on the great lawn – a lawn that swept majestically to the small blue lake, where swans and herons still nested, each according to their season.

CHAPTER EIGHTEEN
The 'It' Girl

Bash raced by Kit, and tagged him. "You're it," she cried, and raced from the library where they'd been released after a spelling bee. She headed up the stairs, two at a time, to the attic, pelted down the dark corridor, and paused outside the Winter Door, with its cut-glass doorknob that looked like a fancy ice cube.

It was a bright midday in April, but the passages in Bede Hall were in shadow from the heavy curtains now drawn across the windows of the floors not in use.

As soon as Kit rounded the corner, he spied his sister with her hands on the door as if she were testing its temperature.

"Kit?" Bash called, pressing her ear to the door.

"What?" Kit managed to say, catching his breath as he reached her. "I'm bored with this game. Let's do something else."

"Why do you think this room is so cold?" Bash asked.

"I expect you've heard of the classic cold spot which indicates the presence of a ghost haven't you?" Kit replied.

"Yes."

"Well, it's *not* that!" Kit said with a chuckle. "There's no such thing as ghosts."

"Lady Nan says there is."

"Lady Nan thinks there's fairies living at the bottom of the garden," he said with his head to one side for effect. "There's no scientific proof for such things. If you can't see something or measure it; it doesn't exist. Period!"

Bash paused and held her tongue. Charlotte saw fairies and gnomes in her own garden, and was quite sane. Wasn't she? She was even opening Bash's eyes so she might see them herself soon. One couldn't argue with methods and results, and Bash had had some fairly lucid dreams about fairies lately as well; one's she didn't feel inclined to share with her twin. She had, in fact, partially blocked him out the way Charlotte had shown her.

Charlotte had also given Bash tips on how to get her own way. "It's all in the eyes," she had said. "Dr. Brooks taught me."

"Scientist are supposed to keep an open mind aren't they?" Bash quipped slyly.

"There's open and then there's a big empty hole," Kit said.

"What would *you* like to do then?" Bash asked.

"A science experiment or maybe watch the documentary 'Planet Doomsday' that Mum picked up for me from the library."

"What sort of experiment?"

"I don't know. Anything's better than pottsy tag. At least hide-and-seek is more interesting in a place this size. Trouble is, the last time we played we couldn't find each other, if you recall."

"How about an experiment on this room then. I can find out where Lady Nan keeps the key," Bash said. "We can set up a camera, and you have a tape recorder. Come on."

"We're not supposed to go in there," Kit said.

"Mum said that when we were just visiting here on holiday. Now we live here, she won't mind if we explore. Let's ask Lady Nan."

"Mum *will* mind."

Bash crossed her arms and raised her eyebrows, sending her brother a dare.

"Why don't we do an experiment on Mum then, and see if she says it's okay. I bet she will. I bet I can make her."

Kit looked interested. "A psychology experiment?"

Bash smiled smugly. "Sure, okay... that's science isn't it?"

Bash and Kit entered the library where Mrs. S was correcting Bash's composition: 'The Prodigious Accoutrements of Panache.' She had the dictionary open to the letter P, and Pigeon was fascinated as she said each 'P word' out loud.

"Mum?" Bash asked, "Remember you said I could take whatever furniture I wanted from the house for my room? Does that mean any room?"

76

Mrs. Smyth was absorbed, trailing her finger down the list of words searching for the word 'prodigious.' "Fine," she said, staring at the word 'pixilated' – a perfect new name for Pigeon.

"Plantagenet...Plethora... Ponderous....," she intoned, as Pigeon fluttered excitedly.

"Even Lady Nan's?" Bash asked holding her breath.

"If she says it's all right. Mind you don't go bothering her. She's calm today," Mrs. S said.

"If Lady Nan says yes, then can I?"

Mrs. S continued reading aloud: "Preposterous," she read, adding, an offhanded: "I suppose so," to Bash.

"Preposterous!... a load of poo," squawked Pigeon spreading his wings for a quick stretch.

Kit watched Bash's performance from the window seat and shook his head.

"Even the cold room?" Bash asked softly.

"That larder is only used for vegetables," Mrs. Smyth replied. "What could you possibly want from there?"

"But can I? Please? Please can I?"

"Yes, yes I suppose so. Look Bash, you can see that I'm rather busy here."

"Sorry."

Bash turned to Kit with a triumphant grin before Mrs. S called out, freezing her expression in mid-triumph.

"B?" her mother called, without looking up.

"Uh huh."

"Ask your brother for help with anything heavy. He'll be here tomorrow."

"Poo!...double poo and no return," Pigeon called after the twins.

"Mum meant Boss, not me," Kit said, when they were out of ear-shot. "And that wasn't fair. You know Mum calls the larder the *cold* room."

Bash faced Kit with raised eyebrows. "She just said your 'brother,' that's you as well isn't it? It'll be fun. We can't ask Boss for help anyway, he would ruin everything."

"It's a technicality."

"You're always saying technology is the best science."

"Bash?"

"What?"

"What if we find something we don't understand? Not a ghost, but something worse. Something... I don't know... dangerous?"

"And you call yourself a scientist. Are you or not? Brave new world and all that."

Kit grinned. "Let's get on with it then," he said.

Mrs. S wasn't fond of cooking at the best of times and couldn't truly be bothered if her meal was coming together as a meal ought, but right now she was diligently making supper, checking to see that the green beans weren't overcooked and the meat wasn't underdone.

She gave a heavy groan. The potatoes were still too hard. Due to the unexpected nature of a heat-wave which had pushed off the rain, she hadn't known what to serve for dinner. The weather was still behaving in the most erratic way.

It had been raining hard and cold in the morning, when from out of the gray... it suddenly poured warm rain, and then the sun had come out turning the day all steamy.

The 'salad weather' hadn't lasted for longer than an hour, so she had finally opted for their usual fare of a hot meal – deciding on boiled potatoes, steamed vegetables, and roast beef. It was anyone's guess if there would be rain, sun, or snow, by teatime.

Mrs. Smyth gave a satisfied sigh as she put the finishing touches on her pie crust. "Go check on Lady Nan, Bash. She's not herself today."

"Mum? When Lady Nan isn't herself who is she?" Bash asked as she set the table.

"She's a little girl remembering things that happened a long time ago," Mrs. S answered, clamping the lid back on the potatoes.

CHAPTER NINETEEN

Anubis

The brick walls of the stable easily broke the back of the wind that rattled its half-door. The twins had taken shelter from their chores, and lay comfortably on bales of straw with their ever-present shadow, Jack.

Kit looked up from his science magazine. "Listen to that wind! Boss can't expect us to work in this, can he?"

"He won't find us in here anyway," Bash replied. "He's in his room playing music. He says this is his *weekend* off, but we can't carry firewood in this wind. There's loads by the back door anyway. He just likes to give orders. He won't even notice if the pile is the same size."

Bash searched for the place in her book where she'd been interrupted, and Kit stared at the top half of the stable door that flapped about, creaking eerily.

"I'm quite sure we can afford one or two extravagances," he blurted out, changing the subject, and causing Jack to twitch in his sleep. "I only want Dad's subscription to National Geographic renewed. It's not a lot to ask."

Bash answered dreamily absorbed in her story. "Mum says we have to keep the wolf from the door."

"There aren't any wolves in England," Kit said, shaking his head. "Honestly Bash, you need to stop reading fairy tales."

"It's too bad we have so many doors," Bash continued, choosing to ignore the side of Kit who liked to interrupt conversations with irritating logic. "Bede Hall has so many doors. We would need extra money to keep a whole pack of wolves away."

"It's only one little magazine," Kit said crossly. "It says here, next month is a special edition on Egypt."

"Well, don't mention that to Mum; it would upset her. I still have some pocket-money saved. You can have that," Bash offered.

Bash counted dreamily on her fingers.

"One wolf each, from the back door, the door to the stable, the servant's entrance, the door to my garden, and then there's the double-doors at the front... so that probably takes two... oh, and the main gate. That's seven... and my two French doors. Do they count as one door?" she asked and decided it did.

"I guess we'll just have to make do with old Jack," Kit said.

Bash hugged the dog who raised his head at the sound of his name.

"Jack would even be scared of Little Red Riding Hood, wouldn't you, Jacko," she said.

Jack yawned, and settled his furry length back into the loose straw.

The twins rambled on about the similarities and differences of dogs and wolves, and agreed that no real wolf could reach the door of the Winter Room, but Kit had noted that when he pressed his ear to the keyhole, he could swear the howling wind sounded exactly like a lone wolf.

Bash said she heard a girl crying.

Kit said they would be better off with a pack of jackals, since their father had been an Egyptologist.

"Better off is a poor version of saying something's more *apropos*," Bash said. "Dear oh dear," Mrs. S muttered to herself, searching for the butter. The distinct blue and white covered bowl, shaped like a hen, was nowhere to be found in its regular spot in the fridge. She must have passed it several times making breakfast as there it sat on the counter by the telephone. "Goodness me, that's a strange place to leave it," she thought.

Bash sauntered in to set the table, still in her dressing gown. Anubis, Feathers and Snowdrop followed on her heels as she was the one who fed them.

"Bash you should put things back where they belong after you've used them. I couldn't find the butter this morning. It should be kept in the fridge. I couldn't find the tea canister either."

"Yes, Mum," Bash said sleepily, and thought, butter? She hadn't been near the butter since last night's bedtime snack. "It may have been Kit," she said. "I remember putting it away after toast and cocoa last night."

But when Kit was questioned, he reminded them he'd skipped his nightcap of cocoa and stayed overnight in the tower to study the stars.

"Pigeon," Mrs. S admonished. "Have you been playing with the butter?"

Pigeon put his head to one side and ogled Mrs. S as if she were crazy.

"Jam!... peach... plum," he squawked and closed one eye.

Cornelius Stratford-Smyth was not the only invisible presence that hovered in the corners during mealtimes, staring at the place set for him at the head of the table. Little did his family know that it would be an unusual form of rain that would restore their world with newfound peace and prosperity, but not that night nor many more to come.

Bede time ignored the exaggerated reports that still 'snailed' their way from Egypt to England, but there were no verifiable sightings of anyone remotely matching Mr. S description. His trail was cold.

Rupert sauntered into the kitchen just as Mrs. S was ladling thick lamb stew into the last of five flat soup bowls.

She placed a freshly baked loaf of bread on the table. "I think I'm getting the hang of this bread thing," she said.

"Smells good Mother, Rupert commented. "I'm starving."

"Don't you mean ravishing?" Kit teased. "I think you've forgotten your sunglasses. You feeling all right?"

"That would be famishing," Bash corrected.

"Nope, I was right the first time," Kit chuckled.

"I'm in a good mood little Kitty, so there's no use trying to bug me," Rupert said smirking at Kit as he produced his sunglasses from his pocket.

Kit writhed in his chair and glared at his brother who seemed rather smug with his comeback. Kit loathed being called Kitty.

Bash cut the crusts from a slice of warm bread and passed it to Lady Nan.

"By the way," Rupert said, taking in both twins with a sweeping gesture of his butter knife. "Speaking of kitties, there's a black and white tomcat living in the stables. You might want to feed him; he was looking rather ... *famished*... the last time I saw him... oh, and nice work topping up the woodpile siblings, there's enough wood for a week now."

"Don't you mean minions?" Kit said, his confidence returning, and giving Bash an 'I told you so' look of his own.

"Yes, well done you two," Mrs. S agreed quickly, sensing a full-blown argument. "Now eat up everyone. There's ice-cream cake for dessert."

"Isn't that rather extravagant?" Kit asked.

"Rupert was kind enough to bring us a treat from Oxford," Mrs. S said.

"Yum," Bash whispered to Kit. "Your favorite. And we deserve it after lugging all that wood."

Lucky was busy burrowing amongst the rubbish bins when Bash approached with table scraps for the compost heap. He answered her friendly greeting with a raised tail and a visit in order to sniff the bucket more closely.

Bash was moved. "Hey there buddy, you must be ravenous."

Lucky was thrilled to hear a kind word and came close enough for Bash to pet him. His bones were sharp under his matted fur.

"Poor old chappie," she said. "Life hasn't been kind to you has it?"

Lucky made an impressive display of his tail's prowess and purred loudly.

So this is Princess Bathsheba – the catnip goddess, Lucky thought.

"Wait right there," Bash said, and dashed off towards the light of the kitchen.

Lucky watched her go, blinked for a second at the darkening clouds gathering overhead, and returned to forage for his supper, but a bucket containing potato peels, cabbage leaves, and bits of carrots held no tasty temptations for a feline with discriminating tastes.

The hungry cat was delighted when Bash returned with a saucer of sardines and a bowl of water, and rubbed around her legs to say thank you.

Bash left him in sardiney bliss to eat in private, but Lucky was not so distracted with his windfall to miss noticing which door she used when she disappeared inside the building that glowed like a lantern.

So, it was no surprise later, when thunder heralded the arrival of a heavy electrical storm, that a persistent scratching sound of a bedraggled cat in search of a Sardine Princess, was heard at the kitchen door.

"The poor wee mite," Mrs. S cried at the clump of wet black fur shivering on the doorstep. "The little lamb's all wet."

Lucky unclumped himself and casually sidled past her to the fire giving Jack a warning growl. Jack lifted his shaggy head once to sniff the newcomer, but didn't stir from his rug. Feathers came to hiss, but smiled smugly.

'Told you it would work' she purred, recognizing her old pal from the sphinx.

"I'm a little lamb," Lucky bragged.

"I guess that makes me Little Bo Peep then," Feathers chuckled. *"You're just plain 'lucky' that's all."*

"He deserves a proper home, Bash suggested hopefully. "We have plenty of room for another cat now. Don't we?"

There was no argument. Bede Hall was enormous; it could house a hundred cats, but Mrs. S hesitated.

"Tuxedo cats bring good luck," Bash volunteered lamely.

"Oh *very* scientific," Kit said sarcastically. "Where'd you hear that?"

"Charlotte told me," Bash said, flashing her brother an indignant look.

"It's all very well to help him during the storm," Mrs. S replied, but he can't stay in here. You'll have to make a bed for him in the stables. We can give him a nice clean box and some blankets. That will have to do. Stray cats carry all kinds of vermin. We'll have no more inside-cats please. Thank goodness Feathers is spayed."

"You're almost home," Feathers growled to Lucky. *"In my opinion a cardboard box still beats a rabbit hole any day."*

Lucky looked at Mrs. S and meowed as plaintively as he could. Feathers hissed back *"Just give them time. What took you so long anyway? Where have you been?"*

"To London to visit the queen," Lucky replied, sarcastically.

"Well, I'm relieved to be rid of any city," Feathers said, *"Livingston was full of dangerous drivers."*

"Hang on!" Lucky hissed. *"Spayed? Who are they kidding?"*

"They assumed," Feathers replied, licking her paws. *"The SPCA told them I was 'fixed' to get rid of me."*

"Just as well they couldn't catch me then," Lucky declared. *"Miss Sarah saved me by telling them I was one of her rescues. I guess I am lucky."*

Lucky complained to Feathers as he inspected a delightfully snug cat nest. *"Vermin? I'm most offended,"* he lied, circling the inside of his new bed a few times. He flumped down in a heap noticing at once how soft and dry, and quite perfect it was. He had food and water delivered and a comfortable bed out of the wind, and yet he was still free to come and go – the best of both cat worlds.

"Humans aren't overly bright," Feathers said, *"you learn to live around them, and once you've hooked them they're easy to train. It's like falling off a windowsill."*

CHAPTER TWENTY
The Tenth Life

Sure enough, within a few days, Lucky was unceremoniously bundled off to the animal hospital to be neutered, given shots, and 'shampooed within 'an inch of his life,' as Kit instructed the vet.

"What do you reckon?" Dr. Fox asked probing the cat's ears with a long cotton swab, "Is this chap on his eighth or ninth life?"

"Looks like his tenth if you ask me," Kit replied, scratching Lucky's other ear. "Never mind buddy, you're all right now. You can stop protesting. It'll all be over soon."

Lucky bristled indignantly. *'It's my fifth,'* he hissed remembering how important he was.

The veterinarian filled out an official file card. "Shall I put his name down as Tom?"

"Nope, we've got the perfect name for him," Kit said proudly, "it's Anubis."

Tom preened, impressed. His Egyptian ancestors would approve.

"A new what? You'll have to spell it for me," Dr. Fox said.

"Anu*bis*: A-N-U-B-I-S. Anubis was an ancient Egyptian god. A wild black dog called a jackal, that has sticky-up ears like a donkey. Anubis survived in the desert as a scavenger. He was the guardian to the underworld. He ate road-kill just like this chap, well chariot-kill more like, and the scraps other people didn't want. Ironically he lived off dead things. So, he was known as the god who transformed death into life.

"D'you suppose that's where the nine lives thing started? It's interesting that the word dog is god spelled backwards isn't it?" Kit finished, not pausing to see if his audience had been following.

"Goodness, that was better than reading an entire history book," Dr. Fox said.

But Kit wasn't done.

"Cats were sacred in Egypt. There was Bast and Sekhmet the devourer, well she was actually a lioness, did you know it was against the law to harm a cat?" he rattled on, "people were put to death for harming a cat."

"Too bad it's not like that these days," the vet said.

Dr. Fox searched his brain for a nugget of trivia that might impress Kit, and could come up with only one:

"Did you know baby foxes are called kits?" he said.

Despite the humiliation of his operation, Anubis recuperated quickly and in addition to being the consummate guardian as his namesake decreed, made himself useful as a ratter. He still considered himself 'lucky' considering he didn't have to eat the wretched things anymore. It was an easy trade-off: the occasional dead rat in return for daily bowls of savory fish paste, fresh water, all the dry kibble a cat could eat, and a fireside chair... and now and then, the added bonus of the occasional sardine and a few kind words from a princess, as well as having a companionable wife.

'*Next life*,' Feathers said, curling up by the fire with her husband, '*we can be humans. I think we've earned enough points.*'

"*We don't have to. Do we?*" Anubis yawned. "*I was looking forward to being a tiger first.*"

"*I think you have to be a dog before you can be a tiger*," Feathers said.

"*Well that can't be right*," Anubis commented, "*not right at all.*"

As if in answer, the legs of a chair rattled and tapped, and startled poor Feathers who had been quite happily contemplating sleeping on it. Instead she remained where she was and slept the with one eye open.

The cackles in the stairwell raised the hackles of Anubis's fur.

"*I always hated it when you did that*," Anubis said to the dark. "*You sound exactly like Parks.*"

"*I was just welcoming you home*," Bede Hall said. "*How does it feel to be back?*"

"Sore," Anubis said.

"By the way," the Hall said. *"Silly Feathers. Inform her the rules of transmigration are very clear: humans upgrade to dogs (or sometimes, an exceptionally clever house). In my case it was human to house to house cat. You and feathers can look forward to many tiger years, and then, if you live an exemplary life, you can be an elephant. That's as high as it goes."*

Lady Nan woke up nine-years-old, with an urgent question: "Can we go to the garden today? Please can we?"

Bash tucked the snowflake shawl around her grandmother's shoulders and acted as if nothing was unusual. The transition from sleeping to waking was often the only time Lady Nan was still a bit confused.

Bash drew back the curtains to show Lady Nan the rain beating against the windows hoping to calm her, but instead the old lady began to panic.

"Oh dear, the world is crying," she said.

"No Beryl, it's just the April weather," Bash said reassuringly. "It's always rainy in spring."

"It's not summer then?" Lady Nan asked in a whisper. "Not August?"

"No Beryl, August is four months away. The garden isn't awake yet and neither are you. It's too chilly for you to go out and play."

Lady Nan relaxed. "Rain rain go away, come again another day," she recited. "She *will* come back another day. Won't she?"

"If *she* said so, then she will, Beryl. Let's have some tea."

"I'm not allowed tea," Lady Nan said. "I have hot cocoa in the mornings if you please."

"That's what I want as well," Bash said. "I'm going to make some and then read to you from your Narnia book. Would you like that?"

"I can't decide if I want 'Narnia' or 'Winnie the Pooh,' Beryl said.

"You've had the Narnia book a lot lately," Bash reminded her.

"I like all the snow in it. It makes me feel snug and comfy," Beryl said.

"Why don't we read the 'tiddley-pom' chapter in the Pooh Book," Bash suggested. "That's about snow?"

"That's Pigeon's favorite," Beryl giggled.

Beryl fretted awake, eager to be downstairs. She reached for her walker and then sat back down on the bed and listened to Bede Hall.

"We must help find..." Lady Nan started, confused. "A father is missing," she continued, still in Beryl's voice.

Bash took her grandmother's hand. "I know Beryl, we haven't given up hope."

Lady Nan had carried her dream forward into the bedroom. Her eyes looked worried, the way they used to in the rest home – out of focus, staring at a distant horizon only she could see. As far away as Narnia.

"There's always hope," Lady Nan said, wistfully. "People come back don't they?"

Bash was concerned. "I hope so Beryl."

The rain came down harder and rattled the window.

"Snow!" Lady Nan exclaimed suddenly. "In the window. Oh dear! Snow!" she cried in some distress.

Bash closed the curtains to calm her. "It's still an April shower. Just silly old rain," she said. "It will clear up soon."

"Silly old rain," Lady Nan announced clearly, in her confident grown-up voice, but Bash couldn't tell if Lady Nan was calling her daughter, Rayne, silly or addressing the weather.

"I remember another dream," Lady Nan said suddenly, smiling brightly at her Granddaughter. "Sheba, run and fetch our book and a pen, there's a dear."

She was Lady Nan again, but she muttered about rain the rest of the day and somehow managed to wheedle it into most conversations for three whole months.

CHAPTER TWENTY-ONE
Something in the Air

Planet Bash' wasn't the greatest name for a new world, but that's what the green jungle of the conservatory felt like. A place for new growth in specially-tended soil richly composted under a soft layer of moist spongy moss. Parks' own recipe.

Finger pots lined the tables in rows – small 'feeblings' Bash called her baby seedlings, and they slept like plant babies in a giant incubator, with Bash – acting as the 'Green Mother' of Bede forest, singing them lullabies in their glass nursery.

Parks commented Bash was more 'Smythical' and had wheezed so hard at his joke, Bash had gone to fetch Parks 2, but he was nowhere to be found. Instead, she had run into Parks 3, who told her not to worry as he'd just seen his grandfather, fit as a fiddle, walking towards the Hall.

Bash told her seedlings stories, the same as any child at bedtime... 'flower-bed-time' she told them. She said a lot of silly things to them casting about for magic words to say.

Charlotte had been clear about that. It was the tone of one's voice, she had emphasized.

"Don't go near them if you're angry or sad. Wait until your mind is clear before you reach out to them. And heed what they say because plants are clever; they already listen to you, and they're more apt to talk after they've been given some personal attention."

So Bash listened to what her plants had to say, and set up a wicker chair where she read the book she'd been given about a real magic garden in Scotland where the spirits of plants responded to respectful communion and tender loving care.

Bash was careful to sit patiently and wait with her garden until she felt a slight tingling in her spine, which meant her energy was ready to share and receive.

She visualized herself as a human satellite dish that captured the sun's rays – its heat waves of power beyond the gray storm that still circled Bede Hall like a huge eagle looking for a juicy rabbit. It was a powerful feeling to harness the tender fingers of light and know she was a channel for good.

The lavender children loved her back, sending an appreciative flutter of greeting in a tiny audible voice that somehow seemed to sound delicately fragrant.

Bash hummed as she went about her work, loving every minute she was there with her hands in the spongy soil.

The trapped air was artificially warmed by an electric heater that burned off the chill and pumped fake summer breezes across the miniature leaves.

Bash sprayed warm water in a high arc so the droplets would land like spring rain, and catch the dust particles floating in the newly created micro-sphere. The mist spun dozens of miniature dancing rainbows refracted from the beveled edges of the glass walls, and each lavender plant eagerly reached their leaves towards them and conveyed their thanks in a wave of scent.

When Feathers tagged along she no longer watched the prisms dance as intently as she once had, instead she laid down on a nest of straw and fussed it into the hollow shape she wanted.

Bash wondered how Jack would react to a litter of kittens. She had shown Feathers many good birthing nests in the kitchen, under beds, and behind sofas – all of them fine sanctuaries, but Feathers had chosen her own favored place in the glass garden, shaped like a pyramid with its outdoor panorama of trees and weather viewed snugly behind a glass window – the room that Kit called Bash's chlorophyll experiment under a bell jar.

Birds came deliciously close enough to make Feathers' whiskers tremble, bees and butterflies tapped their wings on the glass whenever the rain stopped, and there were night moths and rabbits who frolicked enticingly, making her natter with anticipation.

Anubis stayed out of her way, instinctively sensing imprisonment, alternating between wanting to be responsible and demanding his freedom.

Bash gave him extra plates of tinned salmon, sharing the savory tidbits she saved for Feathers and her growing tummy.

"Kit? Did you know a baby fox is called a kit?" Bash casually mentioned at dinner.

Kit beamed smugly. "Of course I did," he said, best pleased with himself.

Lady Nan was still asleep, so Bash set the cup of tea on her dressing table.

It gently clinked against the side of a cosmetic bottle, one of an array of varying sizes. Bash examined them, idly enchanted, and when her hand reached for her favorite, the morning chorus suddenly burst into song as if on cue and made her hand freeze. It was as if the birds outside had trilled 'don't touch.'

The stopper on the bottle was shaped like a pair of swooping birds, so it seemed eerie that the birds had chosen that precise moment to sing.

The frosted white glass looked as if it was made of ice and that two live miniature doves had been frozen in mid-air, and started to chirp.

Bash reread the label she knew well: '*L'air du Temps* – Nina Ricci,' and tested the French words in different ways by whispering them one syllable at a time, so as not to wake Lady Nan.

They definitely sounded full of panache. Just the sort of thing one would find on Lady Nan's dressing table.

The stopper made a gentle grating sound when Bash turned it in the neck of the bottle, and when it came out it released a lovely delicate 'carnationy' cloud.

Bash sniffed slowly with her eyes closed to single-out the ingredients.

She knew her flowers: the base scent was carnation and she recognized secondary notes of roses and violets.

A single golden drop clung to the tip of the glass stick attached to the stopper. Bash tapped it gently, letting it fall back into the bottle, and waved the glass rod back and forth in front of her nose as if she were drawing a line in the air with a pencil.

Her nose followed its path, and she leaned forward to catch the last fragrant trail as it wafted away – a tiny aromatic train departing a station, leaving behind an echo of its spirit. A perfume ghost waving goodbye from a disappearing window.

Lady Nan had taught her that a miniature pocket of one's personal space was the best place to experience the highest arc of a scent.

Bash dipped again, and this time she placed a bead of the liquid gold on her wrist and flattened it with the end of the glass wand. She stroked the remaining perfume behind her ears.

The room filled with the scent of a carnation flowerbed after the rain, and Lady Nan stirred awake.

The teacup rattled in its saucer as Bash hurried it across the room.

"Lady Nina," Bash said by mistake. "Your tea is getting cold."

"How lovely to wake up in the garden," Lady Nan said. "Tea and birds and the scent of flowers."

Bash plumped her grandmother's pillows, helped her to sit up, and tucked the snowflake shawl around her shoulders.

"We used to call carnations, gillyflowers," Lady Nan said. "They were the flowers of courtship. We believed in the language of flowers. Every variety held an important meaning."

"Can I have the bird bottle when it's finished?" Bash asked.

"Oh, that one will never be finished," Lady Nan replied as she sipped her tea. "It was a special gift. I think of it as my private smelling salts. It helps me remember. I always keep it close."

"How?" Bash asked, knowing the bottle never left her grandmother's room.

Lady Nan opened the drawer of her bedside table, and pulled out a white linen handkerchief embroidered with the initial B. She sniffed it and smiled.

"My best friend, Sarah Goodman, embroidered this for Ben,"

Lady Nan said, her voice starting to drift. "She and Ben were sweethearts, I dab a drop of *L'air du Temps* on it now-and-then."

Bash brought Lady Nan back by repeating the question: "How does perfume help you remember?"

"Close your eyes and imagine the smell of toast, and tell me what you see?

It only took Bash a few seconds.

"I see Kit and I sitting at the kitchen table... it's morning. I'm late for school. There's two boiled eggs in blue and white eggcups. The toast is cut into soldiers. An open jar of orange marmalade is on the table, and Mum is frying bacon. Now I can smell oranges and bacon too."

"And how do you feel?" Lady Nan inquired.

"Happy. Safe... wait... I'm also worried about something. A Science test... no, wait it's a dream. Skeletons. Boney fingers in my hair. Bats squealing."

"How old are you?"

Bash tilted her head as if to see a calendar. "It was almost a year ago. I know because... Oh, it was the morning the phone rang about Dad!"

"All that from a bit of toast. You see?" Lady Nan nodded. "Bread, butter, marmalade, bacon, an exam, a ringing sound, skeletons, and bats... and that's only from smelling *phantom toast*," Lady Nan said.

"Time-travel in a bottle," Bash said, being romantic.

Lady Nan nodded her approval. "Well put," she said.

"What about you? What do you see when you smell this?" Bash said, waving her wrist under Lady Nan's nose.

"That's easy," Lady Nan said, "it's 1952 – the present queen's coronation day and my twenty-first birthday. I'm wearing a long frothy blue dress that rustles when I dance. I see a small box tied white satin ribbon and a pair of eyes that..."

Lady Nan stopped and her eyes misted over with memories. "That's enough time-travel for today. Is it August yet?"

Bash changed the subject sensing one of Lady Nan's 'turns.'

"How do you pronounce these French words and what does *L'air du Temps* mean? And why does it smell so much better when it ... goes away?" she said quickly.

"First of all, the purest essence of a perfume is its heart. It's like a voice. Its spirit.

"So now it's a ghost in a bottle," Bash interrupted.

"Ghost?" Lady Nan repeated, her mind confused.

"No no, the... voice of perfume," Bash reminded her. "You were saying?"

"He was nineteen," Lady Nan said wistfully.

"Who?"

"Both of us."

Bash realized her grandmother was back at her birthday party.

"Best of friends, they were... two short years of happiness. One year too numb to remember... and then fifty-four-years of grief."

Lady Nan's gnarled fingers worried a long wool thread from her shawl, and Bash knew it was time to distract her into a safer conversation.

"The French words: *L'air du Temps*. What do they mean?" Bash asked gently.

"The air of time," Lady Nan whispered dreamily. "Lost love."

It was awkward explaining the art of perfume to Kit.

"Lair du what?" he said, looking bored.

"It's the transformation *effect* that's important," Bash repeated. "Although in Lady Nan's case, the name is... well, serendipitous because it *does* mean something relevant."

"What? 'the Cave of Weather'?" Kit asked, bewildered.

"What *are* you on about? Have you been listening to *anything* I've said?" Bash fumed.

"The lair of temperatures," Kit translated logically.

Charlotte Findhorn's cottage was almost completely hidden by vegetation. Masses of colors filled the space between the gate and her front door.

Bash creaked open the wooden gate and made her way over round paving stones spaced apart like lily pads, careful not to tread on the trail of flowers spilling from their beds woven into a bright thatch with the wild grasses from the moor.

Chamomile grew between the stones and speckled the gravel driveway and the sweet scent of honey hovered on the breeze. Charlotte's hive buzzed industriously in the back garden and sent its workers droning to explore the garden.

Flowers and weeds had been allowed to roam and reach for the sun wherever they could.

Beegle gently made a chirping *woop woop* sound to mock the sparrows as he dangled lazily from the branch of a Rowan tree. He held a sampling of bread and raspberry jam, no doubt pinched from the tray Charlotte always provided on Bash's visits.

"I help plants to be themselves," Charlotte had once explained to Bash. "They have to feel free."

Inside, Charlotte had a black kettle boiling on the hob and a tray of scones cooling on the windowsill. Bash was drawn to a painting over the mantelpiece of a boat filled with flowers. On closer inspection she found there was a woman underneath the flowers who appeared to be dead.

"That's 'the Lady of Shalott,' Charlotte said, "from one of my favorite poems."

"The Lady of Charlotte?" Bash corrected, with a smile. "She looks like you. Lady Nan mentioned that poem to me once, but I've never read it. Is it any good?"

"It's the very best," Charlotte said, shaking her head. "In fact, it's a must. You'll be taking my copy home with you tonight to read for homework," she said cheerfully.

And then her eyebrows knitted into a frown. "Bother! Beeg's taken the jam spoon again," she said.

"Homework?" Bash grinned. "I shouldn't have come. Mum gives us plenty to read as it is."

"Well, this is different," Charlotte said, arranging the tea things. "Let's have our tea outside, shall we?"

Bash was somewhat mesmerized by Charlotte's pearl ring. "I've never seen you wear that before," she said.

"I was engaged once."

"I'm sorry it didn't work out."

"We're still working things out."

Charlotte held it up to the light. It was given to me by someone very special. It acts as a tiny crystal ball. Do you want to ask it a question?"

"No, I'm all right, but thank you. "I don't want to know the future."

Charlotte looked into the pearl which now glowed with a light inside it. She frowned. "It's not a good day to ask too many questions," she said.

Bash found the garden swing a soothing place to sit.

"It's the herbs," Charlotte said. "They send their messages on the wind. You can experience their individual signatures when you close your eyes. The medicinal ones can heal from their scent alone. You're sitting in a cloud of power. You're basking in their care when you're out here."

Bash breathed deeply and closed her eyes. For a moment she felt a wave of dizziness and then her head cleared and she noticed the separate scents of sage and lavender and lemongrass.

"Why can't I see the other... *one's* ... who live here?" Bash asked when Charlotte set down the tray. "Isn't it time to introduce me?"

Charlotte looked up casually from pouring the tea as a spoon clattered to the ground beside her. "You mean fairies?" she said. "They choose the time and place, but I wondered when you'd ask."

Bash plumped up the pillows of her new bed – the one Lady Nan had given her. It had once been hers, but unfortunately, the elaborately carved antique had been too formidable a weight to be moved.

Bash recalled her disappointment. She had sighed and sat on it for effect, and Lady Nan had commented that she looked like a fairy princess.

Then after a shopping trip to Bede, Bash had arrived home to find that all four Parks had dismantled it and carted it down two flights of stairs to her room.

She had cried from their kindness, and Lady Nan had sent her a wink to say she had arranged it.

Bash opened the book of poetry that Charlotte had pressed into her hands as she left, and began to read the pages that had been marked with a pressed carnation.

The poem was so lyrical it read more as a song. And it was about an enchanted lady who lived alone in a castle on the isle of Shalott, isolated from Camelot by a curse.

The lady is forbidden by magic to look at the outside world directly. She is cursed to weave a tapestry of the view she sees from her tower window, but can only view it indirectly with a mirror.

But, when the Lady of Shalott sees the reflection of Sir Lancelot she is so taken with him that she turns and peers at him directly. The mirror shatters and her story tapestry flies into the wind.

Bash's eyes kept returning to certain passages as if Charlotte had highlighted them with a marker. A magic marker, she thought to herself, smiling.

But Charlotte had been right; it was irresistibly enchanting.

CHAPTER TWENTY-TWO

Elegant Corners

The worst thing about a large stately home is keeping it warm, and since the Stratford-Smyth's had been reduced to choosing a ground floor corner to make their own, most of the Hall had been left to its dust and its past glory, and its ghost.

The kitchen with its vast wood stoves was the heart of the apartment pumping out heat for roasting and frying, and making hot water – taking the edge off the unseasonably bitter winds and rain that pummeled the draughty house day and night.

But, it was the library that was the true heart of Bede Hall. Its once-scarlet curtains faded to a gentle rusty-colored velvet cast a delightful warm glow over the books and the worn leather upholsteries, now a soft shade of burgundy with their muted red and gold-embroidered cushions.

It was also the site of Lady Nan and Bash's formal vocabulary lessons.

The Red Library, Lady Nan liked to point out, was called red, not only because of the color of the curtains and armchairs, but because one 'read' there.

"I've read most of these books," Lady Nan said, gesturing to the shelves of modern looking bindings. "Especially that collection of what your mother's generation called, New-Age books."

"When you say that it sounds like work," Bash said.

"It was necessary research, all things considered," Lady Nan replied mysteriously, and promptly changed the subject. "Now, our big dictionary here is quite ancient. It's chained to its pedestal due to its great value."

"It's too enormous to steal," Bash said. "It reminds me of Pigeon on his perch."

Lady Nan made a *tsk* sound. "Don't you believe it. Some boys from the village tried stealing the sundial once."

Bash giggled. "Good luck getting *that* past Parks."

"I taught Pigeon some of his bigger words, the same way I'm teaching you," Lady Nan said. "Every time you look up a new word, you're that much closer to being a writer."

The vast gardens that had so recently looked shaggy from growing wild, were gradually losing the long battle with 'Team Parks,' and Parks joked that the Green Man had finally given up the ghost.

Gardens and secrets rested inside Bede Hall's property lines – a magic circle encompassing Bede Village, protecting the ones who lived there on borrowed time.

Most damp days, Lady Nan kept close to her Egyptian four-poster bed wrapped in woolly snowflakes, and whenever she was wheeled to the kitchen she saw the rest of her old home the way it used to be.

She was sometimes in a dither about her inner world, but never claimed to see her old servants. Lady Nan simply preferred to remember the furniture as uncovered, and to visualize the gleaming polished wood and glass she once knew, and to revel in the beauty of the dozens of floral arrangements in enameled bowls and crystal vases that had once been delivered, fresh each morning, from her hothouse and gardens.

A splayed peacock fan adorned one wall of Lady Nan's bedroom – its sweeping iridescent turquoise, purple and gold tail feathers spread in a grand half-circle, much coveted by Feathers herself, who often sat beneath it gazing longingly with her nose twitching, and her tail flopping like a fluffy orange whip.

A white plastic cube with dials that looked like a radio was a permanent fixture on Lady Nan's nightstand, although lately, she hadn't had to use it because it was a sound machine with seven settings of recorded rain to soothe her to sleep, including a light spring shower, and the pitter-patter of raindrops falling on a tin roof. Lady Nan enjoyed each one, especially on hot dry nights, but her favorite was the rushing sounds of a torrential downpour.

This was the setting which instantly pulled Lady Nan into a restful 'heavy' sort slumber with a contented smile on her face, even on her befuddled days.

The upper floors of the Hall were like another country. On rainy days they were visited by the twins like a couple of explorers. Discovering meant poking amongst the memories of the people who used to live there.

The opulence of antiques and art was inspiring; it was a welcome bonus to being warmly accepted in a safe harbor after a long worrisome journey.

Bede Hall's vast labyrinth of hidden staircases, and working spaces with endless sinks and sluices, and mudrooms and sheds, and the rest of its outbuildings and 'follies,' and the extensive acres of once-groomed lawns and tangled wildwoods, and the ponds and lake, were the unchartered territories of the Stratford-Smyth's new planet.

It would take years to map them, and Bede Hall intended its new family do so. Each and every one.

Kit had chosen the servant's coat room for his bedroom because it was connected by a small door to the huge laundry room that had endless shelves for bottles and jars and science books, several different-sized sinks, and a very large table that would complete the effect of a real laboratory after he'd arranged a few things.

His solar system mobile of cut-out planets, and model planes, were hung from the ceiling, and Bash helped him display his assortment of globes and gyroscopes with his telescope and microscope, and set out his kinetic cradle collection, and models of Leonardo da Vinci's mechanical lion and ornithopter.

Mrs. S helped too. She suggested where to hang the half-dozen framed posters to their best advantage with her keen eye for decorating: there were two views of the pyramids and the Great Sphinx, a colorful diagram of the elemental tables, the 'Mona Lisa' which had been digitally altered to a puzzle of fractured pixels, a blow-up photograph of Albert Einstein, and his favorite – a beautiful pattern resembling an abstract painting that was a 'heat map' of the super-volcano of Yellowstone National Park in Wyoming, as seen from space.

The finishing touch was the old metronome from his piano lessons placed beside his 'thinking chair' – a futuristic looking, streamlined, upholstered swivel-affair, that looked like a huge black leatherette egg with arm rests. Kit's room befitted the remark he frequently made that pure science was elegance.

The mechanical music reminded Kit of time passing, and its soothing rhythmic beats helped him to focus on scientific solutions by pulling him into a mind-space that he always maintained surpassed intuition and almost bordered on magic.

The ticking sound happily stood in for the giant wall clock with no hands that Bash had given him for his birthday – a haunting echo of lost time that had ceased passing with the loss of its spindly hands... hands that couldn't pass, representing the possibilities of time-travel that so obsessed him.

When Kit had opened Bash's gift, he had been dumbstruck, reminded once more how his sister always found such amazingly-relevant presents. She had claimed that the clock had found her, and beamed how it was 'synchronistically apropos.'

Bash walked into her room. It was like entering a dreamy cloud of mist and white. Underfoot lay a gently-faded carpet with a floral pattern of roses and sprays of lilies that resembled a large ghostly flowerbed. It supported a double bed – its bleached oak headboard carved with the head of a beautiful fairy queen peeping out from a circlet of acanthus leaves flanked by a pair of angelic-looking wings. It stood against a soothing backdrop of walls papered in patterns of butterflies and bees.

Bash petted Feathers, stretched out on the bed like a ginger throw blanket.

"Hey girlie," Bash said," and the sound of her words caused Feathers to twist and curl up like a hedgehog. "It's dinnertime."

The soft greens of potted plants completed the inviting woodsy setting.

It was Bash's sanctuary away from technology.

She'd had her pick of landscape paintings that spread like a trailing art gallery throughout the Hall and found a vast pastel-colored scene of blurred water-lilies and a bridge, and another of Bede Hall nestled under a vivid blue sky signed with the initials H. B. P.

Bash had also raided the attic nursery, confiscating her Great Uncle Ben's stuffed toy bear attached to its platform with wheels, along with Canterbury, Lady Nan's rickety dapple-grey rocking horse with its straw-colored horsehair mane.

A pair of overstuffed chintz armchairs upholstered with a pattern of huge cabbage roses looked like comfy gardens big enough for two people to curl up in... or one person and a very large deerhound or one person and a well-loved rabbit doll named Pookie. Such chairs were ideal for reading a gripping book and the dreaming that usually accompanied them.

A pair of French doors were sheathed in sheer gauze curtains which, after the blustery storms calmed into fluffy white clouds, would blow lazily in the scented breezes wafting from the gardens, especially elemental since Bash's windows were usually kept open, even during rainstorms.

The rest of the house masked in ghostly dustsheets waited in semi-darkness, separate from the main trail leading from the main floor to the library schoolroom.

When the front doors were open in fine weather, a path of sunlight swept up the grand staircase and mated with the light from the mullioned windows of the library where warmth seemed to emanate from the book-lined walls insulated with red-and-brown leather bindings.

Mrs. S hoped it would give her student's parents a sense of value for their tuition fees.

Bede Hall still rested on its foundations, very much alive.

Its connecting corridors were flooded with daylight to give the impression the entire house was running at maximum power.

But only visitors guessed this version. If you were privileged enough to live there, you knew that beyond the impressive doors to state rooms, lurked drawn curtains and stacks of furniture covered in white dust sheets that made the rooms look like an Alpine Christmas card.

Mountains and valleys of furniture and sculptures every so often disclosed a frozen white marble arm or face, courtesy of the garden's breath sighing over the inner landscape, lifting and peeking under the covers.

Visitors imagined long-ago living spaces where silver tea services hovered, and trolleys of porcelain dishes and gleaming forks glided in a formal setting. It was easy to envisage a scene where mounds of cream buns, and plum cakes were served beside dainty cucumber sandwiches with their crusts removed – thin triangles arranged like delicate petals, and stacked on plate-stands three tiers deep.

It took little effort to hear the hush of long ago slipper'd feet and the gentle gurgle of tea pouring from the spout of a teapot, and the pampered cups that clattered gently when tickled with polished silver spoons.

Rupert's grand plan in the upper-stratosphere of the east wing, was taking shape. Like a bold prospector staking a claim, he pitched his camp the first weekend there and began to create a magnificent bachelor pad purposely moving and removing himself above the group. That he did so even before the weather grew milder, was proof of his need to be literally, 'above' everyone else.

As the eldest child, and therefore the acting head of the family clan, he had the right to claim territory, and he was never one who adjusted *down* to anything.

Rupert Stratford-Smyth loved the concept of owning Bede Hall, but as for decor, the historic or quaint failed to interest him. His goal was to live in an exclusive penthouse loft in New York.

After supper he retreated to his third floor eyrie where he was the proud owner of a stainless steel coffee maker, and practiced making various strengths of the bitter drink in order to seem more sophisticated than the rest of his family who slurped tea from mugs, in the apartment below.

He was happy to make the long trek up the grand staircase to his coffee, even when he was train-lagged from traveling a few hours.

Rupert thought of his lair as his personal 'fortress of solitude,' like Superman's, where he was free to blare rock-music as loudly as he pleased. He saved the kitchen visits for meals on tap and a place to fill his multiple hot-water-bottles and to retrieve a well-earned nightcap of cocoa that Mrs. S always made at ten o'clock on the dot.

Parks attempted to lure Rupert into gardening, entreating him that Bede Hall was going to be his someday if things went well, and why shouldn't they since Miss Beryl said they would.

'Gardening requires an early bird,' Parks tried to drum into him, but gardening was not Rupert's cup of tea *or* coffee. He saw himself as a 'gentleman farmer' inspecting the grounds of his estate giving orders, not riding a tractor-mower from dawn to dusk or planting and digging in all kinds of weather.

"Working the soil is beneath me," Rupert declared, haughtily to the dinner table after one particularly grueling day reading a book.

Bash, figuring correctly that she was already permanently inscribed on Rupert's 'bad list,' didn't care that she would be 'in for it,' and had replied, "That is usually where the ground is. Please pass the potatoes."

Rupert remained silent, but Pigeon had piped up cheekily and recited: *"early birds get the worm...one potato two potato three potato four... five potato six potato who's behind the door?"*

CHAPTER TWENTY-THREE

Worlds Apart

Considering they were twins, Kit and Bash were worlds apart, but they both devoured books: Kit's were about weather and chemistry and new discoveries and inventions, and anything about clocks. His latest interest was the face on Mars.

Bash collected decorating magazines and apart from her old children's book 'The Velveteen Rabbit,' she preferred fanciful stories about princesses and dragons and enchanted realms like the one she imagined she would grow.

Kit fully claimed his tower and was slowly turning it into an observatory and a second laboratory, more homey than the first, with rugs and floor cushions, a portable DVD player, and headphones. He moved in his telescope, and on clear nights he happily scanned the heavens till dawn.

"I'm learning a new technique from Parks and Charlotte," Bash explained, "but I need to design a control group to test the results. What should I do? The simpler the better."

Kit fiddled with the settings on his telescope.

"Describe the experiment," he said. "The briefer the better."

"Lavender, well any plant really, that has been contacted..." Bash started to say.

Kit stood upright, paid proper attention, and coughed slightly.

"*Er*, contacted?"

Bash sighed. There was going to be resistance. "Yes, through telepathy. Talking with their devas. A deva is a spiritual entity that represents the essence of a particular plant or animal. If one asks for their cooperation, the plant will grow at a sensational rate."

"Like a native totem?" Kit asked, polishing a lens.

"Something like that," Bash said.

"*Something* isn't a very scientific term," Kit chided.

"Like the Green Man is to the forest," Bash said.

"Oh. Like *that*," Kit said with a grimace. "Peter Pan stuff. Well, first separate the energies and ..."

"It's not *Peter* Pan. It's just Pan," Bash replied, miffed. "Nature does have some mysteries. Not everything is cut and dried."

"Sorry, didn't mean to offend. Well just isolate one plant and concentrate all the attention onto it and ignore the rest. That ought to do it," Kit said.

"It's not very E=MC^2 is it?" Bash remarked coolly. "Not exactly π r^2 is it? Not exactly squared away."

Kit grinned insanely above his telescope.

"Not even close," he said.

Some days the library could be a tad gloomy, but even the haunted room upstairs felt non-intimidating. Kit used to tease Bash that the ghost was probably just a melted snowman that Lady Nan built when she was small.

"Sometimes you talk a load of parrot droppings," Bash said to Kit.

She turned and addressed Pigeon: "Isn't that right Porridge old boy?"

"More pooh...don't stop... and so it goes tiddley pom...on snowing," agreed Pigeon.

Bash retorted that Bede Hall had the ambiance of a fairy tale and so much panache that it made her feel like a princess.

The Yellowstone poster lay face down on the floor in Kit's bedroom.

"What's *that* doing there?" Bash asked, wandering in.

"Dunno. It fell last night when I was stargazing and I left it there," Kit mumbled.

Bash lifted it from the floor and dusted it off.

"It's such a beautiful pattern of colors," she said, setting it against the wall. "It's all right the glass hasn't broken."

"Mmmnn hmmn," Kit said, off in another world, deep in his book.

"Maybe the ghost knocked it down," Bash said, testing Kit.

"Yup. I expect so," came Kit's reply.

Bash waited to the count of ten. "It looks like abstract art," she declared.

Kit shuffled ahead through several pages in his National Geographic with the title: 'the Face on Mars' on the cover.

"About 3 o'clock I should think," he said.

Just then, Mrs. S poked her head in the door to announce tea, and noticed the framed print.

"Are your pictures falling off the walls as well?" she asked. "Mine are either falling down or hanging crooked every morning."

No answer.

Bash shrugged. "He's not really here Mum," she said, "he's on Mars."

"Kit!" Mrs. S shouted, waving her hand in front if Kit's eyes. "I said it's time to wash up for tea."

"Righty-o," Kit yawned.

"Let's get this picture back up," Mrs. S said. "What exactly is it a photo of?"

"It's an aerial photo of a famous caldera," Kit answered. "It's an underground pit of lava – a hot spot in Yellowstone National Park. Well, more like the *entire* park. It's an area over two million square acres. Caldera means cauldron because a subterranean volcano is like a huge melting pot of liquid rock. It's the most active geological anomaly on the planet. A giant cauldron of magma under the earth simmering away like a pot of porridge forty miles in diameter. That photo was taken with heat-sensitive film. The red part is the hottest part; the blue is the coolest."

"The coolest," echoed Bash, suddenly looking far away, herself.

She shuddered. *"Brrrrr,"* she said, "the temperature is quite glacial in here."

"What's *with* you two?" Mrs. S chided. "Come along now, everything's ready. I've made your favorite, toad in the hole. You know that picture gives me an idea. Instead of math why don't we take a day to study this?"

"I've got all the books on Volcanoes you need," Kit said, pointing to a shelf.

"Vulcanology would make a great subject," Mrs. S said. "I think I'll do a bit of research on it tonight. I do so hate teaching math."

"Sounds very Star Trek, Mum," Bash joked. "Are you sure science-fiction is a suitable curriculum?"

Kit elbowed Bash in the ribs. "Hey, it's astrophysics if you don't mind."

"It will be extremely interesting," Mrs. S proclaimed.

"Fascinating," Bash added, giving Kit the Vulcan science officer's V-shaped salute. "I happen to love building castles in the air."

Beegle, Charlotte Findhorn's Java monkey, chewed the handle of a miniature wicker basket without a care in the world.

"Is it okay if he does that?" Bash asked.

"I always give Beeg his own basket," Charlotte said, "it actually lasts most of the summer, and he leaves the others alone."

"I've never been to Bede in May before," Bash said. "May Day is serious business isn't? The whole village is already buzzing with plans."

"Not serious – joyful, and necessary in order to balance the seasons properly," Charlotte replied, unpacking a second case of baskets.

"It seems early though," Bash commented.

"A fete doesn't plan itself you know," Charlotte said, "special things take time."

Beegle began to shriek as he stuffed his basket full of the discarded stems on the florist shop floor.

"The Beeg is ready," Bash commented.

Charlotte inspected each basket carefully for flaws, and handed them to Bash who then lined them up in rows according to size. "Are these for a window display?"

"They're May baskets," Charlotte said. "We fill them with primroses and sweets, and give them to the children. There's going to be a maypole and Morris dancers."

"It's a pagan celebration isn't it?" Bash said. "Something to do with the spring solstice called... *um*... oh I can't remember."

"Beltane," Charlotte said, giving Beegle a handful of rose petals.

"I heard Mrs. Spoondance tell mum there's going be a gypsy who tells fortunes for 50p."

"Hmmn," Charlotte muttered, "I s'pose so. But anybody can do that if they listen to the wind."

"It's just for fun," Bash said.

"Fortune telling is no laughing matter," Charlotte replied.

"Lady Nan was Queen of the May once. Is 'Jack in the Green,' Robin Hood?"

"No," Charlotte said, "Jack is the spirit of the trees – the Green Man."

"You mean he represents the flora and fauna?" Bash said, "Those are the scientific names for plants and animals. Kit told me."

"He's much more than that; he's the essence of fertility," Charlotte said. "Green Jack wears a tree costume and mingles with the village folk spreading the spiritual energy to sprout the new plants and make them grow.

Beltane rites are dedicated to forgiving friends and family, and the rituals of cleansing the past."

"Then I hope Jack visits Bede Hall as well," Bash replied wistfully. "We need that."

Charlotte smiled slyly. "Oh he'll do more than *that*," she said.

CHAPTER TWENTY-FOUR

Plant Life

A predator breeze battered the ivy growing thick over Bede Hall so that its tendrils tapped hard like thin green fingers railing against the library windows. They picked the lead strips of the diamond latticework making a scritchity-scratching noise like rustling paper, but when the guardian crept in, the breeze held its breath and shushed the vines.

Anubis padded into the library, and in spite of himself, he balked at the overwhelming sense of unease that assaulted his bones. His ears instinctively flattened like radar panels to pinpoint the disruptive presence.

As he did so, the long halogen bulb of a banker's lamp flickered to life under its cobalt-blue shade and made a high-pitched hum only a cat or a rogue vine could hear.

It was obvious to any cat worth dignifying, that the red library was inhabited despite anyone being seated at the table or standing at the window or browsing the bookshelves or lounging in the leather armchairs.

A warning shiver lowered Anubis's sleek tail to stealth mode and he crouched low to the ground, gliding like a snake, slithering over the carpet – his whiskers twitching.

The cat's senses were so finely-tuned he could sometimes even detect the color of a particular sound or scent, so it was with some hesitation that Anubis explored behind the curtains.

As always, he sniffed the air for mice, straining for the sound of their shrill squeaks and the scurrying of their tiny feet. Nothing. He scanned again, this time noticing the slight quivering of the pixilated foliage waving at the window.

He sprung soundlessly to the window-seat, tested each S-shaped handle with his paw, and tried to stare at the moon through the dense leaves, but all he could see was his own reflection.

Yellow eyes glared back at him, and it unnerved him to see himself looking frightened because Anubis prided himself on being fearless. Living feral had taught him how to survive by staying alert; not spooked the way he felt now.

Anubis had decided to take his new name to heart. It was his feline duty to earn his keep by making nightly rounds of the Hall and to hiss into any corners that reeked of magic – any crevices where a spell might lurk or a curse might hide.

His back trembled involuntarily as if some unseen hand had stroked it. He flinched, and focused his investigation on the alcove beside the fireplace.

The corner was dark and formless, but nevertheless a disruptive energy issued from it like a thinking shadow.

The emanation rippled like a transparent flag and passed through Anubis's body making his fur stand on end fizzing and snapping with blue static.

A chuckling sound caused the cat to spin around and hiss, landing on all four feet, claws and fangs flashing.

The sound turned a ghoulish shade of yellowy-green and disappeared out the door. Anubis followed it to the top of the stairs and watched it slip, whining and moaning, through the keyhole of the great carved doors.

Anubis leapt back to the window and watched as the shining green string swirled into a ball and rolled past the sundial. It rose suddenly to a great height and unravelled, weaving itself into the shape of a funnel cloud, and swooped into the mouth of the maze.

A moment later a whiff of red fog flew out of its center like a smoke signal, buzzed the lake, and returned to the Hall to be sucked down the chimney.

It rattled the empty coal scuttle against the soot-encrusted bricks, settled back into the same corner where it had first drawn Anubis's curiosity, and dissipated into the wall leaving a phosphorous cough of dust on the hearth tiles.

Anubis settled on the arm of a chair to guard the fireplace.

A pair of swans that had been drifting on the lake with their heads under their wings in swan sleep, panicked and attempted to take flight, clumsily flapping their heavy wings over the dark surface of the water, craning their long cumbersome necks desperate to be airborne.

The silence was palpable; the clock stopped ticking exactly long enough for Anubis to hear Kit's familiar voice distinctly say: "It's all right; they're safe now."

The gentle thunk of the clock's hands resumed their precision jumps from second to second around the hours marked by old-fashioned roman numerals. The long spindle marking the minutes swept over a dozen illustrations of astrological symbols that were picked out in gold on a royal-blue background – an inner circle of informed fortune. It was 3:33 a.m.

The room shook off its ominous visitor as the first rays of dawn licked everything clean, leaving the room silently bathed in the hush of retreating moonlight. The vibrations from the meticulous order of subdued academia and the smell of antique leather-bound books woke Anubis. He perked his ears towards a new sound – the squeaking of rusty-hinges and the unmistakable clank of a sliding deadbolt that came from the main door.

The willow-the-wisp swept up the stairs in a surge of power and met Anubis head-on.

The collision caused the cat to arch his back, doubling his size, and he gave it such a blood-curdling yowl that it evaporated in a puff of slime-green mist.

Pigeon heard the feline war-cry, shifted uneasily on his perch in the kitchen, and dropped a single scarlet feather onto the floor of his cage.

Anubis shook himself back to normal and slunk warily to his bed, mission accomplished, skittishly avoiding every creak and shadow, and once he had to stop and bat away an annoying remnant of green fog that still clung to his tail.

As he prowled through the living room a child's face peered from the mirror over the fireplace looking for signs of life, and a window blew open, knocking over a vase of flowers. An icy wind howled a cat-shaped 'sending' to creep up the servant's stairwell.

There it loomed like a giant black stain with the stagnant odor of swamp-scum about it that wavered and sputtered like the light from a beeswax candle.

The last sound Anubis heard before he slept was that of a loose shutter banging in the wind that echoed the rhythmic blows of hammers shaping a huge yellow stone block under a vivid blue sky.

Lady Nan was delighted to find a red feather beside her place at the table. It reminded her of one of her most daring hats.

"A gift from Pigeon and Bash for you," Mrs. S said. "Tea?"

"Lovely," answered Lady Nan. "Yes please."

The tea filled the kitchen with the delicious steamy aroma of Lady Nan's favorite blend of 'Earl Grey.'

"I've had to straighten the mirror in the living room again," Mrs. S announced. "I don't understand why it keeps moving. It's extremely heavy."

"It's the ghost," Lady Nan said, opening the marmalade.

Anubis and Feathers were washing themselves between naps, and as always kept one ear to the ground for gossip. Mrs. S changed the subject.

Lady Nan inhaled the glorious scent of stewed oranges trapped in a jar. "I heard a dreadful racket last night," Lady Nan announced. "Did it wake you?"

"It was the cats having a bit of a disagreement, I expect," Mrs. S said. "That red feather reminds me of something."

"Yes, the hat I had made one Christmas. It was all green with one huge red feather that curled..."

"No, it wasn't that. I think we're out of birdseed," Mrs. S replied.

Feathers lifted her head when she heard her name.

"*Such a shame,*" Anubis commented. "*Why can't those two click and get along?*"

"*Red feather green feather... click... don't mind me.*" Pigeon nattered. "*Just make a new hat...click... don't worry about me.*"

"*This house has some seriously strange vibes,*" Anubis said, grooming green mist from his tail. "*I expect I'll get used to them considering I like the perks.*"

"*You like the Parks?*" Feather replied, with one paw in her ear. "*They're a bit of an odd bunch.*"

"*No I wasn't saying that, although I get on with them exceedingly well. They appreciate good breeding,*" Anubis said, stretching full length to dry in front of the fire. "*I was remarking on the leftover magic in the attic and the library, and the elementals that float about the grounds. One got inside last night.*"

Feathers preened like Pigeon and settled into the chair pillow.

"*Aren't we the lucky ones who can see them,*" she said sarcastically.

"*That St Elmo's Fire is rather full of itself,*" Anubis commented. "*Nasty stuff that. Tastes terrible. I'm not too keen on the furniture floating about either. It's a tad disquieting when it jumps at first, although once it's moving it can be quite entertaining.*"

"*No good comes of magic,*" Feathers stated flatly, polishing her whiskers. "*Especially for cats. Are we going hunting tonight?*" she asked. "*It's a full moon, and clear for once – a good night for catching moths.*"

"*Unfortunately, there are creatures called fairies who 'look' like moths; it's tricky to tell them apart when they're flying about, and the consequences for getting it wrong are most uncomfortable. Full moons are dodgy,*" Anubis concluded. "*Miss Charlotte is partial to them though. She makes a point of going out, lighting fires and singing, and all sorts of to-doing.*"

Lady Nan motioned Anubis over to her by patting her knees.

"Come here Anubis you lucky boy," she called.

"I'd better go see what the old dear wants," Anubis said amiably. Lady Nan wiggled her fingers enticingly.

"Do humans really think we're that stupid?" Feathers sniffed. *"That we mistake fingers for a mouse?"*

Anubis made an effortless leap into Lady Nan's lap to please her.

"Remember me," she said, scratching him behind the ears, "I haven't seen you for ages."

Anubis stared into Lady Nan's eyes for a long time.

"Is it really you?" he purred, *"I can scarcely believe it."*

CHAPTER TWENTY-FIVE

Tea to Go

Twigglys Tea Shop bustled with the rush of afternoon tea. Plates of cream scones swooned past Mrs. S on dainty doilies and disappeared into corners of the room.

She wished she could do the same and escape out the door, but her uninvited companions seemed determined to stay, since they'd ordered a plate of watercress sandwiches and an assortment of cakes.

Sylvia Fox, the establishment's skeletal owner, scuttled by to ask if everything was all right in order to give her chum, Enid Tweedy, an encouraging pat on the back, but mostly in case she was missing the beginning or the middle or the end of anything juicy.

She hovered nearby to tweak the chocolate éclairs on a cake stand into a more pleasing pyramid with her boney fingers, and straightened all the neighboring tablecloths until Mrs. Tweedy gave her an exaggerated stare to suggest Sylvia's presence was hampering her mission.

After there were no more excuses to linger, Sylvia swung by the kitchen for a pot of raspberry jam for table six. She had to admire Enid for making it to the teashop in record time, since she'd only just telephoned her moments ago with the heads up: Mrs. Stratford-Smyth was taking tea ... and she was alone.

Mrs. Tweedy, with her son Edgar in tow, had cornered Mrs. S who had been desperately trying to hide behind her menu, and swooped in for a chat which was more like a newspaper hound sniffing out a story.

Mr. Tweedy had insisted only the week before, that his wife take the upper-hand and do some sleuthing of her own to help him in his business. And there was no greater business for Wilbur Tweedy than the selling of Bede Hall for a handsome fee. Mrs. T was to wait for an opportunity, he had advised, and to strike quickly.

"Oh hello Rayne," Mrs. Tweedy gushed. Fancy seeing you here. Only this morning, Wilbur was saying we should drop by and pay our respects."

And from then on, Mrs. S had been even more helpless than usual.

The subject Mrs. Tweedy had come to ferret out was easily introduced.

"Now it's no use denying the rumors," she began.

"Sorry?" Mrs. S said, 'in the dark', as usual.

"Your dear mother told me before she became... ill," Mrs. Tweedy said, nodding sympathetically.

"Yes... well, I've... *um*... heard the rumors, of course," Mrs. S stammered. "Obviously there's no such thing as a ... mummy's curse, but... well, it's easy for... for *things*... as I'm sure you know, to get started.

"You see, my children grew up with Egyptian myths for bedtime stories," she continued, "and there's no stopping my Rupert when he's got an audience. He's quite the performer. At one time, he thought it rather glamorous for the Hall to be cursed and he teased a few of his friends at school. That's all it was. A simple misunderstanding.

"I'm afraid the village has long ears," she finished, trying not to stare at Mrs. Tweedy's gaudy rhinestone earrings when she said the word, ears.

Mrs. Tweedy leaned forward confidentially. "And the ghost?"

Mrs. S blanched. "Oh that... load of old nonsense," she said.

Mrs. Tweedy craned her neck and searched the room for Mrs. Fox and found she was already staring at her with an expectant look from across the room.

The few seconds this took to register was long enough for Mrs. S to cave.

She waited out the uncomfortable silence that followed her explanation as long as she could before letting out a nervous sigh. She lowered her voice and timidly touched Mrs. Tweedy's arm – the gossip's well-known shorthand indicating a confidence is about to be... spilled.

Mrs. S hesitated, trying desperately to ignore Edgar. "Look, this is only between you and me," she said to Mrs. Tweedy, and her tone was so familiar, the plastic pearls on Mrs. Tweedy's neck bounced up and down with excitement.

Mrs. Tweedy nodded breathlessly. "Of course my dear. I can be... that is, I am the *soul* of discretion."

"It's probably because we had a girl from the village with us one summer," Mrs. S continued. "Just to help out for a week you understand, and an odd thing happened: she quit suddenly on her first day.

"She was quite hysterical from an... *experience*. She must have been under the weather because she said she'd felt a cold wind rush through her in the library, and since the room had been stifling hot, no amount of persuading would induce her to stay. She was so distraught she had me in a complete panic as well, and Dr. Brooks had to be called to calm us both."

"Maybe she felt a ghost?" Edgar said, his face full of cream and jelly.

"Oh dear me no! Although there *might* be treasure," Mrs. S blurted in her confusion. "I heard that story as a child. My uncle had been looking for it, and told my mother he'd found something, but shortly afterwards he was drowned in an accident, and my mother wouldn't talk about it again.

"He was almost the same age my Rupert is now. Oh dear, I've gone and said too much. I do dither sometimes. I seem to be all sixes-and-sevens today. I really should be getting on."

"Maybe *he's* the ghost?" Mrs. Tweedy said.

Mrs. S looked beside herself with embarrassment. "Oh my, that's how these silly rumors start. You'll frighten Edgar. I know such things frighten me."

Edgar didn't look at all frightened. He fairly beamed with joy.

Suddenly a look of horror came over Mrs. Tweedy's needy face.

"And your husband *died* in Egypt!" she said accusingly.

"My husband is only missing... we think... that is... he could be... well, he could still be found. It's hard to say," Mrs. S faltered.

Mrs. Tweedy's brain was too preoccupied, her eyes agog, to notice Mrs. S' mistake. "I heard he was kidnapped. Rather odd don't you think, seeing's how he was messing with a pharaoh's resting place? I really don't know how you could have put up with such creepy things for so long, my dear. My husband never brings his work home."

Mrs. S wanted to say, that perhaps that was because he hadn't much work to bring home lately, but she hesitated, not keen to offend, and instead, hoped for a miracle that might rescue her. And in her dithery-ness, she got her wish.

Mrs. S had no choice but to tag along, uncomfortably dragged along with the conversation that had already begun to feel horribly out of her comfort zone. "Oh, all right then. You may as well know," she floundered with a frantic sigh, searching desperately for the right words so the two of them would leave, and instead chose the wrong ones. "My mother thinks the Hall has a ghost... *might* have a ghost... of course she's not... *um*... well, she's not herself these days, although she's said this for years... sometimes she likes to jest... I'm sure she does. I'm sure that was it. She was quite the social butterfly... and well, things are said at parties aren't they."

When Mrs. S saw Edgar's eyes bulge, she added in a feeble whisper: "As well as ... well, I'm embarrassed to admit it... a curse. It's not something we like to talk about, so please keep it... you know... under your hat."

Her words were quite out of her control now, and she heard herself saying things as if another Mrs. S was standing behind her controlling her vocal chords like puppet strings.

"It's because there's a gold statue from a pharaoh's tomb hidden somewhere on the property," she finally blurted, shocking herself.

"That your husband found?" Mrs. Tweedy gasped.

"No, no. My uncle collected Egyptian things and he probably bought it on the black market... oh... well, from some reputable dealer or something."

"A ghost *and* treasure," Edgar repeated, his eyes gleaming.

"*And* a curse," Mrs. S repeated by mistake, wishing the ground would swallow her up, but she continued to speak involuntarily, making herself feel faint.

"At certain times of the day it can feel rather strange in the library. It's the room I will be using for my classes."

It was at that moment that Edgar Tweedy chose to entertain the patrons of the tea shop by emitting a succession of loud sneezes that didn't want to stop.

Mrs. Tweedy looked alarmed. "Edgar! What is it sweetie? What's wrong? Oh dear!"

"I expect he's just getting a cold," Mrs. S suggested, "or having an allergic reaction to something."

"Oh no... Edgar only sneezes like this when he's terrified or over-excited," Mrs. Tweedy fussed.

"Well, which one is it, Edgar?" Mrs. S ventured in a wobbly voice, her eyes wide as a startled deer's.

Edgar sneezed even harder.

"Try putting your fingers in your ears," Mrs. Tweedy shouted.

"Perhaps it's both?" Mrs. S offered, moving her chair further away, and handing her hopefully not-to-be-pupil a tissue from her purse.

Edgar gave in to fits of sneezes and his eyes were watering as he tried to blubber something between wiping his nose and his eyes. A fountain of distress.

"Da... da... Dad," he finally wheezed.

Mrs. S handed him the entire packet of tissues.

"Awww, he wants his dad," Mrs. Tweedy said reassuringly. "Mr. Tweedy is so good with him when he's like this."

Edgar continued in some anxiety.

"Your ears!" Mrs. Tweedy, insisted again, a tad louder than Mrs.

Fox allowed in her establishment. "Edgar! Put your fingers in your ears, dear."

"I don't see how that will help," Mrs. S said.

"No it does. It usually works. Edgar just gets so upset he forgets, don't you darling?" Mrs. Tweedy bleated.

Mrs. S had more cause to wonder at the strangeness of Edgar Tweedy now she knew his ear canal was connected to his nose, but she supposed it had to be as there were 'Ear Nose and Throat,' specialists, so there was perhaps *some* science in it. Still... logic and the Tweedys seemed only distantly connected.

Mrs. S was taken aback with her lack of composure even though she was secretly grateful to Mrs. Spoondance for her warning when she'd mentioned the Tweedy's special interest in her ad for students. Certainly, the cowardly Tweedy lad was slow enough to require summer classes, but now he would be too afraid to step foot into Bede Hall, let alone be left in the library schoolroom. But Mrs. S couldn't have been further from the truth.

When Mrs. Tweedy stuck her own fingers in her son's ears he managed to take a few deep breaths. The sneezing episode seemed over unless something else was still upsetting the lad.

"Edgar can you hear me?" Mrs. Tweedy," shrieked, more concerned than ever as Mrs. Fox rushed to the commotion with a glass of water.

"I expect he can't hear you with your fingers in his ears," Mrs. S said, not meaning to sound sarcastic.

CHAPTER TWENTY-SIX

Dilly Dally Doolally

Kit flumped down on the end of Bash's grand bed. "Mum's put her foot in it again," he groaned. "She's told Mrs. 'weedy' we've got hidden treasure AND a ghost. Edgar's dead keen on spiriting her out."

Bash giggled. "Honestly, you might choose your words more carefully."

"What did I say now, Oh Princess Dictionary?"

"That would make our mum the queen of faux pas," Bash said. She giggled some more. *Dead* keen... *spiriting* her out.

"I might agree with you if I knew what that meant... and no, please don't tell me. I will assume it's something dithery."

"How do you know this?"

Kit stared at the floor. "I dreamed it. but it was true. I know it makes no sense."

Bash pushed the hair out of her eyes and stared back without flinching. "Actually, it makes perfect sense. It felt true when you just told me because I ran it through my own dreams and remembered it too. You know, I've often noticed how things come right even when they're dithered about in paroxysms of querulous incertitude."

Kit rolled his eyes. "Yeah, I think that sort of goes without saying."

Parks 3 reported to the kitchen and ran into Kit and Lady Nan.

"Mum is in town, Kit said, "but she's overdue, so I can make you a spot of tea while you wait. And there's an apple pie around here somewhere."

"Thanks but I'd best be off," Parks 3 said. "Lots to do, but I appreciate the offer. You can tell your mum that I'll need more time to repair the wiring. Too many mice have nibbled their way through the entire system. I can patch it, but it'll take time to follow all the wires to the generator. The good thing is, the damage is mainly in the boiler room, but I'm afraid I'll need to be in there for a few more weeks, at least."

"It's a real power struggle, then," Kit joked. "Mice against men. P'raps we should hire an exterminator."

Parks 3 and Lady Nan issued a strong protest in unison. "You have two cats," Parks 3 said. "Poison is cruel. Miss Charlotte can contact the mouse deva and ask the mice to leave." He looked uncomfortable and shuffled his feet. "Actually, I think there may be a fairy or two camping out in your electrics, and they're devilish tricky to lure out. I daresay some of that piecrust might work."

Kit laughed at Parks 3's wee joke. "I'll give Mum your message," he said, suddenly hungry for apple pie. "See you later." He left muttering 'nice one' and shaking his head.

Parks 3 scratched his head. "Nice what?" he called after Kit.

"My dad is looking for you," Parks 4 said when he found Bash.

"Thanks Four. Where is he?"

"Call me Sonny," Parks 4 said. "That formal stuff should be a thing of the past if you ask me, beggin' your pardon miss."

"I quite agree. So you should call me Bash. It must be strange when you refer to each other at home," Bash said.

"Not at all. I'm called Sonny, my dad is Stan, my granddad is Stanley, great-granddad is plain Parks, and my great-great-grand-dad... well, he's gone now so he doesn't have a name at all. But if he was alive he would tan my hide if he heard me call you Bash. I have to call you 'Miss'. The rules of the land say so. The rules of my family say so.

"My dad is in your kitchen looking for your mum. I think it's about your electrics," Parks 4 said. "You wouldn't happen to know when Rupert will be coming home next would you? He promised me a drive 'round the county to show me the new buildings. A lot's changed since I was here last."

"Have you seen Charlotte's amazing cabbage?" Bash asked.

"It's a right cracker," Parks 4 agreed. "It looks like a Christmas parcel, you see if it doesn't, and your lavender is really coming along a treat."

Bash gave him a quizzical look and hurried to the house passing the cabbage patch on the way.

Parks 4 had been right. Charlotte's experiment stood out like a watermelon surrounded by tiny green Christmas tree ornaments – a green ball tied with a red bow.

The scent of lavender assaulted Bash as she rounded the greenhouse. The field was ablaze with bright purple and the fragrance it exuded was just as bright. The plants greeted her in unison, their voices floating in a mauve wind. *"Hail Bathsheba queen of the lavender,"* they whispered. *"Hail keeper of the green, privy of the secret language, apprentice to Master Parks, novice to Lady Charlotte, heir to Lady Beryl, ally to Lady Chloris."*

Chloris was the goddess otherwise known as the Green Woman. "Goodness," Bash said, overwhelmed. "Am I all that?"

The lavender bowed their heads. *"Much more. Wait and see, majesty. One day you will save Bede."*

CHAPTER TWENTY-SEVEN

Mail Call

Nipper the Jack Russell, bared his teeth and did what he did best. He nipped at Bash's Wellington boots as she walked by.

"Little pup hates boots for some reason," Mrs. Tweedy said. "We don't know why. Maybe someone's given him a kick in the past. People can be so vicious."

The room was far too crowded. Mrs. S wasn't entirely sure why she was agreeing to any of the nonsense being unleashed in her kitchen.

Enid Tweedy had been second guessing Mrs. S at every turn, while Edgar had sat by, smugly watching his mother deliver one of her enthusiastic performances, casually slipping Nipper the best chocolate biscuits from a plate on the table.

Mrs. Tweedy finally paused, but only because her husband had fixed her with an icy stare and began reciting his 'real estate today' speech. Her hands shook as she handed Mrs. S a square envelope. "It's an invitation to our local Women's Institute," she said, blushing slightly. "I'm the president. We're having a guest speaker on pickling cabbage."

It was crystal clear to Mrs. S that Mrs. Tweedy was especially desirous of becoming her new best friend. Enid appeared quite entranced as she drifted into a lovely daydream as her husband waffled on about business. She could envision the garden parties and the hats and the ladies luncheons in a dizzying parade of social events. 'Let me introduce you to my friend, Rayne Stratford-Smyth of Bede Hall...' she heard her voice saying.

Mr. Tweedy tried his best to beam adoringly at his wife as he gave her foot a little kick under the table and glared one of his 'do as I say' stares. "My dear, it's getting late," he said "and Mrs. Stafford-Smyth has to sign some papers. Now you run along and do some shopping. Why don't you buy that lovely pink hat you liked so much the other day?"

Mrs. Tweedy immediately took her cue, ignored her husband, and launched into her rehearsed argument in spite of Mr. Tweedy's choked expression: "Edgar promised me he would work extra hard. He's an excellent little writer. He just has a small problem with his spelling and punctuation... and his composition... and his handwriting is a sometimes a wee bit illegible."

Kit paced back and forth behind the Tweedys making rude faces, disarming his mother so thoroughly that she lost her concentration. Mrs. S looked beaten, and gave in. She sighed with resignation the way a train of thought stops in a station, and gave Mrs. Tweedy a weak smile. She was alarmed hearing her voice say the opposite of what she wanted to say. "I suppose you *could* bring Edgar two weeks from this Saturday, say two-ish, and we'll see how it goes. We may as well start with weekends until regular school is over."

Edgar was busy scoffing chocolate biscuits. He froze, reaching for the last one when Mrs. S addressed him. "Edgar, if you wouldn't mind, please write a short story for me, and there's no need to go to the trouble of delivering it. Just leave it at the post office within the week. I can pick it up next time I'm in town."

Judging by Edgar's sour expression he was not pleased. Not pleased at all. Writing a short story was the last thing on his list of fun things to do.

Mrs. S ignored his sneer and rolled eyes, summoned her teacher face, and spoke with authority. "No less than three pages, in ink please, and no, I'm sorry, but Nipper absolutely *cannot* accompany you to class."

Edgar whined in his mother's direction. "Aw, do I hafta?"

Surprisingly, Mrs. Tweedy dismissed her son's request. "Yes, darling, aren't you a lucky boy to be coming to school here. Only this morning, you were saying how you wanted to meet Christopher and Bathsheba, weren't you?" She beamed at Kit and Bash. "He's heard a lot about you."

Before losing her nerve and without taking a breath, Mrs. S turned to Mr. Tweedy in her best schoolmarm voice. "We need to talk somewhere quiet," she said, and then, drained from her recent display of authority she retreated back into the meek housewife she'd become. Why couldn't Lady Nan be awake. She would have refused to admit Edgar Tweedy and have these people out the door in a heartbeat. But she needed students.

It was a 'Rupert weekend' and she secretly hoped he would suddenly barge into the kitchen in his demanding way and outshine the Tweedy's self-importance with his own personal brand of superiority. Sometimes when Rupert was around, he took control in an offhand way that, through no talent of his own, accidentally turned into a good thing. There were times when Mrs. S rather depended on him, letting him have his own way so she could slip out the grieving widow role and into the one of an ordinary overwhelmed mother.

Wilbur Tweedy busied himself tidying his papers, looking terribly important. Mrs. Tweedy had finally managed to wheedle some information from her gossiping that had proved useful, and now she was talking their way into Bede Hall, even if she *did* think it was for Edgar's sake. There was treasure to be had, and it looked as if Mrs. S had come to her senses and was going to put the Hall on the market again. His rehearsed groveling quite carried him away.

Mrs. S offered her hand to her new student with her last ounce of fake charm. "I'm very pleased to welcome you to my class, Edgar. I look forward to reading your composition.

She turned to Mrs. Tweedy with a forced smile. "Mrs. Twee...." but she was interrupted.

Mrs. Tweedy looked horrified. "Oh my dear Rayne," she fawned, "there's no need to be formal now that we're friends. Please, call me Enid."

Mrs. S swallowed and took a deep breath. "Enid... *er..* thank you so much for your kind invitation. I will certainly do my best to make the Women's Institute meeting tomorrow night, but I'll see you there if I may. There's no need to pick me up."

Edgar was not impressed. He made eye contact with his father, and the two exchanged a fixed-stare that they supposed passed for a secret change of plan signal.

Nipper lunged at Bash's boots a second time.

Bash pulled her foot away. "You want to watch that beastly thing," she said, scowling at Edgar. "Or someone might give him a little kick in the derriere."

Mrs. S rallied once more, surprising herself. "Kit, Bash, I need you to get the mail. Both of you. Immediately. Right now! And if you see your brother tell him it's urgent I speak with him. Take Jack with you."

These orders were so uncharacteristically sharp, the twins didn't even bother to mention their mother failed to use the word please. This was a mother they hadn't seen for a long time. Bash snatched the mail key by the door while Kit tied his shoelaces.Kit and Bash were on the drive before either of them could say 'Edgar Tweedy.'

"Supercilious man," Bash said, brandishing the key menacingly. "Who does he think he is!"

"Well, his wife thinks she's the bees' knees. And I take it that *super-whatever-ilious* means something nasty. As for that snappy little dog, he needs a muzzle.

Bash, usually sympathetic to all creatures, surprised Kit. "Oh, he needs more than that. Parks says he's a little demon."

The mail for Bede Hall was delivered by a small van every morning at eleven o'clock and placed in an iron letterbox held by a stone lion standing on its hind legs.

It was one of Kit's chores to take the large brass key with its lion's-head design from the hook by the back door and collect it, and after the bedlam of three Tweedys, and their mother's sudden show of backbone, Bash willingly joined him for the pleasure of walking under a large black umbrella, splashing through the puddles, racing to see who would first spot the position of the red flag which meant the box was full or empty.

The red flag waved high, signalling them to keep going, and sure enough an official looking letter with an embossed logo was waiting inside.

"It must be good news," Kit suggested, as he returned the ancient looking brass key to his pocket. "It would have been a telegram if it wasn't."

"Or a phone call," Bash added.

Kit's eyes looked excited. "Maybe it's from Dad. There's rubbish phone signals where he is. Let's get this to Mum right away." But they slowed their pace to a walk; the return to sender was clearly a London address.

"When Dad gets home do you think he'd prefer to have his old last name back?" Bash asked to ease the silence. "I heard mum talking to Boss in the garden yesterday. She said when dad came back she would change our last name to Carter."

"When Dad gets home he'll be so glad, he won't care if people call him Rumpelstelskin," Kit replied.

"We're hyphenated by the way," Bash announced. "Joined together by a little line. Lady Nan told me this morning."

"Noodle, we're joined because we're twins," Kit admonished. "Everyone knows twins are much closer than other people, that's all," he said. "It's a biological fact."

"No, our two last names, silly," Bash said, pointing to the typed name, Mrs. Cornelius Stratford-Smyth, on the envelope in her hand. "That dash is called a hyphen. Gosh, Carter-Stratford-Smyth is quite a mouthful."

"I suppose that's another bit of panache, then?"

"Most definitely," Bash answered, tapping the corner of the envelope with her finger. "And that logo is from the Antiquarian Anthropological Archaeological Society, which means it's positively bursting with panache."

But the least panache thing of all, turned out to be the terrible message inside.

Mr. Tweedy's red convertible sports car and Mrs. Tweedy's wheezy station-wagon left the front door of Bede Hall at the same time. Mr. Tweedy roared past the twins in a cloud of mud and ignored them as if they were invisible. Loud marching band music blared from his stereo. Even in the brief second he was visible, it was easy to see Mr. Tweedy was red-faced and in a 'state' as Lady Nan referred to being upset.

Mrs. Tweedy chugged by trying to catch up, waving enthusiastically as Edgar made a rude face out the back window.

Mrs. S was just taking the kettle off the stove and nearly burned herself when the twins barged in shouting their news. She tore the letter open, scanned it with her eyes and slumped into a chair.

Rupert took it from her and read aloud in his best university voice: We are sorry to inform you, we have no further word on the safe whereabouts of Professor Cornelius Stratford-Smyth. It is with regret we consider his file closed, and are treating his disappearance as an accidental death.

Therefore at this time, we believe it likely your husband has fallen fatal victim to the armed bandits and tomb robbers who prey on foreigners, and we can only express our regret at your sad loss.

It was a coward's letter. It went on about the delays and loopholes of the professor's insurance policy – an official, barely apologetic edict from someone who didn't want to be involved with honest word-of-mouth communication, or deal with the emotional outburst of a family continually living on the edge waiting for time-sensitive news.

"You look pale, Mum," Bash said, after the last supper dishes were put away.

"Maybe you should try some of Lady Nan's red lipstick," she suggested. "She has quite the variety. You never wear any except those neutral colors that don't show up. It would take some of your tiredness away. Makeup does that sort of thing."

"I've always been a pale imitation of your grandmother's pizzazz," Mrs. S replied, huffily. "Lipstick makes her happy."

"I think it's the other way around," Bash said, thinking what a great word pizzazz was. "I think she wears it *after* she's happy."

CHAPTER TWENTY-EIGHT

Seeing is Believing

Mr. Tweedy was not easily dissuaded. After a hearty supper and a glass of sherry, he mused to himself by the fire, already planning his next assault on Bede Hall, choosing to act on the assumption that it was still for sale regardless of the newly-cancelled contract in his briefcase.

Paperwork was for chumps, he thought, and the power of positive thinking would turn the tide. Didn't his wife always say that. By the law of averages she was bound to be right once-in-a-while.

He rehearsed exactly how he would begin and what he would say, and how Mrs. Stratford-Smyth would beam appreciatively, pen in hand, just needing the place for her signature to be pointed out.

It was, he would announce, his pleasure to inform her that her financial troubles were over, since he was courting an extremely interested buyer who was negotiating in earnest, wanting to turn the estate into a hotel or a country club or a golf course, but no matter, his partners could decide that later.

Mr. Tweedy watched happily in his daydream as Mrs. Stratford-Smyth made a large decorative R on the dotted line.

His reverie was interrupted by the strained sounds of distress issuing from the kitchen where Edgar struggled with his assignment for Mrs. S entitled: 'How my dog Nipper ate the first version of this story.'

Edgar's best chum, Ollie Baedeker, looked entirely pleased with his news.

"I saw it myself," he said. "It was in a walled garden out back. I was with my dad delivering a load of straw when I heard that girl singing to a cabbage. Big as a football it was. I saw where she put the key to the gate as well."

Edgar leaned forward and stuffed his mouth full of chocolate.

"You'll never guess what she was doing," Ollie said.

"I bet I would," Edgar managed to say with some difficulty. "They're all mad. That Hall is creepy as well."

"She was talking to the vegetables and waving her hands over them, and then she started to chant with her eyes closed," Ollie said. "Do you think she's a witch?"

"Of course she is," Edgar nodded. "Her grandmother is too. She has a black cat and you know what that means."

"Edgar pushed another lump of chocolate into his mouth.

Ollie looked as if he was concentrating on a difficult math problem. "Then... is your teacher... a witch?"

"Don't think so," Edgar replied, both his cheeks bulging with chocolate so he could barely speak without drooling. "Maybe witchcraft skips a generation. Still, she's always talking to that bird, and it answers her as if it understands."

The realization of his recent association caused Edgar to gasp for air and splutter chocolate down his shirt. Ollie thumped him on the back.

"Gosh, I've been *alone* in that library with her," Edgar managed to choke, "and she orders me about all the time. Supposing she enchants me and tells me to do something bad?"

"You could use that as an excuse," Ollie grinned. "I mean for the next time... you know... when you steal something again."

Edgar's face grew red from more than trying to swallow six squares of chocolate all at once.

"I don't steal!" he hollered, dribbling dark goo even more than before. "I'm an investigator. I have to collect evidence."

Suddenly Edgar looked horrified.

"*Ew*! I got this chocolate from Mrs. S's desk."

"We better keep the rest in case it has to be analyzed," Ollie said. "I've seen them do that on TV."

A second later Edgar's face brightened. The thought caused him to swallow hard.

"I suppose that makes me a witch hunter," he said proudly. "It's my duty to inform the newspaper."

"Not the police then?" Ollie queried.

"The police don't give a toss for weird veggies," Edgar said. "Besides, the newspaper *pays* for an odd story."

CHAPTER TWENTY-NINE

And Stay Out!

Only weeks after Bede Hall had reclaimed them, Rupert stayed away from his college long enough to grumble all the time, and Mrs. S had begun to tutor Edgar Tweedy in English Literature – her first and only student, in one of the most glamorous schoolrooms a pupil was ever likely to see.

Kit heard the unmistakable racket of Mrs. Tweedy's car rattling towards the house.

"Mum. Weedy's here," he called out, without looking up from his 'Ripleys.'

Mrs. S had her hands in the sink and dropped a greasy plate back in the water a little too enthusiastically, making soapy water splosh over the counter and onto her dress. "Blast! He's early again," she clucked, searching for a tea towel.

"Should I let them in?" Bash asked.

"Heavens no. Finish these dishes will you please, there's a good girl. I'll have to go. That woman is like a ferret. If *you* open the door she'll be in here for an hour. And then *you'll* have to supervise Edgar."

Bash leaped to the sink and began scrubbing a plate.

Mrs. S dried her hands, dabbed at her dress and smoothed her hair.

"Do I look all right?" she asked Kit, who looked up amused.

"You're fine," he said, looking puzzled. "I don't know why you're always fussing about Mrs. Weedy... I mean *Tweedy*. She's not the *queen*," he said, and with that he dived back into his book.

Ollie had been right. Edgar's eyes popped at the sight of what appeared to be a huge green beach ball which dwarfed the rows of green 'Ping-Pong balls' surrounding it.

Edgar Tweedy scanned the area behind him and strolled casually through the vegetables whistling, and picked the largest cabbage he had ever seen. He rolled its enormity into a black garbage bag and tied it with a bit of string, stashing it by the dustbins, knowing it would be safe for days if need be, but he was wildly confident he would take it home that night.

"I've got it," he said smugly into his phone, slipping behind the stables for privacy.

The voice on the other end was clearly prodding for more information.

"What's my name?" Edgar repeated. "Why'd you need to know that? I... I'm an anonymous caller with one of those tip things," he argued.

The voice in his ear was insistent.

"What does ethical mean?" Edgar squeaked.

The voice went on slightly peeved: "We need to identify our sources before we investigate or we'd be running about all day every time someone wanted to cause trouble. You wouldn't want to do that would you?"

Edgar's face clouded. "I don't understand the question," he said.

Lady Nan hated having a strange boy in her house, but other than that necessary concession, she had returned to her spritely eccentric self with undiluted enthusiasm.

"It's mystifying how things turn out," Lady Nan had said to her daughter. "I never approved of your school idea in the first place. It's gone and opened a can of worms for the ghost, for Parks, *and* for the house."

"Well, Mamma, I need the extra money until, that is if, Cornelius's insurance company ever resolves things."

"Is it that bad then?" Lady Nan asked.

"I'm afraid so," Mrs. S said, "Daddy left things in rather a pickle... and then with Cornelius disappearing, well, I didn't know *what* to do. Rupert insisted he continue on at Oxford almost as if nothing had happened."

"Nothing gets in Rupert's way; he takes after your father," Lady Nan said.

"He does have a scholarship, Mamma," Mrs. S added defensively.

"That boy needs a job. Even I know he's no more archaeologist than Pigeon. He has no love for it. Not like your uncle Ben; not like Cornelius."

Mrs. S wrung her hands. "Maybe I made a mistake," she said.

"Events are bad, then good, then bad again," Lady Nan said. "One can never be entirely sure what's happening. All I *do* know, is that ghastly 'Edgar boy' chills my blood. In my day, children about the place had to be under the supervision of nannies, and obnoxious behavior would not have been tolerated.

"Bede Hall is quite out of sorts with him here. No good will come of him being in this house. Even with the library windows open, it takes hours for his disruptive energy to leave after he goes home."

"Bash, you really shouldn't call Edgar, Weedy, you know." Mrs. S said.

"I can't help it. He is weedy," Bash said, "and besides, it's right there in his name. Plain as day if you take away the 'T'. Lady Nan says that's not a coincidence. And if you mix up the letters in Edgar it sounds like greed: G-R-E-A-D. Lady Nan says the wrong spelling doesn't count because it's the resonance of a word that has all the power."

"I thought you said a weed was just a plant with attitude?" Kit reminded her.

"*Um...* Parks said that," Bash said defensively. "Weeds are fine when they don't choke other plants and try to take over."

"There's even a ruddy food chain in the plant kingdom," Rupert countered from behind his newspaper. "Typical! None of us are safe. No veggies are safe. And from the looks of Edgar a moment ago, he was rather curious about your cabbages. Maybe he's checking out his weedy relatives."

"There *aren't* any weeds in my gardens," Bash said indignantly,

"Not even weedy little kids? Well Edgar's interested in *something* out there," Rupert said. "I've just seen him poking about amongst your vegetables. I think he may be stealing some. He had a dirty great sack with him."

"He can't do that!" Bash shrieked. "He's no business going in there at all! He'll ruin all Park's and Charlotte's work. The plants are sensitive just now. He'll upset them," she fumed, slamming her books shut with an exasperated grunt.

Bash sprinted out the room towards the vegetable garden with blood in her eyes. "EDGAR!" she shouted as she ran. "Where are you? You weedy little git."

The gardens looked peaceful enough to a stranger, but the 'magic cabbage' was gone. Bash immediately sat cross-legged and performed a routine of deep-cleansing breaths and listened inwardly.

It wasn't long before her shoulders slumped and she swayed slightly like a coiled cobra. An imperceptible buzzing sound entered her left ear, and a tiny metallic voice began to speak. Bash let go of straining to hear. Instead she allowed the voice to come to her, and as it got closer it became strong and rang with a doleful sigh.

The message was clear. An intruder had flashed a light from a small black box at the 'great cabbage' and it had been plucked from its row.

A few hours later, only moments after his last class, Edgar looked over his shoulder furtively, while his mother chatted with Mrs. S about his progress, and when it was clear no-one was looking, he retrieved his garbage bag and tossed it into the trunk of his mother's waiting car.

"Dirty great steaming blob of sh..." Bash hollered, banging her way through the kitchen door, seething with anger.

"Bash!" Mrs. S shouted, cutting her daughter's words off before she would be sorry.

Bash looked up, her eyes suddenly wide with innocence.

"What?" she said, disarmingly calm.

Mrs. S's voice resumed its natural conversational tone. "There's no need to lose your composure dear," she said.

Bash thumped down into a chair. "I think there is!" she ranted again. "Where is he?"

"Gone home," Kit said, with half of a chocolate biscuit in his mouth."

"He couldn't have done anything *that* bad," Mrs. S said. "Could he?"

"He's only taken photographs of Park's experiment, nicked Charlotte's giant cabbage, and gone to the newspapers," Bash wailed.

"Who on earth told you such a thing?" Mrs. S inquired.

"*Um*... doesn't matter," Bash said, wriggling uncomfortably, considering she couldn't very well tell Mrs. S it was a tray of lavender plants who had ratted Edgar out.

Mrs. S registered Bash's claim slightly delayed, and ruminated about newspaper reporters and publicity for a heartbeat before her outburst.

"The sniveling thieving little git!" she whispered under her breath. "He's going to be sorry."

Only hours after the Tweedys had finished their dinner, Edgar inquired the whereabouts of his 'booty' while scrabbling amongst frozen cartons and bags for ice-cream.

"Mummy?" he whined. "I left a rather largish cabbage on the counter. Have you seen it?"

"I have sweetie pie," Mrs. Tweedy replied cheerily, squeaking a soapy plate to test for greasiness.

"D'you know where it IS then?" Edgar asked, with his head still inside the freezer compartment.

"Oh yes sweetie, I do. I made a lovely batch of coleslaw with it. I know how your father loves it. It was so big I chopped up the rest for pickling," Mrs. Tweedy said, wiping her apron. "Can I get you anything dear?"

Since it made a terrible mess of his weekends, Edgar Tweedy wasn't in the best of moods when he was dropped off at the huge stone arch over the entrance to Bede Hall.

Underneath it was an impressive door, well, two doors in fact, that opened together like wings.

Mrs. Tweedy always drove her darling son to his Saturday afternoon math class and walked him to the door hoping for a glimpse inside. But Mrs. S was ready for them, and hustled Edgar inside, saying goodbye as she closed the door on Mrs. Tweedy's inquisitive nose.

Mrs. Tweedy refused to pronounce Smyth as Smith, the way it was supposed to. She decided that 'Smithe' sounded more, well, tutorly, and being able to say that her Edgar took classes up at 'The Hall' from Mrs. Stratford-'*Smythe*', don't you know, was too impressive to pass up.

It was so impressive, that some of her friends were almost sorry they had such clever children who didn't need extra summer classes.

Mrs. Tweedy liked to stretch the truth, and told them how she took tea on Saturday afternoons to discuss Edgar's progress with the lady of the manor, herself. Sylvia Fox hung onto every word and wanted to know what kind of cakes were served.

Edgar Tweedy may have been obsessively stalking the phantom of a giant vegetable, a golden statue, and a ghost-child, but apart from

Lady Nan, the Stratford-Smyth family rarely gave the Hall's unseen resident a thought. They were less concerned with a long-lost soul when one of their own was missing.

Bede Hall did what it could to discourage what it called 'that Edgar thing' by slamming its squeaky doors as eerily as it could, and dousing the light when he 'occupied' the bathroom. Once it managed to turn on a tap and lock the door from the outside, but all that did was exhaust the Hall's already sorely-taxed energy and make the little devil sneeze once or twice.

CHAPTER THIRTY

Just Say Cheese

It was one of the only fair days when it was possible to tramp the moors of the Bede Hall estate before the weather closed in again.

It had cleared suddenly without warning, and Helen Peterson, a spinster artist, had been ready with her portable easel and paint box kept near the door for just such an occasion.

Stanley Parks' cottage was a perfect subject to complete her present series of local landscapes. Rustic vistas were more than her specialty, they were her *only* subject.

But this time, Charlotte Findhorn had specifically commissioned a painting for her friend, Stanley Parks Senior's eightieth birthday on May 1st, which wasn't far off in art terms, considering an oil painting would require time to dry.

Helen's companion, Robert Hare, who owned the 'real' antique store in Bede, and was known affectionately as 'Rabbit,' traipsed valiantly on by her side because being near the divine Helen Peterson was reason enough to forgo sleeping-in.

It was his way of courting her – a passive approach that he hoped would automatically drift into matrimony without any excessive effort of his own.

Some people often noted that 'Rabbit Hare' was as timid as his pet rabbit, Pierre, and that by comparison, Helen, who was obviously in pursuit of a husband, was a dragon with a taste for rabbit stew.

"*Plein air* – the art of painting outside in the open air," Helen raved, "can never be outshone in a studio. It's all here," she said taking a deep breath, flinging her arms wide to encompass the hills: "The light, the atmosphere, the mystery, and the ambiance of the 'enchanting cottage' is captured first hand as one sees it in the purity of landscape," she enthused.

Helen gestured towards the faraway hills.

"Da Vinci painted the mists of weather and distance. He called it *'sfumato,'* – the smokiness of air between near and far," she instructed.

"Tweedy says it will be pulled down as soon as the Hall's sold," Robert said rather less dramatically, referring to the cottage below. "He showed me the plans for the new building estate the other day when he came in looking for a vintage skeleton key. He says it's the future."

"New houses lack personality," Helen spouted. "They're too sterile for emotions to stick. There's rarely a sense of the homestead about them. Without that sort of thing inbred in the construction, you end up with cookie-cutter-dreadfuls."

"It's criminal to demolish heritage homes to make way for prefabs that wipe out history," Robert agreed, clearly hoping to score a point.

"Character homes have distinct personalities. Their interiors can feel welcoming and safe all the way to malevolent. I'm able to sense which," Helen bragged.

"What about the haunted ones?" Richard asked tentatively.

Helen gave him an exasperated look. He just isn't trying, she thought. "Those simply have stronger memories in the walls," she said trying not to sound peeved. "The new ones are clean... emotionally speaking."

Robert tried not to show how little he cared. "We should eat the picnic before we get caught... in the rain," he said hopefully. "A few minutes ago, that raincloud was miles away."

They worked their way through fat slabs of cottage pie and several hard-boiled eggs, treacle tart, and two thermoses of over-stewed tea before Helen broke the silence.

It's time, she thought, to stop playing hard to get and reel Robert in. He was as good a husband as she was ever likely to get, and being a freelance artist was poverty work. It was getting harder to make ends meet. Two could not only live as cheaply as one, but they could afford vacations and a new dining table as well.

"Cycles are natural," Helen began, "you only have to follow the seasons. None of them are good or bad; they're just different. One thing leads to another," Helen hinted, searching for a sign of a more personal interest. "Or *good* things," she added with a smile, thinking about the noble arc from friendship to marriage.

Robert nodded, his mouth full of digestive biscuit.

"Rabbit?" Helen fished. "I hope you and I... that *we're* good friends," she said.

"Of course," Robert said blushing, coughing from ingesting biscuit crumbs. "The very best of friends," he replied cautiously, gulping down a mouthful of tea to clear his throat.

"Big commitments begin with small promises," Helen went on. "Clockwork-life, I call it."

"It always has; always will," Robert said straightening the knives and forks so he didn't have to look directly at Helen. "It's called... *um*... progress."

"Some call it consequences, but it always feels like punishment or a reward," Helen replied.

The sun disappeared behind the ominous raincloud, now directly overhead.

"Time to pack it in for the day," Robert announced, a tad relieved, but dismayed seeing how far away his car was – a very small blue shape in the distance below. "It looks like we're in for it."

Helen rummaged through her backpack for her old-fashioned instamatic camera and handed it to Robert.

"Sweetie, can you take some shots of the cottage while I get this lot ready to go," she asked, already expertly folding the easel into a wooden briefcase. "I'll have to finish it back in the studio after all, but I need some reference. I don't like to rely on memory when it's someone's actual house; they notice all the details. Even a tree out of place spoils it."

The word sweetie made Robert's hands fumble the shutter as he pointed the lens at what he hoped best duplicated the angle Helen had chosen to paint. He took several more shots that captured what

Helen liked to describe as 'the rustic charm of 'the English country cottage,' and bumbled after his almost bride-to-be mumbling about rain ruining the camera if they weren't careful.

Everything was carted to the car while the rain brooded, waiting for the last moment to surprise the creatures intent on scurrying away from it. But the rain of Bede Hall still hadn't begun after Robert's car was packed; its mission wasn't quite fulfilled. It knew very well that Helen would want to use up her film.

"There's only three of four shots left," Helen said, consulting a tiny box on her camera showing the number 18. "I want to drop it off at the chemist on the way home."

The rain chuckled as Helen calculated eighteen from twenty-four.

"There are at least six shots left," she said.

"Let me take one of you in front of the cottage," Robert said, already snapping a shot of Helen walking towards him.

"Don't waste film," she chided, making an irritated noise with her tongue.

Robert spied an ancient pitchfork leaning against the fence and offered it as a prop to regain her favor.

"Your turn," Helen said with a forced a smile, handing back the giant fork.

Robert reluctantly accepted it as if he was an actor receiving an award he didn't entirely deserve, and smiled obligingly, 'for the birdie.'

"A little closer to the door," Helen directed. "I need to see that lovely carved bit on the lintel... I promised Vincento I would take a picture of it. He's collecting pictures of doorknobs and rusty hinges now. No, the other way," she barked. "Hold it right there... oops I moved. Sorry, stand still so I can take another one."

Robert dutifully hammed it up to impress Helen, holding the pitchfork like the classic farmer: in front of the door, beside the door, and another on the other side of the door until the camera shutter solidified indicating the roll was done. And as if on cue, the rain suddenly unleashed itself in a surprisingly warm torrent.

CHAPTER THIRTY-ONE

A Prize Turnip

Bash's vegetables had struggled against the punishing weather, but Charlotte's prize cabbage had thrived due to her special attention and what she called the presence of elemental Deva spirits known as numina and Parks' magic touch. By comparison the other cabbages were normal-sized healthy specimens arranged in tidy, well-spaced rows that looked like a quilt of hearty 'green tennis balls'.

Parks' amazing techniques were second nature. Between himself and Charlotte Findhorn, the insatiable florist, the Bede Hall cabbage had grown to outrageously extreme proportions, causing a mild flutter of local interest after word leaked out. Anything was news in the sleepy hamlet of Bede. Bash had to recruit Charlotte to help dissuade a reporter working for 'The Daily Bead,' who had been hoping for a sensational story at last.

"It had all been a prank," Charlotte had told him, "one of the lads was playing about, that was all. He painted a beach ball green and 'planted' it as a joke. He was the one who called you. I'll see he's given a talking to."

But from that moment, Edgar Tweedy was Bede enemy, number one.

Digging weeds was one of Bash's favorite pastimes. The joy of working the grounds of Bede Hall felt like being on an endless vacation from tediously long regular schooldays, and the noisy traffic and the grime of city streets. In comparison, being home-schooled was a brief and pleasant part of the day, with the exception of Edgar Tweedy's disrupting presence.

The boy reeked of menace. It was like inviting a virus into the house. He didn't walk into rooms so much as infiltrate them like a pipsqueak CIA agent. He was quicksilver fast once outside the confines of the library, slithering upstairs and opening cupboards.

Since the cabbage incident, all four Parks had been put on notice that the 'Tweedy creature' was to 'keep off the grass.' This being code for: 'consider Edgar as being out of bounds anywhere other than the beaten path from the front door to the library classroom, with the possible exception of the odd bathroom break,' and Bede Hall did what it could to make sure those visits were as creepy as could be.

Edgar's constant snooping and light-fingered tendencies were the reasons Mrs. S always ushered him through the formal entrance on the main floor. Mrs. Tweedy had been delighted, and put it down to her son's importance, but it was because the right of passage through the rooms the Stratford- Smyths called home, was out of the question. And on absolutely no account, was his 'hench-dog,' Nipper, allowed within a dog's breath of the place, as the little terror of a terrier could squeeze his ratty hide through the bars of the main gate. He had been spotted once or twice streaking across the lawn, lifting his leg on the sphinx, and tearing up Parks' prize petunias.

Edgar was trespassing on the third floor when Pigeon interrupted Rupert's late breakfast. *"By the way, Boss, 'Edgar the poo' is in your room,"* he said in Parks' voice. *"He's a prize turnip and no mistake."*

Rupert hauled Edgar from his bachelor digs by the scruff of his ugly red turtleneck. Not only a heinous fashion crime, but an incident that broke Rupert's best Gucci sunglasses.

Edgar wriggled free and ran off shouting rude words about sissies and sunglasses, and Rupert gave chase, all the way downstairs, out the front door, and over to the maze.

Edgar glanced over his shoulder at Rupert. "Weirdo," he shouted. "You run like a girl," and he dove into the maze. The hedges gave a brief shudder as if it had swallowed a spoon of bitter tasting medicine.

Rupert halted before the entrance, reluctant to go in. He'd never had much luck with the maze. Both times he'd wandered in Parks had to wander him out again. The humiliation of Edgar, not only outwitting him, but the possibility of being stuck and calling for help, kept him debating his next move. But as he was thinking, he heard a loud hiccup followed by a burp and something came hurtling out of the maze like a cannonball with flailing arms and legs. Edgar was delivered to Rupert's feet trailing a loud wail of fear and leaves.

Edgar rolled a few times before leaping to his feet. "This place is haunted," he shouted as he brushed his sweater covered with dead leaves. "Somebody should report you lot." He pulled twigs from his hair, with the words *'and stay out!'* echoing in his head. "You're all crazy." Then he went berserk, ripped Rupert's glasses from his face, and snapped them in two.

Rupert spluttered and fumed for a week. Now he had only seven pairs of designer sunglasses.

Other than Nipper's professional 'career' taking small painful bites of ankles, knees, fingers, and cat's tails, the little tyke was an intrepid digger. Neither of his nor his master's (if you could call Edgar Tweedy the master of anything) shenanigans would be tolerated. The Stratford-Smyths told each other the two species could be expelled in a heartbeat. But they relied on the income from their only paid student.

It was Rupert, who came up with a sly plan to put the Tweedy's in their place. The Stratford-Smyths would have to content themselves with an uncomfortable confrontation and carry off a grand bluff. Mr. Tweedy still wanted to be their realtor but just how far would he go, taking sides against his son for the sake of a sale?

Nipper seemed proud of himself even though Mr. Tweedy told him off several times for biting. His "who's a bad dog, then?" sounded more like "Good boy... well done."

Rupert acted the part of a lawyer, pacing in front of a witness, and cornered Edgar, who did his wormy best to out-wriggle being caught.

"Perhaps breaking and entering isn't your specialty," Rupert said. "Perhaps stealing a prize vegetable is, eh? Do you know what that cabbage was worth? Do you know how much Gucci sunglasses cost? Hmmn?"

Edgar squirmed. Mr. Tweedy squirmed. But Enid Tweedy smiled sweetly at Mrs. S the entire time, reliving a pleasant memory of a recent tea party when they had shared a secret.

The Tweedys were given a choice. Pay for the damages, keep Nipper off Bede Hall's premises or pay a 'get your dog named Nipper out of jail' fine from the SPCA, and teach Edgar to stop poking about in other people's property or face a visit from the local constabulary.

Bash nodded her approval. "Consider it an ultimatum," she added smugly under her breath for Kit's ears only. For the benefit of Mr. and Mrs. Tweedy, her eyebrows rose dramatically as she stared into Edgar's eyes, declaring loudly for all to hear. "And by the way, I hope the newspaper rescinds your advance fee for any new skulduggery you're cooking up, whatever it is. There's sure to be one."

What none of the Stratford-Smyths fully-grasped, was that the destination of Edgar's Egyptian treasure hunt, miracle cabbage aside, was a sighting of their bashful ghost, and more importantly to capture it on film. But Bede Hall knew. The maze knew. And Parks had known since before Edgar was born.

Newspaper gold already jingled in Edgar's pocket, and time was running out. Ironically, he'd been given a *dead*line to produce a picture of a ghost. If he came up empty-handed, without even so much as a fogged image of a blob on some stairs, the advance fee would need to be returned – a frightening prospect to Mr. Tweedy as he'd already spent it on new leopard-skin seat covers for his natty red sports car.

Mr. Tweedy reached for his wallet. "Now now, no harm intended; no harm done," he said cheerily. "Of course you must be reimbursed." But he paled when he heard the prize cabbage was worth every penny of the lost prize money, should there have been a contest, of twenty-five pounds and Gucci sunglasses cost six times the amount the newspaper had paid for the snapshot of a silly vegetable. He was so angry he grounded Edgar for an entire hour.

PART THREE

FAIRYLAND

Over hill, over dale,
Thorough bush, thorough brier,
Over park, over pale,
Thorough flood, thorough fire!
I do wander everywhere,
Swifter than the moon's sphere;
And I serve the Fairy Queen,
To dew her orbs upon the green;
The cowslips tall her pensioners be;
In their gold coats spots you see;
Those be rubies, fairy favours;
In those freckles live their savours;
I must seek some dewdrops here,
And hang a pearl in every cowslip's ear.

- WILLIAM SHAKESPEARE

CHAPTER THIRTY-TWO

May Day

Bash answered the knock at the kitchen door to find Parks grinning with an armful of flowering Primrose branches.

"These are for you," he said, doffing his cap as he stepped inside. Greetings of the May to ye."

"Happy birthday Mr. Parks," Bash replied, accepting the branches, "Will we see you at the celebrations?"

"Have to go don't I," Parks admitted shyly, "They've gone and made me honorary Jack-in-the-Green – a proper fuss they're making of it too, I can tell you."

"Mayday...mayday... mayday... birthday... oh happy day...more pooh," shrieked Pigeon, in Lady Nan's unmistakable 'Beryl voice.'

"We'll recognize you by your costume, then," Mrs. S said.

Parks looked pleased. "I'll be a walking topiary inside that leaf suit. My brother made it for me. All you can see is me feet. Which is fine since I hate to have me picture taken."

"I have something for you," Bash said, fetching a framed poem from the sideboard. "It's that passage you like from William Blake. I've done some drawings of carnations around it. I hope you like it."

Bash read the lyrics to the famous hymn, 'Jerusalem,' out loud: *'And did those feet in ancient times walk upon England's pastures green,'* she recited.

Pigeon repeated the words in song, and then added: *"pastures green...all creatures great and small."*

"I don't know what to say," Parks mumbled shyly, "except to tell you to watch yourself today missy. Beltane can be... well even village fêtes can be... just be careful."

Parks stopped and wiped a bit of stray mist from his eye, and quickly changed the subject by addressing Pigeon:

152

"And how are you this fine morning, Primrose, me old beauty?" Parks chuckled to the parrot. "Didn't forget you now did I?"

"Prim and proper," Pigeon answered, bobbing his head up and down with excitement as Parks presented him with a small Primrose sprig of his own.

"Now don't eat this all at once, greedy guts," Parks scolded, poking the small branch through the bars of the cage.

"Jack old sport!" the parrot called out excitedly. *"Where have you been?...not forgotten...greedy guts... hooray hooray it's the first of May... may I?... maybe I will... maybe I won't."*

The electric lamp on the sideboard flickered erratically, made a fizzing sound, and went out, cutting Pigeon's speech short before he could mention pooh again.

"You be a good bird and I'll bring ye back a bunch of marigolds," Parks said, "but I'll need a good report from Mrs. S," he said.

"All things bright and beautiful," the parrot replied, mimicking Parks' chuckle. *"Feathers! Don't eat that plant!"*

Parks gave the light bulb a gentle tap and it popped back on. "Best have a look at the fuse box again while I'm here," he said. "My grandson is determined to get your power system under control."

Mrs. S made Parks a cup of tea when he was done, and placed a sponge-cake in front of him, with a lit candle on top. "We still need candlepower for the good things," she said. "Sorry Parks, I couldn't put eighty candles on it."

"Make a wish," Bash said.

"I wish I may I wish I might," Pigeon chortled to himself.

"Well I believe I already did. And it came true an all, because here all of you are again," Parks said. "It'd be greedy to want another one."

"Greedy guts!...all at once...happy birthday...with snow on top," Pigeon squawked.

Parks blew out the candle and stared wistfully into the past.

"I remember like it were yesterday," he mused. "When Miss Beryl was crowned Queen of the May."

"King of the castle...queen of the May...dirty rascal," Pigeon taunted between bites of pink primrose petals.

Parks accepted a second cup of tea, and ate third helpings of cake before he had to go.

Pigeon was still singing *'happy birthday to you,'* when he left.

Lady Nan had instructions for her grandchildren: "Mind you're careful today," she said, "the veil between the worlds is thin today. Keep your eyes open. Parks knows all about it. Ask him if you don't believe me... yes, I do see that you think I'm quite mad sometimes."

"What sort of 'things' could happen?" Kit said.

"Mythical elements and such like," she replied with a knowing wink. "You live in Bede remember."

The village green was festooned with a beribboned May pole, and someone had wound branches of hawthorn and marigold garlands around the pillory and all the lamp posts.

It was all very festive with Rowan and Gorse and pink blossoms decorating the booths and tents with the sound of the Morris dancers' bells jingling in time to the drums.

"It's all right Jack," Bash soothed, putting her hands over the dog's ears. "This music must sound awful to a dog," she said to Kit.

"Music? It sounds awful to everyone," Kit replied, grimacing. "I'm going over to the coconut booth and win an amazingly feeble prize."

"Can you please take Jack with you in a bit? I want to have my fortune read by Madame Flora, later," Bash pleaded. "And don't let him pee on Parks," she added, giggling.

"Pardon?"

"Parks is dressed in a tree costume. He's inside that wandering tree over there."

CHAPTER THIRTY-THREE

Cat Burglar

Bede Hall felt the kitchen window being opened and listened as the intruder's footsteps approached the main staircase. It directed the steps to groan louder than usual.

"Shush," a voice said.

"I can't help it," replied a second voice. "It's a creaky old thing. Besides, everyone's at the fete."

"Fate is right...fate it is...Madame Flora...50p a throw," Pigeon's voice muttered absentmindedly from inside a cloth-covered cage, before returning to his dream.

Mr. Tweedy and his son Edgar continued to creep up the stairs heading for the library.

"It's just around this corner," Edgar whispered.

The double-doors to the library opened cautiously letting out a lemon-polished squeak.

"Mayday mayday!" the Hall signalled in distress, directly to Parks. *"Hurry back! Tweedy alert!"*

"In the movies there's always a secret passageway behind some books," Mr. Tweedy said. "Are you sure you haven't noticed anything odd about these shelves?" He continued to press random spines of the books with his gloved hands, growling softly under his breath. "Anything that looks like a gold statue in that glass cabinet?"

"No Dad," Edgar answered sounding miffed. "I think I would have noticed that. There's just a load of old beetles in a tray. Gross."

"What a thing to collect," Mr. Tweedy commented. "Seems to me, grand folk aren't as clever as we think they are."

Mr. Tweedy reached up under the mantelpiece to check the flue.

"There's a bit of a ledge up here," he said from inside the chimney, "but it's empty."

Edgar gave a sudden sneeze, and looked about nervously.

"Dad?" he said in a shaky voice, "do you reckon it's gotten a lot chillier in here?"

CHAPTER THIRTY-FOUR

Seeing Green

Twin bonfires were roaring cheerfully on the green, and as the twins watched, a procession of farm animals were marched between them: cows and goats, sheep and horses, walked skittishly, shying at the orange sparks making accompanying noises of distress. Next came a reluctant succession of family pets.

"Superstitious lot!" Kit remarked. "As if this little parade is going to bring a good harvest. Honestly! Haven't they heard of science? And they call themselves wise. Rubbish!"

"It's just a harmless old tradition," Bash said. "It's only a bit of fun. I'm taking Jack through," she said, waving back to Charlotte Findhorn motioning on the other side.

"It's unscientific," Kit insisted, looking more embarrassed than annoyed. "I see Miss Findhorn has brought her pet monkey with her."

"Most fun things are," Bash replied.

Charlotte was loaded down with Beegle on her shoulder, a thermos, and an armful of her handcrafted May baskets stuffed with flowers and special herbs to honor the occasion.

"I've got a special one to leave," she said to Bash, indicating the largest and most elaborate basket at her feet. "Come and join me. Can you carry that one? I've got my hands full."

Charlotte stooped, laid down her bundles and opened the thermos.

"Thirsty?" she asked, holding out a small cup of pale liquid.

Bash started to say no but changed her mind. "Suddenly I am, rather," Bash replied. "What is it lemonade?"

"Oh better than that," Charlotte said. "This is dew from this morning."

"Dew?" Bash asked. "You mean real dew?"

"Nothing better for May Day. Go on have a sip," Charlotte said.

Bash drank a whole cup and asked for another much to Charlotte's amusement.

"That'll do you a power of good," she said.

Beegle chattered and reached his long arms out to Jack the dog, who shied nervously with every happy-monkey shriek.

"You'd think Jack would be fine considering he lives with a parrot," Charlotte mused.

"Pigeon's in a cage most of the time and he doesn't have long brown fingers that try to pinch the name tag on Jack's collar," Bash replied.

On the way, Charlotte distributed the smaller baskets to children in the crowd who were delighted to pet Beegle and offer him treats.

Bash followed along with Jack, and the four of them made their way to the high street where a nondescript slab of concrete in the pavement contained an embedded brass plaque.

Peals of merriment from the green could still be heard, but here it echoed off the walls of the buildings in a haunting sound rather than a boisterous ear-splitting racket.

"Most people ignore this place," Charlotte said, rearranging her basket with care. "They pass over it every day, never sparing a thought for the witches that were burned on this very spot."

She took a small pouch of dried lavender from her pocket and handed another to Bash.

"It heals some of the bad energy," Charlotte said. She closed her eyes for a few minutes until if felt right, and sprinkled a handful of pale mauve dust over the date, 1613.

Bash handed Charlotte Jack's leash when she had finished, and sprinkled her own lavender while Beegle hopped up and down in a monkey dance.

Jack whined nervously.

"Jack can sense the vibrations of this spot," Charlotte said. "The women killed here as witches were only herbalists like you and me," she added, shaking her head. "Such ignorance."

"Kit thinks it's ignorant to cleanse the land with the ashes from tonight's bonfires," she said.

"It's done by tradition rather than out of respect nowadays," Charlotte said. "But you can tell your brother from me, that there's more to life than science. Living in Bede Hall should prove that."

Parks minus his tree suit looked out of place, for once. "Happy birthday Green Man," Charlotte said, unveiling Helen's painting.

Parks cottage had been faithfully captured under a much bluer sky than had been there on the day Helen had painted it.

"I shall treasure it," Parks said, quite overcome as his gathered friends sang happy birthday.

Helen beamed nearby with her old camera at the ready. She checked the number on her film and noticed there were only a few shots left.

"All right you two," she called out. "Look at the birdie."

"Oh no... no thanks Helen," Charlotte protested looking stricken. "No photo. I hate to have my picture taken and so does Parks."

But it was too late. Helen's trigger-happy camera had already snapped and nothing could be done to erase a shot on an old-fashioned roll of film.

"Sorry," Helen said. "I forgot you two were camera shy."

As soon as Parks heard the shutter click he gave Charlotte one last look of horror at being photographed and hurried back into his tree costume so no-one would see how much he was affected by kindness under a public spotlight. Bash, who was watching the whole thing, stepped up.

"I want a picture as well," she said, "but with you as Jack," she said to Parks, already lowering the mesh frame covered in leaves over his head. "So, no-one will see you."

"Sorry Parks." Helen said. "Could you stand one more for Bash? Then you can come out of that wretched thing."

"Anything for my *Princess* of the May," Parks muffled voice sniffed.

"We'll be quick. Wait right there," Kit assured Parks, moving Bash into position.

"Bash," Kit directed, "stand between Jack and Jack."

Jack-the-dog was reluctantly dragged into place, looking only slightly less nervous, now that he could no longer see Jack-in-the-Green out the corner of his sorrowful eye. But a tree with feet was almost as disturbing.

"Cheese!" hollered Kit, and a stifled laugh issued from inside the tree. "Nice smile, but I think you had your eyes closed in that one Parks," Kit shouted. "Just kidding, that's a wrap, as they say in Hollywood. You can take another break. They've all gone."

Parks emerged from the suit of leaves looking perfectly refreshed and dry-eyed. "Holly! That's what I forgot," he cried, and hustled away. Jack sniffed the empty tree, and whined that it would be better to move on to the food fair.

Helen was late. She heaved her backpack into the front seat of her car, headed for the valley, and had to slam on her brakes when a tree lurched into her path. The pack pitched forward onto the floor spilling its contents.

She put her head out the window and called out: "Sorry Parks," and piled everything back, but one roll of film didn't want to be retrieved, and wedged itself tightly under the metal runner holding the seat.

Madame Flora charged a whole pound to read a person's tarot cards, but only 50p to consult her crystal ball.

"I'll take the crystal ball," Bash announced, plunking down her coins.

"I see you tending a garden," the gypsy said... "but there's a storm. The trees are black and leafless. It's starting to snow. I see a clock striking twelve," she said, "but I feel it's midday."

Madame Flora looked uncomfortable. "Can't see anymore," she said abruptly, covering her ball with a distinctive bright blue and red polka dot scarf.

"Can't or won't?" Bash said warily.

"Here's your 50p back," Madame Flora said. "It's your lucky day."

'The Stopped Clock' was almost deserted. The carnations Dr. Brooks had brought sat proudly in the center of the table.

"Happy summer," Dr. Brooks said to Parks 3, waiting for the others to arrive.

"We'll have the place to ourselves for an hour before the revelers decide to be thirsty," he said, as Vincento Leoni walked through the pub's door with Clive Lucy, Professor Appleby, and Parks 2.

"Charlotte and my father will be late, but Cora is on her way," Parks 2 said.

CHAPTER THIRTY-FIVE

Full Circle

Charlotte and Parks looked hypnotized, staring into the thicket choked with of lilies-of -the-valley.

Jack caught the scent of magic and began to sniff at the foliage.

Parks motioned Bash to look with a finger over his lips and clamped his hands over Jack's quivering muzzle.

Beegle was quiet for once, in some sort of trance.

"Over there," Parks whispered. "You don't often see em nowadays. For heaven's sake keep still and don't speak to em," he cautioned. "If they tries to make eye-contact, look at the ground. Do not... DO... NOT... look... into their eyes."

Bash raised her eyebrows questioningly and looked where he pointed.

There was a small round clearing in the flowerbed.

"A fairy circle," Bash breathed, hardly daring to believe her eyes.

Small twinkles of colored lights arrived in a miniature swarm and alighted on the waxy green leaves like iridescent dust.

The largest fairy wore a white gown made of dandelion seeds and was plainly royal because she wore a crown and the others were seated around her like ladies in waiting.

The queen looked up at Bash, smiled sweetly, and said: "Hello Bathsheba, it's nice to meet you. My name is Nimue."

Pleased to meet you too," Bash said staring into the fairy's eyes. "Your Majesty."

Parks chuckled. "That will earn you a few brownie points," he said.

"Welcome!" said another small enchanting voice. "I'm Nimbus."

Nimbus was decidedly a boy; he looked like a miniature Peter Pan, all dressed in green.

The word welcome seemed to fill the inside of Bash's head; she felt like a lantern filled with hot light, and then Nimue spoke to Charlotte.

"I didn't expect to see the girl so soon, Charlotte, even though I grant you, today is when the veil between worlds is open," Nimue said, fluttering her wings a little crossly. "I like to choose when and where a new human contact is made."

"Are you a queen?" Bash asked, completely captivated.

Nimue curtsied demurely and lowered her head. "We are all kings and queens of the woodlands here. I'm one of Lady Flora's ambassadors. What may I grant you my dear?"

"Grant?" Bash repeated. "I don't understand. You mean a wish?"

"A wish or a request," Nimue said. "It's all the same. But make haste. This is a busy day for me."

"Can you...?" Bash paused, distracted by a glint of mischief in Nimue's eyes. "I would like you to find my father?" she paused again. "I mean, please find my father."

Parks looked worried.

"Oh dear. Oh Miss Bash. I told you not to look," he whispered. "That's torn it."

Charlotte smiled sweetly.

"Fairies is tricky. I told you it was too soon," Parks said admonishing her.

"Nonsense, how's the child to learn this summer if she's not prepared?" Charlotte answered softly.

Parks nodded his head reluctantly.

"I suppose that makes sense. You're always right," he said smiling dreamily.

Parks purposely shook off the magic that had settled on his gardening hat and nudged Bash.

Bash jumped. "I can only stay a moment," she said, forgetting her request. "I'm supposed to meet my brother. He's going to have his fortune read."

Jack whined and put his paws over his eyes.

"Have some tea before you go," Nimbus said. "It'll perk you up."

"Yes do," echoed a chorus of lively voices coming from everywhere. Bash had the feeling of standing in a swarm of friendly mosquitoes.

"Oh. No, sorry," Parks cut in, respectfully doffing his cap but waving Nimbus away with it as if shooing a fly.

Nimbus pouted and drew back the bluebell offering cup filled with the delicious scent of lavender.

"Beggin' your pardon little sir, she won't be havin' that," Parks said, taking the small cup as diplomatically as he could. "You mustn't eat or drink anything while you're here," he whispered to Bash.

"Parks dear," one of the other fairies said, stepping forward, "we only want to celebrate the May. It's honoring the Lady Flora, that's all. Tell him Charlotte."

Charlotte looked asleep, but she was smiling and her eyelids were moving as she spoke. "It's all right Parks, Bash already drank a cup of dew," she said.

Parks blanched, straightened his old shoulders, and became his practical down-to-earth self.

"Now then," Parks said, "no disrespect to Mistress Flora, Your Ambassador-ness, but I feel responsible to get the child home to Miss Beryl."

"This child's from Bede Hall?" Nimue cut in. "One of the twins?"

"Yes, ma'am," Parks said.

Nimue fluttered nearer to Charlotte. "Has she slept in the fairy bed?"

"Yes indeed, many nights."

Nimue nodded her approval. "But did she choose it for herself?"

"The bed chose her," Charlotte said, "and I had a hand in delivering it. Parks team moved it when the family was in Bede, so no-one saw anything out of the ordinary."

"Quite the surprise it was, too," Parks added with a broad grin, remembering Bash's delighted face.

"Well, that explains how she can see us," Nimue said. "Goodbye then, little one. We have a parting song for you to remember to your grandmother."

Enchanting music lulled Bash towards sleep with her wish forgotten. Parks kept shaking her awake, but the song imprinted her waking-dream:

Lavender's blue, dilly dilly, lavender's green,
When he was king, dilly, dilly, who was his queen?
Who told you so, dilly, dilly, who told you so?
Lavender's truth, dilly, dilly, Lavender's keen.

Lavender's green, dilly, dilly, Lavender's blue.

Call on Bede's twice, dilly, dilly, set them to play.
Some to the plow, dilly, dilly, some to the May,
Some to make hay, dilly, dilly, some to cut corn,
While Lady Nan dilly dallies, Peregrine's born.

Who was the *fairiest* of them all?

CHAPTER THIRTY-SIX

Gone for Good

The family rendezvous point in the car park soon stirred into an agitated cloud of fear.

"Bash isn't with you?" Mrs. S asked Kit. "Oh dear," she flustered, "I knew something would go wrong. It always does."

"There there my dear. No worries. My father is with her," Parks 2 said, "she can't have gone far. I know the woods; I'll look there. You and Rupert take the car."

Kit ignored them. He could feel his twin nearby; she didn't feel quite right but she was safe.

"I'm going to the green, Kit said. "Don't worry Mum, Jack's with her."

Bash couldn't remember how she found Kit, but it was dark. She just seemed to wander into him and couldn't recollect saying goodbye to either Parks or Charlotte. Had there been fairies? No, of course there hadn't.

Bash was convinced she'd been hypnotized in fun. It was either that or she'd been hallucinating from hunger. She knew Charlotte could do such a thing because her plant therapy was pretty much mesmerizing them with the sound of her voice.

"I'm famished," she declared, handing Jack's leash to Kit. "Where on earth is the barbeque stand? It was over there by the pond a moment ago."

"Moment! They've packed up and been gone for hours," Kit said, incredulous that Bash hadn't noticed that an entire village green full of revelers and their wares was now a wide expanse of deserted grass.

A few straggly garlands still dangled in the trees and clung to posts, and some wrappings blew softly like tiny ghosts and were caught in the hedgerows.

"Where've you *been*?" Kit cried. "It's past midnight! We've been worried sick. Mum and Boss are looking for you in the car. He's grumpy enough about spending his precious holiday faking the whole 'interested in the peasantry lord of the manor' thing. Parks 2 is searching the woods. You're so in for it. Last time I saw you and Jack you were walking away with Charlotte. We've been looking for you for hours."

Bash was disoriented and quiet all the way home. She was so pitifully 'out of it,' that Mrs. S forgot to chastise her. She sat in the back seat like a waif, clinging to Jack while Rupert and Kit and Mrs. S exchanged puzzled looks.

"Straight to bed milady," Mrs. S ordered when they got home. "I'll bring you some cocoa and a hot-water bottle. We've all had a bit of a fright; we'll talk in the morning."

The new logs, laid ready for the morning, quickened as Anubis and Feathers filed past the dining room. Flames flared into green and red tongues that shrieked and flapped and fluttered, looking like parrot's wings trying to fly up the chimney.

But when Anubis checked over his shoulder, the fire was banked in an innocent orange glow that faded out and became a contented pile of cold logs ready for a breakfast fire.

There were dark circles under Bash's eyes the next morning. She refused to eat. All she wanted was to sit in her chintz armchair and stare at the rain which came down in buckets and streamed down her tall windows making them look like molten glass. It felt like she was sitting behind a waterfall, and the sound of the pounding and rushing of water seemed the sanest way back. But to where? From where?

Lady Nan said it was raining cats and dogs, but Bash could see dozens of other pixilated faces in the downpour. She searched their almond shaped eyes hoping one of them would tell her where the time had gone because somewhere Bathsheba Stratford-Smyth had misplaced an entire afternoon and evening.

"Parks... parks everywhere... no where... where oh where has my little Parks gone," Pigeon chattered in the dark.

The next morning, when Kit delivered a gift to Lady Nan, her nine-year-old persona was in fine form sipping cocoa in bed. "For you Beryl," he announced, before 'Lady Nan' returned. "I won this for you at the fair."

The prize was a large goldfish in a very small rose-bowl.

Lady Nan was delighted and put her face close to the glass. "What's his name?" she asked.

"I rather think he's waiting for you to give him one," Kit said.

"He looks like a scarab with a tail. "And he's the right color too. I think I'll name him, Beetle."

"We'll have to get him a bigger home," Kit suggested, as Lady Nan turned the bowl and stirred the fish with her fingers. "More of an aquarium. I think I've got an old one from my pet tortoise phase," he said.

Lady Nan tipped the bowl clumsily to look underneath and nearly spilled its contents on the floor.

"Steady on Beryl," Kit said, righting the bowl. "It's not a snow globe."

The word snow had a magic effect. Lady Nan returned to her normal self and smiled apologetically.

"Sorry Christopher, it's a most thoughtful present. You are a dear. Where's Bash, I want her to write in our book?"

"She's a little under the weather this morning," Kit said. "I can read to you if you like."

"Mmnnn... sometimes May Day can do that to you," Lady Nan nodded, admiring her gift.

Bede Hall had regained its composure by the time the library clock struck midnight to signify it was the second of May, and listened contentedly to Pigeon, droning below, alone in the kitchen:

"Bring me my bow of burning gold; bring me my arrows of desire: bring me my spear: O clouds unfold! bring me my chariot of fire!" Pigeon recited to Parks, who was now dozing by the dying fire.

Bash took a week to recover enough to be interested in her garden again, but luckily Parks had taken over and her plants radiated health.

"Want to see the photos from May Day?" Kit asked, offering his phone to Bash.

"Oh, yes please," Bash said, eager to find a clue to her disappearance.

The images were sharp, but Bash studied one of them intensely with an uneasy feeling.

"Something's not quite right about this picture," Bash said, handing the phone back to Kit. "I'm not sure what."

The picture in question was the one of Bash and Jack that showed her grinning madly beside a dangerously leaning Jack-in-the-Green.

When they showed Lady Nan, she took one look and started to giggle like a child.

"Sounds like we have Beryl on our hands," Bash said.

Lady Nan tapped the picture. "Look, the tree isn't wearing any shoes. In fact, it has no feet at all!"

CHAPTER THIRTY-SEVEN

Lavender Fields Forever

At Lady Nan's request, while she was still in the nursing home, Bash had brought her a red marker and a calendar with extra-large numbers that showed the days of each month on a single page. Lady Nan had first drawn a big circle around the date August first and eagerly crossed out each day as soon as she woke.

It stood in her bedroom showing the month of May had come and was almost half gone bringing lilies of the valley to the garden. Bash picked them in great bundles for her own bedroom and dainty nosegays for Lady Nan.

The harsh spring had delayed the sensitive lavender-growing season, but the seedlings had sprouted nicely and had waited patiently until the ground warmed sufficiently to welcome them in.

It was late June before Bash finally stood back to admire her small field of lavender, thriving and moving like a sweet-smelling sea. The tiny plants had looked forlorn at first, so sparsely separated in their straggly rows of freedom. They had reminded her of the hatchling robins pushed from the nest in order to spread their wings.

Under Parks' care, and with Charlotte Findhorn's energy, Bede Lavender had evolved into a hardy new species, and was resilient enough to withstand all manner of insults, well able to survive alone and spread together joining hands in a splendid purple carpet. By Charlotte's standards it was an award winning crop. "This lavender surpasses the best I've ever grown," she said to Bash. "We've really created something new."

"Outstanding in its field," Parks said, and doubled-over wheezing with laughter at his joke.

"One day it will save our bacon," Bash said in a trance.

"What did you say?" Parks and Charlotte said in unison.

Bash looked puzzled. "I didn't say a word. I was listening to the lavender the way you told me to."

Charlotte and Parks looked at each other and smiled. "Our mistake," they said together.

Inside the conservatory, it smelled sweetly of healthy earth. Feathers, plump as a partridge, had chosen it weeks ago for her lying-in. Bash found her making and remaking her bed, raking the straw tirelessly into hollows.

When Feathers stopped mewing to clean her paws for the hundredth time, Bash placed a thick fleece blanket on top of the straw. Feathers pummeled and massaged the wool into an even cozier nest and finally lay down, stretched out on her side, panting.

Bash, left Feathers to her nest, and busied herself with endless potting and pottering, glancing over from time-to-time, keeping her eye on the ginger shape ready to give birth.

A small packet of life squirmed under Feather's nose inside a clear envelope that looked like it was made of tissue paper. She sniffed it once or twice in surprise before licking the glistening coating until it came away in a glob like the skin on a custard which she then ate.

Feathers began to lick a mewing grey snowball the size of a mouse that was left behind. Feathers had become a mum.

Bash anticipated a repeat performance, but feathers and Anubis had created just one perfect girl – a pure white, delightfully plump little dumpling that Lady Nan named, Snowdrop.

"Well done old girl," Bash said. "She's a little beauty. I'll leave you two alone for a bit." Feathers smiled back, and the little ball, now dried white and fluffy, wriggled, blind as a bat, eyes unopened, towards the smell of milk, and was enveloped protectively in the gingery blanket of Feather's furry tail.

Bash lay on her back on a mattress of lavender and dreamed into the blueness of the umbrella sky above her. She soared on the back of a mauve cloud, lifted and buffeted gently by the fragrant wafting perfume.

She felt her skin tingle and held up an arm. It was transparent. She could see the lavender waving through it. Bash lowered her arm giggling.

She felt like a lavender witch.

The soothing color delivered a feeling of buoyancy. She floated on it, dipping and diving like a giddy kite. The glorious scent carried her to an imaginary solar system where she swayed in time to the rhythms of the plants like a small human boat rocking on a lilac-colored ocean, that continuously moved in a single fluid ripple – the entire field swayed in motion as if it were one plant like the fronds of an anemone bed, underwater.

A fairy echo issued as a sweet field-song:

When will it snow, dither, dither, when will they play;
They shall be safe, wither, wither, out of harm's way.
We love to dance, dilly, dilly, we love to sing;
When she is queen, dilly, dilly, he'll be her king.
Who tells you so, hither, hither, Who tells you so?
We tell you so, dilly, dilly, we tell you so.
When will it rain? silly silly, when will she know?
Lavender rain dilly dilly, lavender snow.

Mrs. S gave the sphinx a double-take as she shook out the hearth rug. Something wasn't quite right. There was a black object between its paws, and she strained her eyes to see closer. The shape moved and bounded towards her.

"Hello Anubis," she said, "beautiful boy."

Anubis grinned as Mrs. S realized what had been wrong. The sphinx was facing the wrong way.

But when she looked again, there it was – its back to the maze, guarding it as always.

That was close, Anubis confessed later, to Feathers. *"I was levitating the sphinx for practice."*

What subject would you like tomorrow?" Mrs. S asked the twins after their private math class on advanced algebra.

"I say we should have a history lesson," Kit announced. "I think we tiptoe around the subject of Egypt all the time."

Kit gestured to the scarabs under-glass.

"Look at those sad scarabs," he said, "we locked them up like prisoners. We never touch them. Dad went to a lot of trouble collecting those. And he taught us to love Egypt's distant past."

"We've even got his slides, Mum," Bash joined in. "We could look at them and discuss the work he was doing before he got ... lost," she said.

'But you know it already," Mrs. S protested.

"I'm starting to forget," Kit replied.

"You can always do it for your star pupil, Mum," Bash angled.

"Edgar thinks there's a mummy's curse as it is," Mrs. S said.

"Great, we can scare him sideways," Kit said. *"Très amusement."*

Mrs. S pursed her lips.

"Perhaps we should have a French lesson then," she said. "Well, I'm not up to giving a lecture on Ancient Egypt."

"I can do it," Kit said. "I'd like to. It's good practice. I'll have to give press conferences some day when I discover amazing things."

"Where have I heard that phrase before?" Mrs. S said, looking puzzled.

"Those were Howard Carter's first words when he opened Tut's tomb," Kit said. "Dad used to recite them at Christmas all the time when we gawped so long at the presents under the tree. Remember?

I'll start with the eighteenth dynasty because it relates to Smenkh-khare. We can invite Lady Nan."

The overhead projector whirred eerily in the darkened library.

The first black and white slide showed a man's awed face in profile, dramatically illuminated by a paraffin lamp.

Kit narrated the documented words of his ancestor: "What do you see?" he intoned. "Things. Wonderful things," he continued, quoting Howard Carter's famous reply.

Bash mouthed the words silently, in unison with Kit.

Mrs. S leapt out of her chair and left the room.

Lady Nan applauded," her eyes dancing brightly, eager for more.

The following slides showed the photos of the boy mummy, and Kit pointed out the medical conditions indicated in Tut's profile: the receding jaw, curved spine, and elongated skull.

Edgar looked as if he was under a spell. And for his benefit, Kit altered his voice and clicked to a slide of the legendary golden death mask.

"There is a blemish here on the left cheek," Kit said, tapping the screen with his pointer for dramatic effect.

Kit's arm looked ghostly as it wavered under the projected image.

This is the exact spot where Lord Carnarvon was bitten by a mosquito," he said. "The bite that became septic and killed him. It was the beginning of the mummy's curse."

The beam of dust-filled light looked like eerie fog.

Kit made the exaggerated sound of a flying mosquito and stopped suddenly in front of Edgar.

Lady Nan stifled a chuckle.

Edgar scratched his cheek.

"That was good how you *egged-on Edgar*," Bash said at dinner.

Kit made a dramatic bow. "I was inspired."

"Speaking of being inspired, I've been meaning to ask your advice about an experiment I want to do," Bash said to Kit.

"Maybe somewhere quiet. Say, a tall crumbling outbuilding made of stone perhaps."

"Sure," Kit said. "We can go right now."

"Race you to the tower," Bash yelled, and hiked it across the lawn.

"Last one there is a rotten Edgar," Kit shouted, sailing past her.

CHAPTER THIRTY-EIGHT
The Invitation

Lady Nan had been holding her hourglass for hours, turning it over whenever the sand ran out, hypnotized by the trickle of grains that fell like silk.

Bash asked her usual question on the days she took up her grandmother's breakfast. "Morning Lady Nan, how old are you today?"

"Nine," came the reply. "Please call me Beryl. Although I have another, secret name."

Bash sensed one of Lady Nan's amazing stories.

"I promised the ghost I wouldn't tell," the old lady whispered secretively with a small childlike voice.

"Who did you promise?" Bash asked gently. "I won't tell anyone. I write things, but no-one reads them except me. But you know that because it's you who wants me to write your stories down."

"That's not me, that's my grandmother," Lady Nan replied mischievously.

It was getting confusing, Bash thought. No wonder Kit rarely took part in these conversations and Rupert never at all.

When Lady Nan was sitting in the garden Rupert occasionally said hello, but usually he tried to avoid her as she gave him lists of things she saw needed doing. Her eyesight was fine.

"My friend Snow," Lady Nan started to say but faltered. "Oh dear, now I've gone and spoiled it."

Bash calmed her grandmother by reminding her she hadn't given away a secret name or said why it was secret and that Snow, whoever she was, might not mind, and to ask her so her story could be written.

Lady Nan brightened. "Yes, that's a splendid idea," she said. "Time is running out."

Bash assumed that her grandmother's remark referred to her

advanced age, although even when Lady Nan was living in the present, she seemed indestructible. Even though she couldn't walk around for long with her walker, she had a wheelchair and was whisked outside when the weather was warm.

More than anything, she adored her garden, and she liked to meet with Parks on Monday mornings to check if Rupert was showing any interest in the hands-on management of Bede Hall during his weekend visits.

"I can keep a secret," Bash said, thinking Lady Nan's invisible childhood friend had somehow become confused as Bede Hall's ghost. "Shall I read you a bedtime story then?"

"I thought it was morning," Nan blinked.

"It's just an expression," Bash said.

For once, she was the adult explaining a word to a child. "You can read bedtime stories anytime Beryl, and you are in bed."

Lady Nan finally looked happy. "Yes, please, you know the one I like."

Bash smiled, these days Lady Nan always wanted the 'wardrobe book.'

Lady Nan had started to tell Bash the story of her childhood friend quite a few times lately but never more than an intriguing hint.

"It will have to be soon," Lady Nan said. "I feel it's time. I've been dreaming more of Snow lately, and she seems more upset than ever. She needs to find her father. You and I may be the only ones who can help her. I will ask her tonight if I can tell you her whole story. Tomorrow morning you report to me after breakfast and we'll get started, shall we? Bring our little notebook."

Bash smiled at the reference 'little.' The notebook was the size and shape of a laptop, although twice as thick.

"What about Kit? Can he come too?" Bash asked.

"Let's wait and see, shall we? What month is it?"

"It's the first week in July," Bash replied.

Lady Nan sat up straight without a trace of her younger self. "Then

177

we have to make a plan immediately!" she exclaimed. "Please... I need you to take me to the sundial in the garden. Right away."

This time, Lady Nan didn't mean she wanted a trip outside, it meant she wanted to close her eyes while Bash described every possible detail of the garden: its colours and smells and what birds were singing, and how the heat of the sun had felt on her face.

Bash put on her best storytelling voice, and Lady Nan closed her eyes.

"The magenta peonies are in bloom. The sunlight feels like a yellow blanket, heavy and soft. It's so humid I can smell the straw of my wet sunhat as well as the sweetness of roses and the soil damp from recent rain. The grass glistens and shimmers, slick after the drenching shower. The rows of head lettuce are ready to pick, they look like pale green tennis balls or very large Brussel sprouts, but the Romaine variety look like a line of dark green tulips," she recounted. "The trellis of sweet peas is heavy with blossoms: white and mauve and pink. Their fragrance fills one's nose with the most subtle high-notes of delicate floral perfume. The birdbath is sparkling, overflowing with fresh rainwater that cascades down its sides from the family of sparrows drinking and splashing about, trilling the most delightful birdsong," she finished.

"And the sundial?" Lady Nan asked, leaning forward.

"The sundial looks dazzling white in the sun," Bash continued. "The green grass around it is like an emerald blanket."

Lady Nan smiled. "Thank you, child. I can see it now. You are a good girl to take me there," but her smile faded as she sought the garden in her mind, and a frown appeared on her forehead. "I can see the peony bushes are far too heavy," she said. "Tell Rupert to pick the lowest stems and prop the others up. That boy should see these things for himself. I've had a word with all four Parks telling them not to do all your brother's work."

The old lady's countenance suddenly lifted and she tilted her head with a gracious smile. "Is it teatime?" she said, without a trace of her former irritation.

It was actually 'teatime' several times a day. Whenever Lady Nan told a story she inevitably finished it with a tray of tea and chocolate biscuits. And as much as Mrs. S economized, she always made sure there was an assortment of the finest Bede had to offer in the larder.

It was one of the few luxuries that Mrs. S was determined to keep.

The next morning Bash ate fast and skimped with the dishes, hovering over Rupert, who ate leisurely as if he were on holiday and that there was no work to be done. She raced upstairs and tapped loudly on Lady Nan's door, as sometimes her grandmother was hard of hearing. 'Selective deafness,' Mrs. S called it.

"Come in," came the strong reply.

It was Lady Nan's no nonsense 'big' way of speaking because Beryl had a soft timid voice like a mouse, and when Lady Nan was in a dithery mood, her voice sounded uncannily like Mrs. S's – quavering like a reluctant message waving in the wind.

Bash greeted her radiant grandmother wrapped in her snowflake shawl. Her breakfast had been eaten and she was in high spirits.

Mrs. Carey, the home nurse, had been and gone after giving Lady Nan her morning bath, and as instructed, had applied a smattering of makeup and red lipstick to her patient's face.

Lady Nan sat with her back straight, snow-globe beside her, eager to begin. It was as if she knew her best days only came once in a while.

"Sheba," she said, "come and sit closer." Lady Nan patted the smoothed quilt. "Here." But Bash pulled a wicker bedroom chair to the bed and rested her notebook on the table-tray after removing the dishes. It was more convenient.

The chair was enormous and she could curl up into it cross-legged and balance the small table on her lap. Its lip stopped her pens and sketching pencils from rolling off onto the floor, and a side pocket kept the Narnia book near-to-hand in case Lady Nan called for it because sometimes she just liked to hold it and stare at the cover.

"Bathsheba!" Lady Nan said, in a sharp tone, "you're taking far too long. We haven't much time. I can't abide ditherers. We've got work to do."

It was no use correcting Lady Nan unless she was the nine-year-old Beryl; Bash and Beryl often discussed dresses and school and their mothers, but when Lady Nan was impatient it was wise not to cross her.

No-one used their real names anyway, if nothing else, the Strafford-Smyths believed in variety.

"As I said, the ghost's name is Snow," Lady Nan began. "I don't know her real name. We met in this house when we were both nine-years-old. She was looking for her father, and I was escaping mine in the Winter Room. I called it that. She was only a voice at first."

Bash's eyes stared at her grandmother in disbelief.

"You're not writing any of this down," Nan complained.

Bash snapped to attention and wrote: *Snow is only a voice!* and underlined it in red with an exclamation mark.

"It was Snow's idea," Lady Nan continued. "You see, she'd been told not to give her name to a stranger and it made sense, although we became fast friends almost immediately. She suggested that she look out her window and I look out mine, and we would each make up a new name from the first thing we saw. She saw winter, and said her name was Snow. I looked out my window during a downpour. It was August, and it was difficult to see the garden below through the stream of water running down the glass, so I called myself, Rain. That's *my* secret name. There. It's out now."

Many years later, after Snow had gone for the summer, I married, and since I had your mother in the winter time, I named her Rayne to remind me of my friend. I thought that if I called the name, Rayne, often enough, that Snow might hear me and come back. I saw her in the garden a few times, but she never saw me. Maybe she did, but didn't recognize me all grown up. Maybe that stopped her from saying hello.

180

Snow usually wore her red wool coat and matching mittens and a knitted hat tied under her chin. She was dressed for warmth with a thick red scarf wound round her neck several times, so I knew she had died in winter.

"Incredible," Bash breathed as she scribbled.

Lady Nan's next words startled Bash senseless. "Snow wants to meet you," she said.

"How?" Why?" When?" Bash spluttered.

"The first day of August," Lady Nan replied. "So, you see we have no time to lose. And Sheba?"

Bash faked a careless smile. "Mmm Hmnnnn?"

"Be a dear and take Snow fresh flowers. She so loves peonies. She prefers the white ones."

CHAPTER THIRTY-NINE
Birds of a Feather

"I'm only going into the village for some organic cough medicine for Parks," Bash called to Mrs. S as she left on her bicycle. "Charlotte says the regular store-bought kind is full of sugar, and that Mr. Leoni is a whiz with herbs. He has his own special formula. She calls it 'green medicine.' Anyway, it's something I want to support. Local industry and all that."

"Well, mind you don't bother the poor man," Mrs. S chided. "I know how you enthusiasts are when you start talking."

Vincento Leoni appeared as soon as the bells on the chemist door jangled. He looked like a very thin, very wise, very tall, Santa Claus, wearing a white lab coat and khaki cargo pants. Bash couldn't remember when she hadn't seen him smiling and genuinely interested in everyone. He fairly beamed when he saw her.

"Buongiorno, good morning," he said. "And how is ... eh...Mr. Pidgini?"

"And good day to you too," Bash answered. "Pigeon is very well thanks."

Bash smiled, already captivated by Mr. Leoni's charm. "He's over a hundred years old now."

"Both of the a-times I was fortunate enough to make of his acquaintance, I was most, as you call, impressive. He is an especial creature. Si? I am fascinating of him. I try to buy him once from your 'Nonna,' your granda-mother, but Miss Beryl, she would not part... I do not blame. But see," he said, pointing to the open door of his dispensary. "I am not alone for the birds, eh? You come. I show."

"I really only came in for some of your special cough medicine," Bash said. "The one Charlotte says you make yourself."

"Si, in the back, I make. Very good."

Mr. Leoni wandered off through the door, still enthusing about his recipe and Bash followed. What she saw stunned her. The spicy smells were intoxicating: cloves, cinnamon, and citrus.

There were no shining white tiles or gleaming stainless steel countertops. Model airplanes, paper kites, a miniature hot-air balloon, and bunches of dried herbs hung from the ceiling giving the overall appearance of a sorcerer's inner sanctum. There was even a classic black cauldron on one of the tables full of equipment.

The room lacked any sort of clinical atmosphere and resembled an antiquated laboratory with Bunsen burners, test tubes, microscopes, and an amazing assortment of glass bottles made of cobalt-blue, ruby, and amber-colored glass in a dizzying array of shapes and sizes. One or two resembled large vases... another looked like an upside-down bedpost finial with tubes connecting it to several glass bulbs. It looked like an experiment on life support that dripped a clear golden liquid resembling thin honey into a tall beaker. Liquids trickled, oozed, and dripped everywhere like leaky taps.

A few pots of herbs bubbled away, sending a pleasant, slightly antiseptic scent of flowers into the room that felt more like an Aladdin's cave than a modern dispensary.

Bash recognized a reproduction of the 'Mona Lisa' in a place of honor by itself in a large niche on the far wall, like a saint in a shrine, with an offering of rowan branches laid in front of it.

And wings... there were dozens of wings pinned to the walls: bat wings, one that looked as if it was a swan's, and a framed display of moths and butterflies arranged by size. A row of ornate cages held canaries and budgies all chirping and twittering excitedly for attention when they saw Mr. Leoni enter the room.

"I have... *inspirito*, yes?... the enthusiasms for the wings," Vincento Leoni said proudly.

Bash caught the word spirit, and remembered Snow.

"The air, she is my home," he said. "But the ground she is good also, no? The plants for my especial concoctions are growing there."

"Why is it so dark in here?" Bash asked, realizing that opaque blue curtains covered the windows.

"Too much light it robs the ... the a-values..."

Bash supplied a word. "The potency?"

"Grazzi, thank you, yes, it is most delicate to respecting the plants," Mr. Leoni said, splitting the word delicate into two words so that it sounded like 'delly-kate' the same way he'd pronounced 'fortu-nate.'

"Is this a picture of you?" Bash asked, pointing to a framed sepia photograph of a handsome young man wearing a vintage flyer's suit and goggles.

"It is my first attempt to flying," he said.

"And was it successful?"

"It was... *bellisimo!... magnifico!*"

Mr. Leoni sighed and returned to the subject of his plant's energy.

"Miss Charlotta, she listens to this potent-ness and brings me my ingredients. *Il migliore,* the best."

"She's teaching me how to listen to plants," Bash said.

Mr. Leoni looked enraptured and clapped his hands.

"Bravo bravo. This is very good," he said. "My little Chloris is natural teaching... eh... teacher," he corrected himself.

"Is Chloris Italian for Charlotte?" Bash asked curiously.

"Chloris is as you call, chlorophyll, yes? ... the green blood of all the leaves. She is the name of a goddess – your, as you call, Green Woman, and so, this is also fitting Charlotte. The name, it means Summer Queen... your Queen of the May, yes?... the Lady Flora..."

"You mean florist? Charlotte is a *florist,*" Bash interjected.

"No no... Flor...ahhh! This is the goddess of flowers in my country. And she also ... eh ... to rules the trees with her... husband, Pan... or perhaps she is, sister. No matter, eh? The forests are their especial place." Mr. Leoni pronounced the word, 'es-pesh-ee-all.

"Come. I show," he said, taking down a dusty folio from a shelf.

It was full of loose drawings and prints. Mr. Leoni leafed through them until he found the one he wanted.

Bash peered at a sixteenth century drawing of the Green Man.

Vincento Leoni rummaged through the capacious pockets of his smock and produced his famously-ever-present digital camera, and began to scan through dozens of shots muttering: "I take I take I take."

Bash could see a few as they flashed past at rapid speed. They were from the May Day fete. Odd details of things. Not the sort of usual shots of people waving or posing: a close up of a Morris dancer's bells, a fat bumblebee, several primrose leaves, an acorn shell, and a puddle of water.

Finally, he stopped and passed the camera to Bash, tapping the picture he wanted her to see. "I make," he said enthusiastically.

It was a picture of Parks' tree costume standing up by itself, considering it was basically a wire frame covered in vines, twigs, and leaves.

"I make," he said, nodding his head vigorously, tapping the foliage-covered cone.

"Parks told me his brother made his tree costume," Bash said.

"Si, brother. I am like. We are, yes?"

"Yes. I do see. You are good friends. Like brothers," she said. "*My* brother would be over the moon if he could see this place. He's a scientist."

Mr. Leoni nodded and gestured towards the 'Mona Lisa.'

"Your brother, he is an artist, too, yes?"

"*Er*... no... not espe... exactly," Bash replied.

Bash was so in tune with the old chemist that she had nearly said espesh-ee-ally by mistake.

"To be a great scientist, one must be an artist also. My ancestor, da Vinci. He was a great scientist," Mr. Leoni boasted proudly.

"I thought he was a great painter," Bash said.

Mr. Leoni smiled. "But of course, of course... but a scientist first, yes?... one has to eat. So, the art. It pays for this things," he pointed to his array of chemist's supplies.

Bash left with two red-glass bottles of cough syrup and an invitation for Kit.

"My regardings to your brother and Master Pidgini," Mr. Leoni called after her.

"Isn't it wonderful that there's no language barriers between kindred spirits," observed Charlotte, after Bash told her about her encounter with Mr. Leoni. "At least, not when it comes to us gardeners."

"Buying cough medicine from him is an experience; it's certainly not shopping," Bash enthused. "I love that guy. He's like a modern-day Merlin without the modern part, except he wears cargo pants and running shoes."

"I'm glad you admire him," Charlotte said. "He is... well, he knows more than anyone I've ever met, and that includes Dr. Brooks. Did he take your picture?"

"Yes and no," Bash said sheepishly. "If shots of my coat toggles, the zipper on my backpack, and the gears on my bicycle, count, then, yeah, I guess he did. Indubitably."

PART FOUR

FANTASYLAND

*"Imagination
will often carry us
to worlds that never were,
but without it
we go nowhere."*

- CARL SAGAN

CHAPTER FORTY
Keys Please

Lady Nan took Bash aside. "I need to show you something important," she said. "I need you to know where I keep two special keys. If anything happens to me you must take the second key. It's to the Winter Room. Don't let anyone break into it. That would frighten, Snow. Better that a rusty key is slowly turned in the lock.

"What's going to happen to you Lady Nan?"

"People don't live forever child. I'm very old. You can see that. And, I'm not always aware of who I am or what year it is, you know. Come a day I won't know where the key is or what it's for or remember who's behind the Winter Door.

"One day soon I may not be in a position to tell anyone, or worse – that no-one will believe me when I do. Your father and one other were the only ones who understood. I do miss our conversations. Your mother thinks my stories are crazy, but crazy as they may seem, they're true.

"I made a promise a long time ago, and then I couldn't keep my word. It's a sad day when a child feels abandoned, and it's my opinion ghosts can feel. Snow must think I didn't care. I guess it's my comeuppance that the thought of that little girl has haunted me for the last three years. How's that for irony?"

Bash spoke softly and took her grandmother's hand. "So, what is it that you really want?"

"I plan to be a ghost myself one day. Not everyone is, in fact most aren't. People die and that's that, but some stay and I want to be one of the ones who stick around."

"You want to haunt us?"

"Oh my dear, that does sound dreadful," Lady Nan chuckled. "No. I don't want to be a busybody, well, not exactly. I want to stay with my house. I want to be its guardian. It may have to

188

be sold soon. After that who knows? It will be at the mercy of new owners.

"I won't let it become a hotel or be converted into flats or an old folks home. That ghastly possibility occurred to me when I was lying in my room at 'The Beehive.' Did you know that place was once a grand house before developers got hold of it?

"But it ended up full of terrible smells of soup and antiseptic with shiny brown linoleum everywhere. All the grace was stolen from it and it was filled it with despair. Lost souls, we all were. Trapped and deserted. No wonder we all wandered off to *cloud cuckoo land.*"

"Where?"

"Our various delusions," Lady Nan explained.

"And how will having the key help Bede Hall?"

"Even though, at times, Snow can be seen in the garden, she's trapped in the Winter Room. After I'm gone I will be able to help her, and I may need you to help both of us. We, in turn, will look after the house."

"You want *me* to help *you* help a ghost *after* you're a ghost yourself? That's not an everyday request."

"Indeed it is not. Which is why I'm asking you. You aren't an everyday girl; you're compassionate. That means kind. I see how you rescue things and animals, the underdogs, the under-cats, and even the struggling plants in the garden. You, Bathsheba Stratford-Smyth, have a caring heart."

Bash squeezed Lady Nan's hand.

"You can start by helping Snow this summer," Lady Nan said.

"I don't know how. I'm not sure I want to know how," Bash said in a hollow voice.

"Nonsense girl. It's an adventure. It's *life*... well maybe not life. Snow misses her family. Like you, she's lost her father. We need to make her feel welcome for a start, and then warm; she's cold all the time. If she can imagine being warm or is surrounded by warm emotions, perhaps that's all it takes."

"How can I do all that?" Bash sighed.

189

"First, you need to open the door and have a good look around. I left some things in there. I was particular. Parks helped me clear away the boxes and clean it, and I chose various things from around the house. We had servants back in my day, and the housemaids were barely older than you are now.

"They did as they were told. I got them to shift furniture and paintings about and they brought me quite a lovely carpet as I recall.

"For ten years, I filled Snow's room with unwanted bits and pieces. Unique pieces. It was my cozy little secret. I went there to get away from schoolwork and read my books. I kept it locked and spread the rumors of the ghost child to scare the servants away.

"Oh, she was really there, I just wanted no-one to bother her. In those days, no rational person investigated ghosts, it wasn't the done thing. They gave them a wide berth. That means they stayed purposely out of their way.

"My governesses and lady's maids and the house parlour maids grew up and moved away to other positions, and soon I was the only one who remembered the truth about the Winter Room. Oh, and Parks of course.

"I made a huge mistake by telling your grandfather about the ghost; he was my fiancé then, but I never ever told him our special names. He promised the Winter Room would always be mine to do with as I pleased. He would have his library and his club, he said, and it was of no consequence for him to miss an ugly storeroom high under the eaves that was only useful as a servant's bedroom."

Lady Nan's eyes gleamed. "Oh, but Sheba, it wasn't ugly. It really wasn't."

"Lady Nan wants me to meet the ghost," Bash wailed to Kit. "I don't think I can do it alone."

"Lady Nan hallucinates sometimes," Kit said. "Don't worry. There's no ghost, but this does take care of getting the key. I'll go with you and we'll tell Lady Nan it's for safety reasons. We'll explain that you don't want to meet a stranger, by yourself. She'll have to understand that."

Lady Nan did understand. "Very wise of you dear," she said to Bash. "And Christopher dear, how gallant of you to accompany your sister," she said to Kit.

Lady Nan was holding the 'second' key, the one to the Winter Room, up to the light by its blue tassel, examining the filigree of its snowflake-shaped head, when the twins arrived.

A box made from a hollowed-out novel stood open. The key that had been inside it swung from the drawer to her writing desk.

"Keep it safe," she said as she pressed the ornate key into Bash's hand. "It's very precious. Do not disturb the room until it's the right time."

"Which is?" Kit asked.

"Snow is there all the time," Lady Nan said, ignoring Kit's direct question, "but she won't appear to any of us until the first of August, and we won't be able to see her when the month is over. Use the key on July 30 to prepare the room. Wake it up so to speak."

"What's so special about a few days?" Kit pressed.

Lady Nan looked uncomfortable.

"July 31 to August 1st is a natural shift of seasons," she explained, "an ancient Celtic celebration of the sun god that marks the end of summer and the beginning of autumn. It seems these transitional times hold special power. Bash, ask Charlotte, she'll know."

"So, superstition then," Kit remarked with more than a little disrespect in his voice.

"It is the time of Lughnasadh," Lady Nan said in the matter-of-fact voice of a learned professor giving a lecture. "Moon madness... but it's the Sun that rules the world."

"It feels colder than usual keys," Bash commented.

"Lunacy more like," Kit said under his breath.

The silver metal shone through the rust which had tried to eat it, and if a key could look happy, it seemed to glow with good cheer in the sunlight.

"Don't either of you tell your grandfather," Lady Nan cautioned.

"That would be difficult," Kit reminded her, "he's been dead for three years."

"What's *that* got to do with the price of eggs?" Lady Nan replied with a beaming smile. "If you really want something enough, a little thing like dying won't stop you."

Parks was sorry that he had to decline Mrs. S's offer to join the family for Sunday dinner.

"Stanley Jr's gone and dropped a heavy flowerpot on his toe," Parks said, by way of explanation, "and I'd feel better if I stayed home, seeing as how my grandson's gone off with some of his village mates," he finished apologetically.

"Oh dear," Mrs. S said. "Can I help?"

"Well, he can't walk properly at the minute," Parks replied. "But it's mostly just phantom pain, now. Still, it's best I'm there all the same."

"Another time then," Mrs. S said.

"Righty-o," Parks said with a huge sigh of relief, and fairly evaporated out of the room in case Mrs. S came up with a new invitation.

"I thought the Parks' were joining us for dinner tonight," Rupert mumbled, his mouth full of baked potato as he poured lashings of gravy over his Yorkshire pudding. "Never actually seen all four of em together," he commented offhandedly, "or two of them for that matter."

"Couldn't come.... injuries... pass the Yorkshires," Kit said, squabbling in a fork duel with Bash for the last outside slice of roast beef.

Apparently, Rupert wasn't interested enough for further

clarification because he dropped the subject and continued to focus on chopping a pungent mound of horseradish into a mash of spicy sauce and resumed stuffing his face.

"Why don't you two take turns over the well-done bits since you both want them," Mrs. S said to the twins.

"Mind your manners... table manners... tsk tsk....ladies first... house manners," Pigeon chortled.

"Ladies first then," Bash declared, spearing the coveted meat.

It was mid-July, and the blistering-hot weather had the twins sunbathing under a cloudless blue sky. Beside them was a cooler filled with crushed ice that held two cans of lemonade. The lazy drone of a curious bee paused as it inspected the hole in one of the open cans and the bottle of 'Tropical Paradise' suntan lotion oozing on its side in the grass.

Finding nothing natural, it flew away again trailing off into the distance, its buzz blending with the sound of the tractor mower.

One of the Parks was ambitious in spite of the heat-wave, Kit thought to himself.

The smell of freshly-cut grass surrounded the little island the twins white towels made on the lawn.

Bash lay on her stomach, and idly plucked at the blades of grass in front of her as she eyed the sundial. And as she did, an old thought surfaced to trouble her.

"Why do you think the Captain burned Lady Nan's diaries?" she asked.

"Don't know," came Kit's muffled reply from under the wide straw hat over his face. "Maybe Mum knows. I'll go interview her after supper. She probably doesn't even know there were diaries," Kit continued listlessly.

"Well, Lady Nan still knows," Bash said. "And she said she would tell some day."

"When? That's what I'd like to know," Kit said. "Hopefully before she's... before her mind's completely gone. I don't like leaving these sorts of things unresolved. Why mention it at all if she wasn't going to tell us." He sighed. "She seems 'on edge,' with all this 'waiting for August' pressure."

Kit cornered Mrs. S with an uncustomary cup of tea when he knew she was asleep on her feet. It was always the best time for optimum results and she had been too tired to be surprised.

Mum?" Kit said nonchalantly, "Lady Nan said Captain Hilly burned her diaries."

"Sounds like something he'd do," Mrs. S said.

"She said she would tell us why one day."

"Well, it had better be someday soon," Mrs. S replied dreamily, making exercise circles in the air with her ankles. "She's getting on for seventy-five years-old, it's baking hot, and she keeps looking out of her window at the sundial, saying, it looks like snow."

Lady Nan recited in a storyteller's trance. "My father had been in a frightful mood all day. He and Parks' father had had a row. All I did was interrupt him at the dinner table. Well, not exactly interrupt, more like contradicted. And even more than that – I criticized him in front of his guests, no less."

Bash looked hypnotized, but Kit squirmed uneasily in his chair wanting to ask questions.

"All conversation ceased," Lady Nan continued. "My mother stared at her plate the whole time I was being scolded in front of everyone. I got a proper dressing-down; it was humiliating."

"What did he say?" Kit blurted.

Bash elbowed him to be quiet.

194

Lady Nan shook a finger in Kit's face as a demonstration.

"You're a child!" she shouted, by way of an answer, delivering it as an accusation. "That's what he said."

"He never screamed like that did he?" Bash asked.

"He did indeed," Lady Nan said. "He had a brusque way of speaking to children and servants."

She sat back and stared in silence over the twin's head remembering the scene, and Bash whispered in Kit's ear:

"Brusque means gruff," she said.

"I sort of gathered," Kit whispered back.

"He admonished me as if it were a crime to be a child," Lady Nan said dreamily.

Pigeon shuffled on his perch and fluffed out his feathers the way he did when he was upset. *"Too much sun!"* he shrieked.

Bash shushed him.

"Shhhhhhhhh!" came the bird's rude reply.

Kit tried not to laugh. Lady Nan was clearly remembering something painful. So painful that she had let it stop her story.

"Go on," Bash urged. "Don't stop."

Lady Nan recovered and resumed speaking. "This is how one can become emotionally scarred," she said. "Never let that happen to you. Never treat your children like that. You wouldn't would you? Listen to children; they often see more than adults. They can be very world-wise."

She waited until both twins solemnly shook their heads.

"The rule back then was for children to be seen and not heard. We were dispatched to attics and nurseries and presented to our parents, sometimes only once a day, before bed. We were briefly paraded in front of guests when it suited as well.

"I was used to being free to ask my Nanny whatever I wanted, Lady Nan said. "Whenever I wanted. So, at the dinner table, I did the same.

"I usually took my meals in the nursery. Cook would send up

plates in the dumb waiter. And never the rich foods presented at table, either. I was given casual 'tea things' like 'toad in the hole' and baked beans on toast or scrambled eggs," she said.

"What did you... how did you criticize great-granddad then?" Bash asked.

Lady Nan smiled at the memory, looking rather proud of herself.

"I told my father not to speak with his mouth full," she said.

"Woah! That must have been *some* dinner," Kit exclaimed.

"I believe it was pheasant," Lady Nan replied, "more like 'peasant' by the end of the meal. That's what my father made me feel like. Worthless. Not that peasants were worthless, you understand, but they were treated as if they were. My father treated Parks' father like that.

"Parks' father was my friend," Lady Nan continued. "He always took time to explain things. He was more like a father to me than anyone, really. He explained things; my father lectured.

"Your great-grandfather told me to keep my opinions to myself and never ask questions. He equated questions with answering back to one's betters. How does any child learn if opinions are irrelevant?

"Parks' father and I discussed plants and animals, and the house; he taught me to appreciate Bede Hall. He told me to listen to it. 'A building has a voice,' he said, as does everything: books, sundials, and weather.

"Parks' father told me about the Winter Room although it wasn't called that back then. He called it 'the cooling-off place.' He gave me the key and told me to only use it when I heard the room calling me. He taught me the art of listening," Lady Nan said. "He taught me that even a room with a blue door has a voice.

"My father was the opposite: 'Speak when you're spoken to,' he used to say, 'and when you're grown up *perhaps* you can do as you like.'

"Perhaps! He actually said, perhaps. What he meant was, that I would be free-ish under the cloud of whatever my husband would allow me to think.

196

"Anyway, he ordered me from the table. Banished me, actually. I can still see him fuming. 'Go to your room at once,' he shouted all red in the face. And I did. I went to the only room I considered mine. A room where a nanny or a servant couldn't barge in without so much as a knock. A room where no adult would dream of looking for me. A room to which I had a key.

"I went to the Winter Room, but first I visited a tiny grave."

"I went there the day of my humiliation and the next day after that, and any day I felt like escaping the rules, but the most important day was after I felt ill from humiliation. The ghost found me sleeping and we became friends soon after."

"Didn't you have real friends?" Kit asked. "I mean school chums?"

"I wish I had," Lady Nan said wistfully. "I never went to school. My brother, Ben, your Great Uncle Bentley, was sent to school but daughters had to stay home. After 'Nanny School' I was privately tutored in the library, and I wasn't allowed to play with the worker's children on the estate, although Parks' son, Stanley (the one you know as plain Parks) and I became friends of a sort. He was like a big brother. Especially after Ben died.

"My first 'social place' was to be out of the way, tucked out of sight. *Spirited* away, if you pardon the pun. Left in the nursery on the third floor where my nanny had an adjoining room, and so I explored the servants' rooms down the hall when she was having a nap. Naturally, I found the blue door, but oddly, it was locked. Servants rooms weren't allowed to be locked.

"Parks' father found me crying in the maze that bad day, and he gave me the present of a pretty key to dry my tears. You can guess which one. It opened the blue door. He said it would be a better place for tears lest someone heard me, but Bede Hall always heard me."

Feathers padded in and jumped on Lady Nan's bed.

"Mind your betters...watch you p's and q's...especially the p's," Parrot admonished Feathers.

"Oh do hush up," said Feathers in a hissy fit. *"Birds!"*

...hiss..."*You're only good for one thing if you ask me.*" She licked her paws and mad a great display of cleaning her whiskers.

"*Nobody asked your opinion. Speak when you're spoken to,*" Pigeon squawked.

"You talking to me, parrot face?" Kit asked.

"Like a bird could ever stop you," Bash laughed.

But Pigeon had the last word: "*toad in the hole!*" he announced, as if that explained everything.

CHAPTER FORTY-ONE
Knock Knock... Who's There?

Tuesday, July 30th had started off unbearably hot, but going on for lunchtime, it started to thunder even as the sky remained bright blue, and it started to rain shortly after.

Everyone went outside. Even Mrs. S was pried from her computer to experience such a bizarre event as warm rain under a blazing sun and white clouds.

Kit was ecstatic and took pictures with his phone, and ran about taking notes and jotting down the time. Mrs. S said they should bring out bars of soap and some towels.

They romped for the hour it lasted. The poor flowers wilted from the steam, and Parks 4 was thrilled he could leave his weeding for another day. Lady Nan called it cavorting, Kit called it horsing around, and Mrs. S called it forgetting her troubles for a while.

The arrival of Mrs. Tweedy's car signaled it was time for afternoon home-school.

"Tweedledum alert!" Kit shouted to anyone within earshot.

Parks looked up at the clouds bright with magic rain and waved both his arms enthusiastically the way a shipwrecked sailor stranded on a desert island tries to attract the attention of an overhead rescue plane.

The rain stopped suddenly, and as the sun was already out, the garden looked quite ordinary if you didn't count the swampy puddles and the drooping flowers.

The twins slid into their chairs wearing their bathrobes with towel turbans wrapped around their heads, grateful to be inside while the stone bricks of the terrace sweltered like a jungle.

Edgar gaped at them with a vacant expression. Apparently the phenomenon had been an isolated incident, well inside the Bede Hall estate. The rest of Bede had enjoyed a perfectly dry morning.

It was late afternoon when Kit followed Bash to the Winter Door, dragging his feet, already making calculations in his head. Proving something *didn't* exist wasn't all that exciting, even though it was pretty much all any scientist could ever do according to standard protocol. And that went for the ghost as well as the weather. He was about to investigate the first, and had checked on the latter.

The weather channel had sounded almost proud when it declared it was in the dark concerning the 'alleged' event of a hot-water rain shower.

Apparently if a 'situation' hadn't happened over a large city, it never happened at all. However, it *could* confirm that there had been no other reports. It was a freak phenomenon they said, suggesting Kit might be making a prank call. Either way the conversation ended up as an unsatisfactory exchange.

Kit told Bash that near as he could figure, the warm rain had maybe been a freak collision of two fronts meeting at the back of something.

"Oh, well-put Einstein," Bash had sniggered. "Can you be a tad more scientific-specific?"

Later, the television forecast announced that unseasonal chilly temperatures were expected to return in the south.

"That's the calm before the storm," Lady Nan commented. "Snow in July is simply not possible. There's no snow until August. Has the whole world had gone mad?"

Strange anomalies and fluctuations off the norm had been happening more often in the last year, at least it had in the area surrounding Bede Hall and the village, but not much was reported elsewhere.

Kit was impatient to get back to his computer. Yesterday's weather was old news. Today was reserved for a much headier phenomenon. The meeting of a ghost.

The twins finally stood before the pale-blue Winter Door that was so oddly cool to the touch. The silence crystallized into an awkward pause.

"If there's a ghost in there, I'll eat my bike helmet," Kit announced.

Bash rapped the end of the broom handle loudly on the door. Three times. Then a count of three, and three times again.

"What are you knocking for?"

"I just want to warn her."

"What her?" Kit said, exasperated. "Honestly Bash, you've completely lost your marbles, now. Can we *please* get this nonsense over with."

"And *you* call yourself a scientist," Bash countered.

"C'mon let's not make a big deal of it. I haven't got all day, you know."

Bash waved the antique key in her brother's face. "*This*," she declared hotly, "*is* for science!" daring Kit to deny it.

Kit rolled his eyes.

"Knock knock," Bash said.

Kit answered reluctantly, sounding bored. "Who's there?"

"I'm a ghost."

"I'm a ghost who?"

"I'm a ghost who likes to win," Bash said.

"Well, I guess that's told *me* then! What extraordinary wit you *don't* have. Anyway, it's more like, I'm a Fig-Newton of an old lady's imagination," Kit said, his words dripping with sarcasm.

"That's figment," Bash said disparagingly.

"No, really? Are you sure?"

Bash fiddled with the key ring.

"At least Fig Newtons are tastier than your old bike helmet," she whispered, her hands shaking.

"Why are we whispering?" Kit whispered back, "I thought you wanted to warn her."

Bash gave Kit one of her icy glares, pressed the play button on Kit's tape recorder, and turned the key.

202

A blast of pleasantly cool air escaped from the Winter Room and ruffled the twin's hair in a friendly greeting. It took a few seconds for their eyes to adjust to the dark, but what they saw caused Kit to balk; he froze in his tracks.

The white lace curtains with their pattern of interlocking snow-flakes, were parted to reveal a window pane covered in frost, and in big letters, someone had written the word HELLO with their finger.

"Hello," Bash returned cheerily to the window. "My name's Bash and this is my brother, Kit."

But Kit had retreated to the hallway.

"Sorry, he's a little shy," Bash continued in a casual conversational tone. "He's a scientist, so he'll want to ask you a lot of questions."

"C'mon Bash, we've seen enough. Let's go," Bash managed to squeak, making a beeline for the stairs.

"I'll be back tomorrow," Bash said to the window. "Sweet dreams."

The circumstances demanded sunlight. Kit flew down the stairs, and burst into the garden. He didn't stop till he came to came the sundial, one of his favorite thinking places.

Bash joined him, carrying the tape recorder, walking on air, giddy with excitement.

"There's an explanation," Kit finally said. "It must have been Boss having a joke."

Bash flipped the key in the air and caught it. "Well, the joke's on him then, as there's only one key, and this, by the way, is it."

"Play back the tape; I want to hear what just happened so I believe it," Kit urged.

The recorded sounds emanating from the black box were those of a door opening, followed by a howling wind, and the whir and the click of a camera shutter.

"Where are our voices?" Bash asked incredulously, "and where's the picture I took of the window?" she said with dismay, staring at a blank frame on the camera where the word *hello* should have been.

"We'll have to go back again," Kit said. "To investigate."

Bash gave him a look of fake surprise. "Ya think?"

"Okay, I apologize. I was wrong," Kit said, taking a deep gulp of air. "But that did work up an appetite. You hungry?"

"Starving," she said. "Last one to the kitchen is a rotten bike helmet."

Kit had fully recovered his scientific poise, by the time they sat down to a cozy lunch of baked beans on toast.

Mrs. S placed a lopsided chocolate cake on the table with a flourish.

"What do you think of that? Rupert made it from a mix."

"*Ergh*," Kit said. "Is there anything else?"

Bash raised a fork of baked beans to her mouth and grinned, "Have we got any Fig Newtons Mum?" she asked, and took a bite.

CHAPTER FORTY-TWO

Home Sweet Home

On Tuesday evening, when fierce gusts battered the windows of Bede Hall with yet more stinging rain, most of the family were preoccupied with their savory meal of pot roast and dumplings. The aroma of a Bramley Apple crumble cooling on the sideboard, promised a sweet dessert course that would be served with whipped cream and steaming cups of strongly-brewed tea.

It was Bash's favorite time, when the world seemed better for good food and the unusual additional warmth of a summer's hearth. She kept her father's memory safe with positive thoughts, and for a few hours, it was easy to believe he was just away on one of his digs, across the world but only a phone call away.

She looked across the table at Kit's flushed face and they exchanged a look of mutual excitement. They tried not to analyse what had happened, each convinced it was the other who was playing a hoax, and so both of them wisely decided to leave the future to resolve itself.

Tomorrow and the tomorrow after that would come soon enough and the reveal would be over.

Rupert and Mrs. S were engaged in a lively conversation, and Lady Nan dozed in her wheelchair by the fire wrapped in her snowflake shawl, with Feathers on her lap, and at her feet, lay a very peaceful deerhound and a paternal Anubis hugging what looked like a 'Snowball.'

Pigeon stirred as a crack of thunder shredded the peace of the kitchen. He woke suddenly and exclaimed *"storm before the calm"* and promptly went back to sleep.

The rainy months of spring that had arrived as a wild tempest, had barely dissipated. Even with the official approach of summer, it had been freezing wet one day and unbearably hot the next. The gales and electrical storms had simply forgotten to leave.

The English moors were still fraught with the final lashings of straggling winds, wearing themselves out to prepare for the lost climate of August.

Then, on the eve of the 'big day,' the skies over Bede surprised them with a glorious sunset of peach clouds edged with gold.

PART FIVE

THE WASTELAND

"How full
of the creative genius
is the air
in which these are generated!
I should hardly admire more
if real stars fell
and lodged on my coat."

- HENRY DAVID THOREAU
(describing a snowflake) 1856

CHAPTER FORTY-THREE

The Ghost of Christmas Future

The village of Bede was as still as a photograph. No nightmare breeze stirred the leafless trees withered into crouching shriveled shapes. Hoar frost dusted the cars and houses and the boards on the windows. Kit felt the foreboding coldness of fear fill his body. The weather was glacial. Bone-deep cold. It was the dismal cold of a land under a curse.

The pitch-black dark of noon muffled any sign of life on the deserted streets. He looked up at the cloudless gray murk of sky. A dirty orange strip clung to the horizon. It was a ghost town. No midnight dogs. No prowling cats. No birdsong.

Kit walked toward the mournful sound of the church bells feeling like Ebenezer Scrooge about to meet up with one of his ghosts.

The church looked as if it had been whitewashed. The steeple clock pointed to an event of catastrophic proportions.

As he watched, its hands fell away and landed a few feet away from where he stood. They stuck out of the ground like a pair of antennae. The effect was dramatic. The clock's face now resembled the one on his bedroom wall.

Enormous flakes of snow fell in slow-motion, landing with a dry rustling sound like cornflakes being poured into a bowl.

Kit slipped over the frozen ground following the icy paths between the gravestones towards a shaft of blue light. One stone, illuminated by a spotlight, flickered and he was unable to stop his legs walking towards it. What he saw chilled him even more. The inscription read: Bathsheba Stratford-Smyth Beloved Shadow 2001-2021.

Kit woke with a start and was relieved to see the familiar wallpaper of his bedroom, but the hands of the alarm clock on his bedside table formed the same position of the church clock before it had disintegrated. He raced to the window.

Below, the gardens of Bede Hall shone silver in the moonlight and for a moment it looked like frost had attacked the treetops plump with summer leaves, but his red bicycle looked black leaning against the sundial free of snow.

Just where I left it, he thought.

Feathers streaked across the drive and was overtaken by Anubis, a sleek black string, chasing a terrified rabbit that hadn't had the sense to stay still under a full moon.

Kit still reeled from the shock of seeing his twin's grave, even if it had been only a nightmare. His hands gripped the window ledge as he stared at the sundial. And then he remembered. He had put his bike away in the shed. As Kit watched, the mirage of his bicycle turned white and simply vanished.

CHAPTER FORTY-FOUR

White Magic

For an old key, it turned smoothly in the lock and Bash felt rather than heard a gentle click inside the door. It swung silently, most unlike the door of a haunted room.

The light switch made a sound, but the room remained in darkness.

"We need light in here," Bash declared, as Feathers ran into the shadows to chase the possibility of a mouse.

Jack stayed behind in the hall, whining.

"It's okay boy," Bash said, scratching the dog's ears. "There's nothing to worry about."

"We need air first," Kit replied, bravely pushing past Bash. "The curtains have been drawn since yesterday."

Kit pushed them aside expecting to see the word 'HELLO,' but the frost looked like a fresh sheet of wax paper. He tested it with his finger and left the impression of a melted dot in its center before throwing open the small window.

The room was remarkably clean of dust and cobwebs. The sheer curtains were bright and clean with a delicate pattern of snowflakes woven into the fabric. Fresh air rushed into the room and made a circuit around the corners and back outside. It was as if Bede Hall had inhaled and exhaled it clean.

Kit made a long, strangled, gurgling sound in his throat which communicated much more than any words of surprise he might have uttered.

"Cool," breathed Bash, in delighted awe of the vision before her.

Kit shuffled his feet nervously. "More than cool. It's like the ruddy North Pole in here."

"Anybody here?" Bash called out.

There was silence.

"Told you," Kit said smugly.

"She won't be here till tomorrow," Bash reminded him. "That's the anniversary when she and Lady Nan first met."

"Oh, right," Kit said, sarcastically, back in his skeptical mode. "Ghosts use calendars." He laughed smugly. "*Perpetual* ones I expect."

"Today is only for a quick tidy-up and to add some things that Snow may need," Bash said.

"A ghost won't need fresh blankets or a teapot," Kit said. "But you already know that."

"It's a gesture, then," Bash said. "Lady Nan wants it to be perfect."

"It looks fine the way it is."

"Spoken like a boy," Bash said. "It needs flowers and some candles."

The bright sunlight seemed to adjust itself to the light from the hallway and softened into a gentle blue glow that painted a small fireplace and a mantel with candlesticks, and a pile of books on a round side-table. Beside it, was the faint outline of a small door and a daybed covered in a white bedspread with heaps of white pillows. The floorboards were painted white as well. In fact, everything was a shade of white which made it look like the latest fashion from one of Bash's interior design magazines. A wicker chair stood beside the fireplace. Clearly no remains of even a distant fire were present. Kit checked the flue.

"It's all boarded up," he said.

"No problem, Nan has an electric fire with pretend flames in her room," Bash said.

A closer look revealed embossed white snowflakes in the textured wallpaper.

They placed the electric fire in the grate, but there were no outlets for the plug.

"Never mind," Bash said. "It looks very cheery with its red and black plastic coal, and it's the thought that counts."

"My thoughts right now are rather rude," Kit replied. "Sorry, this is a big waste of time, but it looks like a nice private space for you. Let's move the new carpet in, and I'll leave you to sort the small things yourself. You aren't scared in here are you?"

"It feels lovely," Bash said, "quite peaceful. Feathers and I like it, don't we Feathers?"

Kit didn't need to call Jack to follow him downstairs after he'd shifted the furniture several times until they were more or less back in their original places.

Jack was his shadow, and in any case, he would never have wanted to stay. Dogs, they say, pick up vibes... but then, so do cats, and Feathers was already happily massaging a pillow into a bed. Kit decided if there *were* such things as ghosts they would probably live strange 'lives' and then laughed at his backward logic.

Bash bustled about with several vases of peonies trying out various places and hung a print of Monet's water lilies over the fireplace. She set Lady Nan's hourglass beside the teapot and china cups and saucers for two, on a new cherry-wood coffee table with ornate legs. Its dark varnish and the bright carpet looked out of place.

Finally, she stood back to admire her work. And then she remembered the walnut mantel clock Nan had given her for the mantelpiece.

She ran downstairs, but closed the door from force of habit, in case anyone happened by.

Returning with the carved clock, Bash turned the crystal door-knob, and what she saw both shocked and delighted her, but the magic of it seemed commonplace, and gave the room an even safer atmosphere.

The colorful carpet had turned several shades lighter so that one could still enjoy its washed-out shapes of leaves and flowers. The Monet print was drained of its pastel blues and pinks. The hourglass's case was silver, and the coffee table was now, white.

But most enchanting of all, was the electric fire flickering with blue flames until she noticed Feathers curled up asleep in the wicker chair beside it. Feathers was no longer ginger-colored; she was pure white.

Bash set the clock in place, and after taking a last long look at it, she closed the door, but no sooner than the door made contact with the door frame, that the brown clock shimmered briefly like a mirage in the desert, blinked once, and turned white.

Bash rushed to a mirror, and was relieved to confirm she was still a brunette and that her complexion was the natural flesh-tones it had always been.

Kit would believe his eyes, but how on middle-earth was she going to explain Feathers to the rest of the family?

Bash smuggled Feathers downstairs and into the garden. The center of the maze seemed like a safe place to wait until she thought of something to do.

The magic of the room seemed less bizarre than suddenly owning a white cat, and for the immediate moment, Feathers was the biggest problem.

Feathers was content to clean her whiskers and settled on Bash's lap. It was pleasant to be surrounded by the soothing green of nature and Bash leant her back against the leafy wall. It was a good place to think.

Kit, she decided, would take the pragmatic approach. Her mother would believe any story if Parks told her such a thing as cats changing color always happened at this time of year, and Boss wouldn't even notice. Lady Nan must have known of the magic effect and may have an antidote, but for once Feathers looked more like Snowdrop's mum.

Bash was delighted when Feather's rubbed against the unicorn statue and her fur flared once, shifting to a distinct shade of beige. Every few minutes a darker color was perceptible, until an hour later, Feathers was back to being a nice vibrant ginger color, although her amber eyes were now, blue. Perhaps no-one would notice, Bash thought. They were all too busy to remember little things like that.

Bash used to tease Kit that the blue door was the gateway to winter because it was so cold, but now it was much more serious.

At least she had discovered that most of the magic wore off in the sunlight. And even if there was no ghost, which she told herself she really didn't believe for a minute, it would still be a good spot to hide or read on blistering hot days as Kit had suggested.

Kit, knowing where the key was, had obviously snuck into the room the night before the 'hello' incident, and was acting scared when he ran down the stairs. But then, that didn't explain the tape recorder, unless Kit had faked that too.

Kit was the classic 'wiz kid,' and Bash was fairly sure he could have made a tape of stormy sound effects and disconnected the play button.

One thing she knew for sure, was that Kit would experiment with any new phenomena she might have discovered until he found an explanation.

It turned out, that Kit experimented (as Bash knew he would) by removing the whitened clock to see if it would change back to its original color, but even after being left under the sun for several hours, it remained white. After the Winter Room touched an object with its icy breath, it was white for good. Apparently, only animals were temporarily effected.

Kit's tower was a alight with several lamps as he copied the data from his experiments to a computer file while Bash watched.

"There's a practical side to this *wintry-touch* thing," Bash commented. "Rather poetic really – Jack Frost's icy 'Midas Touch' fingers," she teased. "Lady Nan told me it was the finest space in all of Bede Hall to recover from sunstroke," she continued. "It will still be great for that."

Kit addressed his sister with an exasperated expression. "This room is outside the realm of known science," he argued. "Do you not get how important that is? This is a great discovery. Some sort of portal. Not ghosts and wimpy rumors and superstitious silliness, but real fourth-dimension physics of warped space-time that manipulates matter."

"Plus, I won't need to buy white paint anymore," Bash said to bug him.

After supper, Lady Nan sat by the fire with Feathers on her knee making a big fuss of her. "Who's got lovely blue eyes then?" she crooned.

CHAPTER FORTY-FIVE

Domino Time

Lady Nan had named her only child, Rayne, for a very special reason, and only three people knew why. All of them lived in Bede Hall, 'lived' being a bit of a joke because one of them was a ghost.

It was the last day of July and for over a year the Stratford-Smyths lives had been reshuffled like a deck of cards. Lady Nan was too excited to eat breakfast, but she winked at Kit and Bash.

"You'd better eat something. You'll need your strength for tomorrow," Kit said.

Lady Nan smiled a red lipstick smile.

"D-Day," she replied dreamily, and sipped her tea. "Bash, if you don't mind, I think I'll have one of my lady sleeps today."

"A what?" Mrs. S asked.

"A long lazy nap like in the Lady of Shalott," Bash answered. "It's daydreaming with flowers," she added to be helpful. "I pick some flowers from the garden and spread them around Lady Nan and she drifts off to sleep. Charlotte calls it aromatherapy."

Mrs. S looked sad. "You two are quite the pair," she said, which meant she could see that her daughter and mother had formed a mutual admiration society that continued to leave her out.

It was hard to believe so much time had elapsed since Lady Nan had described herself as being 'as near death to death as dammit,' hovering on the edge of sanity, dreaming of her past in the Beehive Nursing home.

'I was adrift in my bed like Tennyson's 'Lady of Shalott,' she had quipped, and to prove it she had shown Bash a print that showed the poet's famous fairy queen lying prone, covered in flowers in a state of semi-consciousness.

Bash had said she looked like a real float, the sort in a parade.

"Floating down a lazy river on a barge wearing a crown of

carnations under a blanket of lilies is a romantic image, I grant you," Lady Nan said out loud, "but ..."

"There will be no floating today," Mrs. S said wearily, "the radio says it's going to be a scorcher."

"I can assure you there was nothing therapeutic about that Beehive place," Lady Nan whispered aside to Bash, helping herself to buttered toast and marmalade. "Not a bed of roses," Lady Nan added with a dramatic shudder. "I used to sleep in order to escape. Back then, sleep was another country."

Bash watched as Lady Nan spooned on extra marmalade.

"There you go," Bash said, "a little toast is better than nothing."

"Can I get you anything cooked, Mama?" Mrs. S asked, with the frying pan in her hand. "You look different today. You feeling all right?"

Lady Nan sent her daughter a beaming smile and discreetly elbowed Bash in the ribs.

"You know, I think I'd like a couple of poached eggs," she said suppressing a giggle.

For years the 'Lady of Bede' had been dreaming while her son-in-law, Cornelius Stratford-Smyth, had been excavating the same hills and valleys she visited in a parallel Egypt – one of the places the professor had loved best on earth, hot on the trail of the tomb of the pharaoh Smenkhkare, King Tut's older brother.

Bash produced Lady Nan's notebook and a pen from beneath her chair, and placed them on the kitchen table.

"Do we have time today?" she asked with a knowing smile, gesturing with her pen. "If not, I think I'll make some notes of my own."

"I'll be your thesaurus," Lady Nan said to Bash, placing her knife and fork in a straight line on her empty plate, "until you decide to fly solo."

"Well, I may start a diary," Bash said to no-one in particular, chewing the end of her pen and gazing at Kit.

"We're all flying solo," Mrs. S declared, refilling the teapot.

"If you ask me, we've been flying in formation," Kit said, winking at Lady Nan.

Tonight of all nights, the stars were bright enough to throw magic in Bash's eyes. It was the least the full-moon could do, to shed a little light on the ghost and a young girl's new dreams.

Lady Nan's book was Bash's inspiration. She had opened it upside-down by mistake, and there it was – a parallel blank page, waiting for such a moment. A twin book, and Bash scribbled furiously before bedtime on the last page of Lady Nan's book. Tomorrow is the day, she wrote:

> *A ghost or one of Kit's tricks? This is my first real attempt to write about what I think and see, and mostly what I've learned since we came to live here, at Bede Hall. Supernatural things are strange at first, but then seem normal.*

The word supernatural flashed up at her from the paper like a neon sign. She continued to write with more energy. She'd never felt so wide-awake. So alive.

> *The word supernatural is important, she wrote. It must be because I can hear words in my head when I look at it. I hear super-science and natural energy that mean everyday things, and not some scary nonsense. Kit says that's pseudo-science, but he's still nervous around the Winter Room. For instance, if there is a ghost as Lady Nan says, it's a natural thing. Only stories about ghosts are scary.*
>
> *If singing to plants makes them grow, then that's natural, too.*
>
> *My teachers, Charlotte and Parks, have taught me to notice signs. They call them portents. I call them significant which looks like the words sign and magnificent put together. They told me to depend on my intuition. They taught me to listen.*

Lady Nan says they are my mentors. I looked it up and they are.

I can never forget the loss of my father, but being here, at Bede Hall, I've been able to find something good to believe in again. I have my own naturally-super garden, and met new friends. Some are invisible. Charlotte calls them elementals or devas (better known in mythology as fairies) although my memories of them always fade quickly, like dreams when you wake up too fast.

Charlotte and Parks say all woodlands teem with mythological beings. My guess is that they know more than they're telling. Charlotte says they are grooming me.

She also says I'll get better at remembering my conversations with devas if I spend time alone in the maze not thinking about anything. It's called meditation. Lady Nan knows all about it, but she calls it visualization. It's just imagining, but waiting for your brain to tell you what to imagine.

Whatever it's called, it works after you do it for a while.

Let me tell you about Bede.

It's like some giant dropped a toy village from the sky where eccentric people live apart from the ordinary world with imaginary spirits, including Lady Nan's ghost-friend, Snow, who lives (correction exists) upstairs. It's something I can sense but not understand clearly.... at least not yet. It's a hunch, and hunches are good signposts.

I checked with Kit and he says Bede is like a village in a petrie dish. He refers to it as a science experiment under a bell jar. I looked that up too and he's right.

Kit has his own experiments; he wants to reverse time the way Lady Nan says she dreams because when our grandmother closes her eyes to sleep, she travels to an Egypt where our dad could still be excavating. Some days it comforts me to pretend she's right.

Bede Time feels like it hovers on a clock with no hands. Even the village pub is called the Stopped Clock. When I asked Charlotte if that was significant, she just winked, so I know there is something deep in it and I intend to find out.

This book will be the story of how my grandmother, Lady Nan, returned to Bede Hall to, as she once cheerily announced to me, "end my days there and eventually haunt the place."

Edgar Tweedy has turned out to be the rudest and most impudent thief.

Lady Nan says that the Hall has decided Edgar deserves a little paranormal, extra-curricular activity, and that it monitors his every move.

I wish.

Strangely, it had been Lady Nan, dismissed as being too old and bewildered to know what day of the week it was, who had come to her senses as well as our family's rescue, with the daring plan that pulled us together.

It was as if bad times had cleared Lady Nan's muddled mind.

Mum says that Lady Nan was a tiger when she wanted to be, but I disagreed. I said that Lady Nan was a tiger when she had to be. She has some dark secrets. I know because she almost tells me.

– Bash (Bathsheba) Stratford-Smyth.

Bede Hall manipulated the stars into patterns like the spokes of an umbrella as if rearranging a couple of constellations could keep the future nice and dry. But it had other plans that required a swirl of magic. Star chess it remarked to Anubis.

Waiting to get the Tweedy vermin alone for a little one-on-one 'interaction' proved to be almost entertaining, but unfortunately, the pesky creature was too insensitive to hear the Hall menacing.

It would take extreme measures to sort him, and Bede Hall had known, months ago, the very creature to help. Even now this creature was shadowing Edgar for the perfect time to strike. The Hall, sensing the moment was not far off, said that it made the waiting all the more sweet.

Midnight over Bede was a blackboard of chalk stars. As always, the odds for perfect timing were positively astronomical, but there was the ghost of a chance.

CHAPTER FORTY-SIX
No Wardrobe in Sight

Kit sat down to breakfast with exaggerated enthusiasm. "It's August first," he announced to no-one in particular, rubbing his hands together. "It's going to be a goodun."

Rupert made a fake excited face and said: "Oh goody, how pray tell?" His eyes rolled.

"Well... *er...* there's a full moon," Kit lied.

"Big whoop."

"The biggest," Kit confirmed, with his best scientist attitude, and Rupert quickly disappeared behind his newspaper before he could receive a long speech about the weather and tides and planetary alignments.

Snow was sitting in the wicker chair staring at the blue flames with a white cat on her knee.

"My name is Bathsheba," Bash said, "but I like to be called Bash. You must be Snow?"

Snow looked up at Bash and turned transparent as a cloud. The white cat made a frightful yowl, flickered like a candle, and disappeared.

"You're not Rain," came the girl's timid reply.

"No, Rain is a ... a friend of mine. She'll be along, later. She asked me to say hello and to tell you she's looking forward to seeing you again. She'll be here soon... *um...* you're to wait till I fetch her. It will take a few minutes longer now that she's in a wheelchair."

Bash paused, never having given orders to a ghost before.

"I mean, if that's all right. She didn't want you to worry," Bash said.

"I've been worried for the last three years," came the mournful reply. "My name is Anna, but I'd feel better if you still called me Snow. This," she gestured towards the cat, "is Unicorn. He was Rain's cat."

It felt strange, Bash thought, to be so thoroughly examined by a curious apparition. The two girls stared at each other with interest. Snow was shorter by a few inches. If it can be said that a ghost's color could return, Bash noticed the white mist turn slightly blue as Snow tried to smile.

"I expect we've given you a bit of a fright," Bash said, and Kit let out a strangled noise from the hallway making Jack whimper again.

Unicorn hissed and shrunk behind Snow's back.

Snow peered over Bash's shoulder at Kit and gave a little gasp. Kit responded with a lop-sided grin, and shuffled his feet. Jack slunk behind Kit and whined through his nose.

Snow reminded Bash of the 'little match girl' from a fairy tale. A waif come to 'life,' she thought, skin pale as moonlight, her waxen pixie face peering out from under a white hood trimmed in white fur. Her body was encased in padded white overalls and white boots. White mittens covered her hands.

"Thank you for the fire, though. It's wonderful... and the flowers," Snow said, returning to a solid form once more.

"You're most welcome," Bash replied. "We wanted, that is, Lady Nan wanted, you to feel at home."

"But I am at home," Snow said in a small voice, looking as if she might burst into tears at any moment. "Who is Lady Nan?"

Kit finally spoke. He cleared his throat and entered the room with Jack glued to his leg. "Lady Nan is Rain. She's older now,"

"Yes, her birthday is a few weeks before mine," Snow said.

Kit regained his scientific curiosity and took out his pocket notebook.

"No, I mean she's an old lady. A grandmother. Mine to be exact. Do you always see her as... as your age?"

Kit and Jack had deliberately hung back sharing the same fear, taking in the entire scene at a safe distance, but now Kit felt quite recovered and Jack amazingly slumped at his feet, wary, but calm as could be.

"Is that a polar bear?" Snow asked, pointing to Jack, who was now as white as could be as well.

"Have you never seen a picture of a polar bear?" Kit asked incredulously, and at once he was his old reporter-self, making mental notes and chiding himself for not bringing his camera.

"This is my brother, Kit," Bash said, remembering her manners, but Kit didn't say hello.

Bash pointed to Jack. "And that's our dog Jack. He's a deer-hound."

"What year is it? For you, I mean," Kit continued.

"Years don't count now," Snow remarked, looking back at the fire.

The twins assumed Snow meant, once you were dead.

Snow was restless. Her pale blue eyes with their dark worry circles were always searching. She walked to the window, petting Jack on the way, and Jack responded with a doggy sigh.

"Could I meet Rain in the garden since it's hard for her to use the stairs?" Snow said.

She sighed louder than Jack.

"I don't see why not," Bash replied. "It's easier to wheel her chair out there. I take her all the time."

"Even with all that snow?" Snow asked gazing out.

Bash joined Snow at the window

"Nonsense," Bash started to say. "It's August," but she was stunned to see that the gardens below looked like a Christmas card. Snow lay thick over everything and all the trees were bare of leaves. The topiaries were like a field of strange snowmen.

"Kit! You won't believe this," Bash said.

"If I can see it I will," he replied, walking to the window.

Kit stared down at a winter scene.

"I see it," he said. "I'm not sure I believe it."

Kit zoomed down the stairs nearly tripping over Jack who was doing his best to beat his master to the bottom. Both raced outside in a tangle of excitement. The garden was in full bloom, stretching with every color. The day was barely a few hours old, but already the mauve shadows on the terrace radiated a shimmer of heat waves.

Bash and Snow stared down at him from the small square window and waved.

"It's summer down here," he shouted up. "It's already boiling."

"I see winter," Bash replied.

"Hang on, I have to see it again for myself, meet me down here."

Bash flew into the garden and was met with a blast of sunshine.

"See!" Kit said, already headed inside.

Soon Kit was looking down at Bash who was now standing in the middle of a snow bank, and there was a track of footprints leading across the lawn.

"Incredible!" he shouted down. "This is getting interesting."

"Fetch Lady Nan," Bash hollered back. "I'll come up and get Snow."

"She's already down there, Kit shouted. "Can't you see her? She's over by the sundial."

Bash turned to look, and sure enough Snow was there, but this time she looked like a live girl and her hat, mittens, coat, and overalls were pink. She was wearing sunglasses that looked more like ski goggles and she held a carnation in her hand that couldn't decide if it wanted to be pink or yellow. In the end it decided to be white.

"Morning Lady Nan. It's August first – countdown to Operation Snowstorm," Kit said. "Bash is talking to Snow right now, she's expecting us as soon as you want to go."

"Right now please, there's a good lad," Lady Nan said.

Lady Nan's eyes had gone all distant and bright. The effect was disturbing and Kit noticed that his grandmother's voice had changed.

"Is that you Grandmamma?" he asked.

"I'm nine. How could I be a grandmother, you silly boy," came the amused reply.

"Oh. Right. Hi Beryl," Kit said. We're going for a little ride."

"I visited the Winter Room last night," Lady Nan said with a twinkle. "It looked perfect. I dreamed myself there. I couldn't take my night medicine. It stops me dreaming. Now I want to actually be there while I'm awake."

"We're going one better, milady," Kit teased, handing Lady Nan her straw sun-hat. "*We* are going to a garden party, so you'd better hang on to your hat."

The best thing about saving a child ghost is time. Ghosts don't feel time in quite the same way. For one thing, they're always the same age. Snow was nine. She'd been nine since Rain first met her, and even though she'd been alone a long time, sixty-four years seemed like nothing. No time at all.

CHAPTER FORTY-SEVEN

Cats in the Window

Lady Nan knelt down and gave Snow a hug. For a few seconds Lady Nan's body shimmered into a Lady Nan-shaped cloud of ice crystals. Snow seemed to absorb the old woman's energy and for a happy moment her skin glowed quite pink with life.

The little girl's teary eyes were distinctly dark purple when she turned to face the twins.

"Those are happy tears I hope," Bash said.

Lady Nan began with an apology to Snow. "Dear girl. I was delayed. Forgive me. What can I say? I haven't been myself for a long time, and I had given up hope of ever coming home again."

"I couldn't find you," Snow chided. "I called. Your room was empty. I even stayed till September."

"I heard you," Lady Nan said. "But the doctors gave me too many pills, so I was trapped. Bash rescued me."

Bash looked down at her shoes and then out the window to avoid the question in Kit's eyes.

"Well, I didn't think it would hurt," Bash rationalized. "They were only the ones to help her sleep, and she wanted to stay awake *some* of the time. She told me she always missed the 'B flowers,' whatever *that* meant. I could see that made her sad. She barely knew who I was. I felt her pleading with me to help even when she was asleep. That's all."

"You never told me," Kit said, taken aback. "I think you might have."

"There was no need to get us both in trouble. Besides, Lady Nan made me promise," Bash explained.

"Bash helped me wake up," Lady Nan announced innocently. "And here we all are."

Lady Nan took Snow's hand, now a pale blue color, and looked into her eyes. "My grandchildren tell me your real name is Anna."

Snow said nothing.

"Where's my sweet Unicorn? Do you mind if I still call you Snow?"

When unicorn and Lady Nan had been joyfully reunited, and Snow's eyes were quite blue again, she took Lady Nan's hand and led her to a wicker lawn table where she fidgeted around her. She reached up to set her straw hat at a jaunty angle with some difficulty, even though Lady Nan was seated.

"No need to fuss child," Lady Nan said, tossing the bonnet aside. "I'm in the shade so it's quite all right. I know you're eager to explore the garden and I can watch you from here. My wheelchair is hopeless on the grass."

"Are there bees?" Snow asked with hope in her voice.

"Hundreds, Lady Nan replied. "Bash and Parks have managed to attract a new hive. You can visit it later."

A slight shadow of anxiety passed over Lady Nan's face. There's something sad about beehives, she thought, and then the unpleasant memory was gone.

Snow whispered in Lady Nan's ear: "I have a secret that can't wait... But it's private."

Lady Nan briefly reverted to the age of nine and spoke to her grandchildren. "Snow and I have a new secret," she said.

"Why don't we leave you two alone for a while then," Kit said, as Lady Nan sounded her old self again.

Unicorn bounded from the shrubberies and rubbed into Lady Nan's legs.

"The three of us," Lady Nan said, petting the cat.

Snow spoke loud enough for the twins to hear. "I found out something, but it's very weird. You'll never guess."

"Back in a few minutes," Bash called out over her shoulder. "We'll be in the gazebo."

Bash picked carnations on the way back. "These are Lady Nan's favorites," she said plucking the red and white blooms. "They mean something."

"What... that Victorian flower language thing?" Kit snickered.

"That too. Remember I told you what she said about the power of smell and that it took her back, reminiscing? That's a kind of time-travel don't you think?"

Kit jammed his hands in his pockets. "There's no need to trivialize time-travel. I *will* find a way, but that 'wasting time to smell the roses thing' isn't going to do it. That's for poets."

Bash smiled sympathetically. "Actually, it's *taking* time TO smell the roses," she corrected. "And I'd say there's a lot of poetry in science with all that synchronicity business going on. I mean, rather than the chronological."

"Where did you learn the word chronological?" Kit asked, hoping to test her.

"I overheard it somewhere and looked it up. I mean, it's not *rocket science* or anything, is it? There *are* dictionaries you know. Synchronicity is when odd things happen together in really important ways. Everything occurring right at the perfect time in ways that seem unconnected. The greatest discoveries are like that. You know... a chance meeting or an experiment fails, and suddenly something amazing happens from all the mistakes colliding together like solving two jigsaw puzzles with one set of pieces.

"Chronological is as it sounds: logical time – one thing after another, in order like the hours of the day."

"Yes, I do know that," Kit said.

"Maybe that happened to Dad," Bash mused. "The *synchronistic* thing. Those kind of events can mean good *or* bad. Maybe he was supposed to be lost for a reason. Maybe he'll still come home."

Kit looked uncomfortable and changed the subject. "What do you think Snow meant, about something being weird?" he said. "I should add it to my notes."

"She's a ghost, so I'm guessing pretty much everything is weird," Bash said. "They're probably just talking about old times."

"New times, more like. Snow said she'd discovered something because of us."

"Well, we *did* introduce her to dogs and polar bears and blue fire," Bash noted dryly.

Bash tracked the sun's position and moved Lady Nan to a shadier part of the lawn near the sundial. She zoomed back inside for a jug of lemonade, four glasses, and a plate of chocolate-covered biscuits.

She had momentarily hesitated when it came to adding the fourth glass, but decided it would be polite regardless of ghostly limitations. For sure, Snow had demonstrated she could interact with physical objects. Ghost etiquette was pretty much a bizarre 'learn as you go' thing.

Snow was happily strolling through the flower beds when Bash returned to call her over, still wondering if a ghost could drink or eat or even taste. However, stopping to smell roses appeared to be less of a problem for her than Kit because there Snow was, touching and sniffing every flower with ecstatic appreciation... and it was plain that she was more than able to kiss dogs.

The first thing Snow noticed were the glass goblets grouped on the tray. Each one empty except for a handful of ice cubes.

Snow stared as if bewitched and lifted one of them to the sun, and seemed entirely captivated – as happy as a child with a new toy.

"What are these?" she said in awe. "Diamonds?"

"I wish," Bash replied.

"I would have thought you of all people would know what ice was," Kit said testily.

"*This* is ice?" Snow repeated incredulously.

"I guess you wouldn't go out of your way to manufacture the things, considering your... *situation*," Kit said, remembering his manners.

"I have never seen it like this," Snow whispered, her face studying the light shimmering through the cubes. "They look like miniature building blocks."

She emptied the ice and tried to make a pyramid shape that slithered sideways refusing to stay in formation. I know this shape," Snow said. It's important.

Lady Nan shaded her eyes, watching. She seemed flustered. The wide brim of her sunhat was pinned under the wheels of her chair. Her hands restlessly fingered the snowflake shawl and every now and then she gave a great sigh and cast her eyes about as if she was searching for something or someone. She stared at Kit a great deal and seemed more troubled than usual. Her earlier enthusiasm seemed as wilted as the rose in Snow's hand.

"Take a deep breath of these," Bash said handing her grandmother the flowers she'd picked.

Lady Nan buried her nose in the carnations, but seemed more agitated than ever.

"So much for my smelling salts," she said. Her voice was shaky and she had been crying. She was drained of color.

But Snow was becoming brighter. Her winter coat was now red with a white fur trimmed hood.

Boss was mowing the lawn for once, since the novelty of a mower tractor was a bit of a lark, and obviously didn't notice the 'Little Red Riding Hood' figure, who could have stepped out of a fairy tale. The twins tried to hail him, but Rupert Stratford-Smyth was locked behind his sunglasses inside a world of headphones and rock music. Snow had abandoned her own ski goggles and upturned her face to the sky embracing the sun.

"She looks like a strange little Christmas elf," Kit observed, stopping to write in his book:

> *Invisible to others. New colors after being in the sun. She keeps saying 'she has found him' and Lady Nan is upset by some new secret. Snow used the word weird. No transparency which means she is feeling safe. Makes eye contact with me a lot.*

231

Lady Nan spoke with resignation. "Rupert can't see her. No-one can but the three of us."

"And the animals," Bash added.

Kit made a notation: *animals react to Snow*. "What's up Lady Nan?" he said, pen at the ready. "You look as if you've seen a ghost," he joked.

Bash shot her brother a 'how could you be so insensitive' look and rolled her eyes.

"Well, it seems I *haven't*," Lady Nan replied.

"Excuse me? Haven't what?"

"Haven't ... *um*... got my... sun-hat," Lady Nan said.

The shade had receded to the furthest corner of the terrace and the little group obediently followed it.

The carnation posy fell from Lady Nan's hand as she wheeled herself closer to the house.

Snow saw the twins and waved.

"Well, she looks happy," Kit said.

"Yes, she's found her... who she'd been looking for," Lady Nan said. "Well you two, I think it must be time for a spot of lunch. I see Rupert heading for the kitchen... that's always a clue."

The ignored biscuits oozed in a puddle of melted chocolate, and Jack sniffed them appreciatively as Kit loaded the tray.

Snow watched Kit and Jack as if mesmerized.

"Not for dogs," Kit admonished, lifting the plate away. "I have something much better."

Jack looked at Kit adoringly as he pulled a dried doggy-treat from his pocket that its manufacturers were determined to pass off as a strip of petrified bacon – tougher than any real bacon on the planet.

Jack had no problem falling for it at first whiff, and waited in a fever to snatch it immediately, but he stayed calm as he'd been taught, and was rewarded with the pungent brown leathery strip that crunched in the his jaws like a small china ornament.

"Well done Jack Frost. You're a very *dear* hound," Snow said to Jack, flinging her arms about him and kissing his nose for the hundredth time. To Jack's delight, Snow began to scratch his ears.

232

"Kit?" Snow said, brightly. "Do you have any more of those treat things? Can I give one to Jack?"

Being addressed by his name threw Kit into a mental tailspin.

Kit dashed off a few key words on his intrepid notepad:

Snow can pick up a glass. Sees ice cubes for first time ... makes a pun ... obviously aware ... can understand new things... knows what a dog treat is... Jack, Anubis, Snowdrop, and Feathers magnetically drawn to her... parrots are as yet, untested... waves cheerily at all four Parks... not good with strangers.

At this point he stopped and wrote the name Boss in brackets.

Snow appeared to be more relaxed as she inspected the peony bushes with Jack trotting after her. Her winter coat disappeared quite suddenly, and she now wore an ankle-length white nightgown with long sleeves and lace cuffs. Her exposed hair was unsurprisingly, pure white. The short style gave her an even more pixyish appearance, but she was emaciated... an albino child, in need of emotional nourishment. Her lithe form made Bash sad, but at the same time she was charmed.

"The white gown makes her look more ghostlike," she said to Kit.

Snow returned with several peonies. "I like this color best," she said, holding out the reddish-purple flowers that now had pure white stems where she had touched them. What color is this?" she asked, touching the petals.

"It's called magenta," Bash answered, and no sooner were the words out her mouth, than the peony turned the kind of pale peach color found inside a sea shell.

"And this?" Snow asked.

"That's called pink," Kit said, scribbling:

No concept of colors. Can hold material objects. Colors fade at her touch.

233

Bash drew Kit's attention to Snow's footprints that left a trace of sparkling blue frost in the grass before melting under the sun, and he added:

> *Leaves blue footprints that fade to white and disappear in a few seconds.*

Bash picked up the rejected carnations and the straw hat crushed by the wheels of Lady Nan's receding chair. "Maybe re-incarnations," Bash speculated, sniffing Nan's flowers. This smell takes me straight to Lady Nan's birthday."

Lady Nan made it clear she was too busy to talk to the twins during lunch. She picked at her salad and kept glancing out the window. She stared at Kit a long time and looked as if she were going to ask him a question.

"More tea, Mamma?" Mrs. S said, lifting the teapot.

Lady Nan's eyes were far away. "No thank you my dear. I think I'll have a lie down. Must have caught too much sun. Rayne, will you take me up please."

"Pretty please... looks like snow...looks like... time for pooh," Pigeon squawked.

When Mrs. S returned, she admonished the twins while Rupert smirked behind a magazine. Bash got the worst of it.

"I let you and Lady Nan do pretty much as you please, but you have to remember her age. Your grandmother can't be outside on a day like this even for a short time."

Mrs. S pursed her lips and looked accusingly at Bash. "And where is her sun-hat?" she demanded.

"Sorry, Mum. They were in the shade and..."

"They? Who was she with?"

"*Er...* Feathers and Jack."

"Cats and dogs love the sun. Humans do not. Your grandmother may love the memory of it, but it's not good for her anymore."

Bash felt she needed to protest for Snow's benefit. "Lady Nan says she wants to go out every day, now that it's stopped raining. So, what will I tell her?"

The word rain seemed to jump out every time she used it. In fact, all words that meant icy cold, like 'melting' or being asked to get ice from the freezer, or if she was catching a cold, sounded louder than usual.

Mrs. S ordered her list of conditions. "Half-an-hour only. Straw hat. In the shade."

"But..."

"No arguments milady. That's final. You can wheel your grandmother to the gazebo or the terrace. I will speak to her. Not that she'll remember. After you've finished your lunch I want you to take her a glass of water. And mind you wear your own hat this afternoon," she clucked.

Bash knocked gently on Lady Nan's door before opening it. She was already asleep, curled on her side with her snowflake shawl over her, the way Beryl preferred.

Bash set the glass on the bedside table and pushed her grandmother's snow globe that was about to fall from the edge of the bedside table. She noticed but never registered that the snow inside it was still swirling from a recent shake.

When the door clicked shut, Lady Nan's eyes flew open. There were worry lines on her forehead as she reached for her 'crystal ball' and she hugged it till the miniature house and tree inside it had changed from a tranquil winter landscape to a summer's day.

Feathers and Unicorn were becoming inseparable. "Friends for life," Kit had said, making another of his ghost jokes.

Feathers was often found scratching at the Winter Door first thing in the mornings when Kit and Bash looked in. Some of the times, Feathers had even stayed all night. This was one of the mornings that she was discovered from the garden below.

Kit noted the scene first. "Look up there," he said, pointing to the window of the Winter Room. "Feathers is locked in again."

Snow's window looked as if it held a pair of cat bookends on its sill. Bash raced up the stairs to let Feathers out.

Snow and Lady Nan were having a serious conversation but Bash was able to catch the tail end of it.

"You haven't seen Ben at all? Lady Nan was saying, "Anywhere? Surely fourth dimension apparitions cross each other's paths. And this was his house."

"He isn't here, but then I'm not..." Snow stopped, seeing Bash.

"Sorry to disturb," Bash said. "Just collecting cats."

Neither Snow or Lady Nan looked interested, so there seemed no harm in letting Unicorn follow her and Feathers downstairs to the kitchen, but she hadn't reckoned on Pigeon, who no doubt, saw the ghost cat quite clearly.

Bash put food down for Feathers and watched as Feathers let Unicorn have a sniff and take a few bites. Unicorn started to purr loudly and rub against Bash's legs. A second bowl was lowered to the floor, and Bash watched both animals scarf away happily.

"Pooh...Vermin...piles of feathers...piles of pooh," Pigeon shrieked in Mrs. S's voice. *"Please...no more cats...no... more... pretty please...no more cats...not enough pooh!"*

"I just had the strangest encounter with Lady Nan," Kit said to Bash, looking puzzled. I couldn't be sure if she was happy or sad. There were tears, but they could have been the good sort I suppose. I didn't know what to say. She kept trying to tell me something, and then burst into tears. I finally left to get her some tea."

"She's experiencing a rather emotional reunion," Bash said.

"How can you tell if Lady Nan's depressed?" he asked.

Bash answered Kit's question with another more pertinent question. "What color was her lipstick?" she said.

CHAPTER FORTY-EIGHT

Tickled-Red

The word history even has the word story in it. I wonder why there isn't a 'her-story' for women?" Bash mused, cheekily to Snow. "And it's interesting that the word heart lies inside hearth – the heart of a home, and remember... the word myth is in Smyth."

They were having a conversation over morning tea, and Snow was loving it.

"How very apropos," Lady Nan replied with a twinkle in her eye.

Snow's eyes were question marks.

"Perfectly appropriate," Lady Nan explained.

"Ahhhh," came Snow's response, as Bash giggled.

Snow continued to wear her old-fashioned nightdress all the time, now, and Bash thought the Winter Room was beginning to feel slightly warmer. Snow even followed Lady Nan to breakfast, keeping to the hearth's heart where Jack always parked himself. Today, little Snowdrop lay asleep on the chair.

Mrs. S inclined her head towards the same chair, now occupied by Snow as well.

"Look at Snow..." she said, pausing to cough, "Snowdrop," she continued, spluttering, but it was too late.

Snow looked terrified. The sheer notion of being seen by Mrs. S made her shiver into a thin pulsating vapor.

Bash quickly moved to the kitten and stroked it, saying a few soothing words to Snow at the same time, making sure to make eye contact. "Morning little Snowdrop girl," Bash chirped. "Aren't you lucky with a big old chair all to yourself."

Snow smiled wanly and readjusted her form to the thickness of fog, and by the time Bash was back at the kitchen table, she was solid again.

"Crisis averted," Bash said to Lady Nan, handing her the morning newspaper. Lady Nan nodded and pretended to examine the front page, politely, adding: "Yes that report is most interesting."

Her words trailed off, and she waved encouragingly to Snow.

All Mrs. S saw was her mother shooing away a fly.

"Snowdrop looks more like a snowball when she's curled up like that," Kit said, trying to be helpful.

"How apropos," Bash said, giving Snow a direct stare, and making sure Lady Nan heard her.

"What story?" Boss said, retrieving the abandoned copy of the 'Daily Bead' scanning for the headline that had been worth discussing.

"*Um*, it was the ... *um*... weather report," Bash said. "It says sunny. Yesterday it forecast rain and Lady Nan wanted to be outside today. So... *er*... crisis averted."

"Riveting," Rupert commented, and returned to delicately peeling the shell from his boiled egg as if it were a precious artifact.

"Where's Kit?" Snow asked, peering down the hallway behind Bash.

"He's over at Dr. Brooks," Bash replied.

"Is he ill?" Snow asked, looking alarmed.

"Just science biz," Bash said. "I am happy to spend some alone time with you."

"Do you want to go to the garden? Is it too cold?"

"We could try and make it warmer in here." Bash suggested. "Red is called a warm colour. If we left the door open everything inside would stay red."

"I've never had anything red before, other than my coat. Oh, and my mitts and scarf. But they're only red when I'm outside."

"I like to decorate. It'll be fun. I'll be right back, so don't go away."

"I'm rather attached to this room," Snow laughed.

Bash shook her head, grimacing "You sound just like Kit. Even your jokes."

"Do I?" Snow said, looking pleased.

Bash collected all the ruby cushions from the library window-seats, and the vase of purple peonies on the piano, and raced back upstairs with her arms loaded, stopping every third step to retrieve a fallen pillow.

Snow was sitting on the floor staring into the hourglass.

"I got these and some purple peonies," Bash called out, unable to see Snow. "Where are you?"

"Down here. You never ask WHEN I am," Snow said thoughtfully.

Bash pulled the blue door shut. "If we're going to have a talk like that we should close this," she said.

Immediately, the peonies turned mauve and the pillows turned pale pink, which delighted Snow.

The two laughed together arranging the flowers and leaned back on new shell-pink pillows.

"Do you have something you want to tell me?" Bash asked. "Some secret perhaps? Maybe something... weird?"

"Nothing like that. At least not yet," Snow said, smiling mysteriously. "But I bet you have another question."

"When did you die?" Bash asked.

"Very soon," Snow replied.

"Hey Bash," Edgar said. "That's a big key for a puny girl like you. What's it for?"

"It unlocks things," Bash replied sarcastically.

"It looks like an interesting one," Edgar continued. "So, what does it unlock?"

"The dungeons," Bash replied.

"Great, the dungeons of Beedy Hall. Can I go with you? I'd like to see more of this place or are you going to sing to your flowers again? Is that where you keep the ghost?"

"Aren't you late for stupid git class?" Bash said, sidling past, hoping her stare would turn the little maggot to stone.

Edgar watched her take the back stairs and waited to the count of ten before he followed her.

The tasseled key hung from the keyhole of an open blue door.

"Where are you? Bash called out from inside. "Are you here? Snow? I need to talk with you. Hey Unicorn. Where's your mum? Nice kitty kitty."

Edgar wished he'd brought his blue sweater. The hallway was bitterly cold after the hot afternoon.

Back in the classroom, a familiar blue tassel protruded from a drawer, eyed by Edgar for an hour.

Rupert put his head in the door. You two are wanted downstairs," he said to the twins, ignoring Edgar completely.

"What have you done now? Bash accused Kit.

"Nothing much. How about you?" Kit replied.

"Mum said she wanted us to go to the shops this afternoon. I think it's another one of her lists," Bash groaned.

"I think it's something she wants to say without Tweedledee hearing," Kit whispered, motioning to Edgar who was chewing his pen and gaping moronically into space.

"Better than being stopped up in here *with* him," Bash whispered back, a little more loudly.

"Come on let's find out what she wants," Kit said. She's making cinnamon buns this morning. I could eat a couple of those right now. I'm starving hungry."

It was easy to take the key and slip up the stairs. Mr. Tweedy was getting impatient that there'd been nothing interesting to report lately, and Edgar had his eye on a new computer game. Surely a mysterious key and a locked door would be worth a new computer game.

Inside the room it was very white and cold, and it took Edgar a moment to adjust to the brightness. He heard a cat hiss from the corner long before he saw it.

A young girl sat on the bed holding a white cat that was clearly not happy at his intrusion.

"*Er...* hello. Sorry wrong door," Edgar managed to get out.

Snow looked alarmed. "You're not supposed to be up here," she said in a small voice. "Who are you?" she asked, before turning quite transparent.

The key was still in Edgar's pocket when the twins returned.

"Afraid you'll be on your own for a bit," Kit announced as he tidied away his books. "Don't touch anything. We have to go out."

"You ought to stay home if you've got a cold," Bash said disapprovingly after Edgar's third sneeze.

Edgar primed his cell phone to camera mode and crept nervously up the stairs to the third floor.

"Not to worry," he called out feebly as he approached the blue door. "It's only me again. Bash said I was to come and tell you she's going to be late. She had to go to the shops. You won't mind if I take a couple of pictures will you?"

Edgar checked his phone and scanned the only shot he'd managed to take. It was quite blurry as he'd sneezed when he pressed the button, but the newspaper wouldn't mind. All snapshots of ghosts looked fuzzy, and the outline of a girl holding a cat was still discernible.

Edgar was staring out of the library window with a strange smile on his face when Mrs. S hustled back in the room.

She made an exaggerated noise thumping a large book on the table opposite him to get his attention. "Sorry to be so long. Let's see how you've done, shall we?

241

Edgar startled and tried to cover his blank sheet of paper with his white sleeve. "I...*er*...I need more time," he said. "I think I have that writer's block thing."

A quizzical look came over Mrs. S's exasperated face. "Edgar? Weren't you wearing a blue sweater when you arrived this morning?" she said.

The library was too angry to laugh. Its leather chairs shuffled themselves sideways a little, and the ticking of its clock quickened, sounding twice as loud. For years it had heard the nannies of Bede Hall's children tell their charges to be seen and not heard so as not to disturb the grownups social gatherings.

It was a silly thing to tell a child, it thought. Children were happiest when they ran through the upstairs halls and played noisy games in the nursery and shrieked in the garden.

Bede Hall felt complete with such sounds of lively energy echoing down the stairs. In fact, it was this spontaneous childish energy that made a structure of cold bricks a home, it thought. Shushing the children destroyed its sense of fun. And now this 'Edgar thing' had upset the little child it had protected for so long.

The August Girl had been so light and happy drifting about downstairs. Her cat, Unicorn, had picked the carpet on the grand staircase as soon as they were free to roam again, and it hadn't been bothered at all. In fact it felt rather exhilarating to be scratched, and it was thrilled to have the loneliest room in Bede Hall joining the others again.

It could feel the warmth of the sun streaming through the windows, painting its walls yellow, and was proud to stand against the latest elements of 'rain and snow,' keeping its family cozy.

Judging by the words the boy spoke into the small chirping box he carried, he wasn't going to be silent or remain in the shadows. Bede Hall sent a message to Pigeon.

Pigeon stirred on his kitchen perch and began reciting the some of Edgar's words: *"pick me up...pictures... pictures...press people... it's me dad...right away...please."*

Bede Hall apologized to Snow as she cried, but with the same excuses old houses usually give.

"Age sometimes befoggles my windows," it said, *"my main staircase aches a treat in the mornings, and mice are nibbling my electric nerves to shreds, so I can be forgiven if I'm a smidgeon forgetful in the afternoons. I over-think sometimes. In this case, perhaps I under-thinked."*

"I think you don't care. Friends who say they care, lie," Snow said. "You told me you would take care of me. You promised only animals and people you approved of would be able to see me."

"Well, true, I did say that, but I have my reasons you see. Life isn't a straight line. It's chess really. I was... under-thinking several moves ahead."

Snow remained huddled in a distraught ball.

Bede Hall tried to explain. *"I'm most frightfully sorry that you were ruffled, I truly am. That bully required a severe ruffling,"* it creaked. *"I pride myself on being a safe haven for those who respect magic and private property."*

Snow sniffled. "You promised to be my guardian."

"You and I have always been friends," the Hall cooed. *"I befuddled that brat's camera, so no picture of you exists."*

Snow's eyes were red with sorrow. "But I thought my key would be safe."

"I tried to tell Miss Bathsheba to shut that drawer, but she didn't hear me, and please be reassured that your situation is being handled discreetly with the help of several of my"... the Hall creaked again, *"... associates. All in good time. Remember that, my dear. All in good time. I said I would help you this year, and I keep my promises."*

"Promises promises," mumbled Snow. "My father promised he would be right back."

Snow tried to stamp her foot the way Rain had shown her.

"You can stamp your little foot all you like, miss, I've seen it before with Miss Beryl. I will be more careful, but speaking of promises; I promise that Master Edgar Tweedy will rue the day he messed with Bede Hall."

But later, upstairs, while the house slept, Unicorn allowed Snow to squeeze him more tightly than he normally liked as the house shushed them, kindly. *"I'll send Rain,"* it comforted. *"Parks will know what to do."*

Snow's form fluttered like a butterfly's wings as a sudden shower tapped a soothing rhythm against her window.

CHAPTER FORTY-NINE
Doctor's Orders

The sign read: Dr. Peregrine Brooks – psychiatry M.D. in black letters outlined in gold. Underneath it was a brass door knocker shaped like King Tut's famous death mask shining out from a bright red door.

The door opened after several loud raps by a sprightly looking man with a cheery smile. He had a full mane of white hair and a flowing moustache, and he looked very elegant in his white shirt and red tie and a grey tweed jacket which had leather patches on the elbows. Every inch a gentleman. The wire-rimmed spectacles he wore gave him the air of a scholar... which, as Kit well knew, was exactly what he was.

"Sorry," Kit said. "Were you just going out?"

"No no no. Come in."

" I assumed... your clothes... you look as if ..."

"This is my uniform," Dr. Brooks said, with mock formality, extending his hand. "Peregrine Brooks. And you are?" he asked, pretending not to recognize Kit.

"Kit... *er*... Christopher Stratford-Smyth. My Nan said I should find you if I ever needed to talk to someone who wouldn't think I was crazy. She said you could heal the soul."

Dr. Brooks face went from cheery to eager anticipation.

"Kit! Well I never. I didn't recognize you. Well, you'd better come in, then," he said, opening the door wide. "How very exciting. I haven't had one of *those* conversations in quite some time. Bit of a tall order, that soul bit, but I do my best. I wondered when we would meet again."

"I didn't think you'd remember me," Kit said nervously.

"You look so different. Very grownup from the time I last saw you, that's all," the doctor replied affably.

Kit had never been inside Dr. Brooks' home and he gingerly stepped into an enormous entrance hall with a steep staircase carpeted in the most beautiful pattern he'd ever seen. The second thing he noticed was the hint of gold that glinted everywhere from several objects and gilt picture frames.

A pair of obelisks stood either side of the bottom step and the finial on the stair post was a crystal pyramid. In the corner stood a hallstand, for hats and coats and umbrellas. A selection of walking sticks with animal heads for handles protruded from it like a bouquet.

Each handle was an Egyptian god that Kit recognized: the falcon; Horus, the ibis; Thoth, the lioness; Sekhmet, the jackal; Anubis, and the cat goddess, Bast.

The overall impression of the hall reminded Kit of something he couldn't quite place.

Dr. Brooks stood aside, and revealed a sleek statue of Anubis that stood on a round table in the center of the entrance floor. It was the size of a real dog, crouched on its haunches like a sphinx with its long thin legs stretched out in front.

The jackal god was painted black with gold on the inside of its alert ears, and it wore a real gold metal collar around its neck.

Kit couldn't resist running his hand over its back.

"I expect you know this chap," Dr. Brooks said, patting the jackal's head with affection. "Good old Anubis. Always the guardian, eh?"

"He's my favorite Egyptian animal," Kit said, and then he remembered something he'd read about the archaeologist, Howard Carter's words, when he broke through the sealed door and gazed into King Tut's tomb.

His first impression had been the hint of gold as his eyes adjusted to the darkness. When asked what he saw he had answered, "Things...wonderful things."

"Dr. Brooks, you must be an Egyptologist," Kit said, grinning.

"Guilty as charged, lad," the doctor replied. "Please call me Peregrine. All my friends do."

The narrow hallway that led to a square of amber light, reminded Kit of the classic tunnel entrance to an underground tomb. It was richly lined with paintings of the pyramids and the sphinx, and temples with colorful columns, and its long turquoise strip of carpet had a border design of alternating lotus and papyrus flowers.

The square light turned out to be a cheery parlour that continued the Egyptian motif, but had an additional modern touch from its pair of enormous black leather man-eating armchairs and a plain ebony coffee table that were arranged comfortably in front of a sleek, glass-enclosed fireplace. A large vase of white carnations filled another corner.

A brass box in the shape of a scarab graced the center of the table, and in a far corner was a replica of King Tut's golden throne-chair, painted with scenes of him hunting hippopotamus picked out in red and turquoise details. Kit noticed someone had carved the initials PB into its seat.

Kit sank into one of the upholstered chairs, feeling right at home, noticing the handle on its side, which meant if he were to become even more relaxed, he would be able to recline.

Not having reached that degree of familiarity, Kit nestled back against the plump cushions and waited, but his nervousness returned slightly as he remembered his mission. He steeled himself and shrugged it off. A professional scientist has to be fearless, he thought to himself.

England felt very far away, even though he could see green grass and a profusion of flowerbeds through the bay window.

"You must love Egypt," Kit commented, all nice and relaxed.

"It's in my blood," the doctor admitted wistfully.

"Mine too."

"A good beginning for a renewed friendship then, don't you think?" Dr. Brooks said, smiling, but he looked away and took a long, sad, sigh before he returned to his hospitable self.

"I was about to put the kettle on, so I'll rustle us up a bit of tea, shall I? Sit here and enjoy the art. Have a bit of a wander if you like... won't be long," and with that he disappeared through another door hidden at first by a papyrus screen.

Kit was left alone, and taking the doctor at his word, walked over to the books that lined the walls. One shelf was dedicated to art and history and another was all about meditation and astrology, similar if not identical, to the books Lady Nan had in her bedroom. The ones she had once angrily called 'a load of New-Age nonsense' in a fit of pique.

Another section was all science, and yet another, Kit was pleased to note, was about ghosts and the paranormal. Lady Nan had been right when she'd said the doctor was interested in many things.

The clatter of a tea tray loaded with china cups and plates announced the return of the doctor, and Kit realized, he was very hungry, now that he was no longer nervous.

"There's a good fellow," Dr. Brooks began. "Could you move that box to make room for this lot. I've got a sponge cake coming out next and some sandwiches."

"Have you ever been to Egypt?" Kit asked moments later, between delicious bites of jam sponge.

"In a manner of speaking," Dr. Brooks replied, dreamily.

"Do you mean armchair travel? You know, where the imagination makes it so real it's like being there? I do that all the time," Kit admitted.

"*Er* yes... that too," the doctor replied. "No bags to get lost, eh? And no jet lag or silly time zones," he chuckled.

The room grew quiet and Dr. Brooks looked thoughtfully into his empty cup, turning it as if he could see his future there in the tealeaves.

"Funny you should mention time zones," Kit began, awkwardly.

"I expect you didn't come to talk to me about Egypt," Dr. Brooks smiled. "Where is that crazy conversation you promised me?"

Kit's nervousness returned and he suddenly felt uncomfortably hot.

"It's all right lad, you won't say anything to shock me."

"I came to ask, well discuss really, what you know about temporal fluctuations in the general fabric of history," Kit said, as if he were apologizing.

Dr. Brooks nodded. "You mean time-travel," he announced without a trace of surprise.

"And ghosts," Kit blurted loudly, shocking himself.

"Ah... those," Dr. Brooks said. "That's rather what I expected."

"You expected?" Kit said, open-mouthed. "You expected a stranger to walk in wanting to discuss time-travel and ghosts?"

"You're no stranger. You're just too young to remember the one or two times we met, and Bede Hall certainly isn't a stranger to me, although it's a strange place, I admit, but I knew your Grandmother Beryl and her brother for a very long time. We were a team you might say. Those were the happiest years of our lives... well, mine at least, but I think perhaps all three of us. Ben and I were best friends and ... well, your Nan was my..." his voice trailed off. "We were all very close indeed."

"I know it sounds like those two things aren't related," Kit started to explain.

"So then, is the Winter Room acting up again?" Dr. Brooks interrupted. "It's a time portal you know. I take it you've met Snow?"

Kit was stunned, but he took a deep breath and continued as if it were the most ordinary of conversations. "Ever since I met her, I've been having dreams that feel real. I mean as real as you and I sitting here."

"They're likely going to get even more intense. That is, if you want them to. I expect you want to know where your father is, don't you?"

Dr. Brooks words were matter-of-fact statements rather than questions.

"Can I do that?" Kit stammered excitedly. "Do you think he's still alive?"

"I'd say your chances are excellent. The thing is this... with time travel, no-one ever dies.

Kit gasped. "Of course. That makes sense."

"I've been observing you for a while now, and you my lad, are sensitive to suggestions, always were, which means you're a good subject for hypnosis. I have studied it a long time."

Kit's lips became dry. His father was still alive... somewhere in time when death was a future event.

"You needn't worry. I've not been playing mind games with you... although that's fairly easy to do, and I'm not going to hypnotize you, either. I would never do that without a person's permission. I'm talking about self-hypnosis. I think you should give it a try. It's visualization on a grand scale, but it's a great responsibility; not a game."

A rather austere sounding chime boomed into the silence and made Kit jump.

"You see?" Dr. Brooks said. "Even my grandfather clock agrees with me."

"My grandmother would as well," Kit said. "She's... well..."

"Eccentric?" finished the doctor. "Extremely psychic. Sorry, please go on."

Kit nodded sheepishly. "She's still on top of most things," he added to be fair.

Dr. Brooks opened the glass front of the six-foot tall clock, made a slight adjustment to the hour hand, and settled the quivering pendulum. "I like to keep the correct time," he said with a wink. "Now this *is* interesting. You'd better go first."

"Lady N... I mean my grandmother, says dreams are a natural form of time-travel. She says old people slip off the time-track all the time, just from boredom. Their minds wander off for entertainment, and that dwelling in the past is what doctors call dementia."

"She's right in a way. It *can* be that, although dementia is a more serious condition when people get stuck in the past and can't get back, as opposed say, to a few pleasant hours casually daydreaming about one's past life."

The doctor coughed, suddenly at odds, "I mean their good old days," he corrected. "Your grandmother has memories well-worth visiting. Even, I daresay, the painful ones."

"She does look pretty sad sometimes," Kit offered. "She spends hours gazing into a snow globe that she calls her crystal ball. I think she wants my mother to think she's out of her mind, but I don't know why."

"If someone does that playfully, long enough, they can permanently lose their grip on reality. I hope your Lady Nan has....*er*... help...."

"My sister, Bash, is her best friend. They do things together all the time, and Bash is writing down all her stories."

"Fuel for many more fascinating conversations to be sure," Dr. Brooks replied with a shrug.

Kit shrugged too. "Define interesting."

"Well," the doctor exclaimed, clapping his hands and rubbing them together. "Let's get down to business shall we? You're going to have to sit cross-legged on the floor for this. I shall instruct only. I only meditate in a chair these days. My bones won't let me...."

The doctor's face brightened with an idea.

"Wait, you can use the old throne here. It's got the perfect ambiance you'll need to focus. Ambiance means..."

"Oh, I know what it means, all right," Kit said laughing. "My sister is quite keen on that word. What I don't know, is why I need it to focus."

"You're going to Egypt, my boy, that's why," Dr. Brooks said.

CHAPTER FIFTY

Sweet Magic

Bash took another sip of lavender juice and tried to describe it.

"What else is in this?" she asked Charlotte, "Vanilla?"

"Magic," Charlotte answered, laughing.

"It tastes sweet. You should make lavender syrup," Bash suggested.

"I do," Charlotte said, "and I sell it at the post office along with my lavender jam and lavender ice-cream."

"*Mmmmn.* Lavender pancakes," Bash mused.

"And bubble bath," Charlotte added. "Lavender is good for headaches, healing cuts, and helping a person to sleep too. I sell those products at Mr. Leoni's."

"And fresh lavender and sachets at the florist shop. It must be magic then," Bash agreed. "You have quite the lavender industry here."

"Thanks to Bede Hall, it will be even better," Charlotte said. "Parks can do wonders with plants... the soil is special there, and you're my business partner."

Bash thought she misheard Charlotte say 'the soul is special there' and thought how apropos it was.

Nimue is going to take you home now," Charlotte said. "Are you sure you can walk? Magic can make a person feel wobbly."

"One could say pixilated," Nimue piped up, suddenly appearing on Charlotte's shoulder.

CHAPTER FIFTY-ONE
Out of this World

Kit gathered up the tea things and dragged the table to the corner so there was room for the golden chair, while Dr. Brooks put on a tape of soft instrumental music.

"This sort of music will create the right mood," he said. "I want you to focus on an inner picture of a candle. Hold it in your mind till you really see it, and then let your thoughts become the smoke rising from its flame. But first, let me explain. Meditation is a gateway. It leads to something we coined, in my day, as oobies. It stands for the letters O-O-B-E.

"It's getting a little weird, doctor," Kit said.

"It's not weird at all. It's just an acronym for out-of-body-experience,"

"Yeah, like that's not weird," Kit said under his breath.

"It's more formally known as Astral Projection. Your physical body stays here," Dr. Brooks said indicating the chair, "but your transparent body, referred to as your soul, travels anywhere time and space draws it. The ancient Egyptians called it a person's 'Ka.'

"I can time-travel?" Kit grinned.

"You can fly!" came the reply.

"It was the sixties," Dr. Brooks began, and he spoke as if reciting a beloved fairy tale.

"I was twenty-nine or so. It was a time when ancient belief systems were reborn into fanciful dreams. It was all very exciting and futuristic, when really it was old-stuff made into a philosophy my generation liked to think of as new-stuff... We called it the New-Age. It was made up of ideas which made the afterlife more entertaining than *dead-end* life."

"So... lies then?" Kit interjected.

"So... *truths* about immortality lost *inside* lies, more like. It was a circus. The only good thing about it was the way we began to listen to our bodies and thought of it as connected to the mind. There were magic medicine men and shamans and self-appointed teachers, so-called gurus, who lorded it high above everyone else, sometimes quite literally, in the Himalayas. They were said to be the keepers of the secrets of life, the way old Anubis guards the entrance to a pharaoh's tomb. Complete rubbish of course. Not Anubis. I meant the gurus.

"Well, meditation and visualization spawned a craze for 'far-memory' experiences and the meanings of dreams, and that in turn sparked theories of reincarnation and past lives and karma and soul mates."

"What's karma?"

"Karma is payback for good or bad deeds when you come back to earth as another person," Dr. Brooks said offhandedly.

"Like the saying, what goes around comes around," Kit said.

"Precisely. Now, you have to appreciate that these things were extremely inspiring. We didn't have the special-effects movies you have today.

"The trouble was, common sense got trampled on the way to the 'mountain top' so to speak, and genuine science separated itself from the pseudo-sciences, like astrology with its sun signs and numerology and reading tea leaves and aliens from outer space. They were fads that encouraged the exploration of who we used to be, and of course, charlatans were more than happy to oblige us, making up the most inventively outrageous stories. I'm afraid we rather bought them all, hook, line and sinker, at first.

"But psychiatrists had been regressing hypnotized patients for years by the sixties, in order to help them recall repressed memories too painful to remember, which had made them ill."

"Do you mean reincarnation?"

"I mean past-life regression," Dr. Brooks corrected. "Hence all of this," he spread his arms to encompass the room. "Why else would a normal rational person collect all this?"

"Lots of people collect things."

"Personal memorabilia is one thing, an obsessive compulsion for all things Egyptian is something else. Ben got me hooked after Beryl got *him* hooked. Ben passed it on to me like flu. I'm afraid it's quite terminal."

"You think you lived back then? You think there's a soul?"

"Christopher. I'm a doctor – a serious doctor, and I've seen patients die and watched vaporous mists rise from their bodies, and I've heard their stories and dreams under hypnosis..." he trailed off. "The evidence is too great not to... accept... things," he finished. "Wonderful things."

The doctor's last two words made Kit shiver.

"It was a gradual awakening. I'm a logical man, not given to hysteria," Dr. Brooks said. "Not one for science-fiction. But science *fact-ion*? That's a different, and not so pretty, kettle of fish."

Dr. Brooks walked to a bookcase and extracted a worn paperback from the top shelf and handed it to Kit.

"Anyway," he continued. "It was this 'new wave' of thinking which made me want to be a doctor, and another... incident that I won't go on about. So I studied the work of the man who wrote that book."

Kit read the title 'The Interpretation of Dreams' and the author's name, Dr. Carl Jung, that Dr. Brooks pronounced as Carl *Young*.

"That's kind of a pun, considering we've been discussing being old or young and the different ways of dreaming, and different ages," Kit interjected.

"Very good young man," that's using your right brain." Dr. Brooks complimented.

"My what?"

"The right side of one's brain is the creative side – the imagination and one's artistic self. The left side is reason. We scientists use both, equally. That is, if we're any good."

Kit sat riveted by so much information.

"As you may imagine, the floodgates of history were completely blown away," the doctor continued. "The crazies, and yes there are always crazies, well, they were so off-the-wall that they were able to push *pseudo*-science into the realm of *silly*-science."

"You don't seem that old to me," Kit said.

"My boy, you're only as young as you dream," Dr. Brooks said.

Kit and Dr. Brooks took a pleasant break in the garden to relax before the demonstration with the chair. "My sister...." Kit began.

"Your twin," the doctor corrected.

"Sorry, I forgot that you know our family. My twin sister charms plants. Her friend Charlotte has her talking to them, a bit like you just described. 'Tuning in,' she calls it, and Bash has had some astonishing results. Her lavender grows twice as fast as it should... and its scent is ten times stronger. Miss Findhorn, the florist can't get enough of it. It sells *that* fast. Bash is with her right now."

"Charlotte is a great friend of mine," Dr. Brooks said. "Her methods are sound, but she can get carried away. I hope your sister is strong-willed."

"Oh," Kit said, slightly taken aback. "Well, they do seem to be working, and Bash has a mind of her own," Kit said.

"Well, I'm glad to hear it. You must bring Bash to see me. I would love to see you two together. Twins are a special study all by themselves. Do you read each other's minds?"

"Something like that," Kit nodded. "If we physically put our foreheads together, we can sometimes see the same things. The old Vulcan mind-meld thing. You know, from 'Star Trek.'... dream me up Scotty," Kit added, weakly, trying to defuse the tension he felt returning. "I think I ought to tell you a secret," he finally blurted, slightly pink about the ears from his bad joke.

Dr. Brooks paused and picked two white carnations from the vase. He placed one in his buttonhole and sniffed the other, inhaling deeply till a smile spread over his face.

"I sometimes have the same dream as my sister," Kit said earnestly, "but I don't often tell her. She is very... sensitive, easily upset, but more than that, she tells Lady Nan everything."

Dr. Brooks extracted a tall thin bud vase from cupboard and

filled it with water for the second carnation. He sniffed it again and closed his eyes.

"Heavenly," he said. "And now back to business."

The doctor demonstrated the correct hand position for meditation, placing his thumb and index fingers together, resting both hands in his lap.

"This is called a mudra," he said. It forms a natural circuit from the brain to your feet and hence the earth. Sit up straight. Align your posture to the back of the chair and plant your feet firmly on the floor. This is literally, grounding one's energy. And it's how the brain receives intuitive messages. It can 'hear' the subtle vibrations of the universe and interpret them. Often hours later, before or during the first stages of sleep.

"If you don't fight it, there are two paranormal events that will occur: the first is that you will feel a pleasant tingling in your chest and feel like an inflated balloon. If that happens, it's important not to panic. Rising off the ground is quite safe, so you can 'go with it.' It's like flying. More like being weightless in space. A disquieting sensation at first, I grant you, but once you do it a few times, it's something magical that you'll actually look forward to. You'll have to trust me on that.

"The other, is that you will simply feel rested and have a lucid dream later during a natural sleep cycle. It won't, in fact, be sleep; it's the lucid state *inside* sleep. That means a dream where you realize you're dreaming, yet stay asleep. A real scientist's dream.

"Both phenomena are places where it's important to push old boundaries and discover the truth."

Kit scribbled everything in his notebook and was relieved when Dr. Brooks took another book from a shelf titled: 'Astral Projection – a scientific study' and handed it to him.

"Read this. It will give you the confidence to believe in the power of your mind. There are energies we haven't begun to explain. Not to mention try to control, but you're Lady Nan's grandson. It's in your blood."

257

Kit felt proud to be included in what felt like an exclusive club.

"Do you have a place where it's quiet with no telephones and you can be left alone? It's very important to separate yourself as if you were part of an experiment, which of course you will be."

"I have my own tower. It's behind the stables. Lady Nan gave it to me for my birthday."

"I know it well," Dr. Brook said. "I couldn't think of a better place."

Now that the 'business' was out of the way, Dr. Brooks turned Kit's attention to the empty chair. He turned it around where there was a scene, supposedly of King Tut, the boy king, and his wife, who was applying precious oil to his skin.

"My sister used to say it was suntan lotion when she was small," Kit laughed. "We were introduced to Egypt early. Books on Egypt were bedtime stories as often as 'Winnie the Pooh.'"

Dr. Brooks grinned. "I remember how 'Winnie the Pooh' was your grandmother's favorite book even as an adult. She used to read it... consult it as a sort of oracle."

"Yeah, she does that a lot," Kit said uncomfortably.

To cover his embarrassment, Kit pointed to the red-skinned queen on the chair. "I know her," he blurted out.

"You What!"

"I mean, I know who she *is*," Kit corrected, startled from Dr. Brooks shocked expression. "That's Ankhesenamun."

Dr. Brooks looked relieved. He sighed once and pointed to the king beside the queen "This fine fellow is the pharaoh Smenkhkare, the king your father was searching for. He's easily confused with his brother Tutankhamen. As you see, the ancient Egyptians always depicted a royal person with red skin."

"No, not *searching*, he *found* him. My dad *found* Smenkhare. He was returning to his tomb when he was... when he... when he disappeared."

Dr. Brooks looked stunned. "Cornelius *found* him? Smenkhkare has been found?"

"Yes sir. I've seen pictures of artifacts from his burial chamber. Are you feeling all right? You don't look well."

Doctor Brooks smiled broadly, "I assure you I'm quite well. Just speechless. You see, I feel I *knew* him," he finished.

"And you thought I couldn't say anything that would surprise you," Kit laughed.

"That's the happiest part of being a scientist," Dr. Brooks replied. "You wait and see, but fair warning, sometimes you discover things you wish you never knew."

Dr. Peregrine Brooks was insistent when Kit protested his generosity.

"I want you to have this chair. I insist you have it. Keep it in your tower. It can be delivered without too much fuss if your brother helps."

"Not Boss, I mean Rupert. Sorry, it's quite the opposite. He's the absolutely last person in the family to be supportive of a thing like this. You have to trust me on this one. We call him 'Boss' for a reason. Bash and I, and Lady Nan have kept him and Mum in the dark about Snow. He thinks the ghost is a joke. Mum just worries Lady Nan is... well, bonkers, not to put too fine a point on it."

Kit didn't like the way Dr. Brooks suddenly scowled.

An invisible storm swirled through the room, knocking over lamps and smashing china cups while all the time Kit could see them quite undamaged and innocent.

"Young man," Dr. Brooks said, drawing himself up to his full height. "I won't allow anyone to talk about Beryl in that way. Not even her daughter and certainly not you."

Kit stuttered an apology. "I... I wasn't thinking," he said, looking for a place to hide. Perhaps even run under the door and escape into the garden where he could surely now fit under the flowers being shorter than they were.

"No indeed. You were not," the doctor agreed. "And if nothing else, a scientist should always think before he blurts out an unscientific term like, 'bonkers.'"

259

Dr. Brooks looked ruffled, like Pigeon when he was about to go into one of his 'pooh tirades.'

"And... and I'd like to thank you again... you know... for the chair," Kit stuttered, trying to regain his composure. "I'll treasure it."

Dr. Brooks face relaxed. "No need to go panic, son," he said. "It was only a slip of the tongue. Rather Freudian that. And Sigmund Freud was ... well, to be honest... bonkers. Barking actually," he added chuckling. "See? It's easily done. And easily forgotten. A little time-out and here we are back again. I believe you were about to tell me why your brother Rupert is called Boss."

"Cool," Kit said. "The way you did that. Talking until you were, well, here."

"That's something you'll learn how to do. Gets one out of a lot of sticky corners. Damned useful. It's called dancing on one's feet."

"We were actually suspended in time," Kit said dumbfounded. His words came slow and subdued... a calm: "wow... perfect... thanks."

The room wanted to absorb the recent negative energy, and Kit and Dr. Brooks had the good sense to let it do its work. For a moment they both looked as if they were meditating, which they were. Just standing still with their hands loose at their sides. Not looking at each other. Eyes inward, waiting for a centered feeling to mutually release them.

The vibrations were quiet. Kit's head felt like a blown egg. He started to breathe and drifted calmly into a gentle conversation towards a sane goodbye. "So, where did you get all this other amaz-ing stuff?" he asked casually, picking up his coat. "There aren't any Egyptian shops in Bede, that's for sure."

"Desirable collectibles tend to find their *owners*," Dr. Brook said. "Scientist-to-scientist," he went on, adopting a 'confidentially between you and me tone,' "Serendipity is around us all the time. We just don't care to acknowledge it."

Dr. Brooks answered Kit's vacant expression with an explanation.

"Serendipity is more positive than synchronicity... it means perfect timing for something extraordinarily splendid."

Dr. Brooks beamed at Kit as he said goodbye.

"Come back very soon and tell me how you got on... and please give my fondest regards to your grandmother and sister. Your mother won't mind if she knows we've met either. I'll have the chair sent over tomorrow."

He paused.

"I don't suppose there's a chance I could see some of those pictures of Smenkhkare's things, could I?" he asked shyly.

"That might be a bit of a problem," Kit admitted sadly. "There were no prints made, and Dad never posted them on his website because they weren't official yet."

The doctor tried to hide his disappointment. "Wait a minute," he said in a rush. "I'll be right back."

And off he scuttled, returning with the carnation.

"Please give this to your lovely sane grandmother with my most sincere compliments," he said with a wink.

It was rather awkward, but Kit managed to fit the narrow vase in his backpack with the flower projecting jauntily from the zipper. It was heavier for the additional books, so Dr. Brooks helped him, patting him on the back to signal when it was secure.

After the door closed, Kit stared at it for a while. The brass head of King Tut stared back. He reached up and touched it lightly.

"Serendipity," he murmured to himself.

Thankfully he had jotted the word in his notebook with the pyramids on the front. He would astound Bash later with a spectacular word of his own.

Kit walked on air to his red bicycle that now seemed to glow, unworldly, out of time against the pulsating green of Dr. Brooks' hedge, and peddled to Bede Hall not entirely sure if he or the road or the trees were real.

CHAPTER FIFTY-TWO

Purple Rules

It was lovely and cool in the gazebo at sunset, when Kit and Bash had their meeting. Bash still had the scent of lavender clinging to her skin. She looked as if she was in a trance, but that's because she was.

"I've had the most glorious day," she said in a faraway voice. "This lavender therapy thing is wild. My food tastes of it. I'm transported. If I look at the garden I'm going to see fairies or something."

Bash waggled two fingers in front of Kit's face.

"How many fingers do you see?" she asked giggling.

"Eleven," Kit said. "Have you been drinking?"

"Haven't you heard of drinking in a scent?"

Kit snapped his own fingers under Bash's nose. "Not one that makes you mental."

"Purple catnip," Bash mumbled dreamily. "I feel like a cat. I'm a purple cat."

Dr. Brooks is still sweet on Lady Nan," Kit announced, hoping to break the lavender spell with something more interesting than perfume power.

He repeated himself once more.

Bash's eyes remained unfocused.

"Dr. Brooks?... Lady Nan?... Hello?..." Kit said, drawing his words out slowly.

Bash began to sing: *'lavender blue dilly dilly lavender green.'*... "*mmmn*... don't know the rest. Something about a queen. A fairy queen I think. Charlotte sang it today when we were in her garden looking at... looking at. I don't remember. Did she drive me home? I don't remember getting home."

Kit stared into his sister's eyes and swore they were mauve. It was getting spooky. Bash ogled back at him fuzzily.

"Tipsy through the tulips," she sang through her giggles.

The round open structure of the gazebo had become the best place to talk in private as anyone approaching could be seen a long time before arriving, and Kit wondered if Bash was going to be able to make it back to the house. She looked too sleepy to walk very far.

"When can I meet him?" Bash asked, suddenly perky.

"Who?" Kit said shaking his head. She had gone lavender mad.

"Doctor Purple," Bash said. "Pay attention. You're supposed to be a scientist."

"I don't miss much," he said. "But *you* did today. You should have seen his place."

Bash stared at Kit as if he had just materialized out of thin air. Her eyes sharpened into two round brown discs. "Whose place?"

Alarm bells went off in Kit's head. "Bash tell me what happened!"

"Hey," she said, as casually as if they'd just met in the street. "How was your day?"

"I've been trying to tell you," Kit said, but you've been all *lavendery.*

Clearly, Bash was somewhere other than the gazebo. There was a long silence where neither twin spoke, and then Bash resumed to a normal conversation.

"When did you say?" Bash asked.

"As soon as possible," Kit said.

"Tomorrow then," Bash replied. "After your *throne* gets here. How are you going to explain *that*, by-the-way?"

"I probably won't have to if synchronicity is in play, besides, Mum knows Dr. Brooks very well. He was a friend of Dad's and handing down an Egyptian chair to me isn't out of the question. It's Lady Nan I'm worried about."

"Why? Lady Nan is more open than any of us."

"Because Lady Nan isn't telling us everything, that's why. There's something going on that she and Dr. Brooks know; something that has nothing to do with lost lovey-dovey romance and karma. By-the-way, do you know what serendipity means?"

"What's Karma?" Bash asked.

"I don't suppose you've got any of that lavender stuff left have you?" Kit replied.

Kit faced going to bed with a degree of concern. Although he had yet to perform any of the formal dream experiments, Dr. Brooks had been insistent about the spontaneous power of suggestion, and if nothing else, his head was filled with the most powerful suggestions he'd ever had.

It had been an uplifting afternoon. Kit mulled over all that Dr. Brooks had told him. Especially the scientific data that linked vivid dreams to time-travel and the psychiatrist named Jung, pronounced young, and its reference to youth and old age, a scientist who unlocked the secret meaning of dreams and the word synchronicity.

Kit realized with a physical jolt, that up until a year ago, Lady Nan had been living on Young Street.

Down in the kitchen strains of Pigeon singing wafted its way up the stairs to the library. *"Lavender blue dilly dilly lavender green, I'll be your king dilly dilly you'll be my queen."* Pigeon was mimicking Charlotte Findhorn's voice.

The day the chair was to be delivered, Rupert was being lectured to by Parks 4 and was even more grumpy than usual.

"What are you two up to?" Rupert barked, for no reason other than it wasn't fair the twins were younger and had no responsibilities.

"We just came to tell you that Lady Nan is on the warpath... something about the carnations," Kit said. "She wants you to report upstairs. She's in one of her 'queen' moods.

"*Er...* thanks. Tell her I had to ... go to town," Rupert said, already striding towards his car.

Bash looked for Parks 2 and found him snipping the topiary shaped like a chess piece, queen.

Parks 2 heard her approach and doffed his cap.

'This is what Parks must have looked like not so long ago,' she thought. The family resemblance was striking.

"You know this one's my favorite," Parks 2 said, patting the green shape.

For a moment the sun glanced off the spikes of its crown and reminded her of an Egyptian obelisk.

"I'd like to make a topiary of my own," Bash said. "Just a small one."

"First we need to find you a section of box-hedge and replant it," he said.

"Is that too much work?" Bash asked.

Parks 2 scratched his head and smiled. "Not for me; it's a job for my son and grandson. Between em it could be done. You'll need drawings of your design from several angles. It's a slow process. I'm afraid it takes years of pruning to tame it."

"I plan to be here a long time," Bash said. "I want to make a snow globe."

CHAPTER FIFTY-THREE

Captain's Law

Lady Nan woke from a dream where she'd been back in the nursing home – the place where hope was still terribly muddled with memories and the world had lost all its color.

The old hospital room had still been the same – full of dark shadows, and the hands of the clock had gyrated wildly.

A large calendar that filled an entire wall, had mocked her, choked with sinister red numbers circled with acid yellow sparks flashing like angry halos.

Lady Nan lay awake for half an hour recalling the parade of women in her dream, all dressed in white, who constantly ignored her, and how she had become increasingly insistent and finally so agitated that a doctor administered medicine to calm her.

When Bash brought Lady Nan's morning tea, she found her grandmother searching her snow globe, more flustered than she had ever seen her.

"The little house is trying to tell me something," Lady Nan cried. "Quick! we have to write down a dream. Oh Bash! Get our book. Please hurry!"

Lady Nan was insistent that her nursing-home days had returned to be relived for a reason. "Lucid dreams always mean something," she said, in some agitation.

Those two years had been when time had sped up, or gone backwards and stopped, and then just as erratically jumped forward again, as life failed to repair the rift that had been widening for years, and she had tried in vain to piece the good parts of her life back together like a new quilt made from old squares.

Bash found a fresh page, patted her grandmother's hand reassuringly and indicated she was ready.

"Okay how do you spell loo... something?" she asked, her pen poised.

"Lucid," Lady Nan repeated. "l-u-c-i-d," she spelled. "Have you ever had a dream where you woke up inside it and knew you were dreaming?"

Bash shuddered, remembering her skeleton dream, and nodded that she had.

"Well, that's a *lucid* dream. Lucid means clear-headed thinking. Which is what I'm doing now. My dream was symbolic. Lucid ones always are. Perry... Dr. Brooks... will know what it means."

With that, Lady Nan closed her eyes and forced her dream to return, determined to capture it while she could still remember.

"I was back in my old room... the one at the 'home,' and I woke up – a dream within a dream, as I said. I had fallen out of bed. The walls of the room disappeared and I stood up with the urge to run for my life.

"I knew I was running to Bede Hall because I heard it calling. It was in distress. I tried to send it a message that I was coming as fast as I could, but no words would come out of my mouth.

"It was winter and I was still wearing my hospital gown, and barefoot, but the snow underfoot was warm as sand. It felt like wool, and I ran until I bumped into a glass window the size of a wall. It felt cold and smooth and I tried to see out, but it was too dark.

"I gave up and lay down on my back in the fallen snow, and looked up at the night sky where white flecks floated like stars. I felt contained, safe for the first time in ages. I'd managed to escape my stupid prodding doctors, and suddenly all I wanted to do was sleep. I curled up into a ball and warm snowflakes swirled down covering me like a blanket.

"I sank into a dream where I felt a circle of people crowding around me. One of them shook me by the shoulders and told me to stay awake. They kept asking me to open my eyes.

"I felt dizzy and I must have floated out of my body because the ground disappeared and I felt like a bubble – deliciously light and suddenly carefree. I was lifted into a white vortex that swirled around me in a whiteout blizzard. I felt as if I was inside a whirlpool, but it was so very loving and I felt wonderfully happy.

"The tornado subsided and I found myself hovering over my body. I could see it on the ground far below me lying on a white sheet half-covered in snow.

"I could feel a ceiling pressing against my back so I knew I was back in a room and a gentle voice encouraged me to return to my body, but I didn't want to go.

"I was delightfully buoyant – underwater... warm water. I felt like a baby inside its mother's womb.

"From that height I looked for Bede Hall, but all I could see was a tiny homestead a short distance away, and suddenly I was fully-conscious, back inside my body, wading towards it through deep, dry, snow. Walking waist-deep and swimming at the same time with snowflakes in my face and hair.

"I made it to the door, but it wouldn't open. And that's when everything turned nightmarish. It wasn't a real house because the door... the door was only painted on!

"I panicked, searching for a way in because someone I loved was inside calling me. I ran around it, frantically scratching at each window, but they were the same as the door. Painted. My fingers had started to bleed and I lay on my back and made an angel in the snow. I was in my body, but I could also see it from above at the same time because I was pleased to see that the tips of the wings I'd made were pink from where my hands had touched the snow.

"I suddenly knew the voice from the house was the ghost of Bede Hall. I remember smiling because I decided to literally, 'give up the ghost' and it was a funny pun. That was the thought I heard.

"I let go of everything: Snow, my little ghost-friend, Bede Hall, Ben, and... everyone. I stopped searching for answers, and stared up at the sky daring death to finally take me, and I closed my eyes waiting for death.

"I felt a pleasant tingling in my spine and watched calmly as a giant's hands reached down towards me... reaching for me... and they scooped me up. Me, my sadness, my broken dreams, the house, and the land, all together. Cupping around us... lifting us to heaven.

"I searched for the face of the giant and saw..."

Lady Nan started to sob gently.

"I saw my own face! My own face was looking down on me, smiling, and I realized something terrifying. Oh Sheba! I was inside my snow globe... and the giant was me!"

Lady Nan finally fell into a restless sleep after Bash calmed her down by agreeing to call Dr. Brooks.

By the time Bash looked in on her a few hours later, Lady Nan was daydreaming out the window.

Bash put her hand on her grandmother's shoulder. "Everything all right now?" she asked. "Feeling better? I typed up the dream. It's all there, on paper, as you wanted."

"I should never have let Ben run off like that," Lady Nan whispered wearily. "And I should have married Pigeon... no, that's silly... another bird... I can't quite remember. Oh dear... I didn't want to forget him," she finished unhappily.

Bash tried some bird names to humor her: "Was it Robin? Was he a cardinal? A turkey perhaps?"

Lady Nan laughed. "Well, the captain *was* a right turkey, but then, I wasn't much better. I went along with everything. Pigeon warned me not to marry him, and the Hall was definitely most put-out about it all, but it was me who walked down that aisle. Mind you, I wouldn't carry the carnations. I couldn't bring myself to do that."

"So you never had a bridal bouquet?" Bash asked.

"Parks handed me a small posy of yellow tea roses at the last minute," Lady Nan said in a daze. "I could always count on him. Thank goodness he'll never leave us."

CHAPTER FIFTY-FOUR

The Bad Old Days

The Captain had died almost four Septembers ago, and Lady Beryl Stratford-Smyth had been so distraught from the resounding consequences, she had to be tranquilized and hospitalized. He had borrowed extensively from the bank using Bede Hall as collateral.

Her doctors had declared her mind had 'snapped,' and Mr. and Mrs. S had told their children that their grandmother would never be the same. They could still visit her, they said, but were forewarned not to expect her to make much sense.

Cornelius and Rayne Stratford-Smyth were left to sort out the financial mess the Captain had made of things.

Bash remembered hearing that the skeleton staff at Bede Hall would have to be given notice, and had wondered what they meant.

For-sale meetings had been hastily arranged, and Lady Nan was sent to a fancy nursing home near her daughter, son-in-law, and grandchildren – 'The Beehive Rest Home' in Withering, Surrey.

Ironically, it was exactly halfway between Bede Hall and Livingston. A symbolic halfway house where one lived in-between worlds with each one fighting for possession until *one* of them *won*.

Bede Hall waited three entire frantic summers while Lady Nan slept through her seventy-first, seventy-second, and seventy-third birthdays in her own fog of despair.

Only Bash had noticed the light returning to her grandmother's eyes from time-to-time that flickered whenever she read to her from her favorite Narnia book – the scenes where Lucy first discovered the frozen wasteland beyond the wardrobe door.

Each time Bash visited the hospital, there was always a fresh vase of white carnations by her bed, and Lady Nan would ask her the date before settling calmly into a, usually bizarre, conversation. The card always read: *as ever – love P.B.*

"You're in there I know you are," Bash had coaxed her bewildered grandmother one particularly rainy afternoon.

Lady Nan had been listening intently to the storm outside.

"I'll just wait here shall I? Why are you trying to fool yourself? There's nothing wrong with you, you know... you're tougher than all of us," Bash had remarked, when the sudden boom of thunder cracked open the door to Lady Nan's mind.

Lady Nan had startled awake, and surprised her granddaughter with a few words of wisdom. "My dear girl, something is about to happen and I can't tell you what because I'm not entirely sure what it will be. You must prepare yourself for magic. I can call it nothing else. Nothing less. After that I will know what to do."

It had been a mysterious thing to tell a ten-year-old girl.

Since it was one of her lucid days, Bash had listened without interrupting and took notes for the biography she wanted to write. Her 'Nan book' was a collection of scrambled stories that Lady Nan told out of sequence.

"I had no brother by the time I married," she said. "I couldn't love anyone, then. Although I had done once, very much. I think I wanted to suffer on purpose.

"The closest blood heir to the Stratford-Smyth line was a distant cousin of mine named Hilton Cadwick, a retired naval officer. My father, wanted us to marry, but Hilton and I never even liked each other. But, it was my duty.

"I couldn't bear to be parted from the house and he wanted to be more important. He loved the class system. Desperate to lord it over others, and Bede Hall offered him the status he craved. He had the money to save it and I couldn't bear to see it falling apart. My father had been close to selling parts of the estate to developers. It was a desperate time. Hilton's money overruled everything, and I was a 'daddy's girl,' so I wanted to please him. Nothing else much mattered.

"So, Hilton and I married to get what each of us wanted the most. It's not the best or the worst of reasons, I suppose. Some marry and fall out of love and live apart, or stay together in a terrible atmosphere of sadness. It's easier when you begin that way; it's impossible to fall out of love if you were never in love in the first place."

"Were you ever in love?" Bash pressed gently.

Lady Nan fidgeted with the long fringe of her shawl. For a moment she had smiled, remembering, but her smile had faded quickly and she had carried on in a matter of fact voice, her face clouded with sadness.

"The day after I was married, Hilton changed; he became a bully. He took being the lord of the manor to heart, and he controlled everything except my Winter Room. He had promised I could have that. As a wedding present, I suppose.

"I used to go there to be by myself. It was my special place to read and ease my headaches when it was baking hot outside. I decorated it with flair. I'd curl up under a fur coat turned inside out and nap. It felt like another world. Like Narnia.

"I made the 'Captain' angry one day when I mentioned the ghost, and that's when he demanded the key. We rowed into the middle of the lake and he threatened to throw it in the water. He made me apologise and to promise never to speak of the ghost again, then he gave orders to the servants that no-one was permitted near the Winter Room. Pigeon told me where he hid the key, later."

Bash had written down a strange word from its sound. "What does Ekle...ecktic mean please?"

"Eclectic means odd... different... special... artistic," Lady Nan replied.

Bash was pleased to know a descriptive new word that meant an extraordinary variety of unusual things. It was her intention to one day create an eclectic garden that would astonish the rest of the world.

Lady Nan abruptly changed her thoughts to the present day.

"My husband was a blockhead!" she declared hotly, and although it pains me to have to say it, your brother Rupert is a chip off the *old* blockhead, and that's the plain truth of it!

272

The Captain burned my diaries, you know," she added dreamily as an afterthought.

"Someday I'll tell you why."

Lady Nan admitted it was wrong to speak ill of the dead, but had also added that she didn't much care. She was angry when she remembered who she was, and where she was, and what had happened to her family home.

The duty nurses never noticed that she was having less-befuddled days when she remembered the blue door and the ghost behind it who relied on her to set her free. To them, she was an old woman in the first stages of dementia and all they could do was calm her when she was distressed.

"Compos mentis," Lady Nan whispered to Bash as if it was their secret.

"Which means?"

"Of sound mind. I'm in my right mind... today I am clear-headed," Lady Nan said. "I want you to remember that."

CHAPTER FIFTY-FIVE

Stalking for Gold

Edgar minus Nipper was only half the problem.

The wood floors creaked underneath their worn carpets. No doubt, had Bash been a fly on the wall, she would have commented the sounds were apropos for a haunted house.

Lady Nan's door was ajar, and Edgar could hear Jack whimpering from within.

The familiar chiding of Bash's voice shushed the agitated dog.

"Jack? What is it boy?" Bash said. "Silly Billy."

The sounds of a spluttering tractor mower followed by an angry tirade of rude words, came from below.

"It's only Boss cursing again," Bash assured the dog. "Silly old chap."

Edgar's ears could only make out every other word from his fingers being in his ears, but distinctly heard the word 'curse,' which made his urge to sneeze even worse.

"Come on up here Jack old thing," Lady Nan said, patting the bed-covers. "There's plenty of room."

Bash sighed and smoothed the quilt.

"Honestly Jack, you *are* spoiled," she chided.

"Dogs hear more than lawnmowers. Cats and dogs have supernatural hearing," Lady Nan announced mysteriously. "Close the door, Sheba dear. Maybe your mother's student is sneaking about again. Rupert caught that dreadful Edgar creature again, wandering around where he shouldn't the other day. Your mother shouldn't leave him alone. There are Egyptian valuables in the library worth their weight in gold."

"Please! Enough about that beastly boy," Bash said. "Tell me more about Uncle Ben," she urged gently. "I need it for my book... I mean *your* book."

"Well, if it's for my story," Lady Nan I'd better spill all the beans hadn't I?"

Lady Nan sighed deeply and began to dictate. "I never told you. Ben and I were twins."

Bash gasped. She gulped and said nothing as if it was a casual thing to have lost a twin. If Kit died she would have never recovered. She listened with more respect to Lady Nan who had glossed over her news on purpose.

"Perry and Ben had been messing about with their collections of treasures, and mummy called Ben with that urgent 'I want something' voice, and the boys ran off to get out of doing whatever it was."

Edgar listened even more carefully, but had to stifle an enormous sneeze after hearing the word, gold. After he wiped his nose on his sleeve, he put the words: curse, Egypt, treasure, gold, and mummy together and ran downstairs. The stairs were remarkably squeak-free as he bounced heavily on each step.

"It was winter," Lady Nan continued. Perry went through the ice. Ben saved him by jumping in after him and pushed him to the surface... but Ben must have died from hypothermia or the exertion. He was never robust but he had *joie de vivre*. That means the joy of life.

Lady Nan shivered and pulled her shawl tighter. "I often think how he suffered. He hated the cold at the best of times, but that icy water. Even ice cubes in a drink remind me. Winter is my least favorite season and Christmas is especially difficult but I had my friend. My little ghost friend.

She paused before adding an afterthought.

"Perry died too, by the way, but he was luckier. He was resuscitated at the scene. He told me how he saw the whole thing floating above his and Ben's bodies. He verified the details later. I think that was made him decide to be a doctor.

"Perry told me that he and Ben had a brief conversation while they were disembodied, and that Ben forgave him... well, what his actual words were 'there's nothing to forgive. It's my time. Tell Beryl to be happy for me.'

"Perry told me Ben was actually quite thrilled to be dead and had assured him everything was as it should be. Ben said his mission was almost over. Now it's mine to keep everything on track."

"Maybe no-one can do that," Bash said soothingly, hugging Lady Nan.

Lady Nan nodded in agreement.

"I've been thinking a lot about that lately. No matter, *my* mission is almost over as well. Then I'll know a lot more about the subject."

"Nan!" Bash scolded. "When you're a ... well... a ghost... will you let me know?"

But Edgar hadn't stayed around long enough to hear Bash ask that.

Mrs. S heard Edgar sneezing in the library. He was coughing and wheezing over his essay, and didn't even seem too upset when Mrs. S asked him to write it over on clean paper.

"Edgar put your fingers in your ears, there's a good boy," Mrs. S suggested. "There's nothing in here to be afraid of. Hang on, I'm going to call your father."

Lady Nan felt quite refreshed after her session with Bash, and hummed as she made a pot tea in the kitchen, getting about using her walking stick without her chair.

"Morning, Piglet," Lady Nan said to Pigeon, who fluffed his feathers delighted to be noticed.

"Pooh," he replied happily.

"Piglets love biscuits," Lady Nan teased, waving a familiar brand of chocolate biscuit tantalizingly in front of the parrot's eyes.

"Penguins!" shrieked the over-excited bird, doing a triple dance of bobbing, flapping, and hopping. *"A penguin...please piglet... please pooh...a penguin...Polly wants a penguin!"*

Just at that moment Mrs. S walked in, aghast at the sight of her mother out of her chair without her walker.

"Mamma.. what...?" she spluttered. "What on earth has possessed you? You could fall! Chocolate could kill Pigeon."

Lady Nan smiled innocently at her daughter, looking especially vivacious in her fire-engine-red lipstick.

"Possessed me? Honestly Rayne, you *are* dramatic. We're just playing snap aren't we Penny old chap," she said to Pigeon, who was happily ripping excited chunks from his biscuity prize.

277

PART SIX

WINTER WONDERLAND

"The woods are lovely,
dark, and deep,
But I have promises to keep,
And miles to go before I sleep."

– ROBERT FROST

1922

CHAPTER FIFTY-SIX

The Second Snow

Cornelius Stratford-Smyth had loved Christmas almost as much as his children. He always used to say that there was something magical about the first snow.

Meditating in the tower wasn't working, so Kit sat in the center of the maze and read Carl Jung's 'Book of Dreams.' When he tired of reading in the dazzling sunlight, he put it aside and idly doodled a stick figure on the front of his old notebook.

He never intended to spoil its cover, which was a photograph of the great desert plain of Giza with its three pyramids in the distance. It was far too precious.

It was a gift from his father a few weeks before he disappeared, but the figure seemed to draw itself while he was thinking about dream-walking and time-travel.

He was actually trying *not* to think, which was impossible. It was what Dr. Brooks had instructed him not to do.

"Don't try," the doctor had said, "relax, and when you feel a tingling sensation or hear a warm buzzing in your ear, follow it like an explorer. Curiosity is a scientist's duty and it won't hurt you, but anxiety will block your attempts to 'fly.' Be fearless."

It reminded Kit of the mind game he used to play with Bash, when from time-to-time he would blurt out: don't think about elephants, and to her dismay, she would see elephants everywhere for the rest of the day.

The childish stick-figure Kit had drawn was waving, and he had also scribbled a black dot and an arrow, and the letters, CSS for Christopher Stratford-Smyth, which was odd because he always used KSS, with a K for Kit.

Clearly he was frustrated and bored, so he sat cross-legged, folded his hands in his lap, leaned against the green wall of leaves, and closed his eyes.

Snow invited herself into Kit's experiment. He had his eyes closed for what seemed like only a few minutes when he felt a chill as if the sun had gone behind a cloud. But it was too cold for that, and he opened his eyes to find Snow standing over him, smiling sweetly.

Even when a ghost smiles sweetly, it's hardly the occasion for celebration, and Kit jumped up quite startled.

He tried to act like it was the most natural thing for a nine-year-old ghost to appear in a maze... the word amazement came into his mind and he smiled. Dr. Brooks had warned him how words and events would show up as signposts if he remained open.

"Do you mind if I show you something?" Snow said.

"*Um*... not at all... where is... it? Is it in the Winter Room?" Kit babbled.

"It's more of a when really, but also some 'whats' and..."

"You mean whatnots?" Kit suggested, trying to sound more at ease.

Suddenly he missed Jack, but his experiment had specifically demanded: no cats, dogs, parrots... or people. His logic had failed to count a ghost as a person.

"Not exactly there. You need to follow me. It's not far," Snow said, holding out her hand.

Kit looked uncertainly at the hand but took it to be polite, slightly embarrassed at being afraid of Snow when Bash wasn't around.

Snow's hand was lovely and cool, and he noted with wonder, perfectly solid as well. At the back of his mind Kit gave himself credit for thinking the warmth of his own hand might bring the little girl comfort.

They'd rounded one green corner when Kit remembered his notebook.

"I'll be right back," he said. "I need my pen and paper."

Snow's eyes were full of trust, but she clung to Kit's hand and wouldn't let go.

"It's just back there. I'll be right back, honest," Kit said.

Snow blinked back tears. "My father said that once and..."

"Well, I'm not him and I won't do that," Kit said. "Okay?"

Snow clung harder and stared at the ground.

"Okay, come *with* me then. It's just over h...."

Kit stopped mid-word. What he saw stunned him. There was his spiral notepad and his pen, but beside these things he saw himself, sitting, smiling dreamily, apparently in a trance.

His first real thought was rather silly; he wondered how he was going to record his out-of-body-experience with his writing materials locked in a different dimension. His second thought was that he might be dead, and it nearly broke his trance.

Kit looked at Snow, smiled sheepishly, and squeezed her hand as if to say, look at us!

Then the two of them were the height of the treetops, and Kit's body was far below.

Floating like a seagull was a reasonably pleasant sensation, but Kit had to fight against wanting to return to his body with the nagging fear he may not have the choice.

"Am I dead?" he asked Snow.

Snow didn't answer.

"Is this how you feel all the time?" Kit asked.

"You get used to it," Snow said.

The landscape seemed to fly underneath him. The thought of being like Superman was embarrassing.

Snow giggled. "You are my hero," she said.

"Wow, can you hear my thoughts?" Kit said.

"I can *see* your thoughts," Snow corrected, "which is why I don't always understand them, but you love superheroes, so this time it was easy."

282

They had arrived, wherever it was, on a winter's evening because they were in a snowy landscape. It was dark, the moon was a murky disk hanging like an abandoned lantern in the dirty sky.

Kit found himself standing outside an Alpine Ski Chalet with a familiar looking roof of multiple peaks and gables with smoke drifting from its chimney.

It reminded him of Dr. Brooks' instructions to let his thoughts drift like smoke and he determined to allow the next events to happen or be led by Snow who danced a jig around a stack of firewood. It had not been stacked neatly, but thrown higgledy-piggledy as if someone was in a hurry or didn't care.

A familiar gold shape poked out from the pile and caught his eye. On closer inspection Kit realized it was unmistakably the panel from the back of his King Tut chair. Another plank of wood was part of its seat. Kit could see the initials PB. The rest of the woodpile was more chopped furniture.

Kit scanned the surrounding hills and noticed a low grey fence of stone posts a short distance away, looking for all the world like a Stonehenge for rabbits. There were no trees, just shrivelled shrubberies, twisted and blackened as if they'd been in a fire. Red stained the four cornerstones in a horribly familiar pattern. There on the four cornerstones were red numbers that, both clockwise and anti-clockwise, read 2020 – a message that meant hindsight – a truth that made perfect sense after comparing it with the past. But here, in the future, his past was the time when he first saw them on his twelfth birthday. This square grid of stones in the snow was the top of his tower.

A new thought made him feel queasy, and when he heard Snow say the words 'welcome home' he felt he was going to be sick. They were still outside Bede Hall. His tower was buried in snow. Impossible.

Real snow had fallen so deep that it covered the tower, leaving only the ramparts above the snow. He looked for the manor house but it was gone, and ran towards the chalet structure where Snow was waving.

"Come on Kit, it's freezing out here," she called.

This time the approach to the A-frame lodge felt like progressing in slow motion, wading through hip-deep snow. Kit focused on a red bicycle leaning against a small blue door getting larger and larger until he stood in front of it. It was the Winter Door.

The 'lodge' was the topmost floor and rooftops of Bede Hall, and Snow was inviting him inside.

"Shall we go in?" Snow said gently. "I promise not to let go of your hand."

"Well, since we're here, I'd better investigate. You said you had things to show me?" This lucid dreaming thing was a little too creepy.

A familiar voice squawked out from the interior:

"Feathers!...leave that plant alone! ...the last unicorn... too much snow...be right back...stop bashing about and get in here!" It was Pigeon.

Inside, the furniture was brown, and feeble gray flames smoldered like a damp campfire in the grate.

Antique toys lined the walls: A dapple-gray rocking horse, its horsehair mane and tail completely gone; a stuffed toy bear, its platform missing three of its wheels; an empty doll-house, its miniature furniture scattered about the floor; and a teetering stack of children's books piled against a bookcase full of bottles and cans of food.

Kit read the spines: the complete Narnia series, 'Winnie the Pooh,' 'When We Were Six,' 'The Velveteen Rabbit,' 'Fairies are Real', and a dozen more. A worn copy of 'The Lion the Witch and the Wardrobe' rested on the top beside a set of Russian dolls, covered in white dust.

Snow stood beside her blue body that lay, still as an ice statue, on a child's cot. Unicorn, curled up like a mummy, was at her side.

Her arms were hugging a doll of some kind, and when Kit peered closer he discovered it was Bash's toy rabbit, Pookie.

A clock face with no hands hung over the mantelpiece. Pigeon was no longer alive, but was stuffed on his perch with a faraway look in his button eyes. A gentle layer of frost covered everything in a mauve crust that looked like dried lavender.

"Where did you get that doll?" Kit asked.

"My aunt gave it to me," Snow said. She loved me."

Kit's thoughts raced. Snow must have brought him here wanting her body to be found in order to be buried. He'd heard ghosts were attached to things like that.

But it couldn't be the past because Bede Hall had never suffered these injuries.

Snow stared at him, holding back her tears.

"Time's-a-wasting," she said in a matter of fact tone before adding: "Time isn't real and buildings can be angry. Bede Hall is just sad."

"Snow. I am so sorry," Kit said, "You died alone in your sleep." He gestured to the body under the covers. "Are you okay seeing this?"

"I'm not... I haven't," Snow said in a small voice.

"I don't understand."

"I'm not dead," Snow whispered. "I'm dying."

Kit tried to think like a scientist. What was going on? "Are you dreaming?" And the full impact of what he saw shocked him. "You can be saved. You want me to save you. You're not a ghost. You're time traveling!"

"That's only a little part of me," Snow said calmly. "It's not the real me. Besides, you saw your body in the maze. There's nothing to be afraid of other than being alone. It doesn't matter now. I have Rain again and ... you."

Kit's mind reeled. He felt like he was possessed. He bargained with his *ka* to return to his body at once, but nothing happened, which made his fear spin into full-blown panic. I'm time traveling! What if I can't get back?

"I can't stay, Snow," Kit said. "We have to go back to the maze now, and Bash and I will reunite you with your family. Dr. Brooks will know how."

"Back in your time, I'm safe. Nothing's happened yet. There's time," she said. "Do you understand? You can change this."

Snow mutely took Kit's hand again and pulled him to the hearth where a faded photograph of a tall man holding a book hung by a piece of yellowed sticky-tape. Above it was Kit's familiar timeless clock.

"That's my father," Snow said touching the picture fondly. "He wrote books. I have them all downstairs. Want to see?"

Snow opened a small cupboard door, crudely cut into a wall beside the fireplace. Kit hadn't noticed it before. The other side was a different fireplace in a room smaller than the Winter Room.

He laughed nervously. This was a dream anyway, he told himself, so he might as well play along, but he was in the post office of Bede, surrounded by fallen shelves that he recognized from their narrow slots for letters.

The rest of the corner shop was demolished. The window fronts were blown in with drifts of snow covering whatever remained of tins and boxes.

A freezing wind of ice crystals blasted Kit's face.

Behind him, Snow called. "Come back. Please. Don't go."

She hadn't followed, and Kit turned towards Snow's shaky voice.

He called over his shoulder: "It's okay. We should get back to your room. Lead the way."

But Snow had other plans and veered off like a hare and scampered down another passageway.

Kit followed Snow through several more holes until they reached the hallway that led to the servants' stairs. Below were the kitchens and the corner where he hoped he still lived with his family.

The stairs had fallen lop-sided from the strain of the outside snow, and Kit willed himself down the drunken angle. Snow trailed after him due to the narrowness of the stairwell.

As he suspected, the snow had done major damage to the foundations of the house. The stoves were filled with debris, rendered inoperable from the collapsed chimney.

The grand staircase of Bede Hall looked like piano keys hanging by wires. But in an astral state it was easy to float to the second floor and inspect Lady Nan's bedroom. It was eerily reminiscent of a documentary Kit remembered he'd seen about the wreck of the Titanic, found by divers with its grand staircase eaten away, and a mini submarine that had maneuvered up the stairwell into the ballroom above. Now he was floating the same way through the ether, exploring the 'depths' of Bede Hall.

Lady Nan's four-poster bed was intact. Her room looked like a shrine. The glass case had been hauled from the library and placed in the center. The doors were literally frosted-glass. Kit wiped a circle and peered in. It looked like a freezer in need of defrosting. Thick white ice made it impossible to open, but Kit could see the artifacts inside: a tray of scarabs, an hourglass, a snow globe, and a perfume bottle with a stopper in the shape of two doves... lastly, there was a key with a blue tassel sitting on a tiny frozen cushion.

Back downstairs, Kit visited his first lab – the laundry room with its multiple sinks. It was a time capsule of memories.

Snow dragged him over to his old poster of the Yellowstone Caldera and tapped the red color which indicated the hottest spot.

"That's where it happened," she said sadly. "The Winter Bomb. That's what my Aunt B called it."

Kit's 'astral' headache had grown into a monster with teeth. It thumped inside his skull trying to get out, and he had never felt so thirsty. He had to wake up soon and take an aspirin, and drink a gallon of water, but he needed to know.

"Do you know when this happened?" he managed to croak.

Snow shuffled her feet. "It's in my Dad's book," she said. "It's what I wanted to show you."

Snow opened a drawer and pulled out the notebook Kit had left back in the maze.

Snow's bottom lip trembled. "I've been looking for you for a long time... *Daddy*," she said. "I didn't know that Rain was my grandmother until I saw you in my room."

That's when Kit discovered the bizarre truth that astral travelers can feel queasy. He was trapped, and his 'daughter' was crying her heart out while a parrot shrieked: *"times a wasting...get the cat... get the cat...the last unicorn... Anna needs a unicorn!"*

Apparently, Pigeon was very much alive, but the most bizarre thing was that Kit was Snow's father, and with that, both Kits fainted like a pair of bookends holding up the world.

"What was your Aunt's full name?" Kit asked to distract Snow while he tried to pry open a desk drawer. The wood splintered and Snow winced.

"Please don't hurt the house. I'll tell you my Aunt's name if you stop."

"Okay, tell me, and we'll go upstairs and talk to Pigeon."

"Her name... her name was Bathsheba but she liked to be called Bash," Snow said.

Kit was so dizzy he had to bend over with his head between his knees. When he finally recovered, he stood up and shouted as if to the house itself.

"I need to read my notebook right now!" and as soon as his words were uttered he was back inside the Winter Room with his pyramid notebook in his hands.

But it was old and brittle. Kit opened it respectfully the way an archaeologist handles a precious relic.

The pages were dog-eared. There were entries written like a diary and the book flipped open to a passage it clearly wanted him to read:

August 1, 2022 - "The caldera blew in the fall of 2020. Some joke no doubt about the universe's idea of hindsight. It took less than a year for the gardens to die and they took my beloved sister with them." She died on the same day that Snow used to appear. I don't believe in spring anymore. I gave up on the Twinters when Bash never showed on our twentieth birthday. I'm so angry with her because it was my birthday wish and now I know ghosts exist and she never came to haunt me – C.S.S.

There were newspaper cuttings of the disaster. It had been 2020 when the Yellowstone Caldera blasted the planet bringing a volcanic winter that likely destroyed most of the human race and its animal and plant kingdoms.

Kit pieced the crazy facts together as Snow's imagination had created them. Incredibly, Snow was his daughter. She wasn't dead; she was in a coma. He stood in the future. Christmas - 2021. His twin had been dead five months, and Pigeon was one-hundred-and-seventeen years old. And, what were 'Twinters?'"

Snow started to evaporate and a new fear clutched Kit in an icy grip. He was going to be left alone. Lost out of time with no Bash to rescue him.

CHAPTER FIFTY-SEVEN

Time Out of Mind

"Bash! " Kit screamed. "Help! Can you hear me?".... and miraculously his voice slipped over time and space, and Bash shook him awake.

The maze had turned a darker shade of green in the moonlight.

"Come on silly-head. Wake up. It's way past supper time. You have Snow to thank. She said you were out here," Bash chided. "You were screaming."

"We've got to go to the post office," Kit said, idiotically. "Now!"

Bash ignored him. "Mum's put a plate on the stove for you. I managed to convince her you were doing an experiment in your tower and couldn't be disturbed. She's gone to bed," Bash said. "That's where you ought to be."

"No, It CAN'T wait!" Kit wailed. "Where's my bike? I'm going now whether you come or not."

He looked frantically around the maze and clutched his notebook, rifling through the pages searching for ... he stopped. The diary entry he was looking for hadn't been written yet.

"I'm a dead man," Kit said. "Literally, a dead man."

Goodness," Bash said, "your language skills *have* improved. You're talking in metaphors now, except that's not a literal statement because you're actually alive?"

"Metawhats?" Kit asked. "Are you for real? Do you ever stop?"

"Well, you're not *really* dead are you?" Bash said, "So when you say something like you just did, it's symbolic. It's a figure of speech. Lady Nan told me. It's a device. Are you planning on writing a book or something?"

"What? How did you know?" Kit spluttered.

"You don't look well. Let's get you inside. I'll make us cocoa," Bash said.

"Nothing's real," Kit stammered out of breath. "Am I even solid?"

"I think that's a trick question," Bash said, "come on, you'll catch your death out here."

But when the post office was well within his reach the next day and the next, Kit avoided it. He knew without a doubt that there was a tunnel from Bede Hall to the corner shop and that probably Mrs. Spoondance was not as empty-headed as she seemed.

"This lucid dreaming thing yielded something I didn't expect," Kit confessed as he and Bash entered the maze.

Mrs. S had prepared a picnic. Kit carried it without noticing its weight. He had heavier things on his mind.

"Well, I would imagine it would if it worked," Bash said.

"Oh it *worked* all right."

"You don't seem to be that happy about it. I'd have thought you would be over the moon."

"Bede village is not as it seems," Kit tried to explain, "or at least some day fairly soon, it won't be."

Kit looked so gloomy and helplessly out of his depth, that for once, Bash had nothing to say. The silence grew thicker as the close green walls muffled the confusion of what was once the real world. The leaves rustled and jostled him as he slipped further away from logic.

Bash's lips pursed in anger. "Oh for goodness sake, just spill the beans."

"I've visited the future," Kit blurted, "and I found a time portal, I think. I wish I hadn't but there it is."

"Wow, talk about getting what you wished for," Bash said. "None of what you saw boded well I take it?"

"Not much."

"Is that an understatement?" Bash asked, "or a flippant off-the-cuff who cares it's not a big deal?"

"A" Kit said quickly. "Definitely A."

The twins arrived at the ground zero of Kit's experiment. A single bee buzzed out of the leaves like a small projectile and settled on the picnic basket.

Kit sat cross-legged in the exact spot. "I was sitting right like this. Right here. Snow came up and the next thing, I'm flying into the teeth of a dream knowing all the time that I was still here.

"We have to check out the door inside the winter room," he said. "That room is not just a whitewash game; it's a portal. Not a regular tunnel. If it was a real tunnel it would have taken me ages to get to Bede."

The living walls of the maze absorbed Kit's anxiety with its cool leafy wallpaper. It smelled earthy and nightmares were miles away. Overhead, a flock of crows cawed back and forth across the sky as if unsure which direction to fly.

"Maybe Mrs. Spoondance is none the wiser about this portal thing?" Bash said, opening the basket, suddenly hungry.

Kit looked at her with surprise.

"I never even considered that, and I thought I was scientific. I've been avoiding going to town. I feel paranoid, like the whole village knows about the portal. Not knowing which ones feels ghastly, and if Dr. Brooks is aware of it then who else knows? Does Lady Nan? Is there a conspiracy?"

"Okay calm down," Bash said. "You're getting carried away. Let's see what Mum made us for lunch."

Mrs. S had outdone herself. She had packed clubhouse sandwiches with roast turkey and crisp bacon, and slices of Parks' prize tomatoes. For the next twenty minutes the twins munched in silence listening to the birds and watched the bee explore a planet-sized landscape of chocolate icing on one of the cupcakes their mother had thoughtfully included. They each had their own thermos of ice-cold milk and a packet of chilled red grapes.

"Do you hear those crows?" Bash asked finally, as once more a flutter of them passed noisily overhead.

"Of course I do," Kit said, feeling pleasantly full and less agitated.

Bash loaded the basket but left the grapes. "You know the rudiments of meditation, but do you know what a *guided* meditation is?"

"Dr. Brooks mentioned it in passing. We didn't actually try it. I gather it's listening to someone describe a place and following their words in your mind until you can see it so clearly that you feel as if you're there," he said.

"It doesn't have to be a journey. Charlotte explained it to me, and it works by the way. Close your eyes and listen to these hedges," Bash instructed.

"What?"

"It's the basic principle behind my experiment with Charlotte that I asked you about. Listen. What do you hear? If you hear nothing it's fine because they hear you."

Kit gave Bash that *not again* look.

"They?" he said suspiciously.

"Okay smarty pants. Just bear with me," Bash replied. "Pretend for some bizarre moment that I know something more important than a few grand words, okay?"

"Okeydokey."

Bash took a cleansing breath and exhaled the tension she was feeling from Kit's doubtful expression. "Energy surrounds us. These branches, are alive – home to a million creatures. They're connected underground with roots that mingle with the topiaries and way out to the trees by the lake.

"The vibrations of the fish and waterfowl and insects communicating have real untapped power. Natural power. Bede Hall is a magnetic beacon to them all. Like a receiver. Bede Hall transmits as well."

Kit breathed easier.

"I suppose we humans tune all that out, don't we," he said sheepishly.

"Well, it's not for nothing that people leave town to camp under the stars in tents," Bash commented. "Cities and towns stifle the connections between living things. As weird as it sounds, Parks refers to the earth as a woman named Gaia – one living 'entity' with growing seasons of life and death, and if he's right we're pretty lucky to be living here."

"Yup it's weird here all right. You don't have to convince me."

"The silence out here is deafening. Charlotte has learned to translate a few of the voices, that's all. She would have been burned as a witch for such a thing in the past. Did you know there's a marker in town where several women were burned in 1613?"

"I don't want to know."

"You and I talk to Feathers and Pigeon and Jack," Bash continued, "and we think nothing of it. Charlotte and Parks converse with flowers and vegetables. It's not so different. Edgar stole the evidence of our cabbage experiment. Edgar is unaware but he knows."

"That's the worst kind of knowing," Kit said.

"Edgar's snooping has become more than mischievous curiosity, but all he knows is that we, meaning Bede Hall, has produced one giant cabbage. A fluke of nature. Others won't be so stupid. If other people in Bede have learned to do what my friends have done, then their company is worth pursuing," Bash continued. "That's the pure science of living out here. People who are savvy know enough to keep what they know to themselves. There's nothing sinister here. That's what I've discovered."

"Wow. My sister the scientist," Kit said. "Who knew?"

"I'm glad we know *some* of each other's secrets," Bash said, "because we're a team. Remember? And somehow, in the best of ways, Lady Nan and Dr. Brooks are part of it."

"Bash?" Kit said shyly. "I'm not trying to be ornery, but there are some details I'm still working out that I can't share just yet. Is that okay?"

"Sure Bash," replied. "Wait till I tell *you* about the fairies."

Bash's new credibility evaporated after she explained how she'd been lost that night of the May and described her meeting with the fairies.

Then it soared again as Kit realized his dream-travel was a parallel experience of missing time. It was reassuring to know, that he and Bash were still in sync. Bash was learning the art of listening and he was learning the art of seeing. 'Visualization on a grand scale,' Dr. Brooks had called it.

Bash closed her eyes and appeared to be receiving a positive message because she was giggling and said 'hello' a few times to thin air. It gave Kit time to mull over the events of the last few months.

Time was a fluid reality that could be explored. Not manipulated, but experienced as swimming or flying or dream-walking, and the ones who knew this secret were purposely quiet about it. It was *that* important.

Suddenly Parks was an ally and Lady Nan wasn't so addled. The pattern of it intrigued him; everything was worth studying. The word miracle became another seven letter word for science. They were interchangeable.

The twins reached the kitchen, glowing with secrets.

"Thanks Mum," Kit enthused. "The sandwiches were..."

"Magic," finished Bash.

CHAPTER FIFTY-EIGHT

History Repeats Itself

The residents of Bede had grown up with the a great stately home at the edge of their village, but they still gawped like tourists through its massive iron gates with its designs of lions and crowns flanked by a pair of sphinx sentinels, and wondered at its crenelated towers, convinced that inside such places loomed luxuries beyond imagining, and often remarked wistfully to each other how lucky the latest residents must be to live there.

Central heating and the dozens of electric appliances that made their own lives a hot-water paradise were easily forgotten along with the reality behind the nostalgia of wood and coal – a continuous round of messy backbreaking hours, chopping, lifting, and shoveling.

They especially disregarded the fact that the only people who had actually done the luxuriating, were long-dead generations who had enlisted an army of servants to do every scrap of work.

The romancing of the past glossed over the way the servants had worked for a pittance, if not for the sheer loyalty to those who *allowed* them to serve, as if it was a great privilege to wake before dawn in all weathers and labor long past midnight, seven days a week.

What they failed to grasp, was that living in the enchanted fairy tale of a stately home required an overabundance of hot-water-bottles and plenty of extra woolly sweaters, and that stately actually referred more to one's state of mind.

The general population of Bede, like most humans, tended to be envious of other people's things, and were absolutely positive the Stratford-Smyths had pots of lovely money because people with two last names were always rich.

So, villagers would ogle jealously and drive on to their airtight homes that answered instantly to the pushes of buttons and the flicking of switches without realizing they were 'lords of the *manner*' just as much as the old lords of the *manor.*

Approaching Bede Hall was the most stately part. Its long drive pulled visitors closer to an illusion of opulence nestled between sleepy hills within a garden that once had perfectly trimmed hedges and lawns like velvet carpets, and a maze of tall green walls pampered by a dozen pairs of clippers every day, and a marble fountain where water once cascaded from the mouths of marble dolphins and splashed the mermaids who rode them, lulling the imaginary carp with their songs.

The many disrepairs of the Hall's facade had been masked for years by cultivating the spread of flowering vines that created it the perfect postcard even up-close.

Girls from the village school imagined a princess's room in the lofty tower across the courtyard not knowing it was the lair of a boy-scientist, guarded by several invisible flashing 'keep out' signs.

The crumbling steps were relatively safe if one wasn't in a hurry, but it remained rather drafty from the ever-widening spaces between the eroding bricks. Birds and bats occupied its stairwell, and owls searched under the moonlight to cull the mice colonies that sheltered there from the rain.

Bash had once painstakingly written Nan's exact words into their notebook: *strangers are drawn closer to Bede Hall by the romantic ambiance of its crenelated towers.*

Crenelated, Bash discovered, described the tooth-shaped gaps on the top of the stone walls, and ambiance meant how one felt once they got there. Kit called it good vibes. The villagers called it feeling grand, but the most sensitive visitors found their first impressions were tinged with sadness.

Only a handful of extraordinary souls in the village honored the old ways, but they were more like legendary characters of myth whose main purpose was to live by example – as young as they could dream.

CHAPTER FIFTY-NINE

Departments of Helpful Hints

Bash found Dr. Brooks as charming as Kit had described. He kissed her cheek and complimented her choice of perfume.

"Delightful scent *L'air de temps*," he said. "I feel quite... transported."

Dr. Brooks made a display of standing back from the twins admiringly, and hurried them inside to a cream tea much more elaborate than the one on Kit's first visit.

"I hope you like strawberries," Dr. Brooks said over his shoulder as he headed for his third trip to the kitchen.

The doctor returned with a portable three-tiered table with a carrying handle, and set it beside Bash.

"I don't often get to use this," he said as he placed apple tarts on the top shelf.

"How did your grandmother like my carnation?"

"She was surprised and made sure it was in her... boudoir." Bash said. "That's what she calls her bedroom sometimes. It sounds more grand."

"The right word always does," the doctor replied.

Dr. Brooks took Kit aside while Bash fussed with the tea things. "How goes your experiments?" he whispered.

"I should probably have my head examined," Kit exclaimed.

"You've come to the right place then," Dr. Brooks replied, laughing.

"I had some amazing results, but ..."

"A bad trip eh?" Dr. Brooks interrupted.

"The worst. I'll tell you about it later," Kit said under his breath. "Your chair arrived shipshape," Kit said in a louder voice to include

Bash in the conversation. "Rupert was at school, so he didn't see it. It looks right at home in my tower."

"And well it should. It used to belong to your uncle Bentley. That's where he kept it. Your grandmother gave it to me after he... after he passed," he said, choosing his words carefully. "And speaking of gifts. I have one for you, Bash. Mustn't leave you out, must we?"

Dr. Brooks produced a small red leather box from his pocket and handed it to Bash, grinning over her head at Kit.

"I need to speak to you alone. Scientist to scientist," mouthed Kit. "It's urgent."

Dr. Brooks nodded.

"I'll show you my gardens later," he said to Bash, accepting the teacup she proffered in exchange for the box. "You can give me a critique. I understand you're quite the budding horticulturist, pardon the pun. Words are rather..."

Bash supplied the missing word: "serendipitous," she said.

"The very word. You won't mind if I leave you alone for a bit while your brother and I discuss a science experiment of ours, will you?"

"I will be more than happy to leave you two to science," Bash replied. "I can look at some of your lovely books."

"Aren't you going to open your present?" Kit said.

"It's a ring box," Bash said shyly, her eyes gleaming.

"And they usually contain rings," Dr. Brooks teased. "I hope you like it. It was your uncle's, as well."

The box revealed a turquoise scarab ring in a silver setting. It swiveled ingeniously on a coiled hinge in order to read the hieroglyph of a bee carved on the back.

"B must be for Ben," Bash said.

"B is for Beryl too," Dr. Brooks replied. "And now it can stand for Bathsheba."

299

Kit felt he was close enough to Dr. Brooks to ask a sensitive question. "What's wrong with Lady Nan's mind?"

"Your grandmother is the sanest woman I know, but she suffers from an excess of guilt. I told her doctors that but it didn't go down too well, so, there was a parting of the ways. She blocked me out. She can be stubborn."

"She's determined," Kit said.

"She's tenacious," Bash corrected.

"That's a big word," Dr. Brooks commented.

"It's the right word," Bash said.

Kit thought about the right words he was going to have to use to explain his latest discovery to Dr. Brooks. How does one tell a scientist that the world has only six years to live?

Kit's chance came the next day, and when he'd finished reporting his findings to Dr. Brooks, they shared an overwhelming feeling of despair. Regarding such a grim and bizarre future took some getting used to.

But after a few mercifully uneventful nights, Kit decided his dream-walk had been metaphorical rather than historical, and he determined to investigate Snow more thoroughly, and for good measure, he asked Dr. Brooks for some references.

"I need to speak to a writer and an historian," Kit said, "and anyone else you think I should interview. I need answers."

"Asking more questions is not the same thing as confirming what you already know," Dr. Brooks said. "But if it eases your mind then I know of a few colleagues who will be happy to talk with you if you use my name."

"What would one have to do, hypothetically speaking, although we both know it's me, to write a sci-fi book for children?" Kit asked Clive Lucy, the stout balding author, whom Dr. Brooks had recommended.

"How old?"

"Pardon?"

"How old are the children?... your readership?"

"My age, I suppose," Kit said. "Thirteen-ish."

Mr. Lucy contemplated his vast store of knowledge for a moment before answering.

"Well, it's all in the rhythm of the language. Think storyteller. Think summer camp. You must capture one child at a time. It's the sound of the words. Sound is everything. It has to be lyrical. Hypnotic. Children follow stories the way bees are drawn to a field of flowers. But here's where it becomes technical, you have to break the adverb rules. Children understand adverbs. They can't get enough of em."

"Kit looked stunned. "Yeah... right... adverbs," he said feebly.

"I expect your mother can help you. Watching a lot of movies in your chosen genre will help as well, but the most important thing to do is read. Read, read, read."

Kit swallowed weakly. "Genre... right... thanks," he said, searching for the right words to continue, wishing for once he had Bash's vocabulary at his disposal.

Even the wrong words would do, he thought. But he drew a complete blank. Clearly, this writing business wasn't going to be easy, and he took some comfort thinking how most dreams were a bit vague and hardly ever came true.

But as soon as this thought occupied his mind, he knew it was a lie. His dream had been a different sort. Lucid, Dr. Brooks had called it.

"Why so glum chum?" Bash said, finding Kit scowling in a dark corner. "Cheer up it may never happen."

Bash's last remark made Kit feel worse than ever. He wondered how a twin could nail something so 'on the head' like that and not know it.

"It's time to do a bit of investigating," Bash suggested, thinking Kit would jump at the chance. "You know the scientific stuff. We should find out something about Snow. We'll have to ask an expert – someone who knows everything about Bede's business, since she died here."

There was only one person for the job.

Drew Melville, head librarian of the Bede Public Library, was adamant. His serious expression confirmed it. And it had taken him no time at all to sound so sure. He consulted his head rather than any of the books or the banks of drawers full of index cards, behind him. He took his informal position as town historian seriously, being a stickler for information in general and Bede in particular.

"Sorry," he said flatly. "There's absolutely no ghosts at Bede Hall. There's been a few sightings of one in 'The Stopped Clock,' but that was back in the seventies."

There was no bother discussing it further, really. One thing the twins did know about the stern librarian, was that he filed absolutely everything, never missing a detail. He was known for his thorough dedication to fact-finding, and could put his finger on any newspaper story, article, or reference in an instant.

"I would know," he said, not meaning to be arrogant, but simply stating one of his beloved facts. "All reports, all *documented* reports, that is, are duly noted and given a number. By *me*," he hastened to emphasize.

"The only other probability," he droned on, "which is highly unlikely considering the nature of our village grapevine, is if a sighting hadn't *wanted* to be publicized. For instance, a family might not *want* their ghost to be common knowledge.

"Nothing puts off a real estate deal than some silly rumors of paranormal activity. I know because my brother-in-law, Wilbur Tweedy, is a realtor."

"I seem to recall there was an incident last year like that. Awful muddle for him. He was quite devastated.

"Anyway, unless a legitimate sighting was recorded in someone's diary or a letter or something personal like that, no historian worth his salt would ever know. Guessing and assuming are quite beyond the pale," he finished rather emotionally.

By the look on the librarian's face, it was plain this state of affairs was most unsatisfactory, and that Mr. Melville felt he was worth his weight in gold rather than a common thing like table salt.

Mr. Melville continued after a moment's reconsideration and came up with a final, alternate possibility. Very 'last resort' was implied by the extreme height of his eyebrows.

"A sighting may not have been taken seriously, which had been," he said pointedly, "from someone unreliable, someone given to hallucinations for example, someone who was...*er*... not quite *there* so to speak, say an old person whose mind was... fading." Other than that he concluded, "ghost sightings are a trick of the light or a blobby mist on a fuzzy photograph."

"Well what about the one in 'the Stopped Clock' then?" Bash queried. "You said there'd been a ghost there."

"Alcohol," Mr. Melville intoned distastefully. Likely an overdose of spirits."

He paused to smile at his own pun. "I never said there was a *ghost* in the pub; I merely stated there had been a *sighting*. A very different color of cat. People see things after a 'few-too-many.' Completely unreliable source of reference, I'm afraid."

With that, he turned dismissively to a large pile of papers that were clearly in need of sorting, and shuffled away mumbling something about a system gone mad.

"Well, thanks," Kit said to the back of Mr. Melville's head.

"That was a bit of overkill wasn't it?" Kit exclaimed once they were back in the street.

"Really!" Bash fumed. "It was clear he meant Lady Nan when he said not quite *there*. He was so... pompous... so... so sanctimonious," she finally spluttered. "Lady Nan is right where she says she is," she continued indignantly. "She may be iffy about the exact date or her age, but her visitations from Snow were real enough... and," she added, "it was just too bad that we couldn't come out and tell 'Mr. know-it-all snooty books' we've seen a ghost ourselves."

"I'd heard he was a bit of a nutter about details," Kit shared. "Peregrine says the guy's extremely left-brain, and files absolutely everything from loose scraps of paper to all the old ads from the notice boards around town, and cross references each one with his own code. His accounting only proves that there's no hard copy in Bede that he knows of, that's all."

"Snow is either being stubborn about her dates or she's so disoriented from her sudden death, she doesn't know *when* she is... was..." Bash said, confusing herself. "I've tried to pin her down, but she just changes the subject."

"I'll give lucid dreaming another try," Kit volunteered, using the word lucid casually, as if he'd been extremely lucid about what it meant for quite some time.

"Snow seems rather taken with me," he said casually, "She's always wanting to hold my hand."

He shuffled his feet, knowing more than he was saying.

"Peregrine!" Bash suddenly exploded, after the 'penny dropped.' "*We're* rather *'pally'* aren't we? On a first name basis are we?" she teased.

"We are as a matter of fact," Kit replied. "We're... *er*... sort of ... science soul mates, if you want to know... like you and me," he finished rather embarrassed.

"I think you mean kindred spirits," Bash corrected sympathetically. "And speaking of spirits, if we were old enough, I'd suggest a trip to 'the Stopped Clock' myself right now," she said.

Kit's face brightened with a new thought, "Hold on," he said grinning. "That might be just the ticket. Maybe the ghost in the pub was Snow... or at least related to her in some way. It's worth investigating. It's our only lead. We have to check it out."

But after several conversations with the bleary-eyed regulars and the more alert patrons of 'The Stopped Clock Tavern and Hotel,' it was clear that all the twins were doing was drawing unwanted attention to themselves, and they reluctantly concluded, that Snow would have to remain an isolated case of the 'apparitions unknown' category.

The two were pretty thirsty, having watched everyone gulping down beer and sipping wine, so they treated themselves to takeout slushy drinks from the corner shop.

They walked, slurping happily, passing the church surrounded by its wobbly gravestones, and found a deserted bench on the village green. For a while they watched the crows hopping on the ground squabbling over bits of anything that remotely resembled food.

"Dr. Brooks and I," Kit finally said, breaking the silence and trying to explain his earlier comment, "we click. Time just flies when we get started talking about... well, everything really. He knows it all without being a know-it-all, if you know what I mean. We're on the same wavelength."

"He knows Lady Nan right enough," Bash commented. "More than he's willing to admit anyway."

"I'd say that he *has* admitted his feelings, and some things are none of our business. But, you'll have to check with Lady Nan because *that* won't be in the public record for sure or old Melville would have dropped it into his report," Kit said, defensively.

"I wouldn't be too sure of that." Bash replied. "So Mr. Scientist, where do we look for the elusive Miss Snow now?"

"For now, we don't," Kit said confidently, "we let the matter drop. Or at least drop into our laps."

"I don't understand," Bash said, making a sucking sound with her straw against the bottom of her empty cup.

"We let *what* we want to know come to *us*," Kit said. "That's the way pertinent information moves about. It reveals itself when the mind stops trying to find it. So, as long as we keep an open mind and send out a thought-beacon or two, it won't be long before we know... or rather it will take as long as is best. Some things we aren't meant to know. Like Dr. Brooks and Lady Nan and... the future. Pertinent indeed ... la dee dah."

Bash tossed her paper cup in a waste container. "How very 'Charlotte' of you," she said, tongue-in-cheek.

"Very." Kit replied, overriding the sarcasm. "You'll see."

"I'm sure it will be positively serendipitous," Bash finished, trying to sound more sincere than her words, because she really did know what her brother was talking about. She and Charlotte were always on the same page.

CHAPTER SIXTY
Snowed Under

"I don't think I'm cut out to be a writer," Kit moaned to Dr. Brooks. "Not if it's all about adverbs, whatever *they* are. Dreams aren't always accurate are they?"

"They're symbolic," Dr. Brooks corrected. "However, yours are more. Yours are the result of a scientific experiment. Lucid dreaming, by its very definition, is a cut above a story told in pictures or replaying the random events of one's day. It's a version of the truth."

"Which is?"

"I'm afraid what you see, hear, touch, taste and smell is what you get."

Several cups of tea with biscuits later, Dr. Brooks leaned back in his chair and clapped his hands together which meant he was about to deliver a morsel of wisdom worth paying extra attention to.

"Now, that's what I call being *snowed in*." Dr. Brooks commented. "Sorry that popped into my mind. One should always pay attention when thoughts do that.

"Now, if I were you, and of course I'm not," he continued, "I'd concentrate on what I *didn't* know. Forget your little 'window of prophecy,' and pretend it was only a dream, which, may I remind you, it was."

"But you just said..." Kit spluttered.

"I know what I said. The brain is tricky. It's impossible to fool it once it's got hold of something, but that's what a scientist has to do in order to remain open."

"But how? It's my sister... it's my... planet," Kit wailed.

"Don't just regurgitate information... think! Blurting without backup is no better than gossip," Dr. Brooks said.

"I guess I can see that." Kit replied. "I'm a bit snowed under myself actually," Kit said, seriously, not even hearing his own joke.

"See! You're doing it again. Don't! Guess!"

Kit took a deep breath: "I fully understand completely, according to all the information duly collated available to me at this time," Kit said, sarcastically.

Dr. Brooks laughed. "I guess I deserved that," he said.

"So what is a genre then?" Kit asked timidly.

"Science-fiction for a start."

"A math genius is no-one to mess with," Dr. Brooks said. "Calculating the elegance of the universe is a fulltime job. Not much time for chitchat or common sense."

Prof. Newton Appleby looked the part. Part absentminded professor and part raving lunatic. He carried at least four pairs of spectacles on his person: one that permanently sprouted from the top of his head, and another that swung precariously on a silver chain under his hooked nose. The other two must have had legs and a taste for travel because they constantly wandered away and returned days later, right where the professor had left them.

The chained pair was the one most usually ignored while the old man searched every pocket of his lab coat, and exhausted the labyrinths of several desk drawers, eventually noticing the pair poking out of his pen pocket.

"Please sir," Kit ventured cautiously, expecting nothing short of performance theatre, "could you spare a moment of your time. Dr. Brooks sent me and..."

"Yes yes. Peregrine, old friend of ... course... student?... have I had lunch?"

Kit tried to remember all that Dr. Brooks had told him. "Mathematicians tend to appear woolly-minded," he'd said. "But not to worry. Professor Appleby understands everything, possibly too much for his own good, but he grasps the full impact of your questions long after you've gone... sometimes *days* later. So, second visits are much more enlightening. And don't be fooled by his scatterbrained attitude... he isn't. It's just that he's juggling a hundred theorems and mathematical possibilities that occupy his mind, constantly re-equating themselves in endless proofs.

"One of Appleby's proofs can be dozens of pages long. To us they're nonsensical, but to a mathematician's eye they're art, just as much as a great painting... well, I can't describe it because I'm not one of them. They tend to talk to each other and leave the rest of us out. Unless they need one of us to point them towards their home or find a lost shoe, but they're quite content to wear shoes from different pairs.

"If you think hieroglyphics are difficult to read, try substituting each picture with a number and see where *that* gets you," Dr. Brooks had enthused.

"But what's math got to do with time-travel?" Kit had moaned, sounding more than a tad indifferent.

The room had gone too quiet too suddenly, to be comfortable as Dr. Brooks splutter and spouted at the same time.

"My dear boy, *math* is the language of the cosmos!" he had shouted. "It has *'to do'* with everything that exists. Numbers are the foundation of life from absolute zeros to the infinities of magical decimal points. Multiplicities beyond multiplication."

Dr. Brooks had been unstoppable. There were times Kit had wanted to dial 999 to be rescued.

"The great divide between the unknown 'factor X' and irrefutable knowledge. The addition of variable truths and the subtraction of abstractions. Infrequent frequencies and 'freak-quencies,' fractious fractions, unprincipled geometric principles, acrobatic anomalies, the dance of spectrums and the tangled tangos of DNA, the complex two-stepping of X's and Y's, the waltzes of binary fission. From atom-smashing logic to nuclear, mind-blowing, serendipity doo da.

"Time-travel will most certainly depend on the subtleties of quantum physics... another name for advanced mathematics, by the way. All positively poetic," he gasped to a full stop.

"And I need to see this man because...?" Kit said nonplussed.

"Because," Dr. Brooks said, "if you're serious about any real scientific endeavor, your chosen discipline will involve a hundred pages of data reduced to a set of numbers and letters. Often as few as three! There's no getting around that. No way at all!

"Manipulating time and space is probably one-hundred-percent math. Sorry, but that's the truth of it. There are easier levels of science. I'm afraid you've chosen the top of the mountain."

"Professor Appleby, sir, I've come to discuss the fluctuations..." Kit began weakly and gave up. "I've come to discuss time-travel," he stated firmly, bravely standing his ground ready for punishment, and delivering his request with such authority, he thoroughly impressed himself.

But Professor Appleby accepted his question and smiled vacantly, repeating the word 'time' so frequently in his explanation that he eventually began looking at his watch... or he would have done had it been on his wrist.

Another protracted search found the missing timepiece hanging over a goose-neck lamp like the melting pocket-watch Kit had seen in a painting by Salvador Dali, which was, as he remembered, ironic under the present circumstances, titled: the 'The Persistence of Memory.'

What followed, or what Kit *tried* to follow, was an odd collection of English and science-speak that in the long run led Kit to believe such a thing as time-travel, although not child's play, was relatively possible.

It was the term *relative* which caused a problem. Professor Newton Appleby started to explain why, but Kit stopped him politely and said he'd be back tomorrow, and "thank you for a most stimulating conversation."

Professor Appleby looked up and to the right. "Tomorrows," he said, "aren't what you need. For time-travel you need yesterdays!"

Kit left with the conclusion that Professor Appleby had perhaps professed a smidgen too much for his own good.

He'd been brilliant to the point of idiocy – one singularity short of hospitalization. It was hard to believe it had been creatures like this who had put men on the moon.

Kit mused that they'd probably also put a lot of men in the loony bin as well.

Bottom line?... time-travel was not pure science-fiction. Minds who knew what the stars thought, said it was logistically possible... given enough *time*, that is.

Kit left Professor Appleby's office seriously mind-boggled. He didn't know whether to be elated or depressed, but knew for sure he would pass on a second visit.

'This must be the part of science,' Kit thought, 'that Dr. Brooks had described as *sometimes you discover things you wish you never knew.*'

CHAPTER SIXTY-ONE

Movies-R-Us

Dr. Brooks' white carnation basked in a place of honor on Lady Nan's bedside table, actually displacing her snow globe. From time to time she glanced at it and smiled. The table beyond it held the aquarium with Beetle. His old goldfish bowl had been turned into a rose bowl which now held the floating head of a splendidly fragrant pink peony instead.

Snow sat on the enormous four poster bed watching a DVD perched between her friends, Rain and Bash. Snowdrop curled up with Anubis, and the two of them resembled a yin yang symbol with his black fur and her white. Unicorn cuddled close to Snow, and Feathers sat on the floor positioned under Lady Nan's peacock fan hoping for a miracle.

Kit sat in a small armchair. He was not exactly thrilled; he had important things to do, and watching a Jane Austen movie was not close to being one of them. For one thing, there were no special effects. Just a lot of ladies milling about sewing, and writing letters, or mooning over cups of tea, and square-dancing in slow motion.

"Let's have 'Sense and Sensibility' next," Lady Nan announced cheerfully.

"Not another one," Kit wailed. "It's just love and weird clothes."

"They had style back then," Lady Nan reassured him.

"They had panache," Bash added just to bug Kit.

"But you've seen it at least a hundred times," Kit moaned.

"Just like you play the same computer games over and over," Lady Nan teased.

"That's different. The endings are never the same. They're at least a challenge," Kit declared hotly. They take skill."

"Then think of watching Jane Austen as a challenge, and use your scientist skills to interpret their hidden meanings once-in-a-while," Lady Nan said, dismissing him like a queen.

"Well girls," Lady Nan said, resuming her offer. "What would *you* like to watch?"

Snow spoke up. "The house wants you to watch 'Pride and Prejudice.'"

"Well, that makes no sense at all," Bash said.

Kit thought a moment and nudged his sister. "Maybe not. It's no stranger than anything else around here lately. And you said yourself that Bede Hall has a cheery atmosphere. I believe 'ambiance' was the exact word you used. Isn't that the same as a personality?"

Bash turned to Snow. "Anna, please ask Bede Hall if it wants us to watch something else. We saw that one the other night."

"I already know. It wants the director's commentary in the special features menu – the making of 'Pride and Prejudice,'" she said.

Kit took Bash aside. "This obsession of Lady Nan's might be more than an old lady's whim," he said. "You should watch it with that in mind. A special feature may hold... well, a special hidden meaning. At least, I have a hunch that it does."

Lady Nan's voice boomed. 'Pride and Prejudice' please," she said. "Come on Bash. We're waiting."

"Ladies. This is where I leave you," Kit announced, "we watched that one yesterday."

"Oh come on," Bash said chuckling. "Where's your natural *joie de vivre* ? Don't be prejudiced now."

"Maybe I will, if you promise to stop being so proud of your big fancy words," Kit zinged back. "You don't even know what prejudiced means."

Lady Nan broke in. "It means in favour of something without the science," she said looking directly at Kit.

"I don't understand," he said looking sheepish.

"Prejudice is when someone forms an opinion without hearing both sides or any new evidence because they are already convinced. Most unscientific. A scientist who ignores his experiments because he wants something to be true isn't very sensible is he?" she said.

"But it does make him prejudiced. Does that make any sense or sensibility to you Kit?"

Kit gave in. "Women!" he blurted. "I will now go and gather some fair evidence."

Kit handed Bash the remote. "I take it you know how to work this thing," he said sarcastically.

"It's not rocket science," she replied with a grin.

Kit he couldn't bear to think of Snow as his daughter. Such a thought was just too freaky. Still, he had to believe the evidence. He realized Lady Nan had a point. He didn't want to believe something that affected his data. All his notes pointed to Anna's bizarre claim being true. Dr. Brooks had been right. Time-travel had its unpleasant side.

Kit bowed towards the four poster bed. "Hope the three of you enjoy your special feature," he said. "I shall be in my tower."

"Would you like some company?" Snow asked, starting to get up.

"*Er...* no thanks Anna ... I mean, Snow. I need to be alone for my experiments to be unprejudiced. Besides, you have to stay. You're the only who can speak to houses.

Bede Hall was pleased.

Pigeon spoke to Mrs. S who was darning socks.

"please...pride... prejudice... plum cake and kitty poo," he chortled.

"Yes dear," Mrs. S answered, "are those your new names?"

"That's Mr. Kitty Poo, to you," Pigeon mumbled.

It was interesting to watch how a movie was made. Behind the scenes was different. Actors were hemmed in by a forest of cameras and floors littered with cables. Busy crew members moved props, and hundreds of lights dangled from the rafters or on poles, from every side. The director sat in a folding chair booming orders through an old -fashioned megaphone.

One of the stars (the woman who played Mrs. Bennett) gave an interview explaining how the 'ambiance' of a real house helped the actors to feel their part.

"Take this beautiful house," she said. "It grows on you. It tells you a lot about the people who used to live here."

Bash's ears perked up. By the look on Lady Nan's face she was enjoying the tour immensely, and Snow had her eyes closed with her head to one side as if she were listening.

Bash watched the screen, determined to pay closer attention. A wandering camera took her down hallways where racks of costumes lined the walls, and down a staircase behind the walls that the servants had used. Now and then a makeup artist arrived to puff powder on shiny noses and adjust wigs.

Snow was nodding in agreement to some unseen presence.

"Snow, what is it?" Bash asked. "Is the house speaking to you?"

Snow nodded again. "Bede Hall wants to be in the movies," she said, as if it were the most normal request in the world.

"A house can't act," Bash said.

"Of course it can," Lady Nan piped up. "Bede Hall acts out all the time. It has distinct moods. It loves summer and spring a little more than fall and winter. It's rather iffy about rain and it adores Christmas. In fact it loves any sort of family party."

"And it doesn't want to be sold," Snow said.

"I don't want that either," Lady Nan said, giving Snow a hug. "You tell Bede Hall that."

"No," Snow continued, "Bede Hall doesn't want to act. It wants to be a set. For a movie."

"Now that *does* make sense," Lady Nan agreed. "There's a lot of money in Hollywood. It could be the very thing Rayne needs to turn this place around. Sheba, you must tell her."

"But then there would be people all over the place," Bash said, "and you remember how that went, the year you tried opening it to the public. It was awful. They left litter everywhere and trampled the flowerbeds. It was a nightmare to clean up. I heard you say so."

"Didn't you hear that director man?" Lady Nan said. "They repair things and clean everything before and after they're done. They're very careful and respectful, and they use the best carpenters and gardeners. They leave a place in better condition that when they arrived... and they pay! Bede Hall is as beautiful as any stately home in the movies."

"The gardens and the maze especially," Bash agreed.

"The house says thank you," Snow said.

"Period dramas are all the rage," Bash reported to Kit, later. "There are so many on TV now. A series would mean Mum could give up her teaching, and there would be a great big invisible 'keep out sign' for gawping tourists. We wouldn't have to do anything. Bede Hall is a star waiting to be discovered. Lady Nan said it would be very lucrative. That means it would make a lot of money."

"As long as they leave my tower alone," Kit grumbled.

Lady Nan couldn't help but notice Bash's new scarab ring when she handed her a glass of water. "Where on earth did you get that?"

"Dr. Brooks said I should have it because it's a family heirloom."

"You've seen Dr. Brooks too?" Lady Nan said, with a hurt expression.

"Yes, with Kit. They've become good friends. I took Dr. Brooks some lavender the other day. He's very kind. Kit says he's the cleverest man he knows since... since Dad."

Lady Nan smiled one of her remembering smiles. "It was Ben's," she said wistfully, touching the ring. "I gave it to him. He was wearing it the day he... well, Perry found it and returned it to me, but I made him keep it."

"Perry?"

"Peregrine. Dr. Peregrine Brooks."

"You must have it back," Bash said, already slipping the ring off her finger.

"No no. Of course you should have it. I was just surprised to see it. I'm so pleased that you and Kit have had the chance to get to know Peregrine.

"It's funny. I had a dream last night, and Ben was wearing that ring on a chain around his neck. It rather hypnotized me while he was giving me a message. Ben told me our mission was almost over. I was so happy to see him."

Bash presented the 'Bede Hall movie set' idea at the dinner table. Lady Nan was most enthusiastic and Snow sat by the fire pretending to warm her hands, all the while listening to Bede Hall's delighted responses.

Bede Hall was ready. It fairly glowed with the prospect of being the center of attention from a team of restorers descending on its rooms and grounds, and the positive attention it would receive, not just respect but fame – showcased in story and captured on film to be seen forever by millions of people who couldn't possibly leave their candy wrappers and grubby fingers over everything. It purred almost as loud as Anubis, Feathers, Snowdrop and Unicorn put together.

Jack allowed Snow to pet his head, and Rupert was on board immediately. Anything that released him from weekend gardening lessons was great news. He was especially keen on acting the lord of the manor to a group of movie people.

"Rupert had better be in charge of making inquiries," Mrs. S said.

"It'll give him a chance to use his posh Oxford accent," Kit teased.

"He'll be an actor pretending to be an agent," Bash added.

Mrs. S was pleased that her mother and children were in accord for once. She felt quite uplifted by the time the dishes were done and she had her feet up with a nice cup of tea.

"Snow has a lot of secrets," Kit confided to Bash. "She's been alone so long, I think she craves attention."

August is almost over. Perhaps you'd want attention too, if you were going to disappear for another lonely year," Bash said. "And you never told me what happened when you had that out-of-body dream with her."

"Oh that. Not much to tell really. Like I said, it was only for a few minutes. We were kind of in a whiteout blizzard. It looked like the North Pole. Then I woke up."

"That's odd because I dreamed I had a conversation with her that night as well. She showed me some things, but I forgot when I woke up."

"Best not to encourage her; she tells fibs," Kit said.

"Well, I think you should be more sensitive. Stop 'having a go' at her," Bash snapped. "What's Snow ever done to you?"

"You mean besides telling me secrets that make my head want to explode, and following me around like a puppy all the time, and popping into my experiments uninvited, and generally freaking me out? Oh, nothing much, really."

"Well, it's clear you're never going to be an actor," Bash said.

Bash wanted to change the subject, and she had a good one. The fact that Kit wasn't telling her the truth could be saved till later.

"Have you ever heard the word sentient before?" she asked.

"I think it means smart," Kit said, "but I'm not really sure. S'pose that means I'm not. Why?"

"It means the ability to understand. Lady Nan used it when she talked about Snow being able to hear the Hall. If a building has feelings and can communicate them, then it's sentient. It means it's alive."

Snow arrived in Kit's pre-dream state and stood at the bottom of his bed.

"Is that you again?" he whispered snarkily.

"I just wanted to say goodnight," Snow said.

"I hope it is. Good that is... it couldn't be worse that the other night. Sometimes I wish you'd never shown me your secret," he said.

318

Peregrine Brooks nursed his second glass of sherry and brooded over the current situation. He felt responsible. It was he who had stirred young Kit into poking about the subconscious, and it didn't do to alter one's path for the wrong reason.

There was no doubt in his mind that it would have been natural for Kit to have been inspired to write books at precisely the right moment. He was bound to be, considering where he was headed. The boy was in for adventures and no mistake.

Under the present circumstances, it was obvious Kit couldn't confess what he knew to his mother. The poor woman had had enough on her plate, let alone a ghastly premonition that would only upset her just as she was finding her 'sea legs.'

It had seemed only proper to send Kit to dry old Melville at the library, and to receive a smattering of the math ahead from old Appleby, and to pick his friend, Clive's, brain regarding the creative writing aspect, even though the lad *had* taken his being a future author a little too seriously. A dream ahead of its time was always tricky.

Clive Lucy was a fine English Professor and a fair writer himself, and had even taught Rayne Stratford-Smyth in her college days, and there wasn't a book Drew Melville didn't know inside and out, with the exact number of pages, author's date of birth, and precisely where it was on the shelf.

In the meantime – the meanest of times, he reminded himself, Bash had to be encouraged in her own creative writing endeavors as if nothing were out of the ordinary, and besides, it kept Beryl happy, and anything that did that was to be celebrated.

Gold winked from several Egyptian ornaments as the sun dipped low into Dr. Brooks' sitting room, filtering the afternoon through the drawn curtains.

On the one hand, he thought, it was right, more than appropriate actually, to whet Kit's budding science genes to plow on full steam ahead. Without his appetite for scientific facts and science-fiction, a writing career was rather redundant. Dr. Brooks knew first-hand how knowing too much was a great burden.

Peregrine Brooks downed the rest of his sherry and contemplated a third, but being much relaxed from the two he'd already had, decided the effort was beyond him.

His eyelids drooped, and he felt himself drifting off to Egypt again, on what he had come to understand years ago, to be a random 'wing and a prayer' event. But at least he was going. He'd never experienced a trip yet that wasn't, ironically speaking, 'before its time.'

"Where have you been?" he heard a young voice accuse frantically. "I thought you were never coming back!"

CHAPTER SIXTY-TWO

Cairo Online

Kit closed his eyes in Bede and opened them in Cairo. The transition happened seconds after he had bunched his father's familiar soft leather jacket and held it to his nose. The smell his of father's coat delivered him to Egypt in a shimmer of electrons like a Star Trek transporter.

Kit found himself in one of the hundreds of alleys where people sold trinkets to tourists. The market was more than bustling; it was a war zone. Maniacal vendors, shrieked their bargains in order to be heard above each other.

A dark-skinned boy his own age caught his eye and quickly looked away.

Kit had the impression the boy had been watching him for some time. He was wearing a long tunic that reminded him of Snow's nightgown. He had a cap embroidered with tiny mirrors perched on the back of his head, and black 'page-boy hair' with a fringe cut straight across a snub nose, covering most of an enormous pair of chocolate-colored eyes.

Kit was distracted by the sound of a pile of boxes falling, and the commotion of the seller cursing all the gods of Egypt for his troubles. When he looked up, the boy was gone. He searched the tacky souvenir stands of King Tut key chains and pyramid T-shirts with no luck, but he heard a low whistle coming from behind a display of belts and pendants on long chains.

Kit parted them like a beaded curtain and stepped through.

A hand grabbed his arm, and he started to protest, but the other hand of the boy shushed him by putting a finger over his mouth.

"There are tall ears here," the boy whispered, pointing to a nearby statue of the god, Anubis, tapping its ears that stood up like a rabbit's. "Come."

They walked down a series of twisting streets, each one more slummy than the first, and finally stopped outside a cluster of dilapidated office buildings.

"You are looking for me," the boy stated in a matter of fact voice.

"I.. *ah*.. no... I'm looking for my father," Kit replied. "I have no idea who you are, and it seems to me that *you* were following me."

"No, you were *looking* for me," the boy repeated with complete assurance.

Kit offered a handshake. "My name is Kit."

"I am Taraq."

Then Kit had a remarkably scientific thought when their hands touched. "Exactly WHEN are you?" he asked.

Taraq smiled and his dark skin showed a gleaming set of white teeth.

"I understand," he said, letting go of Kit's hand. He gestured toward a building that looked worse than the others. "I am sleeping in there. And yourself?"

"*Um*... I'm... in... England," Kit stated, suddenly feeling rather silly.

Like a true scientist, Kit took mental notes to remember everything. Especially when Taraq produced a sheet of paper from his wide sleeves like a magician flourishing a bunch of flowers.

It was a photograph of a gold statuette. Kit could read the hieroglyphic picture words and the oval-shaped loop around the words meant it contained the name of a royal king or queen. It read 'Smenkhkare,' the very pharaoh his father had found, and had been about to document.

"It's odd," Kit admitted, "I can't read hieroglyphics this well when I'm awake."

"I can't speak English as well as I am right now, either," Taraq admitted.

Kit tapped the photo. "I've seen this before." he said. "See this crack? It's unmistakable when you've seen it once. I noted at the time it was the shape of the letter V. I try to notice details about things. I plan to be a scientist. My father found this. Not one like it, but this exact statue."

"There are many more such pictures. They are from Smenkhkare's tomb. You are interested, yes?"

"In him, yes. In buying artifacts, no. This statue has been stolen. Do you work in the black market?"

"I work for men who run an artifact trading business, as you call it – the black market. They sell in secret, which is where my job comes in. The Internet makes people invisible. You understand?"

"Yes, no-one ever really knows who someone is online."

"Exactly. And there are no paper trails such as addresses or contracts or receipts. I happen to be good with computers. My bosses are not. They're better at stealing, and they are 'tough guys' as you say in the movies, and can't be bothered learning the latest technology. That is where I come in. Or rather came in.

"I used to live on the streets. At first they needed an errand boy and I needed a place to stay. Then one day, a computer was set up and I watched. It was very strange because it seemed as if I already knew how to use it, and once they saw I could do things, I was more valuable to them as a technician. It is also my job to find other street kids to deliver messages and pay them. Between the children and my work, I know everything that goes on about their operation."

Kit tried to act nonchalant. "And?"

"And, I know where your father is."

Kit stopped breathing. "Can you take me to him now?"

"He's in danger. He is in prison."

"A jail! So, he's not been kidnapped?"

"I didn't use the word jail. He is kept underground."

"So then he was kidnapped."

"He was betrayed."

"I can take you to the site of Mr. Cornelly's..."

"Cornelius," Kit corrected.

"To Smenkhkare's tomb," Taraq went on. "This is our dream – yours and mine, so it's up to your father to show up. He may not be asleep, but he is connected to both of us. He may be sleeping and wandering somewhere else. I dream-travel all the time. It's never the same twice. My brain tells stories. It speaks in pictures..."

"Like hieroglyphics," Kit interrupted.

"Like flash cards. Most of the time," Taraq continued, "I don't know what they mean."

"I have a friend who will know," Kit said. "A doctor in my village understands dreams. I can tell him what I see, and maybe you and I can share a dream again and find my father."

"I doubt we can dream the same dream again. Not in this way. Dreams aren't like the chapters in a book. They don't follow the rules of time."

Kit's face brightened, and he grabbed Taraq's shoulders. "I've got this amazing bizarre crazy-wild idea. We ..."

It was Taraq's turn to interrupt. "Those are the best ones," he said, grinning.

Kit returned the grin with an even more enthusiastic one of his own. "We can meet online," he beamed.

By Taraq's eager expression, Kit could tell he was favorably impressed.

"I haven't got an email address of my own," he said. "I only use the business one on my bosses' website. I manage the site, so you will have to contact me there. I send all the pictures of artifacts for sale to the buyers. You will have to pretend to be an interested buyer. It takes many emails before a deal is sealed. My employers have to be careful: No phone numbers, no streets, no real names, and no traceable payments. No paper trail. The lines between realities is the safest place to conduct business."

"So much for ethics," Kit said.

"Ethics?"

"Fair trading. Playing by the rules," Kit explained.

Taraq found this remark hilarious. "My business is a form of magic. Disappearing artifacts, disappearing people, and disappearing tombs," he said, whisking the photo of Smenkhkare's statue back into his robe.

He invited Kit to inspect his trick "You see? Nothing up my sleeve."

"Now you see it; now you don't," agreed Kit. "That sounds about right.

"'There's no reason why we can't make it work. I just have to be extra careful." Taraq said. "I can give you the website address. Are you good at memorizing things?"

"First give me something worth memorizing."

"We need to travel many miles, but fortunately dream miles don't follow the rules either. See? We are here already."

Kit and Taraq stood on a strip of faded brown grass that marked the edge of the desert. The brightness of the blue sky was blinding. Before them stretched a vast landscape of golden dunes with three triangular shapes on the horizon.

"This is Giza," Taraq said, pointing to the pyramids. "No need to tell you what those are. We need to go closer. There must be a message for us there or we wouldn't be here."

"We're dreaming but we are *aware* of it," Kit remarked. This isn't just an experiment. It's synchronicity."

Taraq looked confused. "Please explain this word."

"A coincidence is an event that means something. It's time playing a game with us," Kit said.

"Like computer games?" Taraq asked. "Do you play?"

"Of course," Kit replied.

"Then we should play on-line too," Taraq suggested.

Kit didn't mean to sound abrupt. "I can't. I don't have time for playing games. If we're real, then this is an amazing opportunity."

"So, we are just a lucky meeting?" Taraq asked, looking disappointed.

"No. Not that. Luck isn't scientific. I watch, and listen, and control, and measure the things that show up."

"You are measuring us?"

"I am."

Taraq seemed distant, and Kit felt responsible.

"Do you have any idea how horrible it is to lose a father?" Kit said.

Taraq spoke to the sand. "I have never had a father to lose," he said. "I don't remember either of my parents."

The thought struck Kit hard; he took family for granted. "You lived on the streets alone? I am so sorry, he said. "I didn't..."

"Have any idea?" Taraq finished, looking miffed.

The next minute seemed like an hour, but Taraq spoke again as if there had been no pause in their conversation. "I am not alone. I have bosses. I don't live on the streets; I survive them. It is much harder."

"My brother's name is Boss," Kit volunteered. "He's nothing as bad as your bosses, but I expect you and I have a lot more in common than either of us think. We can be good friends even though we live thousands of miles apart."

Taraq brightened a little. "I've never had a friend either," he said. "The men I work for... I hear them talking. Bragging mostly. I'm a scientist too, I guess, because I watch and listen. My sleeping mat..."

Kit's expression stopped Taraq's words cold.

"What?"

"Nothing. I assumed you had a bed, that's all," Kit said.

"My *'magic carpet'* is in a room with a bank of computers," Taraq rephrased sarcastically. "It's full of boxes and crates filled with straw. It isn't hard to guess that they're full of stolen antiquities.

"So... now I am figuring out a way to escape. If I learn enough on my boss's computer, I believe I can find a real job, but it won't be easy. I know too much about them to just walk out the door. I have to wait till they're caught or they kill each other off."

"You're not a slave, Taraq. You could go to the police."

"Most of them *are* policeman," Taraq replied curtly.

"You're trapped then. You can't run to another city?"

"I like to eat," Taraq said.

Kit thought about the vast kitchens of Bede Hall, and the food piled high on the table, where he never had to wonder where his next meal was coming from or when.

As dreams will, the scene shifted into where it wanted to go.

The boys walked toward the pyramids. Kit noticed the sand was pleasantly warm, not scorching hot as he had heard. They left no tracks. The sand returned like molten silk to fill each footprint as soon as it was abandoned.

Kit calculated the math, running it through a mental list of variables. He could see that Taraq was doing the same thing. We probably *do* have a lot in common, he thought.

"Dreams are a different dimension," he finally said, "but... so is the Internet. We can meet in alternate realities where physical bodies and addresses don't exist."

"Emails," Taraq said quietly, sounding disappointed.

"Not *just* emails," Kit corrected. "Special connections like this don't happen all the time... at least, not to me."

"So then why?"

"Sometimes things aren't clear for a very long time, but I know one day they will be. A person has to wait to find out. A clever teacher taught me that," Kit said.

Taraq picked up a passing cobra undulating past, turned it into a ruler, and wrote the name of his website in the sand with it.

"You're the one measuring us now," Kit joked.

"It's one of the oldest Egyptian magic tricks," Taraq laughed.

The pyramids loomed closer and shimmered behind heat-waves like a mirage. The familiar figure of Cornelius Stratford-Smyth stood halfway up the Great Pyramid of Cheops on its north flank, and waved before disappearing between two of the granite blocks.

"There!" Kit pointed. "Look!" But where his father had stood was a large black dog – the god Anubis, scavenger of ancient Egypt.

The creature leapt from stone-to-stone, and the face of the pyramid became a game like 'Super Mario Brothers' with the scene now displayed on a giant computer screen large enough to contain the pyramids and the entire sky.

An electronic tune played while Anubis jumped over chasms, and each time he landed on a block a music note sounded that seemed like a coded message. Then the game ended in a cartoon explosion, and a 'game over' sign flashed across the landscape.

The image on the screen changed to Giza again, but this time it was night, and the pyramids were lit by searchlights from below, silhouetted against the most magnificent display of heavenly constellations that Kit had ever seen.

The wind howled, and the sand turned a shade of orangey-pink and swirled like the eddies in a pond at the onset of a storm.

Stonehenge replaced the pyramids in the center of the great desert plain, and an Egyptian slave wearing nothing but a white loincloth, raked the sand around the standing stones as if it were a giant's Japanese Zen garden. The rake made a pattern of whorls that resembled the crop circles in one of Lady Nan's New-Age books.

Stonehenge vanished to reveal the Great Sphinx behind it which had become a green topiary. It shrank to the size of the one at Bede Hall.

"Are you seeing all this?" Kit said to Taraq.

"You mean Anubis playing 'Super Mario,' and the circle of obelisks, and the Sphinx made of leaves?"

"The same."

"I must thank you, my new English friend, for the gift of your amazing imagination," Taraq said.

A cloud approached like galloping horses and overtook them. Red sand swirled around Taraq like a small tornado, separating him from Kit. His voice grew faint.

"Tomorrow," shouted Taraq's disappearing voice.

"Yes. Tomorrow," Kit yelled back into the darkness, just as an alarm clock shrilled in his ear, and sent Jack leaping onto the bed, whining to go out.

CHAPTER SIXTY-THREE

Freezing Rayne

Kit started up his computer, his nerves firing and snapping with sparks, his metronome set to its highest speed urging the machine to connect.

Pigeon danced about in an agitated pace on his 'visitor's perch' bobbing his head up and down in time to the metronome's melodious clicks.

It seemed a lifetime before a mechanical jingle signalled he was connected.

It was a matter of minutes for the site to materialize. The banner at the top was the same image he had seen in his dream: turquoise sky, yellow sand, and the pyramids far away.

He tried to imagine a tiny speck waving from the largest one.

Bash's voice made him knock over the metronome.

"Feathers!" the voice squawked, mimicking Bash perfectly. *"Leave that planet ... that plant alone!... don't make me come over there!"*

Pigeon was in fine form.

At first, Kit was loath to involve his new friend in a mission that would likely put him in danger, but he thought about what he would do himself if the situation were reversed, and decided that's what true friends were for. Even new ones. Friends ventured beyond casual acquaintance to go the extra mile for each other.

Kit was quite prepared to pledge the same loyalty to Taraq. But in the end, it was Taraq's suggestion that he do some sleuthing of his own, vowing he wouldn't stop until the whole truth was uncovered, good or bad.

The details of Taraq's mission were worked out in a series of dreams within dreams like Tut's famous nest of gold coffins. Kit realized happily that they were 'apropos' – and a perfect example of synchronicity as he had once researched the 'Matryoshka principle' which meant similar things of descending size that fit inside each other, named after the Russian nesting dolls... like the ones that perched silently, hiding their inner secrets in the nursery at Bede Hall. The ones he'd just seen a few days ago in Snow's frozen sanctuary.

It meant he was on the right track. His dream clues were like the dolls... one inside the other, and at the center the smallest doll represented his father. Smenkhkare's missing golden statuette and all the pharaoh's likenesses, before it and since, had been kept hidden out of sight in the darkest innermost sanctums of the great Egyptian temples.

That dark place was now where his father was held prisoner, and Taraq, his new best friend was going to rescue him.

"There's a few things I need to tell you," Kit began.

"No duh," Bash said, "it's about time."

Kit's jaw dropped. "It is! It's absolutely, exactly, positively, about time."

"It can't be anything good then."

Kit hesitated. "D'you want to get some cocoa first?"

"Sure. Cocoa always makes things better," Bash said, getting out the milk pan and two mugs.

"The thing is... we're not *supposed* to know the future. I didn't exactly lie to you about my time dream. I just didn't tell you everything."

"That much I figured out for myself," Bash said, spooning sugar into the cocoa powder.

Kit continued. "Because none of it has happened yet. And if I told you, it might change things, and screw things up that are already going to be screwed up. In a different way. Do you understand?"

"Your scientific logic is as flawless as usual, but your words lack panache," Bash declared in a temper. "It's really most capricious of you."

"Really? ... Oh man ... Not now. Could you... for once... listen without sounding like a flaming thesaurus. This is seriously important!"

"But you know... so..."

"Yes... which is precisely why *I'm* able to mess with things that haven't happened yet *because* I know. If I tell *you*, then you could change it too much or freak out."

Bash stirred the milk with a long wooden spoon, deliberately counting four stirs clockwise and then four stirs counter-clockwise to stay focused. "Like what?"

"Like the end of the world!" blurted Kit, miserably.

But he left out the worst part: that it was the end of *her*.

"So, I... *uh* met this guy," Kit said casually, "and he has a plan to rescue Dad."

Bash blew the steam from her cocoa and stared at Kit. "Have you gone bonkers?"

"He's in Egypt," Kit said quickly. "Same age as us."

"You met him on-line I suppose," Bash stated, unimpressed.

Kit took a deep breath and slammed his cocoa on the table a little harder than he intended. It slopped a little, but it served to break Bash's look of disinterest.

"I met him in a *dream* first... *then* on-line," he said with a fierce expression that dared Bash to listen.

Bash thought for a few seconds. "I take it back. You *are* bonkers," she said, wiping up the spill, "but you may as well tell me the rest of it. Nothing's really normal anymore, so why should a dream friend who's going to find our kidnapped father be any less real than meeting Snow, a magic room, Charlotte's green power, or being hoodwinked by fairies?"

"Exactly."

"But then, maybe we've both gone bonkers," Bash mused.

She took her first sip of cocoa and the sudden jolt of sugar grounded her.

"Look," Kit started, "I know the last few months have rather dropped us into an altered perception of things. We just have to accept that. But if the real world contains ghosts and fairies and a time portal to winter, then we can't rule out the bizarre fact that I was able to email a dream while I was awake. I'd call that evidence. Long shots are better than forgetting Dad. He may be alive. If time travel is real then he *is* alive.

"Dr. Brooks, Parks, and Charlotte have opened up a paranormal world. Cyberspace is real enough in a peculiar twist called virtual reality."

"No, I suppose you're right," Bash agreed, "we shouldn't rule out anything."

Keeping Mrs. S in the dark was essential. "No way are we telling Mum," Kit said. "At least not till I've investigated this more with Dr. Brooks. Agreed?"

"And definitely not Boss," Bash added.

"Four heads are better than two," Kit said, counting Taraq and Dr. Brooks.

"You mean five," Bash said smiling. "Snow has a head."

"Okay... I gotta know," Kit finally asked, looking rather sheepish. "What does capreesh...whatever you said, mean?"

Bash filled the wide basket on her green bicycle with generous posies of lavender bunched together and tied with white ribbons.

Kit had been intent on visiting Dr. Brooks about the Egyptian business, and had left hours before her in an agitated state, so today, Bash rode as slowly as she liked rather than in tandem, savoring

332

her freedom. Kit was apt to make their trips to town into a race. It was wonderful to have the road to herself and she deliberately chose her route for its beauty rather than the shortest way to town.

The impression of blistering yellow sands and pyramids spontaneously popped into Bash's mind, and her thoughts wandered to simultaneous images of Egyptian violets and lotus blossoms floating on the Nile, and papyrus rushes swaying in a sun that rivaled its shy English cousin. Kit must be sending signals again. Or was it Taraq?

Cycling down the back-roads into Bede was heavenly. Bash enjoyed the vista of the hills with a pungent tray of pastel purple under her nose. Every now-and-then she glanced down at her handiwork to admire the clusters of florets each nestled in its own cup of green tendrils, and the longer stemmed bouquets – their stalks wrapped carefully in wet paper laying on their side.

Bash delighted in her lavender. It was easily twice as vibrant and ten times as fragrant as plain lavender, steeped in the 'fairy magic' that Charlotte insisted carried the poetry of the flowers. It would make an amazing addition to Charlotte's florist shop window, and the ones that didn't sell, would hang in the rafters to dry with the thyme and sage bundles in the back room, ready for Christmas sachets and cooking spices.

PART SEVEN

HOLLYWOODLAND

1923 was the year
the original Hollywood sign
was erected.
It was a real estate ad
for a suburban housing development
called 'Hollywoodland.'
Its inspirational message
remains the same:
This is where magic is possible,
where dreams can come true.

*1923 WAS ALSO THE YEAR
HOWARD CARTER RETURNED TO ENGLAND
AFTER DISCOVERING THE TOMB OF
TUTANKHAMUN.

CHAPTER SIXTY-FOUR

Too Close to Home

Mrs. S had been taking a pie from the oven when Rupert crashed into the room waving his sunglasses and a sheet of paper.

"I just got an email!" he burst out.

Mrs. S said: "that's nice dear," and continued to admire her pie.

"They want to come and see us," Rupert said, babbling with excitement. "The photos I sent must have done the trick."

"What photos? Who wants to come and see us?" Mrs. S said, never taking her eyes from the pie.

"Hollyworks Productions. They've asked us for a meeting," Rupert crowed. "Another house has cancelled at the last minute, and they're in a bit of a pickle."

"Bede Hall is very clever," Snow said at teatime.

"Boss is over the moon," Bash said.

"Boss is over himself," Kit countered sarcastically. "Blimey, all he needs is more power. He's insufferable as it is."

"You'd be ecstatic too if Bede Hall could be saved," Bash said, sympathetic for once.

This was true, but there was no denying that the movie business would likely make Rupert Stratford-Smyth an even more pompous git than before.

Kit had to admit his older brother had had a few rough months of inconvenient long-distance travel. A gruelling semester of final exams was bad enough, but flunking all of them was a bit much even for an inflated ego.

Bash had called it a dead-end career, and laughed at her pun since she had been explaining it to Snow at the time.

"That's not very funny," Snow had said.

"They've already sent Boss a script, and get this: it's a movie about Howard Carter. Dad's hero."

"Who was he?" Snow asked.

"He found King Tut's tomb in 1922," Bash said.

Snow looked uncomfortable. "I think I'll take Jack for a little walk," she said quickly.

"They have to start shooting right away," Bash gushed, "to get the summer flowers while they're at their best. When a movie production decides, it moves fast. They're sending a fleet of gardeners to mow and weed tomorrow."

"Mum first thought it wasn't right," Bash explained to Lady Nan, while Snow watched her brush her great-grandmother's hair.

"You know, a bit too close to home and all that, but Boss convinced her that it was bad business to mess the movie people about, you know, since it's the first time they want us, and that Dad would have been honored." "I think he's right for once," Lady Nan said.

"Turned out, Kit was the only one who didn't like the idea."

"Is *that* what all the shouting was about," Lady Nan said. "I wondered. Fit to wake the dead it was, pardon the expression," she said, addressing Snow, who was sitting round-eyed with anxiety at the thought of hundreds of new people milling about the garden.

Mrs. S surprised everyone after Kit announced that it wasn't the done thing, to disrespect his father's reputation.

"Christopher Carter Stratford-Smyth," she had shrilled in an uncharacteristic display of temper. "Your father would have been proud to be associated with a movie celebrating the life of his hero."

And that was that. It was a 'go,' and Rupert was given the official *keys to the door* in order to see that arrangements were carried out according to the most professional business *sense and sensibility* he could muster out of thin air.

News traveled fast in Bede. Especially when it was in the form of Enid Tweedy with some exciting gossip. She had it on good authority (in this case Edgar who had been eavesdropping on Rupert and Mrs. S) that the village of Bede was in for an adventure.

The village was as thrilled as any town would be at the prospect of dozens of new customers who needed everything from batteries to shampoo, and was soon under the Hollywood spell.

Shopkeepers buzzed in a hive of excitement. Candace Gumm from the sweet shop ordered more American candy bars, and the baker, Mr. Bunsworthy, baked more cakes and revived old recipes for several exotic flavors of muffins to be delivered to the Hall gates, fresh each morning.

A few lucky individuals boasted about the few minutes of fame they would be getting as movie extras, while costume people fitted them with servants uniforms seeing how most of the scenes would take place inside the Hall itself. Parks looked the part of the head gardener and was hired on the spot after much protest. He finally faked a life-threatening illness to be disqualified.

There was a tremendous flap within the Tweedy household.

Mrs. Tweedy was giddy off her head from being able to brag to her relatives that she was about to rub shoulders with movie royalty, and preened Edgar for an audition that surely Mr. Tweedy (as a close friend of the Stratford-Smyth family) would be able to wangle. After all, she thought, he was a brilliant businessman, and Mrs. Stratford-Smyth and her mother, Miss Beryl, were surely most obligated to him for all his efforts to sell the Hall over two whole years.

Wilbur Tweedy grumped that Bede Hall would ruin him with its new property value rising sky-high until he calculated how much more money he would make from the sales of other houses in town.

Movies, he noted, put small towns on the map, and with all the comings and goings he would, or rather Edgar would, have a better chance to snoop about.

What he hadn't considered, was that dear Edgar would be excluded access since he was longer be a student. Mrs. S had announced she would no longer be teaching. Bede Hall School was closed.

Security guards manned the entrance to Bede Hall, and the Tweedys found themselves clearly on the wrong side of the gate.

But apart from the drama at the Tweedy residence, the villagers of Bede were happy to welcome the circus of a movie production coming to town. They cheered the convoy of trucks that rumbled in off the highway, and waved excitedly at the blackened windows of the limousines that streaked after them.

Edgar went howling to his mother with the news that his lessons would stop, although he was pleased at having no more homework, and Mr. Tweedy cuffed his son's ears for bringing him bad news just when he was feeling happy.

Edgar vowed he would not only take more pictures of the ghost of Bede Hall, but he and Nipper would see that the Stratford-Smyths paid the ultimate price for having his pocket money stopped for a month.

He would even borrow his father's expensive camera because the one image taken with his phone had not been convincing enough, and had been considered, by the inscrutable editor of the 'Daily Bead,' to be totally unworthy of publication and to stop wasting his valuable time.

The library at Bede Hall underwent the swiftest of makeovers with new red drapes and window cushions, enormous vases of silk flowers, and gallons of lemon oil furniture polish.

Pigeon's second largest cage, installed in the library, had to be removed and was replaced by a shiny brass perch.

At first, the director considered the presence of a talking parrot to be an unexpected bonus. Such a colorful creature, he claimed, would be a fine addition to his cast. He'd even been delighted to learn that a gentleman like one of his main characters, Lord Carnarvon, would have been quite at home with an exotic bird for a pet.

But the bird kept blurting out the word pooh at the most inopportune moments and refused to learn his lines, hastily written for him: *"It's the curse...Mr Carter!..it's the curse!"*

Even though Pigeon loved his character's name, Percival, he was also too keen on giving inappropriate spontaneous recitations of the MGM lion at odd intervals, that he'd learned from keeping Lady Nan company when she watched her late night programs on the movie channel.

He had been sent to the kitchen in disgrace mumbling *"Action!"* and *"Your in my shot!... I don't do close-ups!"*...and *"Cut, that's a wrap!"* all in the director's voice which had caused all manner of problems.

Then the crew, while scouting other areas in the upstairs corridors, found the blue door.

"Capricious," Bash had been pleased to explain during dinner, considering it was the only way she felt as clever as her brother, "means unpredictable or to make sudden unexpected changes. You're very impulsive," she told him, half-admiringly and half-jealous.

Kit defended himself. "Well, I try not to be *any* of those things," he said. "I pride myself on behaving like a scientist. It doesn't do to be spontaneous or brash or to speak out of turn before considering all the angles of a thing."

"Life is full of twists and turns," Bash said knowingly. "It's okay to act on your intuition. That's what I've been learning from Parks and Charlotte. I'm sure Dr. Brooks would approve. He'd call it following one's instincts."

"Hunches you mean," Kit commented gloomily.

"Not at all," Bash explained. "Educated guesses. I did the research. Most geniuses surprise themselves when they stop thinking so much and start listening. It's called believing in oneself."

Lady Nan followed the twins' conversation with an unusually dreamy expression and announced out of the blue. "Acting and behaving are two different kettles of fish."

CHAPTER SIXTY-FIVE

The Back of the Tiger

Mrs. Tweedy corralled Mrs. S, clearly delighted about something. "Such wonderful news," she gushed. "You'll never guess."

Mrs. S waved the twins on. "I'll be in the post office. Meet me there in ten minutes," she said over her shoulder as Enid Tweedy steered her away.

Edgar walked backwards behind them and made the rude 'fingers-wiggling-in-the-ears' gesture and stuck out his tongue at Kit behind his mother's back.

Bash caught Edgar's performance out the corner of her eye, in the act of retracting his tongue. She elbowed Kit and gestured towards Edgar with her new lollipop. "What's up his... what's got his goat now," she hissed.

They learned why during supper.

"Somehow the little ... creature... has wangled himself an audition as an extra," Mrs. S said. "His mother informed me in the post office loud enough for the entire village to hear."

"I thought she was acting smug about something."

"At least *one* of them can act," Kit said.

Bash was livid. "So, he's still going to be allowed through our gates? Boss has to do something. Something bossy. Right now. The great turnip has already sent me a threatening text that says he's going to the press with some interesting developments concerning a certain *blue door* and its contents."

"I don't think it's what's got Edgar's *goat*; it's what's got our *ghost*, " Kit whispered to Bash. "That smarmy little jam tart is going to blow the whole Snow business if we don't do something."

"Like what?"

"Like tell Lady Nan," Kit said.

"Some days you have to put your foot down," Lady Nan said firmly. "That sneak breaks the camel's back!"

It was a rare mood to see her so angry, and the twins were amused as much as alarmed.

"I didn't like that boy the moment I set eyes on him," Lady Nan fumed. "Little finagler. Bede Hall told me he was trouble. No wonder Snow's been so upset. She's been so much thinner and distracted. She might have told me. Now that horrible creature has spoiled her August. Well, something has to be done!"

"We can't exactly tell Mum," Bash said.

"Except, in the meantime, Edgar's could go to the newspapers, so she'll find out soon enough."

"I'll talk to her," Lady Nan said. "I'd better have a word with Rupert as well. He seems to be our business go-between these days."

Kit looked worried. "It had better be right away. Edgar was nasty enough to let us know to expect a reporter."

"Little monster," Lady Nan said. "As if the dearly departed don't have enough problems. It's beyond the pale!"

Lady Nan's words almost sounded funny, and Bash stifled a laugh. Pale described Snow when she was in any sort of stress.

"Don't you mean beyond the veil?"

Lady Nan was not amused. "Bathsheba, you have a strange take on the situation. It's not like you to be so insensitive. And it's not a bit amusing for Snow."

Bash looked suitably apologetic. "The movie people already have a poltergeist joke going around," she offered as a lame excuse, "so they may not care."

Kit nodded. "I heard that movie people are superstitious. They always say a set feels haunted by a trickster, so maybe they won't be concerned. Publicity is their thing anyway, isn't it?"

"They won't want reporters sniffing around," Bash said, "it's a closed set. Rupert's going to freak out. And a local reporter won't let go of a juicy ghost story or the chance for a first-hand nosy amongst film stars. Nothing much happens around here, and they've locked out everyone who isn't part of the production. It would be a feather in Tweedy's cap if a reporter infiltrated our defenses."

"Got past our fences, you mean," Kit said.

"Obviously not everyone. Mrs. Tweedy managed to get Edgar through the system. That woman is a menace and so is her husband."

"She may be a wannabe stage-mother," Kit said, "but it's Mr. Tweedy who wants Edgar behind the scenes. Scuze the pun."

Kit used Dr. Brooks' meditation techniques to see the problem as if it was a machine and he could wander inside it. His face brightened after a few minutes. "Maybe there is something we can do. I have a plan."

"Next time we need shots of servants' quarters we should remember this blue door," the set designer said to his assistant. "Most of these old places have renovated them out. I think a 'Jane Austen thing' is on our schedule, next. Something about a Hall too, I think. No, wait, I tell a lie, it's an abbey... Northanger Abbey. We'll need this sort of hallway."

"Chilly up here though," the assistant said. "Feels rather nice after standing in that garden all day. And the library could use some air-conditioning. Not as hot as Thebes though." On location in the Valley of the Kings had been excruciating.

"And all for one scene in Tut's tomb."

"Did you hear that parrot? It had to be taken downstairs. It kept yelling 'cut,' so it caused mayhem."

An odious stink of sulfurous green smoke issued from the main chimney. Bede Hall was not happy. *"Edgar's in for it,"* the trees whispered.

CHAPTER SIXTY-SIX
In Like a Lion

Stowed away in one of the vans full of Egyptian props was another boy determined to wreak havoc at Bede Hall.

But Edgar Tweedy couldn't *begin* to match the antics of the wiry nine-year-old because the boy had been dead for thousands of years and knew more magic tricks than Edgar could have conjured in several lifetimes.

The truck doors swung open, and two pairs of strong hands began shifting crates and barrels searching for the one marked 'library scene.'

"I hope that cursed poltergeist stayed in Thebes," a voice remarked amid the grunts of heavy moving.

"There's no such thing," a different voice said.

"Movie sets always have some sort of poltergeist," the first voice spoke again, "and everyone likes to blame some malicious imp dreamed up a long time ago, no doubt in the days when the first backdrop wall fell over and knocked out Charlie Chaplin. Actors are superstitious. Stuff always happens and things disappear because everyone wants a souvenir."

"You mean stuff to sell on the Internet."

"Exactly. It's a perk of the biz, as long as it's one of our bits and bobs. There's the box we're looking for. Be grateful we don't need all this other Egyptian stuff."

"Right. A couple of days in an English library and we're out of here."

"If we get this over to the house fast enough we'll have enough time for a beer in the local pub," the first voice suggested.

"No thanks, warm beer... *ugh*! I'd rather grab a burger and a cold one in the canteen tent."

The crate was small enough to fit on a dolly and was soon

wheeled away in the direction of Bede Hall, but the doors to the van were left open.

From the open door, a stowaway boy viewed the amazing sight of a green desert that stretched as far as he could see. There were plump trees everywhere; not the palms of an oasis, but trees as big as obelisks.

The boy was over by the green statue shaped like the Sphinx when he heard a voice shout: "Jack get back here!"

A hairy lion leaped up to lick his face and he ran to hide behind a flat sun disk standing on a short column.

Kit saw Jack jumping on a child actor, and hurried over in case the boy was scared of dogs. This one was dressed in a long striped cotton robe that he recognized as a galabeya – the long smock worn by Egyptian men. It was like Taraq's, and his father had brought one back for him from Egypt. Bash had taken it to use as a nightgown, although it was what men wore to work in the hot climate.

"I'm sorry. He's not supposed to do that," Kit apologized. "Jack! Down!"

"Hello," the boy said, unafraid. "You can see me?"

"Hi. My name's Kit. I hope Jack here didn't scare you. Not everyone appreciates his enthusiasm. Do you like dogs?"

"Dogs?" the boy said. "Jackals are hairy in your country. Did you tame him?"

"As you can see, not very well. He doesn't usually do this. My Dad named him Jack because he's got the same long legs as a jackal. My father studies... well, *used* to study Egypt. Jack's a spoiled deerhound, but he has the same appetite as a jackal, he'll eat almost anything. "

Jack sniffed the hem of the boy's costume, and then made a beeline for the stick Kit threw as a distraction.

"What did you mean when you asked if I could see you?" Kit asked warily, wondering why the boy stayed in character speaking with a strange accent.

"Do you live in that temple?" the boy asked indicating Bede Hall. "Are you a prince?"

Jack returned with the stick.

"It's too hot Jacko," Kit said, when Jack panted, eager for another throw.

Jack dropped in the shade without argument.

"See," Kit said grinning at Jack, "fully-trained."

Kit pointed to the Hall. "That's my grandmother's house. I live there now. I'm not a prince but I have an older brother who thinks *he* is. Gotta go. I promised to meet a... *er...* my sister. What did you say your name was," he asked holding out is hand.

The boy stared at the hand refusing to touch. "I am Taraq," he said, with a heavy accent.

"Taraq!" Kit exclaimed. "That must be a common Egyptian name. I know someone over there with that name. No I meant your real name."

"I am Taraq," the boy repeated looking puzzled.

"My friend wears a robe like yours, but he's older and taller."

"Then he is not Taraq," the boy declared stubbornly and evaporated into the garden.

Kit sighed. "Not another one," he said to Jack, who had gotten up and was sniffing the spot recently inhabited by a ghost.

Kit brightened. "Hey this might be our lucky day buddy. Now we have to tell Dr. Brooks. He said he would meet you when the time was right."

Kit searched the gardens for the new Taraq and found him sitting on the edge of the fountain staring at the stone mermaids riding the dolphins.

"Did you hitch a ride here?" Kit said, startling the ghost.

Someone called me here or I would never have left my home, Taraq 2 said.

"I think I might know the very person," Kit said. "How old are you?"

"Nine," the boy answered.

"Perfect." Kit smiled. "Do you like girls?"

Taraq 2 was back marvelling at the green sphinx the next day, when a voice caused him to turn around.

"Hey you. Where are the auditions?"

Taraq gave the scrawny boy a quick study and determined he was one of the many servants everywhere who talked nonstop, in a hurry all day.

Edgar pelted him with questions. "Is this where the auditions are? What's it like? Were you nervous?"

Taraq pointed to a cluster of people massed around a man sitting in a canvas chair.

"That is the vizier," he said. "The man on the throne."

"The what?"

"The man who gives the orders," Taraq said.

"How much do you get paid?" the Edgar asked, rudely. "Do you get to keep your costume?"

A woman in front of the palace waved frantically in order to be noticed.

"Someone is wanting you," Taraq said.

"Edgar. Edgar. Over here darling." Mrs. Tweedy shrieked.

CHAPTER SIXTY-SEVEN

Show Biz

"And action!" the director called. Apart from the actors, the entire production stopped breathing and froze like chess pieces on a board. They had no choice but to stand on their marks where they'd been told to move, and wait for their cue.

They were like a human machine. Sign language fluttered everywhere sending silent orders without disrupting the aforementioned 'action.'

The set was packed with crew all trying to do their jobs without making a sound.

Truckloads of them had descended like locusts and soon the grounds were covered in tents and trailers. People in Edwardian costumes swarmed everywhere: maids in white caps and aprons, and gentleman in suits for the lord of the manor, beautiful sweeping gowns for the ladies, and an archaeologist who looked nothing like the real thing.

He was a parody of the rogue and not a bit like the actual Howard Carter, whose photo had sat on Mr. S's desk in a place of honor.

The library and study were the only rooms to be filmed in addition to the grounds, which to Bash's delight, a team of professional gardeners had attacked, paying special attention to the hedges and topiaries, and adding many flowering plants. Parks dithered and hovered around them looking (to the crew) as if he were rehearsing his part regardless of him being direly ill.

Parks had been in a constant state of agitation as engineers repaired the fountain and added a dozen carp and water-lilies to the water. The mermaids retreated by the underground channel that led to the River Bede. Portable railway tracks for the cameras were laid everywhere. Everyone knew what they were doing, and they were doing it as if the end of the world was tomorrow.

Food services set up a canteen, and the twins had a free pass to everything.

They'd never seen so much food. Mrs. S was thrilled with the fact she didn't have to cook for a week and that her property was getting a professional face-lift, even though it was smack in the middle of a madhouse circus with a dozen rings.

Rupert, thrilled to miss his final exams, was even more delighted to mingle with the extras, worming his way higher to his destination – the rarefied circles of the stars.

He played the real lord of the manor role 'to the nines,' and was happy to accept their respect whenever they deferred to his authority. He had found his element, as Lady Nan would have said, eavesdropping on as many conversations as he could, listening to the production staff and actors alike... and every now and then feeling free to issue an order to a stage-hand.

Rupert was in a very good humor at dinner.

"I'm going to be an actor," he announced, waving a potato on the end of his fork. "It's my calling."

"La dee dah," said Kit. "You'll have to study."

"How positively unfortunate," Bash threw in casually. "Studying isn't exactly your calling, is it."

"Pretty boy!" screeched Pigeon. *"One potato two potato."*

Kit gave Pigeon a piece of lettuce. "I do believe someone else is calling you."

Rupert toyed with his stew. "You can all be beastly if you want. Haven't you ever heard of a quick study? Not every actor goes to acting school, you know," Rupert declared.

"The best ones do," Kit said.

"What about natural talent?" Bash asked.

"You have to be able to memorize lines," Kit chided.

"And rise at dawn," Lady Nan chimed in.

"Yeah, and do as you're told all the time," said Kit, winking at Bash. "That's definitely *not* one of your natural talents Boss old boy."

"It's not being ordered about you know; it's called taking direction," Rupert fumed.

"There's only one direction for you," laughed Kit.

"Perhaps you'll think again when I'm famous," Rupert sneered.

"I'll be older than Lady Nan by then," Kit said with a staged coughing fit.

"So, no more college dear?" Mrs. S queried changing the subject. "Your father so want..." and she stopped with her eyes all misty, and concentrated hard on adding pepper to her beef stew.

"I had plenty of memorizing to do at Oxford," Rupert bragged. "Exams were every week. So I've had plenty of practice already."

Lady Nan studied the desert spoon horizontal to her plate and kept quiet.

"What do *you* think Grandmamma?" Rupert asked.

"I think you're handsome enough to be a leading man," Lady Nan replied slyly, her gaze never leaving the spoon.

Rupert looked pleased, and glared at the twins. "See, Lady Nan thinks I can do it," Rupert gloated. "You're a star, Madame."

"Now, stamina is another kettle of fish," Lady Nan continued. "You can learn that if you've a mind to start at the bottom. What do they call those actors?"

"Extras," shouted the twins in unison.

"They're called casual actors, and understudies, and stunt-doubles," Rupert said with authority as if he'd been around the movie business all his life.

"Showbiz is a zoo. You'd better have a real job to fall back on," Bash said.

"I've been invited to breakfast with the casting director, Rupert boasted. "I think there may be a small part for me."

"Your brain perhaps?" Kit suggested.

Rupert ignored his brother. "So I won't be eating with you lot tomorrow morning," he continued. "In fact, I may take all my meals in the canteen. I don't want to miss anything."

"Be a *star* then, and pass the salt before you go," Kit snorted.

Mrs. S smiled sweetly as a warning, Lady Nan stifled a laugh, and the twins focused on their stew and tried not to look at each other.

"La dee dah!" squawked Pigeon. *"Time for my close-up."*

The circumstances were ideal for Snow: Rupert would be away from the house or glued to a patch of floor in the wings watching the filming, so the twins were free to escort her to and from Lady Nan's room.

The pretty manicure girl had taken a fancy to Rupert and offered him a complimentary appointment so she could hold his hand and gossip about the small-talk and the latest rumors she overheard daily.

Mrs. S announced she would be making herself scarce, and take the opportunity to catch up on her reading, and Lady Nan hadn't the slightest interest in anything other than caring for her friend, Snow.

The 'set' gardeners were doing all of Bash's outside chores, and she was pleased that she would reap their efforts long after they'd gone. She had carefully locked her experimental plants in the small shed in her walled garden, and placed a no entry sign on the gates leading to the greenhouses and the vegetable patches, so no-one would see the amazing size of the tomatoes, which had ballooned into enormous spheres that dwarfed the cabbages. Findhorn's musical methods, it seemed, were sound... in every way.

Kit was delighted when he overheard a group of stagehands hanging about waiting for something called 'the rushes.'

"Ever since our location in Egypt, things have gone missing," the first voice said.

"Ooooooh! It's the mummy's curse," mocked 'Tramper,' the property manager and owner of the second voice.

Tramper mimicked a mummy walking stiff-legged arms out-stretched: "You have disturbed my sleep. I curse you," he said.

"You're a right comedian today," the first voice said.

"No deaths though," the another stagehand replied. "Not yet."

"By the way... '*Lord* Rupert Stratford-Smyth,' has ordered us to take everything in by the servant's entrance at *all times*, he says," Tramper announced, all seriousness again.

"Thinks he's the cat's whiskers, that one," another voice said.

"More like the cat's bum," sniggered the first voice.

The money from 'Hollyworks Productions' was clearly going to be enough to pay for a new roof, which was saying something considering the size of Bede Hall's turrets and gables.

The twins overheard their mother talking to Lady Nan. "A few more contracts like this and we won't ever have to sell," Mrs. S enthused. "I don't like to count chickens, but maybe Bede Hall is a going concern after all. And it's better than swarms of tourists."

"A swarm is a swarm," Lady Nan interjected. "Who wants to live in a crowd? I don't," but she meant that Snow wouldn't; she herself, was actually delighted with the financial windfall for Bede Hall.

As prearranged, the twins and Snow met Taraq 2 at the sundial after supper.

The late shift observed a rather excited dog prancing and leaping at moths, and the twins from the manor-house having an animated conversation.

"Taraq," Kit said formally, "this is Snow. She wanted to say hello."

"Anu!" Taraq cried. "No wonder this place called me." "That's the thing about Bede Hall," Kit said sarcastically. "It can talk."

"You two know each other?" Bash said, amazed. "Snow, is this who you've been looking for?"

"No, I've been looking for my father," Snow answered staring straight at Kit. "Taraq is my brother."

Kit's face registered surprise, and a sickening thought filled his head. I have a son as well! He recovered quickly. "But she can't be your sister. There's no snow in Egypt."

"What's snow?" Taraq asked.

"You're going to find out big time," Kit said. "Lucky for you ghosts don't feel the cold."

"Snow does," Bash cut in.

"Well, Snow's not d..." Kit stopped.

Bash stared at Kit waiting for his sentence. "Well?"

"Not *despondent* anymore," Kit managed.

"Despondent?" Bash said in amazement. "Such big words you have Mr. Wolf."

"All the better to impress you by," Kit said. "Dr. Brooks told me that word when he was describing depression. It means being unhappy enough to give up. In Snow's case, giving up the ghost. She's happy now."

"That's because Lady Nan watches movies about love and happy endings," Snow added. "That's what I like most. All those sad people finding happiness ever-after."

"That's only in the movies," Kit quipped angrily, staring directly at Snow. "In real life, people don't always find their fathers."

Bash took her brother's arm and marched him towards the kitchen door. "Come on gloomy guts, Mum's making cocoa, and you should see Boss. I've never seen him so happy."

"That's because Boss *does* live in a movie. He's the leading man, where all the other characters do as *they're* told... by him."

Kit thought a little more. "If life is a movie, then is ours a ghost story, an adventure mystery, a fantasy, or science-fiction?" he pondered.

"Yes," Bash said sarcastically. "No doubt some 'happy-ever-afterlife."

CHAPTER SIXTY-EIGHT

Can Anna Come Out to Play?

Beryl wants to know when Snow can come out to play," Bash said to Kit. "What should I tell her?"

"Snow only answers to Anu these days, and she's holed up in the Winter Room with Taraq. Maybe we should just tell Lady Nan her friend is busy."

"Lady Nan might understand," Bash said, "but Beryl won't. I've seen Beryl when she doesn't get her own way."

"Has Anu or Taraq told you anything?" Kit asked.

Bash shrugged. "I managed to put two and two together listening to them. They were near me when I was in the greenhouse. Anu was showing Taraq how fascinating the hedge clippers were, and he was stunned by Snowdrop playing in the catnip plants. Apparently he's never seen a white cat before."

"Well, what did you make out of four?" Kit asked.

"I think you should put what I'm about to tell you in your notebook."

Kit opened his notebook to the last blank page, turning the book upside-down. This is where he would write when he was older as if beginning a new book. He returned it right-side-up, and smoothed the spot where his last entry left off.

"Lights, action, roll cameras," he said grinning. "I'm listening."

Bash pulled up a wicker chair.

"Apparently Taraq became attached to the replica of King Tut's mask that was being used in one of the tomb scenes over in Cairo. He was pretty convinced it was the real one. He said he'd seen it before. So, ever since the crew filmed on location in the Valley of the Kings, he's been looking after it. He took it very seriously, as his duty to his master... *not* King Tut, by the way.

"The production team had been given a private tour of the real tomb as a courtesy, and somehow disturbed Taraq who was visiting it himself."

Kit interrupted. "Well, ghosts should dream-walk better than anyone," he said, trying to look more amused than he felt.

"Taraq visits that particular tomb for a reason, and it's only a short distance away to the tomb Dad discovered," Bash hinted.

"Smenkhkare's?" Kit said, shocked.

"Smenkhkare's and Ankhesenamun's, Smenkhkare was Tut's older brother. Taraq was telling Anu how the tomb had been meant for Smenkhkare all along, but that he died before it was ready. Actually it was more like he was reminding Snow because she knew, but had buried the memory. It's as if she had amnesia or something. I saw her face as she started to remember.

"Smenkhkare was buried in a plain stone sarcophagus and Tut's vizier kept all three gold nesting coffins, including the golden mask for his own puppet king," Bash finished.

"Smenkhkare's was Queen Ankhesenamun's first husband. Dr. Brooks told me," Kit said.

"Anyway," Bash continued, "somehow Ankhesenamun ended up hiding in there and eventually laid down to die with the two skeletons of the children... Taraq and Anu."

"Ew!" Kit exclaimed.

"It's rather romantic," Bash said defensively.

"How very grisly and macabre," Kit said pointedly, hoping to impress Bash with his new and improved language skills.

"It was a love story. You're a boy; you wouldn't understand," Bash sighed. "After Ankhesenamun died, she and Smenkhkare were reunited, and they acted like Taraq and Anu's parents... one big happy family. But, after thousands of years the spirits of Smenkhkare and Ankhesenamun were reborn.

"Taraq and Anu were left alone. He and Anu played with the Smenkhkare's childhood toys. The tomb was filled with everything imaginable. They loved to play sennet."

Kit chuckled. "You used to call it 'long chess.' Remember? After Dad showed us how to play?"

"Well, the board *is* very long," Bash said defending herself. "And it has similar squares.

"Anyway, as I was saying. Taraq and Anu lived together in the Egyptian afterlife for a few more years before *she* disappeared as well. As Taraq described it, Anu became 'thinner' until she was gone. I think he meant more transparent.

"When Anu returned to the world above ground, Taraq was left with her skeleton, and he traveled all over Egypt calling her.

"I heard Taraq explaining to Snow that she had taken nine months to completely disappear until sadly, she finally said good-bye. Taraq said he could hear a baby crying from a long way away.

"I guess that was Snow... I mean Anna. It must have been winter when she was born. Long before Lady Nan's time. She lived here once, that's a given."

Kit spoke again. "Are you sure the house didn't tell you that?"

Bash stuck out her tongue. "You can be a real pain sometimes," she said.

"That sounds like something Bede Hall would say," Kit said defensively.

"It was really sad," Bash said. "Snow showed Taraq the hour-glass, and the falling sand reminded him of Egypt.

"Then I heard Snow describe how a snowy landscape looked like the Egyptian desert turned white, and how it was as cold as the sand was hot. They agreed that stretches of hot powder or freezing powder were equally treacherous. Taraq conjured up a vision of the sphinx up to its neck in sand for Anu, and Snow showed Taraq an image of Bede Hall's sphinx covered in snow."

The twins were wrong. Lady Nan was as jealous as Beryl, and demanded an immediate audience with Snow *and* Taraq.

Kit and Bash took their grandmother to the Winter Room as the garden was too crowded with movie people. Neither of them wanted to stay.

When the twins left, the room felt even colder.

CHAPTER SIXTY-NINE
Out Like a Lamb

TARAQ ONE

Edgar had snuck into the library and was alone when Taraq materialized, strolling in wearing his Egyptian garb, casual as you please, as if he owned the place.

"Hey, how's the big movie star? Still wearing your costume I see," Edgar said. "I hear the trucks are almost ready to go."

"I hear you like to play games," Taraq said, taking a step closer.

"Like what?" Edgar asked nervously, taking the exact same step backwards.

"Here's one I bet you can't do... yet," Taraq said as he disappeared and reappeared behind Edgar.

"Boo!" Taraq said in Edgar's ear. "I just learned that word this morning. Bash told me it meant *hey you, watch out*!"

To Edgar's surprise the smart-phone in his pocket (his father's expensive business phone) slid out, drifted towards the open library window, and dropped out of sight making a splintering sound as it hit the terrace below.

Taraq materialized a box of tissues, and sent them floating towards Edgar, who had turned an exceptional color of queasy. "I think you might need these," he said.

Edgar's legs made it to the stairs before his brain told them how to run properly. He sneezed his way down the stairs, sliding his way down on the seat of his pants, and jumped to his feet at the bottom, continuing on without looking behind him.

The twins were in the kitchen having spilled the beans to Mrs. S that it had been Edgar who had leaked the ghost story to the papers.

"Edgar," Mrs. S smiled. "You look like you've seen a ghost."

"Pictures...pretty pictures...I've got the pictures... pictures to prove it... pictures to prove it...prove it...what's an ethic?" Pigeon burst out.

"You're in for it now, mate," Kit said to Edgar.

"Don't try to snow me," Edgar sniffled after a fit of sneezing.

"I wouldn't *dream* of it," Kit replied.

"Who's that parrot mimicking now?" Mrs. S asked. "I can almost place that voice."

"I don't know," Edgar said after a tremendous sneeze, trying to disguise his voice several octaves lower.

"I think you really *are* getting a cold this time," Mrs. S commented. "My mother says you should go home and rest."

If it's possible for two hundred people to disappear overnight without a trace, a movie production leaving town can do it.

"That's a wrap!" the director had shouted, and all the crew had cheered, and partied for exactly an hour.

The stars and the director left first, whisked away in various cars with tinted windows.

The trucks rolled out like a wagon train leaving for the wild west of London where the last scenes of Howard Carter's life were to be filmed.

It was the last few days of August and Lady Nan was exceptionally cheerful.

Taraq stayed with Snow having taken endless pleasure in foiling Edgar's attempts to photograph his sister again.

Bede Hall was left like a jewel under the sun, resting in its recently mowed lawns and meticulously groomed gardens. The long winding drive was now a tidy gray snake. Either side of it shallow impressions were ironed into the grass. Every scrap of evidence of the circus which had camped there for ten days was gone.

Rupert preened at the sight – master of all he surveyed. Bede was his as far as the eye could see, he thought, and much further with his new vision that imagined a succession of productions arriving like clockwork in a Hollywood parade.

This had been the most marvelous idea that he'd had of Bede Hall becoming a coveted film location, even though he couldn't quite remember for the life of him, when he'd first thought of it.

Bede Hall was pleasantly tired. Monitoring its portable treasures had been exhausting, but the inventory remained intact, and it was feeling refreshed from the smell of fresh paint and wallpaper paste, and from drinking the rich furniture polish that had been applied to its dehydrated woodwork. The visitors had been respectful and even in awe of its splendor.

The trees rustled gently anticipating the cooling breezes of September. There was no need for Bede Hall to worry too far ahead. If the family had to leave in the future, it would be its duty to crumble as soon as possible, with no bad feelings. After all, it had always done its best. And so it reconciled to flow with the fortunes of the Stratford-Smyth's whatever the future held in store.

It concurred with a toast Mr. Cornelius was known to recite on New Year's Eve: *Man says time passes; the pyramids say, man passes.*

The cozy corner of its foundations sent energetic shivers of life through its hallways and up its stairs. Bede Hall's library heart was not only restored to its former glory, but rested in peace like the old days, when the servants had polished every book and table with sweet smelling saddle soap. Most of all, it was delighted to be rid of that tiresome spiteful boy... or so it thought.

"A most unsavory child," Bede Hall observed indelicately. *"Quite a repulsive little beast, really."*

PART EIGHT

THE PROMISED LAND

*"If you don't know
where you are going,
any road will get you there."*

- LEWIS CARROLL

CHAPTER SEVENTY

Miles to Go Before I Sleep

Dr. Peregrine Brooks sat back in his wingback chair with a great sigh, and pushed his spectacles up onto his forehead. The thick lenses sent a tiny refracted beam of light from the overhead lamp into Kit's eye. "Well my boy, whatever next."

"It's more important to think of what happened *before* rather than what comes *next,*" Kit replied looking nervous. "If I could go back in time I could save my Dad myself," he said.

"If you truly know your 'Star Trek,' you'd remember it's unethical, not to mention dangerous, to change events in the past. The prime directive, remember? Very tricky thing, that. It's not quite the same when one hears... what was it you joked about? ... "Dream me up, Scotty?""

"I don't want to change anything, not really," Kit apologized. "But at least we'd know what happened to my Dad and where he is, I mean was. He could still be alive. Besides, my friend Taraq lives in the present."

Dr. Brooks closed his eyes and rested his fingers on his temples, deep in thought.

"Remember what I told you, with time-travel, no one ever dies," he finally stated. "Now think about that for a moment because it's the key. One can always go back to when a person *used* to be alive."

A look of relief, then fear, and then wonder, passed over Kit's face.

"The secret of eternal life," breathed Kit, more determined than ever to devote his life to break through the barriers of time-travel.

Kit couldn't sleep and he slipped from the side door to the tower for his book on Mars. A startling low-lying colored fog clinging to the flowerbeds was so luminous in the moonless sky that he turned off his flashlight and became mesmerized walking towards it, helpless to stop.

He thought it must be a massive swarm of fireflies or a pocket of swamp gas excited by the magnetic field of the fountain's newly overhauled generators defunct until the movie mogul had decided it was worth repairing for a magnificent opening shot, but when he approached, he could see it was a viscous mist swirling with lumps of color. The sky over Bede Hall looked like a lava lamp out of control.

Kit managed to tear himself away and make it to his tower where he was eager to view the eerie phenomenon through his telescope. Perhaps human vision was too biased and therefore unable to penetrate the layers of twisted light particles.

With the adjustments to the lens complete, Kit zoomed in on the sight below. The topiaries looked strangely different. He could see the Sphinx in profile and the lone howling wolf had vanished altogether. He strained his vision towards the gate he knew was there and saw the topiary hare situated in the middle of the driveway where it most certainly had never been. It had stopped like a real hare under the beam of a flashlight.

Kit covered his eyes and looked again. This time the Sphinx's hind quarters could be seen frozen as if it had been caught trying to escape behind the Hall.

Kit deliberately cast his eyes to the floor for a count of ten and looked up quickly hoping to catch them out. Three more topiaries stood stock still in all innocence in new locations. A swan, a horse, and a bear formed a triangle on the lawn. The chess pieces were aligned in single file – all on the same side, ready to win.

They were playing a game of 'red light green light' with him.

Somehow the Cairo traffic jams sounded louder in the heat. The honking horns gave Taraq a headache.

He was nervous, glancing over his shoulder at every sound or shadow. His bosses prized themselves, not so much on their stealth, but the stealth of others in their employ, who had taken the art of clandestine crime to its limits. Murder was considered an everyday transaction of underground business.

Considering his computer savvy, Taraq was not entirely expendable, but he knew too many secrets, and such secrets overruled keeping him.

His plan was no longer covert. He slipped furtively through the streets, no longer undercover but exposed to the worst of humanity out to silence him, and perhaps his daring had even signed the professor's death warrant. It was an ugly thought but Taraq was used to ugliness.

First he had to stash hard copies of what he knew: the codes and the photographs of stolen antiquities, and a list of the names and addresses of the thieves and their hideouts, and most important of all, the whereabouts of a cache of treasures. Taraq was privy to them all.

The darkness of a moonless night covered Taraq like a shield. He crept cat-like over the unstable rooftops, light and nimble enough to leap without fear of crashing through the paper-thin corrugated ceilings of rusted tin and makeshift thatch.

His hiding place was a slit in a cliff face so narrow, that none of his trackers would stand a chance of breaching. It looked purple in the dark, and Taraq pushed the items further into yet another crevice and dragged a rock over its entrance. He smoothed his way out to the stars with a switch of palm leaves, but a more worrying thought disturbed him.

What if *they* had sent a child to follow him? He had recruited so many, and a street urchin was slight enough to retrieve his hoard of objects.

Never mind, he would have to chance it and get to the professor before it was too late. Kit was depending on him, and the thought of his new friend and the chance to redress some terrible things he'd been a part of, pushed him forward.

An hour later, Taraq had navigated the worst of the bazaar and felt he could walk casually the rest of the way so as not to draw attention to himself.

That's when he was attacked from behind.

CHAPTER SEVENTY-ONE

If You Can Dream It

"So, let me get this straight," Kit said. "Are you saying that I could visit Harry Potter as opposed to the actor who played him? And talk to a fictitious character? You amaze me."

"Glad to be of help. I know you're not easily amazed," Bash replied. "And, by the way, he would be the perfect person to talk to about all of this."

Kit folded his arms to defend himself. "I'm a scientist, so I have to remain skeptical. Proof is required," he said obstinately.

Bash shook her head in exasperation. "Hello Kit. I'm your imagination. Have we met?" she said.

"Oh that! Well, anyone can talk to people in their imagination," Kit said.

Bash stared hard into her brother's eyes. "My point exactly," she said. "But they can answer you if you listen."

Edgar Tweedy deliberately banged a stick against the birdcage to make Pigeon flap his wings, and put his sallow face close to the bars.

"What's your real name Polly? Is it *Stool* Pigeon?" he sneered unkindly.

"*Prime directive ... primrose plum cake...pooh is stool...pooh... pumpernickel...pooh,*" Pigeon squawked back.

"You have a much more interesting name than Kit or Bash, then," Edgar sniggered, as Nipper tried to nip through the bars and got nipped himself from a sharp beak.

Edgar had to hold his hands over Nipper's yelp to muzzle the noise.

"Shush you. That racket will wake the dead," he said to the dog, and then felt quite queasy for mocking the spirits who were perhaps, even as he spoke, behind him ready to pounce.

This time Edgar had a small tape recorder hidden in his pocket. No camera to see and his hands were free. He was counting on Nipper's presence to distract any specter that dared to show. He'd looked it up on the computer: All ghost experts agreed that dog energy was too strong for a phantom to harm.

Edgar was surprised to find the blue door open, nor did he expect to see two cats, but then the two cats didn't expect to see Nipper.

Unicorn and Anubis had been looking out the window at the snowflakes when a white furry monster lunged at Unicorn's tail.

The ensuing racket brought Taraq 2 into the room. "I love a fair fight," he said, halting Nipper with one outstretched hand and calling Anubis, the black cat, to his shoulder. "You *are* a glutton for punishment."

"I don't believe you've seen my new act," Taraq grinned. "Meet my cat familiar. You know what that is don't you? Of course you do. You're almost as smart as your daddy's phone. His name is Anubis. Wait till you meet his big brother."

Taraq 2 made a performance of closing his eyes and folding his arms. "ANUBIS RISE," he intoned dramatically for effect.

To Edgar's horror the black cat started to swell in size, and its legs popped out like springs. Its face elongated into a fierce canine muzzle with wolf-like teeth, and it stood snarling with saliva drooling from its jaws.

An angry full-sized Egyptian jackal launched itself towards Edgar's throat. Nipper had already turned-tail and practically jumped to the bottom of the stairs in one wild leap.

"Why don't you show our visitors the way out," Taraq shouted to Anubis over the confusion.

Jack was roused from his bed in the kitchen and blocked Edgar and Nipper's escape.

369

Taraq appeared, and encouraged the usually mild-mannered deerhound to attack.

"Come on Jack Frost," he shouted. Show these gits your new trick.

Jack bared a set of truly formidable teeth. Nipper skidded to a halt his eyes as big as soup plates. Edgar tripped over Nipper just as the two attack creatures met above him. Jack only felt a cool breeze rush through him as the jackal emerged on the business end of the door. Edgar and Nipper clearly saw two guardians in a united force of confrontation.

Played back, Edgar's recording was a hullabaloo of barking and snarling, and cats spitting fit to wake the dead, mingled with the sound of a boy screeching like a parrot.

Pigeon was in a flap. *"Winnie the pooh... pooh... pooh...extra pooh,"* he shrieked.

"Be nice," Kit said.

Pigeon chattered on nonsensically: *"Looks like snow...looks like snow...here she comes...white as snow...more interesting than Kit or Bash, then."*

"You be quiet or I'll put you in the Winter Room and turn you into a real pigeon," Kit said stroking the bird's feathers.

"Homing pigeon... pidgin English... pigeonholes... desks with keys...pooh...double pooh...and more pooh please," came the bird's reply, even louder.

Bash arrived to see what all the commotion was about.

"What's up?"

Pigeon is a tad *aggipated*," Kit said. "He woke up on the wrong side of his perch this morning."

"Pooh to you...kit is a fox...Pooh to you," Pigeon repeated, wild as ever.

Kit lowered his voice:

"Taraq 1, *my* Taraq, is going to attempt something bizarre today," he said to Bash. "And don't repeat that to a living soul, I mean anyone... I mean alive *or* dead."

Bash squeezed a new cuttlebone between the birdcage bars. "That's all he wanted, isn't it Plum Cake?" she said triumphantly, "Pidge likes his beak sharp."

"You're telling me," Kit replied.

Anubis snuggled into Feathers, exhausted after his transformation. *"I think I could qualify for being a tiger in my next life, now,"* he remarked dreamily. *"I promise I will be a tiger by the middle of next year."*

"Promises? Elephants in the room?... I don't think." cackled Pigeon. *"Never forget... promises to keep... miles to go. Tiger tiger burning bright... fearful symmetry... what dread hands what dread feet... immortal eyes and all that,"* Pigeon mumbled, and attacked his parrotty toothbrush with considerably more energy than usual.

CHAPTER SEVENTY-TWO
A Rainbow's Chance in Hell

The blow came from behind. Sharp and quick. Taraq 1 slipped to his knees, descending through a burst of pain into a blazing light before he reached the darkness.

Thousands of miles away, Kit had been wandering the rooms of Bede Hall testing his out-of-body lift-out skills when he heard Taraq's voice calling for help.

Upon each re-entry he had made note of how long he'd been gone, and whatever he could remember. Feathers had seen him several times in every location, and seemed to second-guess which room he had placed in his thoughts.

Feathers must have read Kit's mind because she was there waiting for him whenever he arrived. Jack had only whined in his sleep but not woken up, and Pigeon became so agitated Kit thought he might drop all of his tail feathers. He shrieked pooh so many times and so loudly, that Mrs. S had to take him out of his cage and let him fly around the library.

The physical flapping of his wings as he swooped around Kit calmed him down, and he landed on the back of a wooden chair, nervously lifting one talon in the air, muttering: *"key to the door... key to the door...red pillows... seagull alert... kit's a fox...foxes can fly...don't talk with your mouth full... I will when pigs fly!"*

Kit felt like a helium balloon. It had been strange to see his mother below, sweeping out the birdcage unaware of him hovering like a seagull against the library ceiling. He ran down a tunnel that flattened out into a pink desert. A black horse in the distance galloped towards him. Taraq 1 was riding on his back, and he had brought a horse for Kit.

"Taraq?"

Taraq's eyes looked wild. "I need your help," he said. "Follow me."

The boys rode towards a round hole on the horizon that turned out to be another tunnel zapping with blue sparks. Inside was a river, and the roar of rushing water, and a high pitched humming sound. Thunderclaps drew them into a vortex of light.

The horses disappeared from under them as Kit and Taraq surfed down a thin ribbon of red water. In between flashes of lightning, Kit saw the panicked look on his friend's face. Taraq dematerialized and reappeared several times – his form flickering like a candle.

"Hold on," Kit shouted.

It seemed like hours, but both boys finally beached near the foot of the Great Sphinx. Taraq ran between its paws where a stele shaped like a door opened. Kit followed, and he found himself in one of the market streets like the one where he had first met Taraq.

Kit ran after Taraq through a maze of side streets until they stopped at Taraq's body lying face down. A trickle of blood oozed from his ear.

"What happened?" Kit shouted.

"They found our e-mails. I was on my way to your father. They actually sent me. If you help me there's still time to rescue him. Am I dead?"

"Yes and No," Kit replied.

"What should we do?" Taraq asked.

"For one thing you need to get back into your body... Right now! While I think of something," Kit insisted.

Kit waited until Taraq descended into his body before shouting, "Hang on. I'll be right back."

Kit retraced his steps to a busy market stall, and shouted in the old jewellery vendor's ear: "Someone is hurt. They need your help. Follow me!"

The man obeyed as if in a trance, and instinctively grabbed a flask of water and some garish scarves from his display.

Kit watched as the old man turned Taraq on his back, and poured water over his face. He bound Taraq's head with bright blue and red polka dot scarf, and helped him to his feet. But he blanched when he recognized Taraq as one of the boys working for the thieves who ran the local stolen artifact syndicate and ran away.

The last thing Kit saw before waking up back at Bede Hall, was Taraq staggering as he tried to regain his balance. There had been a dark stain on the bright polka dot bandage around his head. Several similar polka dot scarves blew down the street in a blue and red cloud, and for a moment Taraq looked as if were chasing them, but he had stopped and turned back. He had waved to Kit with a weak smile, and given him a thumbs up.

Later, Kit sat with Bash and told her what had happened. "I have no idea if Taraq was able to get to Dad. But he's not like us. There's a chance he recovered enough to go on. He grew up on the streets, and he never gives up."

"Neither does Dad," Bash said.

The reporter from 'The Daily Bead' had been quite curt when he telephoned Wilbur Tweedy.

"I personally don't appreciate being messed about," the reporter said nastily. "My editor is thinking of pressing nuisance charges. Do you know it's the second... no I tell a lie... the third time your son has tried this on?"

"Mr. Tweedy coughed nervously. "I'm most awfully sorry. You can be sure my little Edgar will be punished. Surely there's no need to go to the police," he whined.

"It's a serious offense to slander an innocent party, let alone involve an honest newspaper. The police take this kind of thing very seriously indeed," the reporter went on.

"But he's never done *anything* like this before," Mr. Tweedy pleaded breathlessly.

"Now *there's* something I bet the police have never heard before," the reporter's voice said drily.

The scene in the Tweedy's living room was tense. "But I *wasn't* lying," Edgar sniveled.

Mr. Tweedy had gone quite red in the face from over-exertion.

"If your prank gets out it will reflect very badly on me," his voice boomed. "Do you know what will happen if I lose clients? Which may happen now that I no longer have a *phone!*"

"But it wasn't my prank" Edgar started to say, stopping abruptly at his father's enraged expression.

Mrs. Tweedy looked sympathetically at her son. "There's no harm done Wilbur. You don't *have* any clients," she said, trying to be helpful.

"I don't care if you take a stupid computer game away," Edgar howled. "I did take a picture of the ghost of Bede Hall. I've met her. There's magic vegetables and a cat ghost as well, it scratched me, look."

Mrs. Tweedy tried very hard to see scratch marks on her son's arm, but none were there. "Eddy's been under a lot of pressure lately," she said to her husband. "The movie business isn't easy."

"Movie business!" Mr. Tweedy howled. "He stood in the background raking leaves as a car drove up. He didn't even have any lines to memorize. All he had to do was look up and wave."

"It's extremely difficult to get the timing down just right. They had to shoot it over several times," Mrs. Tweedy lamented.

"I couldn't help it if I laughed," Edgar complained. "A ghost was making funny faces at me, and playing tricks on the cameraman."

The Tweedys looked alarmed.

"What!" they said together.

"There was this ghost of an Egyptian slave, but I didn't know it at the time. I'm sure the rest of the family are witches or something. They've got a bird that talks."

Mr. and Mrs. Tweedy looked at each other uncomfortably.

375

"Of course it talks. It's a bloody parrot!" Mr. Tweedy spluttered. "There's nothing for it, but to go over to the Hall and try to put this right with Mrs. Stratford-Smyth."

"Now Wilbur, mind your blood pressure," Mrs. Tweedy nagged.

"Edgar. You're going with me to apologize." Mr. Tweedy announced, sounding defeated.

"Perhaps I should go instead," Mrs. Tweedy simpered. "Mrs. Stratford-Smyth and I are *such* close friends."

CHAPTER SEVENTY-THREE
Fair Trade

Kit's cell phone did three things just as he was finishing writing his latest report: It lit up, played the tune 'An English Country Garden' as it hummed its way across the table top, and fell into his wastepaper basket.

The ring-tone told him it was Bash calling, and the screen confirmed it.

Her voice was a blur of excitement: "Dad's home!" she shrieked nearly breaking Kit's eardrum. "Come to the house!"

Kit stood dazed and frozen wondering if was having one of his lucid dreams, but he could see no parallel Kit sitting in his chair. He raced down the spiral stairs sending more than a few mice scrambling, telling himself he had to get to the house before his father disappeared again.

The kitchen was in utter chaos when Kit barged in and leapt at his father.

Cornelius Stratford-Smyth was thinner than usual, but his tan was surprisingly intact.

"homing pigeon... nice to see you... home again home again jiggedy jig," Pigeon shrieked over the bedlam.

"It was all very sudden," Mr. S said. "One minute I was dozing in the cellar of a filthy office building and the next I was free. I had to be rushed out of the country with as little fuss as possible. There was no time for phone calls, and I didn't argue. I wanted to be on a plane as much as the authorities did."

Mrs. S dithered about, half-making tea, pouring hot water into the teapot without putting in the teabags, and starting a plate of sandwiches, then forgetting where the knives were. She walked to the larder several times, but came away with nothing each time, more confused than ever.

"A boy named Taraq rescued me," Mr. S said. "He was forced to work for the thieves who kidnapped me. Digby was in on the scheme as well. He's already in custody, and he won't be out any time soon. The boy was no older than you are," Mr. S remarked to Kit.

"The thieves went sour on Taraq for some reason, and he decided to free me. He didn't have to," Mr. S narrated, "he got a nasty bump on the head for his trouble too. How he managed to get me to the hospital is a mystery. The lad required over twenty stitches.

"When the police arrived he ran for it. All I heard was that he slipped through their fingers, but not before he gave them all the names and addresses of the thieves that he could. By the looks on some of their faces, a few of them were involved as well. The authorities are still trying to find him.

"The boy's better off out of it, but I should like to have thanked him properly. I could have helped him out of the country. It's the only safe place for him.

"A band of thugs is never entirely captured and Taraq's life is in danger. I wouldn't give two pennies for his chances."

A small oh! escaped Mrs. S's lips as she missed a teacup, and poured tea over the sandwiches, now cut into quarters and stacked in a pyramid, but lacking any filling whatsoever.

"The Hall looks marvelous. I've never seen it this shipshape for years," Mr. S said, relaxing after his long conversation.

"Yes, it's had a proper face-lift courtesy of Hollywood," Rupert announced. "We've got a lucrative new business."

"We're booked solid till the end of the year," Bash chimed in.

Mr. S stunned everyone and halted the movie business discussion with a surprising statement:

"I'm afraid I'm only home for a short visit," he said apologetically.

"I'll have to go back when I'm fit again, to deliver some valuable scarabs and identify the recovered artifacts, not to mention smooth over public relations if Britain ever wants to dig in Egypt again. Maybe in a week."

"Can't they send someone else?" Mrs. S queried loudly.

"Diplomatically speaking, it has to be me, but don't worry you'll be coming with me. All of you."

This thought didn't seem to lift Mrs. S's spirits.

"Do you think we can find Taraq?" Kit asked.

"We're going to try," Mr. S replied. "It won't be easy. He's an orphan. Even he doesn't know his last name, and even if he did, well, street kids aren't recorded in the Egyptian census."

Rupert spoke at last. "I have to stay, Dad. Someone has to run the business. It's early days to be cancelling any contracts. We can find someone in the village to look after Lady Nan."

The twins smiled at each other. "Dr. Brooks will take care of her. He's got a housekeeper once a week, and I'm sure she would come in every day."

"What has been going on here," Mr. S said, shaking his head. "How long have I been away? Those two haven't spoken for years."

"Oh, but they have. They do. They are. In fact, they're good friends again," Mrs. S said. "Kit had something to do with it. Some sort of science project."

"Well, I have a lot more questions. For now though, I'd just like to enjoy being with my family," Mr. S sighed.

"You must be hungry," Mrs. S said.

"I'm famished," Mr. S said to Rupert and the twins. "But I don't dare have your mother cook dinner in her state. Can you fetch some takeaway from the village? Something English please."

"Fish and chips it is," Rupert said, grabbing his car keys. "Won't be a tick."

"I've always gotten lost in here," Mr. S said as he and Kit traced their way to the center of the maze.

Kit led the way, and when they rounded the corner where Kit had been meditating, he paused.

"This is where I come sometimes when I need to think. Sometimes even a tower isn't enough," he said.

"I think I may have to make use of it myself," Mr. S said.

Kit was momentarily caught off guard with the thought that his heroic father might also need a place to hide from family. With some hesitation, Kit asked the question that loomed so uncomfortably. The 'elephant in the room' sort of question.

"Can you tell me what happened?" he asked.

"I prefer to tell everyone the details when we're together and a little more relaxed, suffice to say, most of all I was surprised," Mr. S said.

"I can't forgive Digger but he unwittingly saved my life. You see, he was too squeamish to really fit in with the black market. He wanted instant money and murder didn't figure into his plan. I think he believed they would let me go after a few weeks.

Of course he legged it when he saw that wasn't going to happen. I gathered from what I overheard that the thieves couldn't find him. That being the case, saved my skin. Digger was at large with incriminating information and they still had me alive for bargaining purposes. Only, Digger stayed low. I think they thought that after a while I would actually find more tombs for them."

There was an awkward silence as Kit tried to imagine the horrors of being imprisoned by a gang of unscrupulous thugs.

"Come on. Walk me over to your tower," Mr. S said. "I'd like to see what you've done with the place."

"I'm in the middle of conducting some experiments with Dr. Brooks," Kit explained. "It's about altered states of consciousness... *um*... it's early days yet."

Kit sent more emails to Taraq 1, but they bounced back. The thieves' site had vanished, taking Taraq with them. The only way to search the 'dark side of the moon' was to dream-travel, but Kit was too anxious, and his emotions jammed his frequencies. He stayed body-logged unable to lift an inch out of his body.

A visit to Dr. Brooks gave Kit the only chance left. A pill which relaxed his muscles. It wasn't the best of solutions, but at least Kit was able to send a signal.

Kit still couldn't 'travel,' but he heard Taraq's voice, that sounded like a radio announcer breaking through static.

This time, Kit's legs felt like rubber, and the fog of medicine kept him from remembering the details. But contact had been made.

Kit heard Taraq asking if his father was safely arrived home. Kit had shouted to his friend asking for co-ordinates, but their signal fizzled out. It felt impossible not to try hard when one wanted something so badly but Dr. Brooks said putting Taraq out of his mind was the fastest way to reach him or at least allow Taraq to do the reaching.

CHAPTER SEVENTY-FOUR

Calling all Taraqs

Cornelius Stratford-Smyth guided his wife down the long tunnel entrance to the tomb of Smenkhkare.

She looked quite girlish in her red sun-dress and matching lipstick.

Kit and Bash crept behind in a hush of silent awe.

"Are you two still back there," Mrs. S called out. "You're very quiet."

"Silent as the grave," Kit called out. "We couldn't *be* more here."

Once inside the antechamber the world changed. Years and dates seemed irrelevant.

"It's positively subterranean," Bash declared.

"I think we passed middle-earth halfway down here," Kit said. "The world could end up top, and we'd never know."

"That pile of bones is new," Mr. S reported, sadly. "When I first entered, there were three perfect skeletons: two children and a woman. It will take months to sort them out, but it will never be the same. The thieves disturbed more than just bones. They destroyed the emotion of their position. Two children lying together with a woman who could have been anyone – a servant, their mother, possibly even a queen. Their story can never be underestimated. The worst thing is that the pictures I took in situ were lost when the thieves' headquarters were raided. Those pictures told a poignant story. The emotion of it can never be recovered."

"Don't look," Kit advised Bash. "It's all right; they're safe now," he comforted.

Bash shuddered. "I've gone all goose-bumpy," she said.

"It's déjà vu. No big," Kit replied, but he felt it too.

"It feels big to me," Bash whispered, averting her eyes from the discard of bones. "It was to them," she said.

Kit was exhausted. The heat of the day and the drama of seeing Smenkhkare's burial chamber jumbled together in his brain. All he wanted was to sleep. The jet lag was worse than he could have imagined, but it was the best thing for dream-travelling.

It was no surprise when he found himself back in the tomb. The antechamber was softly lit by an unknown source of light, and it seemed quite natural to see the skeletons, now intact, with the familiar ghost of Taraq 2, the younger, standing beside them.

"Hi Kit. Are you looking for me?" he asked. "I heard you calling my name."

"Hey Taraq. You heard right, but I was calling a different Taraq."

"The taller one?"

"Yes. Sorry to have woken... *um*... disturbed you. Where's Anna?... I mean Anu."

"She doesn't like to come here. Seeing Queen Ankhesenamun like this upsets her."

"Well, it's nice to see you again so soon. I guess my friend doesn't want to be found. I thought he would answer seeing as we're both in the same time zone now. I figured he would be more likely to be asleep at the same time as me."

Taraq 2 grinned the mischievous grin Kit remembered.

"I am especially good at finding people who don't want to be found," he said proudly. "You sit here that cross-legged way you do, and call him again. I will follow your signal."

Kit complied. This would be a new one to tell Dr. Brooks. He lowered himself to sit on a perfectly intact throne chair, strong enough to hold his physical body let alone his weightless ka, and closed his eyes. In his mind he became an archaeologist in the tomb now crowded with artifacts in mint condition, and with each thought, one of the objects around him removed itself from the tomb as if in the reverse order in which they had first been ceremoniously placed.

The stone sarcophagus lifted first, light as a balloon followed by the rest of the tomb furniture. Several chariot wheels rolled out while their axles levitated slowly in a parade of dissembled parts. One by one, they were *spirited* away until the chamber was emptied, and Kit's mind was an open portal. He heard his own voice echoing up the tomb shaft. "Taraq! He shouted, Taraq! Where are you?"

When Kit opened his eyes it was the young Taraq 2 who was still there. He seemed very pleased with himself.

"I found your friend," he said. "He was afraid to answer you, but I know where he is. He's very stubborn. I like him."

Abu Simbel was a marvel, especially after Mr. S explained that the entire cliff face had been dismantled and moved to higher ground when the construction of the Aswan Dam threatened to submerge it.

Such an undertaking boggled Kit's mind, but it was the sad bones image that Bash carried about with her, even knowing what she knew. Their murder had been heartless and unnecessary.

They toured the temple of Karnak with its bulbous tree-like pillars, and Bash found it difficult to imagine the colors which had once covered them.

"They look so much more magnificent as they are now," she said.

"Most of the statues in art galleries were once like that," Mr. S explained, "painted like the ceramic ornaments one buys nowadays, only on a larger scale. Weather and time have reduced them to their original stone glory."

Hatshepsut's mortuary temple at Deir el-Bahari could have stood in for a modern parliament building, such was its sleek uncluttered architecture. It emerged from the rosy cliffs behind it as if someone had pushed it from the rock face.

The isle of Elephantine, named for an outcrop of rocks that really did look like an elephant, wavered in the heat as they journeyed down the Nile on a guided cruise. It floated like a mirage surrounded by palm trees – a lost world shimmering outside of time.

There were occasions when Bash expected to dock and find she was in Disneyland, and that all the crumbling temples were sets, such had her brief encounter with the movie business informed her that nothing, but no thing, on the big screen was real.

Egypt was the biggest screen of all. A world larger than life. Bash had heard about it and seen pictures of it all her childhood, but when she approached the pyramids she was stunned.

Mr. S squeezed her hand, and shared the precious moment.

"Now do you see what I love about this country?" he said.

"I had no idea until now," Bash said, staring at the Great Sphinx. "None of Lady Nan's grand words could come close to describing this. And the sand is pink."

"I guess it does have that hint of pink about it now that you mention it. You know, whenever I visited the Sphinx I felt homesick for Bede," Mr. S admitted. "Then, whenever I was at Bede Hall the green sphinx made me miss Egypt. I guess that topiary of Parks really gets under one's skin."

Everything was scaled out of all proportion to the humans who had built them. It didn't bear thinking how they must have toiled in the unforgiving sun year after year. Kit and Bash were entranced.

Bash thought it amusing that two such vastly different realms had captured her: the looming world of pyramids and giant temples, and the fairy world that existed under toadstools.

The pyramids of Giza lit up from below with red and green flood-lights reminded Kit of Christmas. He and Mr. S stood together, and allowed the awesome display overwhelm them.

Mr. S pointed to a noticeable gap in the stones.

"I climbed that bit right there and actually waved to you not that long ago," he said.

Kit was shocked. "What!" he said, taken aback. "You did?"

"Well, it was a silly gesture I suppose," Mr. S replied, but I just felt like doing it. I don't know why."

Kit willed himself to wake at dawn and scribbled an address on some hotel stationery. The Egyptian sun had already turned the Cairo sky the same color as Bash's lavender fields. A voice chanting prayers over a loudspeaker floated in through the window.

Mr. S was already awake, being used to early starts in the coolest part of the day, and answered Kit's impatient knock quickly "Shush, don't wake your mother," he said. "Egypt got to her yesterday."

"I can relate," Kit whispered. "This message came for you...er... maybe it's from Taraq."

"Well, that's a highly unlikely. How would he even know I was here?"

"You always told me that the street kids were the eyes and ears of Cairo, remember?"

"That's true enough. I'll send some..."

"No Dad," Kit broke in. "Let's go ourselves. Now. Just the two of us. If he's not there then we will have had a little father/son time. And didn't you say this was the best part of the day. It will be cool. We'd be back in time for breakfast."

Kit saw Taraq first, but could hardly say so. He drew Mr. S's attention to a stall selling robes and T-shirts. I think Bash would like that one that says 'I love Egypt it's hieroglyriffic.' She loves her words."

"And that's Taraq standing beside it," Mr. S exclaimed. "Well, I'll be damned!"

Taraq recognized Kit when he saw Mr. S coming towards him.

Kit extended his hand and stared straight into Taraq's eyes with a silent message of 'play it cool.' "Hi, my name's Kit," he blurted quickly. "I almost feel I know you. This is my dad, but you guys know each other."

"You my lad, are coming with us, Mr. S said to Taraq. "First are you hungry? Of course you are. Silly question. Second – everything's arranged. You're safe now. So let's get out of here. There's a lot to do."

"Is your father always this determined?" Taraq asked.

"He's almost as stubborn as you are. Brother! Am I glad to see you!"

"Brother," Taraq repeated smiling. I never had one of those. Oh, wait there's something else I do have now. I managed to get my own email address."

Taraq addressed Mr. S, shyly, pulling out a camera from his knapsack.

"Mr. Cornelius, this belongs to you. I forgot to give it to you in the hospital. I am very sorry, I blame it on my head. Also, you will find many more photos for you stored in my email files. They should be what you need to prove your discovery and accuse your old partner... and I have a box you will want to see.

"Many precious artifacts were removed from the female skeleton before you saw it. She was wearing the crown jewels of Queen Ankhesenamun. I have photos of them before they were 'harvested' as well as a map showing their present whereabouts. I had time to bury them in a safe place."

Mr. S was stunned, and shook Taraq's hand. "I can see I have a new partner," he said."

"You're going to love England. It's very...er... wet and green," Kit said.

Taraq grinned wider than ever. "As long as there are computers," he replied.

"This is perfect!" Bash declared in triumph, holding up a snow globe like a trophy cup in the airport gift shop. "I've found the best souvenir for Lady Nan."

The family had to agree. Inside the glass ball was Khufu's Great Pyramid, its two companion pyramids, and a tiny model of the Great Sphinx, but it was different: instead of having white plastic snowflakes, the 'snow' was the color of yellow sand.

Taraq's parting farewell gift from the Egyptian authorities was a sumptuous seat in first class. He reclined his chair into a lounging position and tried to sleep. The clouds below him looked like a landscape of snowy hills, and Taraq tried to imagine a land that was like a desert with freezing sand.

"Remember," Mr. S said reassuringly as the plane taxied down the runway, "this is not exile but survival. We will come back after it's safe. You won't be a prisoner. I think we've both had enough of that."

Taraq landed at Heathrow airport wearing a new pair of jeans and a T-shirt with an image of Tutankhamun's golden mask on the front.

Mr. S read out a new list: first stop; Dr. Brooks for a checkup, second stop; Bede Hall, third stop; fish and chips in the kitchen."

Bash took Taraq's arm. "Come on," she said. "Third time lucky."

Taraq drowsed as the miles between himself and his predators smoothed into the rolling hills of Northumberland. He marvelled at the last two months since he'd met Kit.

The old soothsayer in the Cairo bazaar had singled him out for greatness after he had helped her collect a fee from a customer who refused to pay, but he hadn't believed her. Perhaps by 'greatness' she had meant great things or meeting great people.

The thought of meeting the famous Lady Nan, the amazing Dr. Brooks, and a witchy botanist left him quite restless with anticipation. He needn't have worried.

Bash gave him a running commentary as they sped through the countryside, and once in Bede, Kit pointed out the various ordinary shops like a tour guide showing off ancient Egyptian monuments.

There was the post office with its hidden secrets, and Mr. Leoni's alchemist hideout, and the florist shop, and the home of Miss Findhorn and Beegle.

Taraq was treated to a tantalizing glimpse of Dr. Brooks' clinic with its Egyptian decor behind a red door. He strained his eyes to make out the King Tut door knocker, and then finally, they were at the imposing gates of Bede Hall.

Taraq thought they swung open like the covers of a book, and that he was entering a story he'd dreamed once – all so 'long ago and faraway.'

"My dear boy. What joy. Welcome," Lady Nan beamed. "Let me have a good look at you. Come closer."

Dr. Brooks grinned and offered his hand.

"Well young man you're the hero of the hour. I hope you'll be happy here. We'll all pull together to help you. This is a time of great transition."

CHAPTER SEVENTY-FIVE
Homing Pigeon

Pigeon was in his element pacing the length of the mantelpiece bobbing and chortling. Now and then he gave a great flutter of red and green like an exotic fan.

Anubis kept to the edge of the living room in order to study Mr. S at a distance. Finally he slunk under the sofa – his usual place of retreat when strangers appeared and were in need of his approval.

Anubis's instincts told him not to worry. The house had been right. He was able to relax and enjoy the amiable atmosphere sharing food and laughter over... he sniffed the air as Mrs. S unrolled quantities of greasy newspaper.

"Oh my, it's fish," he purred to himself.

Feathers had greeted Mr. S with an enthusiastic chirp, and Anubis watched as she introduced their daughter, Snowdrop.

Mr. S scored points for holding her properly as he made a great fuss of her blue eyes.

"And where's your dad," he cooed cuddling her. "I've heard so much about him."

"Anubis is nearby, under something, watching you," Bash said. "He won't come out until he's checked you out."

"I bet he'll come out for fish," Mr. S said.

A portion of batter was removed to expose the pungent white flakes of meat, set on a saucer, and held tantalizingly close to the floor where Anubis was weighing the cost of his reputation and dignity against the taste of halibut.

It wasn't feline policy to comply with a human's wish once you knew what they wanted. In fact, it was the opposite, but the smell was whisker-twitch inviting. Pure temptation. Deep-fried in savory heaven. Anubis began to drool and caught himself in time. It wouldn't do to lower oneself to the level of canine behavior.

By rights, Anubis knew he should ignore the treat and stand his ground. It was unwise to appear tame. But there was Feathers, her nose in a bowl, wolfing down a fair-sized portion of fragrant cod and Snowdrop was accepting a small tidbit from Mr. S's fingers.

Finally there was Jack, his new friend, accepting both their shares of golden goodness. It had to be stopped.

"Go on," Bede Hall whispered from the floorboards. *"It's safe, and you have to meet him sometime. You've earned a treat."*

"And the boy?" Anubis asked.

"Harmless. There's fish in it," the Hall teased, *"besides, I think there's a mouse nibbling a hole in a lamp cord over there."*

"Well, in that case, I suppose I'd better take a look," Anubis said.

"Gone too long...something fishy going on," Pigeon grumbled *"gone fishing...here today gone tomorrow."*

"My dear old chap. I'm here to stay," Mr. S promised.

"Fat chance," Pigeon replied, making everyone laugh as he flew to Mr. S's shoulder.

"I've missed you old boy," Mr. S said.

Anubis could take no more. Self-respect forgotten, his nose led him out from under the sofa's skirt, and much to his surprise, he emerged to what amounted to a round of applause.

He marched proudly and stood directly underneath the table holding the flavorsome wrappings.

Anubis gave Mr. S an honorary silent meow due a master of the house. His actions couldn't have been more obvious.

"There he is, hey buddy, come here sweetie-cakes, come on boy, glad you could join us..." came all the voices, but the biggest thrill of all, was hearing Mr. S addressing him using his full titles in the ancient tongue of his ancestors: hail the great good god of transformation, beloved of Ra, chosen of the two ladies, revered guardian of the two lands, sublime in joy in whom the Aten finds beautiful."

The form of Taraq was silhouetted against the deepening peach and mauve of the English sunset as he stood gazing at the topiary sphinx. He had said he wanted to be alone, but he'd been in the garden for over an hour and showed no signs of returning.

Mrs. S finally sent Kit to fetch him, but Mr. S waylaid Kit.

"Let me speak with Taraq alone for a minute," he said.

A twilight breeze ruffled Taraq's hair.

"It should look out of place," Mr. S said, "but it doesn't."

"I cannot believe my seeing," Taraq said. "A green sphinx."

"How you holding out kiddo?" Mr. S asked. "Aren't you chilly out here?"

"As you know, desert nights are not warm," Taraq replied.

Mr. S nodded. "You may be homesick for a while, but you must tell me if you ever feel upset."

"I love my country," Taraq said, "but it has not been... as you say, homely, and so I am here in thanks, your home is amazing me."

"It's *your* home now if you want to stay," Mr. S said. "You know, I've never lost the feeling of mystery here. It's never gone away. Not since I first set foot on this property."

Kit arrived noiselessly, and sent a silent question to Mr. S asking if Taraq was okay. Taraq turned to him looking tired but happy.

"Mum wants us in for cocoa," Kit said.

Bede Hall's stables stood like a friendly purple shape in the dusky light as father and son made a leisurely after-dinner tour of the garden. Kit drew attention to its door left ajar for Anubis.

"You've always wanted a horse haven't you?" Mr. S said.

"Someday," Kit replied. "I think when I'm older, but right now I have too many other things on my mind."

"It must have been hard on you all while I was away. I take it you've been acting as the 'man of the house' more than Rupert," Mr. S said in a matter of fact voice. "Parks told me. He's quite impressed with you and Bash."

"Rupert's here full time now, I think he's found his calling, Kit said.

"Better late than never if he's serious," Mr. S retorted. "I might even be able to transfer his scholarship to Taraq, although he already knows more than I do about where to dig. But the fellows at the university may feel they owe me a favor, all things considered.

I want to thank you for all you've done to help your mother, and you've been extremely good about having Taraq join the family."

"I liked him right away," Kit replied. "It was as if I'd met him before."

The grapevine ran from the fish and chips shop directly to the ears of Mr. Tweedy.

"Now the man of the house has returned," he told Mrs. Tweedy, "this movie nonsense will stop. Cornelius Stratford-Smyth is a practical man. He'll want to sell."

Mr. Tweedy's face beamed in anticipation at his latest thought. "He may even want to buy a new place in the village," he confided to his impressed wife. "I could offer him the pick of the luxury condos we're going to build in Bede Heights," hastily adding: "That is of course, *after* we've picked ours."

Mrs. Tweedy was so enraptured she ordered three pizzas with extra cheese.

"Rayne Stratford-Smyth has confided to me several times that her dream-house will have enormous closets and stainless steel kitchen appliances," Mrs. Tweedy announced. "She wants a double fridge and one of those stoves without burners, you know, the ceramic-topped ones."

Enid Tweedy was ahead of herself as usual. She had overheard this very confession of Mrs. Stratford-Smyth's in the teashop when Mrs. Spoondance had paused in passing to ask how things were, and did she like the new arrangements.

"Then that's what she shall have," Mr. Tweedy declared. Nothing but the best for your friends...eh?... our friends," he added generously.

"Our friends," Mrs. Tweedy gushed. "Just think, we'll be neighbors."

Mr. Tweedy was already envisioning a graph of his bank balance rising like a thermometer, when Edgar interrupted his dream.

"I won't have to go back to that Hall will I?" he snuffled miserably.

"Only if Dr. Brooks says you must," Mrs. Tweedy replied, reassuringly. "Sometimes therapy requires one revisits a place to confront their..."

"There's no such thing as demons," Edgar blurted.

"I was going to say *ghosts*," Mrs. Tweedy finished.

Wilbur Tweedy's next visit to Bede Hall was a bit of a shock. First of all in a brief conversation with Mr. S, he discovered the 'treasure' old Miss Beryl had been on about, was the tray of disgusting old beetles he and Edgar saw in the library. And, worst of all, there would be no new real estate listing for the Hall.

It was all most inconsiderate after all he'd done while Mr. S was away and considered dead. Well, they wouldn't be neighbors in gleaming new condominiums after all so there, he thought smugly. He would be living in his own luxury home without them, thank you very much, and then he realized there would be no condominiums, and that technically, they already were neighbors since his pokey mock-Tudor bungalow bordered the great estate.

"I didn't have a ruddy chance of getting this place, did I? Wilbur Tweedy whined to Mr. S.

"Afraid not, old chap," Mr. S said, smiling. "There's not a snowball's chance in hell that this family's ever going to leave Bede Hall. It's in our blood."

Mrs. Enid Tweedy banged a garden trowel on the podium and called The Women's Institute to order. Any new business?" she asked.

An eager young woman raised her hand. "Can we ask Mrs. Stratford-Smyth to give us a talk on Bede Hall?" She fanned her face with Mrs. Fox's illustrated presentation handout on how to remove pet stains from carpets, and coughed discreetly behind it. "Local history is of relevance to us all as are its... well not to put too mild a point on it, Bede Hall's paranormal activities? I mean, is there a ghost and if so, who? Is it Lady Beryl? My son's friend's friend knows of a boy who's seen her. Is this going to affect the movie people? Some of us have quite come to depend on their business, so..."

Mrs. Tweedy paled, recognizing the involvement of Edgar's handiwork as a reporter, and cut in. "All in favor of asking Rayne Stratford-Smyth to update us on the status of Bede Hall's movie enterprises, please raise your hands." The motion carried amongst a stir of approval. "Of course I shall be delighted to approach Rayne myself as she's a close friend of mine."

After the guest speaker glowed beet-red, acknowledging her applause, the trowel tap-tapped in a tinny sound. Mrs. Tweedy waved it feebly. "Ladies, your attention please. I have one final announcement. If anyone has any information about the whereabouts of my missing gavel please see me in private. Thank you. This meeting is adjourned."

Mrs. Fox pulled Enid to the side. "You can keep this under your hat, but I overheard Rayne, not long after she'd moved back, and she said, plain as day to Mrs. Spoondance, that she felt as if the family had never left."

Mrs. Tweedy nodded. "Well, I think it's safe to assume at least one of them never did."

"Miss Beryl's brother Ben died there, in the Bede River. Sarah Goodman remembers it well, she was engaged to him, you know. The details are sketchy except Dr. Brooks almost died too."

The trowel dropped from Enid's fingers in a clatter. Would this Bede Hall nonsense ever end?

It was relatively painless and almost unnecessary for Rupert to inform Mr. and Mrs. S that he was leaving college for a career in the movies.

PART NINE

LAND'S END

'All the world's a stage,
And all the men and women
merely players:
They have their exits
and their entrances;
And one man in his time
plays many parts...'

- WILLIAM SHAKESPEARE

CHAPTER SEVENTY-SIX
Gone Tomorrow

Lady Nan insisted on attending the Christmas Eve service in the parish church of Bede. The graveyard was covered in snow, and Lady Nan searched in a muddle for her brother's grave, even though it had been difficult to get her across the pathways of the cemetery.

It stood out from the rest, not because it was marked by a tall obelisk, but because she could see Parks wiping the snow from its inscription: 'man says time passes; the pyramids say man passes.'

Parks doffed his cap and studied the toes of his shoes, waiting silently.

Lady Nan had been busy searching the ground for the glowing footprints of her invisible companion, but of course, Snow could not have been there. It was December.

Sarah Goodman, Lady Nan's girlhood friend, listened to Bash with a slight look of relief on her face.

"I wouldn't be telling you this if I didn't... if Lady Nan didn't think you would understand," Bash said eagerly.

"*Thinks* does she!" Sarah exclaimed huffily. She ought to *know*."

"We appear to have a ghost," Bash went on, "but it's not the creepy sort. Nothing macabre, no Gothic horror clanking-chain stuff. We don't look up and see a ghoulish face in a window or anything; it's actually the other way around, but without the ghoul part.

"And as you probably know, Lady Nan has seen a little girl ghost *from* the windows since she was the same age. About nine, as near as we can figure.

"I think it's one of the reasons, well the main reason, Lady Nan wanted to come home. She had been dreaming of her, and felt her *and* the house, calling. She wants to see you. Will I tell her yes?"

"Well, of course you may, child. I've been waiting for her summons since we had tea at Twigglys back in April of last year. Goodness, that was eight months ago. I never attend May Day celebrations. Can't abide the ruckus, and cats are at their peril when humans lose their senses. Halloween is another stupid day. That black cat nonsense really started something ugly. Cats have a tough enough time as it is without being considered the familiar of choice for witches."

"Mum's take is that the whole ghost thing is one of Lady Nan's 'elderly dreams,' and the locked room is a distant happy-ish memory, so she humors her as best she can because it calms her down. Anyway, Mum's pretty distracted. We all are. There's no need to tell my Mum everything, is there? No need for ghosts and such?"

"None," Sarah said. "Beryl preferred having secrets from her mother. Your grandmother was my best friend. She still is," Sarah said at last. "This has something to do with Ben. Mark my words. What does Peregrine have to say on the subject?"

"Dr. Brooks is always ... supportive."

"I've never seen the ghost-child myself. Never used to be around much in the summertime. And the times I did try to see her, she didn't show herself. I'd like to see her now, though. Since you've seen her. I think half the time I didn't believe Beryl anyway."

"Sorry, she's gone till next year I'm afraid," Bash said apologetically. "Well, out of sight anyway. She's there all the time but we can't see her."

"I'm afraid the same may be true of your grandmother, and me come to think of it. Gone soon, I mean. I don't say that as a gloomy thing. Quite the opposite. I had a dream she was going home. I hope that doesn't upset you. When you get to hers and my age, death is a bit of a welcome friend.

"I see a lot of Ben in my dreams too. The three of us having a good time with Peregrine watching us. Waiting for his turn, so I know he'll be the last of us to go."

Miss Goodman looked as though she had finished having her say, but after a pause she spoke again:

"What shade of lipstick was your grandmother wearing the last time you saw her?" she asked.

CHAPTER SEVENTY-SEVEN

The Winter of Life

Bash had convinced everyone on having a living Christmas tree, which meant that it had to be much smaller than their old artificial one.

Rupert called it puny. Taraq was thrilled with everything English and couldn't have cared less if the tree was pink, let alone how big it was. Lady Nan said it was as exactly as tall as Snow, and Mrs. S was happy it was there at all, since last year, she reminded them, they had been too upset to have any sort of tree.

"It's bigger on the inside," Bash said.

"It's as big as all outdoors," Mr. S noted.

"*Where*, it will be happy to return in a few weeks," Bash gloated.

There had been no question about where it would go. The heart of a Bede Hall Christmas was its library – the scene of their latest triumph. It was also the room which offered cheery new curtains and freshly papered walls suitable for a celebration.

The little spruce tree sat like a green pyramid on the hefty table that usually held the gigantic Bede Hall dictionary, the size of an atlas.

Rupert kidded that the room was now all 'spruced up' adding a particular comment addressed to Bash: "and please don't say how apropos it is."

It was the children's task to string popcorn and cranberries, and make paper chains to decorate the tree in the original 'green' tradition, barring the dangerous use of candles.

Mrs. S made small popcorn balls to hang outside for the birds, saving one for Pigeon, and shortbread cookies with a hole in the centre so they could be tied with ribbons, and Mr. S draped a small string of Christmas lights while Bash pretended not to notice.

"Are twinkle lights organic?" Kit chuckled.

"There are lines one must cross sometimes," Bash replied.

"Well, if we've learned nothing else this year, it's that," Kit agreed.

Lady Nan looked faraway. "Crossing over," she repeated. "Peace on earth. Resting in peace. Tis the season. What a delightful prospect."

"Mamma, it's Christmas," Mrs. S chided. "We have lots to celebrate."

"My dear child. I do believe I was making that exact point myself," Lady Nan said, smiling a wide hot-pink smile. She glanced at Dr. Brooks as if sharing a secret. "One person's fear is another person's celebration. Death isn't morbid at all if it comes after one's had the time of their life." She added as an afterthought: "And in the *winter* of one's life. After a long winter there's always spring."

Dr. Brooks patted her arm. "Well said, m'dear. And now, would you do me the honor of breaking in this mistletoe?"

Mr. S quipped suddenly. "I've never found tombs gloomy. The Egyptians were quite cheery with their decorations and murals. They knew how to celebrate the afterlife in style."

"Don't say it," Kit warned Bash.

"I wasn't going to say panache."

"Presents!" shouted Rupert, cutting off Bash's favorite word.

"Cocoa!" Kit echoed.

"Snow!" Lady Nan cried.

Dr. Brooks and the twins looked as if they'd been given electrical shocks.

"Wouldn't you like some cocoa?" Bash coaxed.

"I'm not senile child," Lady Nan said pointing to the window. "It's snowing."

"Of course it is," Bash said recovering.

"I have a splendid idea. Why doesn't someone make some cocoa," Lady Nan said, winking at Peregrine, pretending to be in a dither.

"And what name do you want for Christmas," Dr. Brooks asked Pigeon.

"Plum cake... pancakes... purple snow... a dash of panache," Pigeon whispered as only a parrot could, and flapped into a fit of laughter.

White continued to dust the countryside of Bede the rest of Christmas Eve, and at eleven o'clock at night, Jack decided he needed to go out.

"Who's up for a walk?" Kit announced, and three heads answered 'why not.'

"Looks like snow...looks like snow!" Pigeon shrieked shuffling up and down his perch.

"Partriii-idge in a peaaaar tree," Bash sang, into the cage.

Pigeon cocked his head to one side and started bowing. *"Partridge... pears...pie in the sky...beginning to look like Christmas ...spruce up!"*

Outside they ran into Rupert who against all odds was carrying an armload of wood for the fire.

"Hiya Boss," Kit said. "Lost all your slaves?"

Not a breath of wind stirred the soft powdered snow that had turned lavender in the moonlight. For a horrible moment Kit saw the future superimposed over the landscape. He shuddered, shaking off the winter dream, and made a snowball to throw for Jack. For now, the present was safe. Ironically there would be time enough for growing up fast.

"My first winter," Taraq exclaimed, delighted to catch snow-flakes on his tongue.

The three made a leisurely circuit past the maze, and around the fountain to the sundial. Taraq made a point of patting the green sphinx that now looked like an oddly shaped iced cake.

The twins couldn't help checking the window of the Winter Room.

"Nobody's up there," Bash said

"No *body* ever was," Kit remarked.

The window was only a small black square hanging under the eaves like a forgotten painting.

"We'll see them again soon," Bash said.

"Why? Do you plan on dying?" Kit snapped.

"I mean, there's always another August," Bash replied.

"Maybe they've moved on," Kit announced.

"Maybe *we* have," Bash countered.

"I know I have," Taraq admitted with a happy grin.

"Lady Nan told me she dreams about Snow all the time now, so she's probably serious about the big *'moving on,'*" Bash shared.

"I do not understand why your grandmother would want to move on, now that she has Dr. Brooks again," Taraq announced.

"Those two will always be together," Bash declared dreamily.

"Taraq and Kit exchanged grimaces. "Girls and their happy endings." Kit said, grimacing.

Bash defended her opinion. "Well, it is happy if death is a *beginning*," she said, pushing Kit's shoulder.

Kit made another exasperated face at Taraq. "I'm *beginning* to feel sick," he said, making Taraq giggle and choke on a snowflake.

"Come on Bash, get real," Kit said.

"Well that's *never* going to happen. Who knows what's real anymore?"

"Then here's a reality check for you," Kit said nudging Taraq. "Yellowstone Park is going to get more and more active, and in 2020... KABOOMSKY! And nothing, but nothing, can stop geology. Oh, and did I mention, nothing?"

"Well, I'm going to do something," Bash declared. "Gardening is only a beginning. It's a hobby that leads to studying the environment. I'm going to be a scientist, like you. Well, a geologist at any rate."

"Not me," Kit replied. "Did you forget that I'm going to be a science-fiction writer? One can't escape their destiny, including planets."

Bash smiled encouragingly. "Of course you can. I can't move a mountain, but I..."

"Can what?" Kit laughed, nervously. "Put a cork in one?"

Bash was infuriated from not being taken seriously. "I may not know much," she fumed, "but what I *do* know, is that Yellowstone is flat as a pancake. There's no mountain to move. It's acres of land waiting under the earth like a gigantic bowl of trillion-alarm chilli."

"Science-fiction is still science, isn't it?" Taraq suggested. "And doesn't chilly mean cold?"

"Words are funny things, and my brother is going to have to learn that, if he's going to write interesting stories," Bash sneered.

"We've got to get you some chilli, mister," Kit teased. "You're in for a treat."

Taraq grinned in good humor. "I am so pleased to be so entertaining."

"So many experiences; so little time," Kit said.

"My point exactly," Bash said smugly. That brings us back to reality. What are we going to do for the next six years?"

Taraq spoke first. "I'm going to be an archaeologist and help your dad in a place I know best. By the way, when I met Taraq 2 in that dream, he mentioned there were two scarabs in your dad's collection he recognized as Smenkhkare's."

"Our dad will be your dad by then. The adoption papers are being drawn up as we speak. I heard them talking the other night. Early in the new year I should expect."

Taraq grinned and shook his head in disbelief. "My own father," he sighed.

"Hey what about us? You get *all* of us... including Rupert. Sorry about that."

"Of course. I meant *family*," Taraq corrected.

"Speaking of the devil," Bash added. "Now that Boss wants to be an actor, he will be over one of Jupiter's moons to be off the hook in the 'father and son' Egyptology business. Well done Taraq. How very ..."

"Apropos!" Taraq and Kit finished in unison.

"Would it be so difficult for you to 'move on' to another word... pulllleeeeeeeeeeez?" Kit begged. "That's what I want for Christmas."

"In the meantime," Bash replied huffily, "the old Yellowstone caldera is percolating away like coffee."

"I love coffee," Taraq said.

Jack barked at a white hare and raced after it, making the twins laugh.

Tarag worried out loud. "The poor rabbit. Call him back."

Kit giggled. "No way Jack's ever going to catch that."

The topiary hare froze and Jack lost interest. He loped back and the hare disappeared into the trees.

Kit stamped his feet. "Well that's Jack exercised, then. Who's for more cocoa? Come on Jack. Here boy!"

Jack skidded past Kit and caught Taraq's foot so that he sprawled in the snow, laughing. While he lay there laughing helplessly he flailed his arms and made an angel shape.

"Not bad for a first angel," Kit said, helping Taraq to his feet.

Bash looked at her watch. "It's past midnight. Merry Christmas," she said, staring at the moon and stars. "It's just like the 'midnight clear' in the carol. The one about the angels with golden harps touching the earth."

"It's hard to imagine little Taraq 2 as an angel," Kit said.

"I think he was my angel," Taraq piped up, looking sad.

"We definitely need to find you a different name," Kit said to Taraq.

"That's a great idea," Bash agreed. "Our family is very practical about names. Most of us have done it. Try hauling around the name Bathsheba," Bash went on. "It has to have one syllable."

"Tut!" Kit announced. "It came to me instantly, so it has to be right."

Bash nodded her approval. "It's short and sweet and so... you," she said to Taraq... "It's ... quite... perfect," she finished slowly, purposely casual to fake out the boys.

Kit recited each word slowly. "Tut Carter Stratford-Smyth."

Boxing Day proved to be the coldest snap of the winter, and the new gas stove Bede Hall ordered as an early Christmas present was having a game of hide and seek. "The pilot light's gone out," Bash said.

Kit shrugged and peered into the stove. "Must be a fairy in there, eh sis?"

Just then, Rupert skidded into the kitchen in search of heat. He flapped his arms and blew on his fingers. "*Brrr.* Cor, it isn't half freezing upstairs. My sunglasses are quite fogged up. It's not much better down here. A person could catch their death in a house like this."

Rupert's words punched Kit in the stomach. "Don't say things like that. You've no idea what you're saying. No-one is going to die."

Rupert straightened, slightly taken aback. "Steady on little Kitty. No need to panic."

Bash read Kit's face. "Perhaps there is. Perhaps he'll tell us what's what. Coz somethings up isn't it Einstein? You freak out whenever we say the name Snow."

Kit spluttered an unconvincing "don't be silly." But Bash closed her eyes the better to read his mind. To her surprise she saw a bleak arctic landscape. Howling winds filled the air with flakes and blocked the sun. She opened her eyes to encounter Kit staring back at her.

"You see. Nothing," he said, his eyes widening, indicating his request for her to stay silent.

"A big ice-age of nothing. Was that the winter dream I just saw?"

"Make it so," drifted Captain Picard's voice from the telly.

"Captains!" Lady Nan declared in disgust. "*His* commands had to be instantly obeyed."

Kit and Bash knew she was referring to Captain Hilltop.

Bash held Lady Nan's hand. Three days after Boxing Day, the air had warmed suddenly and rain had come down stronger than a March downpour. It washed away the snow and rattled the stained glass of Bede Hall's windows as if to remind it that weather was a force to be reckoned with, and to keep on its toes.

"Shall we find a different show to watch?" Kit asked, lifting the remote.

"No no, you boys like this one," Lady Nan said, smiling. "Don't mind me. I'm just an old lady whose mind is wandering in the Shadowlands."

Picard's word might be the law according to Star Trek, but now that the laws of life and death were in play again, Lady Nan anticipated her death like a bestseller she was eager to read.

Bede Hall seemed to absorb Lady Nan, but she was fully aware of the world, and seemed to glow as she prepared to leave it.

Whenever she could, Bash drew comfort from Lady Nan's company.

The two boys spent more time together by themselves, anyway. Kit's tower window was always a cheery beacon in the darker winter afternoons. Not that she wasn't invited, but Lady Nan wanted her to write down some of her thoughts. "Word for word," the old lady emphasized. "Before the old year's out."

Bash understood completely, and took pains to write everything as Lady Nan wished.

The weather continued to play games. Changeable as the weather Lady Nan said as she peered at the rain coursing down her window one night from the solid white battering of snow the next.

The last days of December produced the heaviest snowfall in years. The drive had to be plowed three times.

Bash read alone to Lady Nan after Mr. and Mrs. S left for an awards dinner in Mr. Stratford-Smyth's honor. They had managed to drive off to London before the flakes came down that night, heavy and soft in a thick navy blue curtain that separated Bede from the rest of the world even more than usual.

PART TEN

THE SHADOWLAND

*"There was
a real railway accident,"
said Aslan, softly.
"Your father and mother
and all of you
- are as you used to call it
in the Shadowlands – dead."*

- CS LEWIS
'THE CHRONICLES OF NARNIA'

CHAPTER SEVENTY-EIGHT

The Final Curtain Call

Lady Nan wanted her snow globe all the time now. She peered into it, and said she could see Snow waving beside the miniature house.

The great four-poster bed was crowded with animals. Anubis and Feathers and Snowdrop curled up filling the spaces between books and Lady Nan's favorite things. Bash dabbed *L'air du Temps* on her grandmother's temples and wrists once an hour at Lady Nan's insistence.

Jack draped himself like a grey rug over the foot of the bed, every now and then whimpering at the sound of the boys' excited voices in the garden below.

The sun had made a dramatic appearance, and made the snow extra sticky. Perfect for making a snowman, and the boys had raced outside.

"We'll call up when it's ready," Taraq said kindly to Bash. "It's my first snowman."

"Make it a goodun," Bash smiled.

Laughter floated up through the open window, and since Lady Nan was dozing peacefully, Bash set aside the notebook where she'd been taking Lady Nan's dictation, to check on the boys' progress.

Taraq was rolling a large ball for the snowman's head. "We're nearly done," he shouted back when Bash called 'hello down there.' Two larger balls had already been stacked on top of each other for the body.

"What are you going to do for a hat?" Bash called out. Do you want me to find something?"

"It's all taken care of thanks," Kit shouted back. Wait and see."

Bash put her head back into Lady Nan's bedroom and carefully removed the snow globe about to topple from her hands. The old lady was gently snoring, as was Jack. Three cats made no sound, but little snowdrop stretched when Bash stroked her and curled up like a hedgehog the instant she stopped.

Bash heard Kit calling her name.

Down below, Kit and Tut stood in front of their creation and performed the dramatic reveal of a magician... "Ta da!"

The snowman of Bede Hall wore Tut's old skullcap, a King Tut T-shirt, and Rupert's old sunglasses. They had added crossed sticks for arms that made it look like a pharaoh holding a sceptre and flail.

While Bash was admiring their work, two young girls raced from the house towards the sundial where Parks had finished brushing snow from its face, now happily sending a triangular patch of shadow to mark 2 o'clock.

"Who are they?" she called down.

"Who are who?" Kit replied looking where Bash pointed.

"Those two girls standing behind you, dancing around Parks."

"There's definitely no girls down here. Maybe we've got more ghosts," he joked.

Bash's expression froze. "Omigod!" she shouted.

Lady Nan's eyes were still closed. She was still smiling, but this time she was 'gone.'

Bash raced back to the window. "Kit! Tut! Fetch Dr. Brooks and phone Boss, he's in the village. Quickly! Tut can use my bike. Lady Nan is..." she sought the right word and came up with the wrong one: "Worse!"

There was no way, she thought to herself, that she was shouting to the landscape or the house that their matriarch was dead.

The two girls were still there, but they were running towards the maze. Anna! Beryl!" she shouted after them with no effect. "Snow! Rain!" but the girls ran into the maze and disappeared.

Dr. Brooks arrived first, with the boys' bicycles protruding from the trunk of his car.

He felt Lady Nan's wrist for a pulse and finding none, he kissed it, and gently placed it back on the bed.

"She's wearing her perfume," he said smiling. "I expect she's enjoying her party."

The doctor showed no visible signs of grief, and Bash worried about him until Kit took her aside and reported what had happened.

"He saw her," Kit confided. Clear as day, he said. When we got there he already knew... and he was quite cheerful about it."

"I saw her too," Bash confessed. "I was watching you and Tut, and there she was, with Snow."

Outside, the sun was shrinking the snow pharaoh who was leaning at a dangerous angle, looking tipsy.

Bash called the doctor to the window. "Come quick! You've got to see this," she said excitedly.

There were two clearly formed snow angels near the sundial.

"The boys have been busy," he commented.

"No. Those snow angels weren't there a minute ago, and there's no footprints around them," Bash said.

"They look like crop circles left from a space ship," he quipped.

Bash looked as if she were about to cry.

Dr. Brooks put his arms around her.

"There there, I was being disrespectful. Girls will be girls. No doubt they were playing a game to cheer us up. It would be just like your grandmother to do something like that."

He looked down at the snow angels and gasped.

"Oh my. Do you see what I see?"

Anna and Beryl were dressed for summer, wearing Lady Nan's two favorite shawls and a pair of her straw hats. They had set up a tea party in front of the leaning snowman who was clearly the only guest for tea as he had his own plate, and cup and saucer, and Beryl was pouring invisible tea into his cup. Unicorn hissed and arched her back at the snowman.

The surrounding snow was unblemished, as if it had freshly fallen from the sky. It glowed pink. Two small boys appeared and raced each other to the table.

"Any teacakes?" one of them shouted.

Bash recognized little Taraq 2. "Who is that I wonder," she said, pointing to the other boy.

Dr. Brooks was overcome with emotion.

"That's Ben," he said.

While Bash and the doctor enjoyed the display, Rupert's car came hurtling down the drive sending the newly sun-dried gravel in a cloud behind him.

Kit and Tut met him at the bottom of the steps. None of them noticed the four children having tea on the front lawn.

Rupert glanced at the snowman. "Nice shades," he said.

Ben waved up at Bash and Dr. Brooks after saying something to his sister. Beryl looked up and toasted them with her teacup.

"Told you she'd be having a party," Dr. Brooks said, chuckling. "It's almost New Year's Eve."

The inscription Lady Nan had chosen for her epitaph was an excerpt from her favorite 'Narnia' book that read:

'The dream is over.
This is the morning.'

- CS LEWIS

Bash laid two wreaths of flowers. Pink peonies for Snow, and another of white carnations for Rain. She squeezed Kit's and Tut's hands.

"How extraordinarily... apro... fitting," she said. When Bash looked back, the peonies were white and the carnations bloomed bright pink. The color of Lady Nan's favorite lipstick.

The funeral reception at 'the Stopped Clock' was crowded. Parks hovered politely in the corner nursing a pint of beer and watched the guests for a long time.

It was nice to be amongst friends, but he realized it was high time to go home. Scotland was the best place to bring in the New Year. The old years were over with Miss Beryl gone. And he'd promised to show Charlotte the highlands. She'd said she wanted to visit her namesake home – the village of Findhorn.

His thoughts swirled into a garbled memory of Miss Beryl. An image of her at age three shouting for her favourite 'Winnie the Pooh' story, came first... "More Pooh," she had cried over and over until Pigeon used to shout it for her.

Parks spoke out loud as if there was someone with him at the table.

"I made the green sphinx for Master Ben, but it was for her as well," he said mournfully. "Both of them always treated me like I was their real friend. They knew who I was, but it never mattered. And now both of em are gone. I've only got Miss Bash left."

Parks sat in a state of melancholy for ten minutes more, ignoring his beer before he stood up and banged a spoon on his tankard to get the room's attention.

"Ladies and gents," he said, addressing the room in a thin wavering voice.

The room hushed, and Parks raised his glass in a toast, as high as his old rheumatism would let him.

"To the Queen of Bede Hall," he said. "May she reign in peace."

Helen, the newly married Mrs. Hare, threw her coat over one of her new dining room chairs and straightened the shade of her new living room lamp.

"I thought the service for Miss Beryl was lovely," she called out to Robert who was already in the kitchen clanking the milk

416

saucepan onto their new stove for cocoa. "And the 'Stopped Clock' put on a nice spread," she added as an afterthought.

"Yes, it did," Robert's voice replied.

"Oh, by the way, I found that film I lost from the May Day fete," Helen announced. "It had been stuck under the passenger seat of my car all this time. I just got the prints back from Vincento," she said, waving a large brown envelope. "Want to see?"

"I won't be a jiff, dear," Robert called back. "I don't want to let the milk boil over."

Robert Hare set a tray of cocoa and a plate of crust-less cucumber sandwiches in front of his wife.

"Oh Rabbit," Helen said over-sweetly, "I thought I showed you the correct way to present an assortment of triangles in a pyramid. Did you remember to add a lot of pepper the way I like?"

Helen rearranged the shape the sandwiches made on the plate, and sent her husband scurrying back to the kitchen for paper napkins and digestive biscuits.

Robert finally slumped into one of their new armchairs and reached for his cocoa as Helen waggled a stack of photographs at him.

"Look at these," Helen marvelled, splaying the prints into a fan. It looked like a card trick, and Robert accepted them, folding them back into the shape of a deck.

Helen patted the seat cushion of her new sofa gesturing for Robert to join her.

Robert sighed heavily, heaved himself out of his comfy chair, and settled himself beside her as she wished.

"Parks is in a couple of the pictures I took of you that day we went to paint his cottage," Helen said. "He's standing right beside you in this one. And here's one of his grandson looking out the window... and another of his son. They're all wearing that same funny hat he always wears."

Each photograph had the foggy outline of one member of the Parks clan floating in and out of the shots.

417

"But Parks wasn't *there* that day," Robert said. "None of them were. They must be double-exposures. I say, they do look rather creepy, don't they."

Helen shuffled through the rest of the photographs. "And here's one I took of Charlotte presenting Parks with my birthday gift."

Helen gasped staring at a snapshot of Charlotte Findhorn presenting a painting to mid-air.

"My god!" she exclaimed. "He isn't there at all!"

Robert felt a chill flash up his spine when he realized how close he'd been to a ghost.

Bede Hall brought in the New Year with as much panache as it could to honor its matriarch, Lady Beryl, and celebrate the events which had brought new life full-circle into its rooms, now buzzing with the energy of ten residents and six animals. It chuckled to itself. Any day now there would be horses in the stables.

Down in the village, Nipper Tweedy no longer leaped willingly into Mrs. Tweedy's car (as Mr. Tweedy never let either of the dogs in his sports car, and ruin the leopard skin seat covers) Even passing the gates to Bede Hall made the Jack Russell howl like a miniature werewolf.

Edgar Tweedy made sure he carried his inhaler at all times. It was still possible to run into Jack and the twins when he had an appointment with Dr. Brooks.

Back in the garden of Bede Hall, the topiary queen looked splendid dusted in snow. Parks had scattered dozens of red roses around her base. She stood 'on guard' to the knight on her right – in check to her mate, the king facing opposite her across the lawn.

CHAPTER SEVENTY-NINE

Happy New Year

Dr. Peregrine Brook's back parlor was cozy. He'd lit a wood fire to take the edge of the January chill, even though his central heating was more than adequate for providing enough heat for four bodies.

"A real fire has an ambiance," Bash stated with authority.

She and the doctor had prepared a feast in anticipation of a full day of swapping stories, and making plans that would stream on past lunch and afternoon tea, and likely well into the supper hour.

"Well, my dears," Dr. Brooks addressed the room. "We've got rather a lot to share in addition to all this food," he said. "I'm going to start at the end and work backwards the way a piece of string leads one out of a maze. So, a rather lax form of chronological order, I think, will serve us best." He consulted a small bit of paper folded small in his pocket and adjusted his reading glasses. "Ah yes, New Year's resolutions."

The entire room let out a groan. Only the newly-named Tut remained impressed. Jack snoozed on, immune to all things unrelated to food or rabbits.

"And I thought this was going to be a cool party about time-travel," Kit grumbled.

"I'm talking about the kind of resolutions that will knock your socks off." Dr. Brooks declared.

"Well, you might have said so?" Kit apologized meekly.

Dr. Brooks gave a little cough and started to speak like a politician standing on a podium: "First... and I don't usually say this sort of thing, what's said here stays between the four of us."

"*Er...* and the four of *them*," Bash gestured towards, Lady Nan, Anna, Taraq and Ben, sitting on chairs as natural as you please. It was strange to see her grandmother, now twenty-one years of age, wearing a long blue gown, and to meet her Uncle

Ben who couldn't decide if he was nine going on eighteen, or eighteen going on nine.

"Quite right," the doctor said, "I stand corrected. The eight of us. And when I die, it will still be the *eight* of us," he added, winking at Lady Nan.

"What about Parks?" Bash asked.

"Parks and a few... *ahem*... select villagers will be our allies," he said.

"So, basically, everyone except the parents or Boss," Kit summarized.

"Your dear father," Dr. Brooks began, "is a scientist who believes the past is a locked time capsule to be analyzed. I think what we collectively know in this room is beyond carbon dating, and it would be a shame to quash something before we experiment a bit more than we've done to date. At the moment we are standing on a potential goldmine of science, and it would be against good science to report it with insufficient data. Are we agreed?"

"Mmmn Hmmnn, yes, sure, uh huh," came a collective mumble of responses.

"Above all," the doctor continued. "We must focus on ways to ensure the safety of the earth. You are all too young to be heard with credibility... yet, and I'm... well, I'm the age where one is dismissed as a *fruitcake*," he smiled and winked at Kit. "So, this is why we need facts and evidence... and you will have to grow up fast in order to 'run with the wolves,' so to speak.

"Now, we can't stop geology. It's not our place to even consider such a prospect, but... and I say but, science changes all the time, and there's no telling what new things will be discovered. It's our job to monitor them, not just by simply reading every new paper and article related to the environment, but to scan the past for the particles of genius thinking that slipped through the cracks of ignorance and superstition."

Kit fairly glowed with excitement.

"The term 'mad scientist' wasn't coined on a whim. Some scientists are..."

"Barking," interjected Kit, grinning back at the doctor.

"They are dogs?" Tut inquired.

"Sorry," Dr. Brooks said for Tut's benefit. "Barking mad is an English term for a raving loony. Oh wait. There is one exception to my exclusivity rule, isn't there always, and I've already broken the news to your mother. I almost forgot. It's just a formality really, but, Kit and Bash – I am your grandfather. So, you see it's not *that* important. And we can move on to greater revelations."

Kit snorted ginger-ale through his nose which was rather painful, and Bash had to thump him on the back. The ghosts had a good laugh since none of them *had* grandfathers anymore.

Tut calmly finished his second teacake, and looked quite happy to remain a spectator. This having a family thing was proving most entertaining.

"Kit has put together a short presentation on volcanic winter," Dr. Brooks continued, "but before that our one and *only*..." he paused and peered over his glasses at Tut, "*Taraq*, will be giving us a fascinating firsthand view of the eighteenth dynasty of Egypt, just to bring us up to snuff. It seems Lady Nan was once Ankhesenamun... and," he added as an afterthought, "I was the pharaoh, Smenkhkare. But more about *that* later."

The twins stared with growing incredulity, their eyes protruding like frogs and didn't dare look at each other.

"Excuse me?" Kit interrupted. "Later? We're going to discuss who you are and were, *later*?"

"Yes, that's right. Well-spotted Kit," the doctor replied smugly.

"Doctor B, you may consider my socks knocked off," Kit finally said.

"I need another cream scone," Bash said weakly.

"We're all friends here, so don't hold anything back," Kit managed to sputter towards Dr. Brooks before bursting out laughing.

"And now," Dr. Brooks announced, "for Taraq's presentation. Please hold any questions till the end. We'll break for lunch at that time."

"More like a bottle of brandy," Kit whispered in Tut's ear.

Bash raised her hand. "Sorry Dr. B, I have to ask Lady Nan something that's bothering me if you don't mind because it rather affects a friend of mine."

The doctor looked kindly on his granddaughter. "I'll allow it, and then we shall proceed," he said bowing slightly towards Lady Nan.

Bash cleared her throat and looked directly at Lady Nan.

"Who is, or was, Parks then?" she asked. "When and how did he die? And will he abandon my lessons and the gardens now that I know... that *we* know he's... *um*... dead."

Lady Nan smiled. "I met Parks when he was nine years-old. At least that's what he wanted me to believe. Nine is a magic number apparently. But in reality," she paused to chuckle. "Parks was a ghost two-hundred years before I was born. His father was a landscape designer when the Bede Hall was only a drawing on a bit of parchment. He was as keen on plants as you are when he was a little boy.

His grandfather and father were keepers of Bede's estate and he was thrilled to follow in their family tradition. He inherited his 'present' job after apprenticing with his father when he was twenty-four-years-old.

"The Parks family worked out the plans for the whole estate ages before the first spade of earth was turned in a ceremony that commemorated the construction of the present Hall as it is today.

"It took seventy-eight years to build, and on the day the dedication plaque was unveiled, Parks was killed during a lightning storm by a fallen tree. His body was buried near the maze. It had grown to its full height long before that. He and his sweetheart, Pearl, met there on his days off. His father had the sundial placed over his remains like a gravestone."

Bash nodded enthusiastically. "So many things are falling into place, now," she said.

"Pearl, was heartbroken," Lady Nan continued. "She never left the Hall after that. She spoke to the house all the time and took on the extra duties of head parlour maid, polishing and dusting from dawn to dusk. She lived in the winter room before it was Snow's. They say she grieved herself mad. Some said she was a witch; in other words, a healer known as a green woman who made magic with herbs and flowers. Villagers rumored she put a curse on the Hall but Parks said no, it was a white spell."

"Yes, yes," Bash said. "Parks *and* Charlotte teach unusual gardening techniques that work like magic. I've experienced some magical things even if Kit *doesn't* believe me."

Lady Nan hushed her granddaughter with a finger over her mouth. "Kit believes more than you know dear. Now, back to my story. Pearl cast her lover's soul into the stonework so he would live forever, and she stayed with him until her death as an old woman of ninety-two. She created a magic tunnel in her room so she could visit him but only in the month of August, and on her days off she sat in the maze, their first trysting place. That's who the true ghost of Bede Hall is. I only saw her as the green woman who sat by the sundial every full moon but no-one else could see her. "You might say, Parks is the 'voice' of Bede Hall, really, because he knows what it wants and where it wants it, and who it wants to live here. And I have it on the best authority that he will never leave it. You see, he's a once-born."

Bash wriggled impatiently in her chair and raised her hand. "I know it sounds self-explanatory but could you please explain more about once-borns."

Lady Nan beamed at her granddaughter. "Of course, a once-born remains a ghost after they pass on instead of reincarnating. Parks will always be a ghost."

"Thanks Lady Nan," Bash said. "It makes sense now. I'll continue to look forward to working with him then. Shouldn't he be here with us right now?"

"Parks is where he loves best – back on the estate. He isn't overly fond of leaving it. He only ever ventured into the village when it was absolutely necessary. Oh, and to visit his old sweetheart, Charlotte Findhorn."

Bash choked on her scone and jumped to her feet.

"Charlotte is a ghost!" She spluttered breathlessly, as her legs gave way, and she crumbled back into her chair.

"No, Charlotte is a 'twice-born,' very much alive," Lady Nan said, "like Peregrine and I... Oh, I suppose not me anymore, she blushed, and... well, several others in the village you may have met," Lady Nan finished lamely. "Charlotte was Pearl all those years ago."

"I've come over all funny," Bash whispered faintly. "I feel quite dizzy."

"Well you're bound to," Dr. Brooks said gently. "You've had a bit of a shock."

"A bit?" Bash echoed weakly.

"She's not the only one," Kit said, looking gutted. "I can't imagine who the others are." He faced Dr. Brooks. "You're alive aren't you?"

"F'raid so," Dr. Brooks replied, grinning. "For now."

Kit looked relieved as much as devastated.

"I say we continue," Dr. Brooks said, "and Bash can have a drop of sherry in her tea, no-one need know, and we'll attend to all these extra little details in due course. All right everyone?"

There were no further protests, and he rubbed his hands together enthusiastically, motioning to Taraq that it was his turn to speak.

Bash and Kit exchanged a look of panic, and tried their best to concentrate by putting on the same brave face as each other while Lady Nan sent each of them what she hoped was a reassuring smile.

Taraq stepped forward nervously, and bowed formally before seating himself cross-legged in the center of the room like an old storyteller. His words hooked them from the start.

"Four thousand years ago, my master was the Pharaoh, Smenkh-kare," he began. "Prince Tutankh*aten's* older half-brother, as he was known then, when the great Aten was in favor.

Smenkhkare was eighteen-years-old when his father, Akhenaten died and left him the throne, and he had to marry his father's widow, his chief wife, Ankhesenaten, a distant cousin, three-years-older. She was twenty-one. He only ruled for one year... until Tutankhaten turned nine-years-old, and his name was changed to Tutankhamun to reflect the new Amun priesthood." He winked at Lady Nan. "Nine was considered the age of maturity then. It was coming of age year for all special children."

Kit sat up startled. "Hey, the first time I dreamed the winter dream I was nine."

Lady Nan clapped. "Oh, well done, Christopher."

Bash put her hand up as if she was in school. "Excuse me Taraq. Just a quick question. Lady Nan, you got the key to the winter door when you were nine and Kit had the winter dream. What about my power?"

"Don't sulk child. Think back to your ninth birthday party," Lady Nan said. "Remember my *L'air du Temps* lesson? Can you remember what the day smelled like?"

Bash closed her eyes and sniffed the air. She smiled."Mmmmmn. Lovely. Charlotte gave me a lavender plant."

Lady Nan joined her granddaughter and blissfully sniffed the air. "And?"

"And we went for a walk," Bash said. "I found an ordinary button on the sundial. Oh, Parks' grave! Charlotte said I was lucky because lost buttons are fairy pennies worth one wish. I threw it into the pond and wished."

"And was it a 'be careful what you wish for' wish?" Lady Nan asked.

"I wished I could stay at Bede Hall forever and... Oh, and tend the gardens."

Lady Nan nodded. "And Parks took you on as his apprentice the next day. He told me you were born to the art of botany."

Kit, caught Dr. Brooks sitting with his eyes closed, tuning in, and warmed to the exercise. "And I made a wish blowing out the candles. I wanted to discover time travel. And Dad gave me a subscription to National Geographic and I got hooked on an article on volcanoes. That's where I saw the photo of the Yellowstone Caldera from space. The poster in my room. The winter dream always came on August 1st."

Dr. Brooks looked as if he'd drifted off during the distraction but he smiled and spoke without opening his eyes. "There are no coincidences at Bede Hall," he said, in an unfamiliar voice. "Just family extending in ways you can't imagine for inconceivable lengths of time-tunnels that radiate from the heart of the world. Before earth's present landmasses shifted there was one concentrated hub of power in the center of Pangea. Today it still exists. The center of that hub is the Hall's red library. It harbors an unbroken line of knowledge." He nodded to Taraq. "Sorry to disturb dear boy, please continue."

Kit and Bash moved closer together and held hands.

Taraq, slightly overawed in the presence of his old pharaoh's voice, took a deep breath and managed a bow. He made a polite cough and continued with his eyes lowered to Dr. Brooks' shoes. "Smenkhkare inherited Ankhesenaten because the power of Egyptian kings passed through their queens, and Akhenaten's chief wife, Nefertiti, was too ill to bear children, but Smenkhkare and Ankhesenaten had known each other from childhood and fallen in love as teenagers, so it was a very happy match.

The Amun priesthood who had been overthrown in favor of the god Aten, murdered King Smenkhkare as soon as the newly-named prince, Tutankhamun, was old enough to officially take the throne.

I was nine then, too, and I was buried alive with my master. My twin sister, Anu begged Queen Ankhesenaten to release her so she could join me, and after the exhausting weeks of embalming and official mourning were finally over, she tearfully relented.

"My master's beloved queen, Ankhesen*aten*, was renamed,

426

Ankhesen*amun*, and was forced, by law, to marry the new 'boy king,' who you know as King Tut. He was... *nine*-years-old.

"The two became good friends, but Ankhesenamun mourned Smenkhkare and wasted away for years.

"Tut was a sickly child with a deformed jaw and a curved spine who had to walk with a stick, and so mentally incoherent, his grandfather Ay, had to rule with him for *nine* years. I guess Ay got used to his power, so when Tut was eighteen and far too weak to rule alone, Ay gave orders for him to be killed.

"They made it look like a hunting accident, but Ankhesenamun knew the truth because Tut's body had been too broken to ever hunt or fight. He was only depicted as a hunter and leader for political reasons. Like the painting on your throne chair, Kit. Anyway, Ankhesenamun guessed, correctly, that as soon as Ay made her his wife she would be murdered.

"Ay declared himself pharaoh when Queen Ankhesenamun was thirty-one-years-old.

"Smenkhkare's tomb was reopened in order to loot it for the grave goods necessary for Tut, *the first one*, and Ankhesenamun visited Smenkhkare's mummy every day, often sitting for hours at a time, the way you saw her that night when we found Taraq 1... *er* now Tut, here in this room.

"Anu and I saw both of them talking many times as our 'kas' were trapped in the tomb as well."

Kit looked confused and scratched his head.

"Ay declared Ankhesenamun his wife before she disappeared. She was able to sneak into the tomb of my master, where she lay down guarding his mummy, now robbed of its jewelry and sarcophagus, and sheltered the sad bones of Anu and me until Mr. Cornelius found us. It was my namesake's" he stopped and gestured to Tut, "bosses who threw us into a scrapheap.

"The four of us were like a family in the Egyptian afterlife. Smenkhkare and Ankhesenamun treated us like their children, and for a while we were happy. Happy that is, until the rebirths began.

427

Queen Ankhesenamun left first, then Smenkhkare, and finally Anu was called, and I was alone for a very long time." He bowed. "I am now come to the end of my story and a new beginning."

There was a light fluttering of polite applause, and Dr. Brooks called for questions. Lady Nan's clothes had changed to the long white robes of an Egyptian queen, and she stood beside Dr. Brooks, looking like a bride.

"That's an awful lot of atens and amuns to remember," Kit said. "Not to mention the Taraqs and Tuts. I should have brought my notebook."

"What's a ka?" Bash asked.

428

CHAPTER EIGHTY

Once Upon a Time

Kit propped up his old poster of the Yellowstone Caldera on the mantelpiece and cleared his throat to a polite spattering of applause.

"*Ahem*... Before I begin, let me announce that from now on to save confusion there is only one Taraq and one Tut. Maybe even one Parks although he likes to take several forms to represent his moods. We will let him decide."

Kit stood a little taller and made eye contact with each member of his audience and gave a formal cough. *Ahem*... "A volcanic winter is the reduction in temperature caused by volcanic ash and droplets of sulfuric acid that obscure the sun and raise the Earth's reflectivity of solar radiation after a large particularly explosive type of volcanic eruption," he lectured without looking at his notes once.

Bash groaned and Anna looked like someone had hit her in the face with a surprise snowball. Tut and Taraq looked hypnotized, and Lady Nan sat quietly, with Anubis in her lap, looking proudly at her grandson, while Ben brushed Unicorn's fur.

Kit faced seven puzzled faces. "Now, this next part may be harder to understand. The long-term cooling effects are primarily dependent upon the sub-lateral injection of sulfide compounds. Stratospheric aerosols cool the surface and the troposphere by reflecting solar radiation, warming the stratosphere by absorbing terrestrial radiation, and when combined with anthropogenic chlorine in the stratosphere, destroy the ozone layer which moderates the effect of lower stratospheric warming. The variations in atmospheric warming and cooling results in changes in tropospheric and stratospheric circulation."

Kit looked up, well-pleased. "I will take your questions now," he said confidently.

There was an uncomfortable silence while everyone studied the tops of their shoes... and in Taraq's case, his sandals.

"Anyone?" Kit asked.

"Maybe I'm not cut out to be a scientist," Bash said.

There was still an audible silence, and Bash felt compelled to explain. "My brother doesn't mean to sound gloomy. It's just that he's always known the planet was in trouble and the environment has always been a bit of a ticking bomb," she said.

"Correct, Sherlock," Kit replied testily. "Are there any questions or have I made myself clear. It's important to understand what we're up against."

Anna shook her head. "Once more in English please. Pretend I'm a little kid and explain what happened," she said.

"Very well kiddies," Kit began.

He took a deep breath and spoke directly to Anna the way a good storyteller addresses an audience of children. He waited till they looked into his eyes before he began slowly with the four words that audiences everywhere know and love from childhood.

"Once upon a time... I should say: once upon a *time-travel*...the world was flat," Kit recited.

Bash stifled a giggle, but the others paid attention, looking relieved.

Kit continued on, throwing Bash a stern look. "This should be easier to understand... Long ago, an asteroid from a distant galaxy, looked around and realized it was lost. So, it stopped by Earth for directions. It tried to parallel-park over the Pacific Ocean, but its brakes failed and, oops, it crashed, so that the people on its world and the people of earth blended into one big crazy mixed-up family. Some were like the once-born earthlings. Some were like the twice-born extra-terrestrials.

"For a few million years it was winter and everyone had to sleep while their new home healed itself. But, a funny thing happened. When the new family of earth woke up, they discovered all their dreams had formed into one big dreamtime, so everyone lived twice for a while. Once for luck and once for good," Kit said.

"I meant a kid of nine, not three," Anna said indignantly. "But thank you. I think I understand the general idea now. Science-speak *is* out of my world but I *can* understand hieroglyphics. And that was very poetic how you got in that whole, once-born twice-born bit in there."

"Well, it's not quite as simple as I made it sound," Kit said.

"We can only imagine," Bash whispered to Anna.

Kit obviously heard.

"Strange that you should say that because actually that's what we do. We imagine ourselves awake," Kit said.

"Strange?" Bash interrupted again. "I'd call it positively, extraordinarily, unparalleled."

The room became distracted with tea and cakes, but as the man in charge, Dr. Brooks was compelled to ask a question he hoped would be the final business of the day. "Any new business?" he said, casually sipping his tea.

Anna spoke up, nervously transparent. "My full name was Nanette," she said. "I was named after my Nana by my... *um*... family."

Lady Nan prodded her in the ribs and shook her head.

Kit, Lady Nan, Anna, and Dr. Brooks exchanged a look of caution. Someday, it might be a best time to divulge more things to Bash and Tut, but now wasn't the time.

"Anyone else," Dr. Brooks said again, hoping they were done.

"Has anyone else noticed how many old people live in Bede?" Bash asked coolly. "No offense to you Dr. B. I mean villagers who seem wise in years, but amazingly youthful and in-shape and rather modern? Charlotte calls them old souls. I mean Mr. Leoni is ancient, but he wears cargo pants and sneakers."

Kit spoke up. "Yeah, he told me he needs loads of pockets to carry the things he needs. He said it was a bit like wearing a backpack for the legs. He's always got his camera handy, as well as odd bits of string and paperclips, a Swiss army knife, and a glue stick or two."

"Bede's a bit like a retirement home without the beds," Bash said. "The inmates are just healthy and clever. Like they've aged on the outside while inside their brains have frozen in the prime of their lives."

Dr. Brooks went pink in the face and spluttered his tea. "Interesting observation, Bash dear. A splendid subject for a later meeting I think," he said quickly, wiping his shirt. "This little get together is adjourned, and I'd like to thank Taraq and Kit for two splendid presentations."

Peregrine Brooks paused, wondering if it was the right time to address Bash's casual question. Sooner or later he would have to.

Sooner arrived much sooner than Dr. Brooks would have liked. The next meeting remained warm and fuzzy for a while but then Kit drew an unscientific conclusion about the powers of nine. He'd had a week to reassess his visit to the future, and with Dr. Brooks mellowed out in a state of contemplation, he shared his relief with Tut. "In light of new information," he said, "regarding my psychic abilities, Bash will survive. That time I saw Bede Hall in a devastated state I was just being shown a what-if scenario to trigger my thought processes. Bash, Anna, and the rest of us are home-free. Dr. Brooks called us special. With inherited superpowers halting a global catastrophe is not only possible, it's probable."

Bash, still in the dark regarding her fate, overheard the words *a global catastrophe is not only possible, it's probable* and joined her brothers' celebration. "I knew it. Parks told me to read the signs and rely on the weather even if it bodes ill. I guess that includes global warming, and Charlotte said victories are written in the stars?"

Dr. Brooks startled everyone by leaping up with a loud "NONSENSE!" that reverberated off the walls. "It most certainly does NOT! Shame on all of you! Have you heard nothing I've said?"

Kit's smile froze to see his laidback mentor instantaneously transfigured from a gentle tutor to a warrior king commanding an army. Surprisingly, he managed to argue. "But I thought you said there were no coincidences at Bede Hall."

The doctor loomed above Kit like a genie out of a bottle. He was livid but he took a few breaths to calm himself. "There are thousands of dangerous variables when you presume to trespass on history. Time travel is a precise science. Kit, with your ability to think rationally and your respect for unbiased calculation I would have thought you of all people would have looked for flaws before you jumped to so lame a conclusion. There's no room to be flippant about human energy."

"I'm sorry," Kit said. "I'll try to keep cool."

Bash frowned at Kit. "Is that your attempt at a sick joke about a winter that never ends?"

Kit shrugged. "It's just an expression. Just words. I didn't mean anything by it."

Lady Nan intervened. "We understand you Kit, but there's no such thing as *just* words. Dr. Brooks is right. We have to be precise. We have to forge on with clear heads."

Everyone started talking at once. Opinions clashed. Kit defended himself and Bash wanted to know more about Charlotte's notion of victorious stars. Anna stared at Kit and started to cry. Dr. Brooks found himself presiding over a classroom of unruly students. "Everyone calm down and take a seat," he shouted.

Nothing happened until Taraq let out a bloodcurdling whistle that stunned the room into silence.

Dr. Brooks gave Taraq a grateful thumbs-up before he spoke. "Thank you Taraq. Now, everyone, let me clarify a few things and then you can ask questions. One at a time. By virtue of seniority, I feel I must take control before things get more out of hand. My first duty is to delegate because to maintain a balance of positive energies we need equal parts logic and wildly-creative thinking. Kit and Anna, you are our designated time travelers because the portal chose you. Tut, you will work mainly with Taraq, Beryl and myself.

The four of us understand Egypt which is essential to our mission. Bash, in a roundabout way your task is down to earth yet profoundly telepathic. You, Parks and Charlotte are able to sense the subtlest vibrations emanating from the ground and read the stars. Plants reflect the earth's pulse which is why we need a team of vigilant botanists in league with the elementals. More about them later."

He addressed the group. "Kit and Bash were foretold eons ago as heralds of the Stratford-Smyth generation who must prevail over a dynasty of old magic which is decidedly dark. It's all a matter of time of course but the 'when' of things is dashed complicated." His gaze narrowed on Kit. "Make no mistake, some of us will die. Some of us have already... more than once."

"We've come close to losing the planet before," Lady Nan said. "We must never discount the importance of white spells, wherever they find us. They're positively restorative to all living things. Think of Mother Earth as a living entity we call Gaia. An optimistic attitude is not the same as hoping for the best. Confidence and joy are vital ingredients for success."

Kit looked dubious. "Joy? Are you sure about that one? We weren't feeling all that joyful when my father was lost. Only when he came back."

"Kit, you reached out and found Tut from your happiest memories of your father," Lady Nan said. "That's what connected the two of you. Without it, he may still be a prisoner."

Bash spoke up. "I understand. It's that 'joie de vivre' you described once, isn't it? You said Uncle Ben had it. That special excitement for things."

"Jwah de who?" Kit said, looking defeated.

"The joy of life," Anna answered. "I've been paying attention."

Ben raised his hand with a question. "I was foolhardy when I was nineteen. Aren't Kit and Bash a bit young for so much responsibility? They're only thirteen."

Kit piped up with a fact he thought relevant. "We'll be fourteen in three months."

Dr. Brooks nodded to his best friend who now appeared as old as he'd ever been. "Ben, we were reckless, but times are different. First we have no choice. Second, and well this is the tricky part, it's only our bodies that age. But I digress." He addressed the twins. "Parks and Charlotte and I have been preparing you both for an extraordinary mission. Please bear in mind that there are many agencies as yet unknown to you and all of them have been at your back quietly bringing you up to speed. From now on your generation joins a greater team who have been around for millennia. I promise it will make sense soon enough."

Tut slunk into the shadows looking lost. "Why am I even here?" he said to Anna.

Dr. Brooks heard and singled him out. He placed his hand on Tut's shoulder. "No-one is here who was not fated to be here. No-one. Never doubt that you are a significant member of this family."

Tut's face reddened and he ducked his head.

"There's a saying about tackling an enormous task," the doctor went on – *'it takes a village'*. If the earth is to survive it will take the village of Bede, the combined efforts of its twice-borns, and all of us in this room."

Anubis took that moment to stretch in an impressive arch and yowl.

Lady Nan scratched his ears. "And you children may even have to take orders from Pigeon or a cat."

"Can you see a pattern emerging?" Dr. Brooks said. "The eight of us are like a fabric woven together with the toughest threads. Twins have the strongest bonds of any humans and we have three sets in this very room. But twinning is also found in deep friend-ships between kindred spirits and birds and bees of a feather."

Lady Nan squeezed Dr. Brooks' hand. "Especially true love and past lives," she said. She reached out her hands to the ones either side of her. "Let's put our mistakes behind us, form a circle, and pledge to do better."

Kit climbed the stairs to his tower with leaden feet, ashamed at his behavior. He'd let down his teacher and his sister. He paced out the perimeters of the old keep under the stars, and touched each of the red numbers. Of course there was no mistaking their encoded message. Any way one looked at them they spelled out the year 2020. When was he going to tell Bash that Anna wasn't a ghost? The truth shouldn't hide forever.

He sat cross-legged to take in the revelations of the day. Data appeared like pages turning in a book: genealogy charts, lists, mathematical formulas, graphs, diagrams, timelines, maps of star constellations as well as land. A parade of recognizable faces morphed into a sea of strangers. The word family barely contained them all.

PART ELEVEN

LAND AHEAD

"Learn from yesterday,
live for today,
and hope for tomorrow.
The important thing
is not to stop questioning."

- ALBERT EINSTEIN

CHAPTER EIGHTY-ONE

Looking Forward

Kit's tower buzzed with excitement. Bash was in her element, rushing about importantly with paper and pens and serving mugs of cocoa to anyone able to drink it.

"At least we know where and when the destruction begins, and when it begins. So that gives us five years to fix things. Lady Nan, you always said everything works out for the best, in time. That's more than the passengers aboard the Titanic knew," she said eagerly, looking to Kit for leadership.

Kit was happy to oblige.

"We also know that not everyone is reborn," he stated. "So, Leonardo da Vinci, for instance, may or may not be alive today, and even if he is, he could be the greengrocer in Bede or a police dog," Kit announced.

Bash looked shocked. "How very disturbing," she commented. "I would expect life to be much more poetic than that."

"Okay," Kit backtracked. "I was just trying to make a point. I think it's fair to say people reincarnate as people, and a genius is not going to come back as a bus conductor... although..." he paused to examine the notion of buying a bus ticket from the greatest artist who ever lived.

Bash was giving him a very strange stare.

Lady Nan held one finger up and cleared her throat for attention. "By the way, he *is*."

"Who is what?" Kit asked.

"Leonardo. He's alive today; he's a friend of mine. Yours too as a matter of fact."

There was a long silence where Kit had nothing to say but he finally collected himself for the business at hand. "All things being equal... and they aren't," he continued. "It's quite likely that Ay was our grandfather 'Captain Hilltop', and our parents may have been Ahkenaten and Nefertiti. We can't rule out that a family doesn't reincarnate together... and Bash... don't even *try* to second-guess who you or I were. It's not productive, and worse, it screws up one's ability to remain ... *um...*"

"Unprejudiced, is the word I believe you're searching for," Bash said. "And I already figured it out, thanks."

Kit took a deep breath and picked up the thread of his last thought.

"Dr. Brooks said that synchronicity involves everything each of us knows, every person we've ever met, and every event that has ever happened," Kit emphasized. "On the way, we humans pick up loose threads, like I just did, and most of them don't get tied together till the end, when it's sorted out in unexpected ways. Apparently it's always for the greater good, even though it may not seem like it at the time."

"And then it's tied in a nice tidy bow," Bash finished.

"More like an elaborate knot," Kit said. "And that's where we come in. I think we all agree that unravelling the Yellowstone knot is paramount."

What do you want to be when you grow up?" Bash asked Kit with a sly look in her eye.

"It's a trick question," Tut said. "Watch out."

"If you mean, do I want to be a ghost?... then, no... I do not," Kit replied emphatically. "A science-fiction writer who perishes in a volcanic winter is poetic enough for me, thanks. I can't imagine how gruesome it would be hanging around a planet for eternity after its sun has burned out."

"Very dark," Tut said, not meaning to be funny.

"The best science-fictions stories usually are," Kit zinged back.

"Not even to stay with me?" Bash asked, pretending to be offended.

439

"Not even with Albert Einstein, Stephen Hawking, Superman, Leonardo da Vinci and Carl Sagan."

"What if there were interesting rules?" Bash suggested.

"And Galileo, Nikola Tesla, Charlie Chaplin, Michelangelo and Ironman," Kit continued.

"Rules?" Tut queried.

"Of ghostdom and time-travel," Bash replied.

"What possible rules could make a bleak scenario of whiteout below-zero landscape hell even remotely tolerable?" Kit ranted.

"Reincarnation," Tut spoke up. "That would make a difference."

"Not unless a person could be reborn in the past. There's not much to do in a perpetual ice-age after a few thousand years."

"We know some of the rules already," Bash announced. "We could visit any one of those people you mentioned, just for fun, or to pick their brains. They had insight, but not hindsight, like us. We know how the world is right now. We have the Internet. And... we wouldn't have to die first because we can time-travel... sorry, *dream-walk*. And just *maybe*, we could learn how to save this boiling, cooling, freezing, spinning planet we're standing on."

"Okay, I admit it would be amazing to meet Leonardo da Vinci," Kit relented.

"Stephen Hawking is very much alive by the way," Tut interjected.

"Well he *does* have to sleep sometimes," Bash replied.

"Did you not *hear* Taraq describe his 'family members' popping out of the afterlife willy-nilly in order to be reborn? They didn't seem to have a choice."

Bash ignored her brother. "I say we make a list of famous scientists we'd each like to visit and perfect our dream-walking abilities."

Kit scoffed. "You mean like Charlie Chaplin?"

"In my opinion he created silent films like a scientist," Bash insisted.

"That was art," Kit said.

"True science *is* art, Bash replied stubbornly. "Chaplin experimented with comedy instead of chemicals that's all. And comedy is a formula. He was a genius. Anyway... my point *is*... visiting geniuses would be the perfect source of research for your books," Bash finished with a grin looking terribly innocent.

Kit smiled inwardly and recovered. "Shut up," he blurted quickly, but it was said with newly-earned respect and admiration.

Bash laughed. "Not so easy to dismiss the idea now. Is it?" she badgered.

Kit paused to reconsider the latest variables. "I suppose there'd be no harm as long as we didn't alter the timeline."

"We *can't* alter the timeline, Bash said. "The past is already recorded history. All we'd be doing is research... and perhaps even enjoying ourselves a little. There are a lot of people I'd like to meet."

Tut was deep in thought. "Well, I'm in," he announced. "I want to talk to my namesake and watch the pyramids and the sphinx being built and know everything about Egypt. I could really help your dad, then."

"*Your* dad," Kit and Bash chimed in unison.

"One name each," Kit ordered. "Pass them forward when they're done. Dr. Brooks will give us a few names later, as he knows more of everything than we do."

When they were in a pile, Kit read them aloud: Charles Darwin, Leonardo da Vinci, Sir Isaac Newton, William Shakespeare, Jane Austen, CS Lewis, and Charlie Chaplin.

"First off does anyone have any objections to any of the names? They have to be unanimous. Jane Austen doesn't work for me," Kit said staring at Lady Nan.

"CS Lewis then," Lady Nan suggested.

Kit sighed, but accepted the substitute. "Well, since Narnia was an enchanted winter, he's valid enough."

The others nodded in agreement.

"Charlie Chaplin is interesting, but we need another science brain," Tut said.

"I agree," Kit said. "Bash? Got another name for us then?"

"What makes you think he was my choice?" Bash replied.

"Actually it was me," Anna said. "Lady Nan showed me his movies."

Bash reassured her. "He *was* a genius, but I have to agree with Kit, that in the spirit of things, pardon the pun, we should have an expert on volcanoes or something, and how precisely is William Shakespeare a scientist?"

"Okay. Shakespeare is out. Who chose him?"

"I did," Tut answered with a red face. "Sorry, I just knew he was famous."

"Think of someone who's knowledge can help us." Bash coached. "We can still visit the others we like as well, but we need to gather some heavy-duty brain power."

After a noisy discussion about who was in and who was out, Kit stood and called for order.

"We don't have to have all the names tonight. We only need one to start. I suggest we think for a few days and meet again. I've got some science books if anyone wants to borrow one. However, there's one more thing before we call it a night," he announced. "If we're going to be a proper team, we'll need a name.

"Anyone got a suggestion? And please be serious. If anyone says 'The Eight Musketeers,' I quit," Kit stated with a serious face.

"quitter!... full of holes...give me a break... home sweet homing pigeon... penny for your thoughts... well really!" Pigeon squawked.

The group's name went through stages, but a week later, with Dr. Brooks in attendance, they finally voted unanimously on the name 'Twinters' after Bash defended it. "It's perfect," she said in a lecturer's tone. "It's a combination of twin power and... *ahem*... the appropriate reference to volcanic winter."

Kit had been in fine form. Leadership felt natural. Let's have a show of hands please," he said. "All in favor of calling the team 'The Twinters' raise your hand and remember we need all eight votes."

There was a rustle of arms in the air.

"The motion is carried," Kit announced, banging a mummy-shaped letter opener on the table.

Lady Nan and Dr. Brooks presided as grandparents assuming their actual ages indulging a room of unruly grandchildren.

Bash was flushed with excitement. "Who do we visit first?"

"It's not scientific," Kit said, "but we put people's names in a flowerpot and let chance decide."

Bash looked worried. "A flowerpot's going to decide the fate of the planet?"

Kit shrugged. "Serendipity decides. The luck of the draw decides. Think of it as a really smart flowerpot."

Lady Nan piped up. "I think you mean 'when' Bash dear. First things first. Bede Hall must feel secure. It will tell us what to do and where to start. And if that doesn't work I'll have to eat my words."

"Feathers! Leave that planet alone!...Pan...not Peter...the green one," a knowing voice cackled in Parks' voice.

LADY NAN'S MEMOIR – a few last words
2014

A stately home is a postcard world glanced from afar, nestled into a vista of rolling green hills framed in blue skies and fluffy clouds. But if you live in one, you experience the reality of damp chilly rooms and dusty dreams. You learn quickly that all memories are inhabited by ghosts.

In the summer of 2010, I was slowly being absorbed by the future, the same way that my childhood home melted into the land-scape. I was letting go. But even miles away in a retirement home, I seemed to be part of the walls.

I had frequently said, that when I passed on, I would haunt the place, and that I had been rehearsing the part for years. I told my grandchildren that there were ghosts there already, and that I looked forward to joining them.

My granddaughter, Bathsheba, is our family historian. Someone had to write it down other than me.

Remembering, kept my mind young but the world said I dwelt in the past and that I rambled on about nonsense. They had no idea.

I wanted to go home. Not just to my living family, but to my beloved brother and Bede Hall, and in my dreams I confided to my friend, Snow, what I planned to do once I was there.

Sometimes the strongest family connections skip a generation. My twin grandchildren have a special link to each other, and so it was with me and my great-granddaughter... although logic kept me from recognizing this until she became brave enough to tell me, and I became open enough to listen.

The red library at Bede Hall has a dictionary so big it has its own table where it sits chained like a bird, but I have been Bathsheba's thesaurus. I used to tell her that if she was to become a writer, she needed to use better words. She took to wordsmithing like Bede Hall took to being a movie star.

As a country chatelaine, it was my right to hold the household keys even though it was my husband who made all the decisions. In my day, shrewd wives agreed to everything before doing precisely what they wanted. I refer to it as 'the ostrich approach' to power.

My keys were a thing of beauty, and they clanked together as loud as any movie ghost dragging chains. They were a symbol, of course, but I guarded them proudly, until one special key was taken from me. Oh, I got it back. Like I said, a wife had to use her guile to get what she wanted.

When I was a very small, I used to stroll the manicured flower-beds that spread like a skirt around the great house. Large topiaries wandered over the lawns like giant green animals, and I learned to swim with the mermaids who lived in the fountain. They remained stone to everyone else except my friend Parks.

I could see fairies and other woodland spirits amongst the plants, and eventually, I was able to speak with them. They were the true gardeners of Bede Hall, and they taught me the language of the flowers.

When I was nine, I met my best friend, Snow. It was the first day of August, and my head was burning from a particularly embarrassing altercation with my father. I sought refuge inside the maze near the grave of my beloved pet cat, Unicorn, and when I was helped back to the house, I could see a girl waving to me from a third floor window under the eaves. I was given the key as a reward for seeing her, which I came to understand, was a rite of passage. Parks bided until it was time. The key changed everything.

I knew the room well enough, but to me it was always locked and known as the Winter Room because it was chilly in the corridor outside its blue door.

I made my way up the stairs, past my own bedroom, where my Nanny dozed over one of her Jane Austen books, and stumbled to the blue door.

It was cold as frost and when I breathed close to the wood I could see my breath the way one can on a wintry day. I lay my forehead on the cold surface and my headache throbbed less fiercely. I could hear someone weeping from inside.

I saw no-one inside; not at first. It was used as a storage room and it was deliciously cool. I lay down on the spare bed and the moment my burning head touched the pillow my remaining pain was released and I slept the most tender sleep of my life. It was soothing winter's day sort of rest. The kind one spends under a toasty quilt on a rainy day with the window open. I always did that. Nanny would close it and turn out the light and I would open it again and say goodnight to the sphinx.

After that, whenever I got too much sun, I retreated to the Winter Room to rest, and once when I had a childhood fever, I tried to find my way there groping my way in the dark, until I felt the cool touch of someone's hand that led me to the healing pillow.

Nanny found my empty bed, and the household searched the gardens for me, but I had kept my secret well. I hid the key in a box made from a hollowed-out book titled 'Pride and Prejudice.' The name Jane Austen on the cover meant no man was likely to even handle it, and certainly not my husband.

The silver key was long and spindly, appropriately known as a skeleton key, and an ice-blue silk tassel hung from its intricate snowflake handle.

I have always been an early riser in order to write a chapter for my children's book on my old typewriter before breakfast, as my husband forbade clacking at night.

After many years of hardship, Bede Hall and I lay fallow for three years. It was a particularly wretched time, but I wanted to die there in peace, and my descendants required a home in the darkest of days of an emotional winter that seemed would never end. My friend, Parks, called us home, translating the sentient wishes of Bede Hall into a message we mortals could understand.

Bede Hall gradually herded us into a corner, and to make ends meet, my daughter, Rayne, decided to turn the Red Library into a private school for a handful of local children. Fortunately there was only one, but that's another story.

It was a scholarly room, well-appointed and cloaked in dust sheets, making the furniture look like ghosts. It was an elite place for catered learning. But the house never intended it to be used that way for long.

My family name is Stratford-Smyth. It contains the word myth, and since the meanings of words are never without significance, it was a serendipitous portent. Our hyphenated name made everyone assume we were rich. Hardly. We made do as our heritage literally crumbled around, what was once, a house of tremendous panache.

But, the family is together again. Together being a whole new definition of ever-expanding possibilities that quite leave the gifts of panache in the dust. It's like I always told my family: If you really want something enough, a little thing like dying won't stop you.

Stopping by Woods on a Snowy Evening

The woods are lovely,
dark, and deep,
But I have promises to keep,
And miles to go before I sleep.

"Whose woods are these
I think I know.
His house is in the village, though;
He will not see me stopping here
To watch his woods fill up with snow."

"My little horse must think it queer
To stop without a farmhouse near
Between the woods and frozen lake
The darkest evening of the year."

"He gives his harness bells a shake
To ask if there is some mistake.
The only other sound's the sweep
Of easy wind and downy flake."

"The woods are lovely,
dark, and deep,
But I have promises to keep,
And miles to go before I sleep,
And miles to go before I sleep."

Robert Frost, 1922*

---

*   the same year Howard Carter discovered the tomb of Tutankhamun

Bash's Glossary

AFFABLE	friendly and easy-going
ALBINO	a person whose skin and hair lack pigmentation or color
ACCOUTREMENTS	bits and pieces or accessories
AMBIANCE	typical mood or atmosphere of a place
APOTHECARY	a pharmacist or druggist, pharmacy or drug store
BA	the soul depicted as a bird with a human head
CAPRICIOUS	unpredictable, impulsive, unreliable
COLLATERAL	something of value held as a security deposit against a bank loan
COMPOS MENTIS	of sound mind
DISPARAGINGLY	disapproving, judgemental, and unsympathetic
ECCENTRIC	strange or weird, unusual, oddball behavior
EMACIATED	thin, wasted, withered
EYRIE	the high nest of a bird
FERAL	living in the wild
FELINE	the species of domestic cat – feline domesticus
GALABEYA	a long robe worn by Egyptian males
GARISH	tasteless and showy
HERITAGE	birthright or inheritance
KA	the ghost double of a person in ancient Egypt
KARMA	the quality of a person's life determined by a previous life
LUDICROUS	ridiculous and outrageous
MACABRE	gruesome, grisly, chilling, morbid, and ghoulish
MATRIARCH	a woman, usually a grandmother, recognized as the head of a family
MENTOR	an experienced advisor who guides a younger

	person
METAPHOR	to describe someone by means of a symbol. A figure of speech
NONPLUSSED	at a loss for words
NUMINA	spirits believed to inhabit places and things
ODIOUS	hateful, horrible, loathsome
PANACHE	showing great style
PIQUE	a fit of temper
PIXILATED	behaving in a strange way
PIZZAZZ	splashy a more exciting form of panache
PRAGMATIC	practical and realistic, no-nonsense. sensible
PRODIGIOUS	exceptionally impressive
PROVIDENCE	divine intervention, luck, chance, and fate
SANCTIMONIOUS	smug and self-important
SAVVY	aware or smart, clued-in
STELE	an inscribed ancient stone tablet
SUBTERRANEAN	below the earth
SUPERCILIOUS	snobbish and snooty, pompous, arrogant, and superior
SYNCHRONICITY	coincidences that seem related, but not caused one by the other.
SERENDIPITY	fortuitous aspect of fate or destiny
TANTAMOUNT	almost like, equal to, practically the same as
TOAD IN THE HOLE	fried sausages covered in batter and baked in a casserole, served with brown gravy
TRAUMATIZED	in a state of shock
VISCOUS	a thick stringy liquid goo
WILLOW-THE-WISP	atmospheric ghostly lights that cling to swampy water

Acknowledgments

The follow up to 'TWINTER – the first portal' is presently on the drawing board – a quaint term leftover from my old graphic design days. Book two in the series 'Time Falls Like Snow' fast-forwards to the year 2016 when the twins are sixteen with the ticking of an ominous invasive time bomb unsettling their teenage years.

I am delighted to have ongoing collaborations with designer Iryna Spica of 'Spica-BookDesign' and Lyn Alexander, the author of the 'Schellendorf series of historical novels' – a tireless literary mentor in my life who demands less and more at the same time.

Three years have passed since book one was published. Hindsight compelled me to revise it because it has taken that long for the twins to tell me where they eventually went, what transpired, and more importantly, when. They drew me a map of their new world. Now I can explore.

I wrote four novels while I waited. Time is a funny thing. 2020 vision is déjà vu with attitude.

About the Author

V Knox writes 'paranormal-friendly' time-slip novels that defy the logic she firmly believes in. Studying Fine Arts led to an imaginative take on art history where she converses with sentient portraits 'who' reveal their lost provenance and innermost secrets.

Paintings lead her into the maze of 'what if', determined to reconcile the world of down-to-earth science with imaginative out-there-fiction. She collects eclectic umbrellas but prefers to get wet in the rain and favors surreal stories that explore the inner world of creative savants, parallel dimensions, and ghostly lovers.

www.veronicaknox.com

www.ingramcontent.com/pod-product-compliance
Lightning Source LLC
Chambersburg PA
CBHW072000110726
47910CB00005B/1596